...y a glorious new world.

"Or what?" said Lewan, and he was proud that his voice didn't tremble, for his heart was beating double-time under Talieth's imperious gaze.

Instead she looked at him and said, "Or I'll see that you're given the best traveling clothes we have, as many supplies as you can carry, weapons of your choosing, and I'll have you taken out the gates and down the mountain. You can go wherever you like.

"And in a few days' time, or a tenday, or perhaps even a month if the gods smile upon us, when Sentinelspire explodes and shatters the land for a hundred miles; when a cloud of dust and ash and fire covers half the known world, choking babes in their sleep, killing wild beasts and livestock, and strangling sunlight from this season's crops—and very likely next season's as well—if you're far enough away to escape that . . . well, then, I suppose you can live the rest of your life knowing that you could have helped prevent it.

"Once the fires have died, the earth cooled, and the ash blown away, you can even come to the great hole in the ground where once we lived, and you can dance on the place where we died. Is that what you want, Lewan?"

I have not sat idle these years.

FORGOTTEN REALMS®

THE CITADELS

THE CITADELS

Sentinelspire

✦

MARK SEHESTEDT

The Citadels
Sentinelspire

Published by Wizards of the Coast, Inc. FORGOTTEN REALMS, WIZARDS OF THE COAST, and their respective logos are trademarks of Wizards of the Coast, Inc., in the U.S.A. and other countries.

Printed in the U.S.A.

Cover art by David Seidman
Map by Rob Lazzaretti
First Printing: July 2008

9 8 7 6 5 4 3 2 1

ISBN 978-0-7869-4937-3
620-21865740-001-EN

U.S., CANADA,
ASIA, PACIFIC, & LATIN AMERICA
Wizards of the Coast, Inc.
P.O. Box 707
Renton, WA 98057-0707
+1-800-324-6496

EUROPEAN HEADQUARTERS
Hasbro UK Ltd
Caswell Way
Newport, Gwent NP9 0YH
GREAT BRITAIN
Save this address for your records.

Visit our web site at www.wizards.com

acknowledgements

First, many thanks to Mr. Ed Greenwood, for creating this vast world for us to play in.

Thanks to the editors at Wizards of the Coast—Phil Athans and Susan Morris—for helping me to get on the *Forgotten Realms*® horse and leading me to the gate. And most-est especialliest to Erin Evans, for helping to whip this book to the finish line. Her many suggestions, research assistance, and never-ceasing encouragement were an indispensable help in crafting this story. Didn't Stephen King once say that the editor is always right? I don't know about all editors, but Erin certainly was!

I utilized many books in researching *Sentinelspire*. My thanks to their authors, especially:
The Horde Boxed Set by David "Zeb" Cook and Steve Winter
The *Forgotten Realms Campaign Setting* by Ed Greenwood, Sean K. Reynolds, Skip Williams, and Rob Heinsoo
The Unapproachable East by Richard Baker, Matt Forbeck, and Sean K. Reynolds
Faiths and Pantheons by Eric L. Boyd and Erik Mona

Special thanks to Gary Larson for "Cow Poetry."

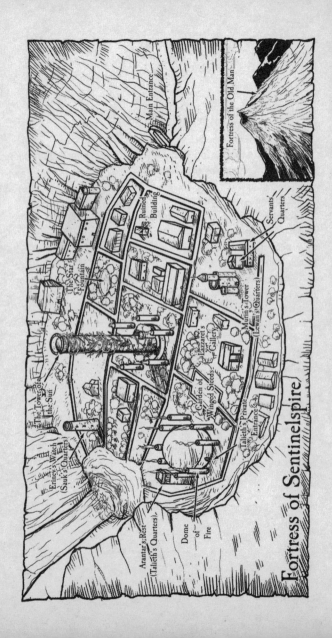

Fortress of the Old Man

Main Entrance

Ruined Building

Servants' Quarters

The Star Fountain

Murin's Tower (Lewin's Quarters)

The Tower of the Sun

Lazzaret's Gallery

Garden of Winged Seeds

Erinec's Watch (Sauk's Quarters)

Talieth's Private Entrance

Arantar's Rest (Talieth's Quarters)

Dome of Fire

Fortress of Sentinelspire

The wise men know all evil things
Under the twisted trees,
Where the perverse in pleasure pine
And men are weary of green wine
And sick of crimson seas.

—G.K. Chesterton,
"The Ballad of the White Horse"

✚

A note to the reader

In the following story, characters appear who do not speak the Common tongue of Faerûn—and sometimes even those who speak Common choose not to do so. Most of the time, the meaning will be clear or explained in context. If not—or if you're like me and love lists of strange words—the following guide will prove useful. Please note that the Orcish phrases are of the dialect of the Stone Tooth clan of Vaasa.

Ash sissaan— "Enter" or (more loosely) "come inside." (Killoren)

Anukh—"Attack!" (Orcish)

Arumwon—"Beast brother," a sort of animal friend given to the sacred rangers of the Stone Tooth Clan of orcs, native to Vaasa. (Orcish)

Berun Kharn kienelleth—"Hope must become vengeance." (Aglarondan)

Dam ul dam—"Blood for blood." (Orcish)

Drassit—Imperative verb, meaning "(you) harass" or "(you) trouble." (Aglarondan)

3

Drekhe—Literally, "Flee!" or more loosely, "Get away!" (Aglarondan)

Dukhal—An insult, meaning "bastard." (Orcish)

Jankhota saalthua—"The time has arrived." (Killoren)

Kumash damun!—"Taste the blood!" (Orcish)

Lur'ashai—"Little lord" or "little master." (Killoren)

Malwun—Literally "oathbrother." The term for a blood brother among the *zuwar*. (Orcish)

Mal karash!—"Oathbreaker." (Orcish)

Neyë—"Come here!" (Orcish)

Ragh ala—"Calm down." (Orcish)

Toch gan neth—Imperative verb, meaning "(you) lead her away." (Aglarondan)

Zuwar—A sacred hunter among the Stone Tooth clan of orcs, native to Vaasa. The *zuwar* are hunters sworn to the service of Malar the Beastlord.

✠

prologue

2 Mirtul, the Year of the Sword (1365 DR)
The Yuirwood

They had come not long after midnight. With the moon and stars drowned in a sea of cloud, the darkness beneath the trees had become absolute. How such a large force had penetrated the depths of the Yuirwood, no one yet knew. It was unheard of. Unprecedented. But to strike so near one of the Circle's holiest sites, to murder the Masters of the Yuirwood and bring fire to the trees, that was sacrilege. Such a crime demanded blood.

Chereth followed the ranger through the wood. Aeryll was the man's name. Man? No, Aeryll was the youngest member of their band, scarcely more than a boy, not even a year out of his *Jalesh Rudra*. Aeryll held aloft a thin chain, a starstone dangling from it. The stone's soft silver glow gave the ranger enough light to guide them to a small clearing, a place where massive slabs of stone broke out of the earth. Little grew here—tufts of tall, sharp grass from the fissures of rock, and mosses in the recesses of stone that saw little sunlight. Chereth and the ranger emerged from the forest just as the clouds let loose a soft rain.

The Masters of the Yuirwood—Triem and the seven of his band who had survived—stood in the lee of a tall boulder.

Someone had bound two starstone necklaces to the long tufts of summer grass that sprouted from crevices in the rock. Just enough light for the humans to see. Another figure, his dark clothes torn and streaked with blood, huddled at their feet, his elbows bound behind his back, his knees and ankles tied before him.

Triem, his hood pulled down on his shoulders, turned at Chereth and Aeryll's approach. "Master Chereth," he said, and bowed.

"This is the only one captured?" asked Chereth.

"Mandel's band is pursuing the others eastward. We've heard nothing so far."

"It took nine of you to apprehend this one?"

A moment's silence before Triem answered, but there was no apology in his tone. "You saw him, Master. What he did. Yes, it took nine of us."

Chereth looked down on the man huddled in the grass. He walked around Triem, and two of the other rangers stepped back to allow him to approach the captive.

"You are Kheil," said Chereth.

The man looked up, his eyes bright in a face masked by blood. A slight gash near his scalp had bled freely, soaking his visage.

"How did you find us?" said Chereth. "How did you come undetected so deep into our sacred wood?"

The man said nothing. His glare did not falter.

"Why did you come? Why bring murder to our Circle?"

The man's back stiffened, pride and arrogance entering his countenance. "No one thwarts the Old Man of the Mountain and lives to tell about it."

Chereth leaned upon his staff and looked Kheil in the eye. "We have much the same rule." He straightened and turned to Triem. "Kill him."

Triem and his rangers dragged Kheil through the woods. The soft rain turned to a torrent as the warm winds off the Sea of Fallen Stars met the cooler air coming down from the Tannath Mountains, creating a thunderstorm that rattled the early summer leaves and shook the hills. Lightning flashed, making the wood a mass of flickering light and shadow. Triem wore his hood down so as not to impede his ears and eyes, and when the band left the woods to cross clearings or crest a hill, the rain hit him like nails, stinging his skin.

They reached the hilltop. There, shuddering in the fury of the storm, stood the Tree of Dhaerow. The tree had died many years before, but its leafless corpse still stood, gray and hard like some withered old sentinel on the hill. It had a foul air about it that made Triem want to walk away and not look back. Perhaps it was the lingering of ghosts or the scent of death upon the grass. Here, the Masters of the Yuirwood hanged the most vile criminals—murderers, rapists, and worshipers of the dark gods. But Triem had long feared that the tree had a presence of its own. Dead it might be, but the old oak had an awareness about it that he had never liked.

"You're going to hang me, then?" said Kheil. He looked up at the Tree of Dhaerow. The hard rain had opened his head wound again, and blood and water soaked him from his scalp down to his boots. "I'm disappointed. I'd heard you Yuir rangers had more imagination."

Aeryll stepped forward, his smile cold in the lightning flashes. "You'll—"

"Enough," said Triem. "Aeryll, say nothing."

"That's right," said Kheil. "Just—"

Dorren, a ranger so big that his brothers in the Circle often taunted him about being half giant, hit Kheil so hard that blood and water sprayed the rangers standing ten feet away.

"Quickly," said Triem. "Before he comes to his senses. Let's not make this any more of a struggle than we have to."

The rangers unbound Kheil, then tied his wrists in front of him. They secured a rope of braided leather over the new bindings, then threw the remaining length over the lowest, thickest branch of the old oak. Dorren hauled on the rope until the tips of Kheil's boots barely scraped the mud. The sudden pressure on his arms and the wind and rain in his face woke him.

Kheil swallowed and said, "Whuh . . . what—?"

Dorren drew his dagger, cut away Kheil's clothes, and tossed them into the mud while Aeryll pulled off the assassin's boots.

"What are you doing?" Kheil asked, his speech slurred. In the light from a distant flash of lightning, Triem saw something in Kheil's eyes. Fear.

"Relieving you of your disappointment," said Triem. "The Masters of the Yuirwood may lack many things. Imagination is not one of them."

The other rangers drew their knives. Cold steel flickered in the storm light.

The storm ravaged all of Aglarond that night. The Masters of the Yuirwood hunted the surviving assassins through their sacred wood, but none were ever found, save the dead.

As the storm passed, breaking itself against the Tannath Mountains and turning its spent fury over the Umber Marshes to the east, Triem's band left the Tree of Dhaerow and the flayed corpse that hung from it. When the thunder had diminished to no more than a low rumble in the distance, and the stars and sinking moon began to peek through the clouds, a lone figure climbed the hill to the Tree of Dhaerow. No one saw the figure cut down the corpse of Kheil. No one watched as he bore Kheil's corpse far away.

He heard singing. A voice, deep and rich, like cedar smoke, chanting in a tongue he could not understand. But the deeper meaning tugged at him, reaching through the pain to that part of him that still remembered a world where pain did not define him. Hope and life broke him like vibrant color breaking shadow. And that color was green. . . .

He gasped, his body taking in a great breath that burned his lungs.

Sounds filled his ears—water dripping from summer leaves, frogs and toads croaking like wet branches rubbing in the breeze, a cacophony of crickets. Beneath these sounds, like the accompanying harp to a bard's song, was the gurgle of water running sweet and clear. He found himself filled with a thirst such as he had never known.

"Easy," said a voice.

He opened his eyes and saw a figure kneeling to one side of him. Sunlight broke through the ceiling of leaves, and a few beams played over the figure. Streaks of gray flecked his long brown hair, but the sunlight brought out a deep green, like moss peeking out from tree bark. His coppery skin was smooth, but his eyes gazed with the wisdom of years, and the ears protruding from his hair swooped up into a sharp tip. Too thick for an elf, yet not thick enough for most humans, this one had to be a half-elf, and with that knowledge, a name floated to the surface of his mind.

"Chereth?" he asked. "How . . . ?"

"How what?"

"How did I . . . ?" He searched his memory and found only broken bits and pieces. Chereth, a druid, one of the Masters of the Yuirwood, that ancient forest so far from . . . where? The mountain. A lone mountain rising to great height above miles of rolling grassland. Sentinelspire. That was the mountain's name. "How did I come here?"

"You would not say," said the half-elf.

He sat up and looked down on his body. The pain—the memory of which made him flinch—was only a dull ache in

9

his flesh, but the scars remained, crisscrossing his torso, his arms, his legs. Looking at them, he remembered—rain and wind, a gnarled tree, and through it all, cold knives glinting in the light of a storm.

"You do remember then," said the half-elf. "I was not sure."

"They . . . they killed me. Th-the knives, they—"

"Yes."

"You told them to kill me."

"Yes."

"Then why . . . this? Why call me back?"

The old half-elf raised his hand, and Kheil saw something dangling from it—a leather cord tied to a knotwork of twisted vines, all braided round three small stones. As Chereth raised it into one of the sunbeams, the light caught in the stones, and Kheil saw that they were jewels of some sort.

"All your life you have dealt death. Now the god of life calls you. Time to answer."

Part One

✠

ASSASSINS

✚

chapter one

14 Tarsakh, the Year of Lightning Storms (1374 DR)
The Northern Shalhoond

Lewan crouched in the cover of the thick brush near the stream. The long tree-shadows and tall grasses made for good cover, but a large predator would detect any movement. Lewan kept absolutely still, save for his eyes, which flitted about, searching for anything on the move. The sound of the stream would hide all but the loudest sounds should he need to move—but it would do the same for anything approaching. Still, he could have sworn that his ears had caught something a moment ago.

The sound came again, off to his right—*wheet-wheet!*—the call of the spotted crake, one of the many small birds that made its home in the tall grasses where the trees of the Shalhoond thinned before fading into the Great Amber Steppes. Lewan answered with a crane's call.

A rustling in the grass came closer, stopped, then moved closer still. A moment later a small green and brown head, scaled and with a tiny horn above the nose, poked out from between tufts of new spring grass. The little lizard's eyes locked on Lewan, the small black tongue flicked out, tasting the air, then the creature was gone, a hiss in the grass.

Berun came in quietly, scarcely more than a whisper himself, crouching low so he didn't breach the surface of the grass. His silence belied his size. Standing straight, he would have looked down upon most natives of the steppes, though he was lean and his features were hard, shaped by years of wind and sun. He held his bow—far larger than the one on Lewan's back—in one hand, though it was unstrung. A treeclaw lizard rode his shoulder, its long tail dangling beside the man's braid.

"You found something?" asked the man.

"Yes, Master," said Lewan. "Down by the water."

They kept to the cover of the trees and brush as much as they could, but nearer the stream it was all grass. Between two tall tussocks was a bare patch of soil that had been moistened by the rain of two nights ago. It had dried since, preserving the four prints quite nicely. Looking at them, Berun's brows knit together. They kept their voices low.

"What kind of animal is it, Lewan?"

"A large cat," he replied. "Steppe tiger, I think."

Berun gave him a slight smile, though he didn't look up. "What else?"

"A female. The rear paws come down slightly to the outside of those of the front. Wider hips means a female—even in cats. Yes?"

Berun's grin widened. "Yes, Lewan. Even in cats. And how big is she?"

Lewan looked at the prints. They were large, as big as his outstretched palm. The soil would have been softer after the rain, and the prints were deep.

"She's big," said Lewan. "I'd guess at least eight hundred pounds. Maybe more."

"A good guess," said Berun. "Well done, Lewan."

"What now, Master? It seems she's headed back into the forest. She isn't spraying any markers, doesn't seem to be establishing any territory, and she hasn't hit any farms in eleven days. She abandoned that last deer half-eaten. She's wandering all over the place. I don't understand."

Berun's smile disappeared and he became grim again. "Nor do I." He looked up at the sun. "We'll keep tracking her while the light is strong. If she keeps heading deeper into the wood, we'll find a good place to bed down. I don't want to hunt a steppe tiger in the dark."

They tracked the tiger throughout the rest of the morning and into midday. They did not hurry, keeping to cover and taking care to move quietly. Although the tiger had taken the deer three days ago and probably wouldn't be hunting again, it didn't hurt to be cautious. Tigers were ambush hunters, and this tiger was already a puzzle, hitting three farms in the last month, slaughtering mostly sheep, but at the last one she'd forsaken the sheep and taken the shepherd. She'd kept to no set range, so she wasn't a newcomer seeking territory. At least not yet.

Just past midday they came upon another stream, one of the many that crawled out of the Khopet-Dag to the west. They were farther from the wood now, and the few trees rising out of the steppe hugged the water where they starved out the thicker grasses. Lewan found fresh tracks near the water and called to his master.

"Look, Master," he said, keeping his voice low. "These are less than half a day old."

The men crossed the stream where the tracks did, moving swiftly so as not to be in open sight for long. The water never rose above their knees, but it was cold; it had probably been snow on some distant peak only a few days ago. As they were about to set foot on the opposite shore, Berun came to an abrupt halt and motioned for Lewan to do the same. He approached the wet soil on the opposite bank with utmost care, crouching low and choosing his ground so as not to step on any tracks. Lewan noted that the fluid grace had left his

15

movements. His master was stiff and hesitant. Something had startled him.

"What is it, Master?" he whispered.

When Berun didn't reply, Lewan stepped forward, keeping low, his hands on his knees to preserve his balance. He followed his master's gaze.

A mass of tracks, many of them trampling others. Among the few clear ones were more tiger tracks. Judging by the size, it was the same beast covering the same ground a few times, but in one smooth patch of soil was a boot print, distinct and undisturbed. It was big and deep. Whoever had made it was at least as tall as Berun—and much heavier.

Scratched into the bootprint—probably with a twig or a thick stalk of grass—were letters. Lewan was by no means a master of letters. In his sixteen years, his master had taught him only the basics, but he knew enough to recognize these. Written in the Thorass letters, they spelled out a word: KHEIL.

"Master, what does this mean?"

Berun swallowed and said nothing. He had gone pale, and Lewan noticed that Berun's fist gripping his bow was tense and white.

"Master? What—?"

"Lewan," said Berun, his voice hoarse. "Go back to the village. Keep to cover. Go slowly. Let no one see you. If you don't make it by dark, bed down secure and light no fire. *No* fire. Do you hear me? You must not be seen out in the open. Get to the village and stay there. Tell them that no one leaves the wall, save in numbers, and everyone goes armed, even behind the walls. Keep the fires lit at night—burning low, but the guards will need to see. And tell them to double their guards. Not just the gate. After dark, every turn of the wall must be watched."

"I . . . I don't understand, Master. We've hunted worse than tigers before. Why send me back?"

"Later, Lewan. You will obey me in this. I shouldn't be more than a few days."

"But I can help you."

"Not this time."

"What do those letters mean, Master? What is a 'Kheil?' "

"Not a what, Lewan. Kheil was a man. Now head back to the village." Berun looked at him. His eyes were equal parts fury and fear. "You *will* obey in this, Lewan. Go. Now."

Lewan looked away. "As you say, Master."

"And Lewan?"

"Yes?"

"String your bow. Travel with an arrow in hand."

✛

chapter two

Berun watched Lewan disappear into the tall grass. He'd hurt the boy. Lewan was confused and afraid, but that couldn't be helped. This job had seemed so simple. Something had been killing sheep around some of the villages that Hubadai, the self-proclaimed ruler of the Hordelands, had established along the Great Amber Steppes. Not all that unusual so near the Shalhoond, but eleven days ago two shepherds had been attacked, one killed, and one saved only by the quick ministrations of the village healer. The villages had banded together and sent out a hunting party. They hadn't been seen since, so the villages had hired Berun to track down the beast. Simple enough. Berun had done many such jobs over the past few years since wandering into this part of the world. The little gold it put in his hand helped to buy what supplies he and Lewan could not take from the wild. But this simple job had just turned into something much, much worse.

Berun's mind swirled. Rising fear told him to go after Lewan, to collect the boy and head south into the deep wood where they could lose themselves. Maybe hide among the *yaqubi*. Let Hubadai's new villages fend for themselves or call upon their new khahan for aid. If Berun's guess was right, then this was no rogue tiger he was following. And those hunters sent out by the village would likely never be seen again.

But another voice whispered round the edges of his fear.

18

An old half-elf's voice. Chereth, his teacher. Berun had spent many seasons with Chereth beneath the boughs of the Yuir-wood, far to the north and west, learning from him the sacred ways of the wild, the paths of life and death, the hearts of growing things. As a Master of the Yuirwood, Chereth had long been devoted to his own woodland home, but as a servant of Silvanus, he was also sworn to protect all the wild places of the world, and that service sometimes took him and his disciple far from home. Over the years, his devotion sometimes turned to obsession, and he walked hundreds of miles, searching for old lore and relics.

Chereth and Berun's last journey together five years ago had taken them into the depths of the Ganathwood, whose long-dead inhabitants shared a common heritage with the ancient elves of the Yuirwood. They had found what they sought and were leaving, were in fact nearing the edges of the wood, when they came upon a large band of marauders, made up mostly of escaped slaves from Thay and Mulhorand who had fled to the Ganath-wood and gone savage. The band had raided some of the outlying villages of Murghôm, stealing supplies and taking captives. They were bloodied and tired, yet they pushed themselves to reach the shelter of the wood. Chereth and Berun hit them hard.

The fight had been short but brutal, the few surviving marauders taking to the woods in different directions. But Chereth and Berun had underestimated the raiders' bloodlust. As the fight turned against them, they'd killed their captives rather than see them freed. Chereth and Berun had only managed to rescue one, a young boy.

"How is he?" Chereth asked.

"Frightened," said Berun. "Looks starving but he won't eat. I barely got him to swallow a mouthful of water. He has the look of a hare before the hawk's talons strike."

"And he fears we are hawks?"

Berun considered a moment. "I don't know that he's thinking even that much."

"Do what you can for him."

Berun heard the farewell in the statement. "Master Chereth?"

The old half-elf looked away. "I must leave you now, my son."

"Wh-what? Why?"

"I found what I sought in the Ganathwood. The final branch of a tree that I have long watched grow. Now that I have it, I must go."

"Go where?"

"To fell the tree."

"Have I failed you in some way, Master?"

Chereth turned back to him. "No, my son. You have surpassed all my hopes for you. Some days I wish you were truly the son of my body as well as my teaching."

"My place is with you, Master."

"Not this time. Not this fight. Tend the slain captives here. Leave the dead raiders for the wolves. Malar must have his offering as well as our Lord Silvanus. Then take care of the boy. Most of all, you must care for this."

Chereth reached inside his shirt and pulled out a necklace braided from thin strips of leather. Fastened on the end was a medallion of sorts, a mass of hardened wood and vine in a twisting pattern that encased three small stones, each just a shade off amber. The bits of wood and vine were dark, obviously ancient and worn, yet they seemed to possess a strange vitality, almost as if they were veins pulsing with life from the three stones within.

"*Erael'len,*" said Chereth.

"The Three Hearts," said Berun, translating. "But Master, you are its sworn guardian."

"Yes. I swore to keep it safe. Where I now go, I cannot keep that oath. But you can."

"But Master, you've only begun to teach me its secrets."

"And you have done well. You must continue now on your own. Guard *Erael'len* with your life." Chereth looked away, and when he spoke again, Berun heard an odd note in his voice. "Do what you can for the boy. He has the look of one of the Murghôm. Head east and ask among the ataman. See if you can find a family for him. Leave word whenever you stop. I'll find you when I am done, if I can."

Berun looked around. Swarms of flies buzzed around the dead, alighting on eyes open to nothingness and clogging wounds where the blood already seemed more black than red. The boy sat still, hugging his knees, his eyes clenched shut.

"When will that be, Master? When will you be done?"

"I do not know. You must promise me one thing, Berun."

"What?"

"Do not search for me. No matter what you hear." Chereth was staring eastward. "If word does not come directly from me, you must. . . let me go."

Berun considered this, and he wondered what had held his master's attention in the east. That way lay the Mountains of Copper, the spider-haunted Khopet-Dag, the great Shalhoond, and beyond that—

Sentinelspire. That was it.

"Master," he said. "This has to do with . . . with Kheil, doesn't it? Kheil and the Old Man of the Mountain."

The tears were gone from Chereth's eyes now, and his gaze was hard. "You must promise me, Berun."

Berun closed his eyes, swallowed, and managed a rasp. "Kheil is dead, you know."

"Even the dead can be raised," said Chereth. "You of all people should know this. Now promise me that you will do as I say. Swear it."

"I swear it, Master."

Chereth extended his staff and turned it. Near the end was a tangled knot of thorns, still green and hale. "Swear it in blood, my son."

Berun grasped the thorns and squeezed until he felt them bite his palm and fingers, then he opened his hand to show

21

the blood pooling there. "I swear I will not come after you," he said. "Save on your word alone. By my blood upon thorn, I swear it."

Crouched amongst the tall grasses and thin trees, Berun looked down upon his hand. The scars from that oath had long since healed—he had worn off many calluses in the years since—but the oath held him still.

He had sworn blood upon thorn not to seek his old master, save on Chereth's word alone. And that word had never come. But what now? He had never sought Kheil's old paths. But now it seemed someone else had. They'd come to him. It was flee or fight. Hunt or be hunted.

Berun strung his bow—a long curve of yew, runes burned the entire length of the wood—and chose a special arrow, the one whose sharp steel head had three tiny holes near the shaft, threaded through with tiny bits of blue hemlock. Not fresh. It had been two days since he'd threaded the fibers, but they'd still do the trick if it came to that. Berun nocked the arrow and took up the trail.

Time to hunt.

✛

chapter three

The tracks led into the deep wood, where the trees grew close, branches from dozens of trees tangling with their neighbors as they fought for the sunlight. Down in the valleys and along the hillsides, the ground was a solid mass of hundreds, perhaps thousands of years of dead leaves, shattered twigs, and trees rotted back to soil.

Berun slowed, proceeding at a careful crouch. The sun had begun its long arc toward the horizon, and the bits of sky that managed to peek through the canopy of leaves and branches had grown pale, thickening the shadows beneath the trees. The tracks were very fresh here—the top layers of leaf-fall were shredded and overturned to reveal the moist humus beneath. If the tiger was growing hungry again, this would be the time of day she'd hunt. The lizard, still riding Berun's shoulder, sensed his master's tension. Berun felt the tiny claws tighten, digging through his shirt and pricking his skin.

"Easy, Perch," he whispered. The lizard flicked his tongue, tickling Berun's ear.

Part of Berun's gift as a disciple of the Oak Father was a unique link to the lizard—a sort of bonding. Perch had the intellect and limited reasoning of his kind, but the Oak Father had blessed the pair with a special connection. Even though Perch's brain could not form words, the comrades had shared

23

the bond so long that Berun had learned to interpret the lizard's will almost as clearly as words in his mind.

But now, the only sensations coming through were unease and inquisitiveness. The bond went both ways, and Berun's fear was leaking through to Perch. *What-what-what? What-scared-what? Where-what-scared?*

Berun did his best to comfort Perch. *Easy. Watch and watch. Taste the air. Watch for danger.*

The land rose as the forest thickened around the broken foothills of the Khopet-Dag. The trees were taller, older—some so massive that Berun couldn't fathom how the winter storms hadn't toppled them. He began to see cobwebs thickening the hollow remains of old logs. Small leaf spiders, mostly. Their larger, more dangerous cousins generally kept to the mountains and higher foothills.

The tracks paralleled a small stream, and Berun followed the trail uphill. Water coursing over thousands of stones drowned out most other sounds, so Berun was very close when he heard it—a growl, so low that it hit his gut more than his ears. He froze. The scream that followed, high and harsh, broke through the gurgle of the stream. A man's scream.

Berun climbed a steep incline of rock broken by tufts of grass and a few bushes with branches tough as iron bands. He pushed his way through a thick cobweb and came to a level clearing about halfway up the hill. The stream filled a small, shallow pool that fed two smaller streams. The smaller rivulet spilled into the stream he had been following. The other fell over the opposite side of the hill.

Crouching amidst the brush, Berun wiped spider silk from his face. The growl hit him again, louder this time. It reverberated in both his ears and the spot between stomach and heart that was the first to flutter when fear hit. Another shout followed—definitely from the ravine. Perch, still riding Berun's shoulder, chattered, and again his claws flexed.

Berun splashed through the pool and then crouched behind a boulder that formed the lip of the waterfall. Holding his bow out of view, he peeked over the edge.

The ravine was not wide—the tiger probably could have jumped across—but it was steep. The constant fall of water had washed away nearly all the soil, leaving a sheer wall of slick rock sloping some twenty feet down. The drum of the water as it hit told Berun the pond below was likely deep. The pool drained into the open end of the ravine that broke the hillside.

Standing on the dozen or so feet of opposite shore, his back to the rock wall, was a man. Not one of the locals, by his looks. His round eyes and the paleness of his skin painted him a westerner. His clothes were ragged and torn. His hands and face bore many tiny scratches—probably from scrabbling through the thick brush—and blood smeared a good portion of his skin. In trembling hands he held a spear, and he kept the steel point low, between him and the massive steppe tiger.

She was a beautiful beast. Her tawny coat was streaked by dusky stripes that faded into a uniform gold along her underbelly. Familiarity hit Berun, a feeling like fear. The fine lines of red ochre painted in intricate designs along the top of her head and down each flank gave her away.

"Taaki," Berun whispered. His throat caught at the noise, but he remembered that the sound of the waterfall would probably drown out normal speech. He'd have to shout to be heard down there.

The steppe tiger crouched, her muscles taut and prepared to spring, kept at bay only by that sharp steel barb.

Berun swallowed, considering. If Taaki was here . . .

Maybe she was alone now. Maybe that explained why she was roaming the Amber Steppes and the outer Shalhoond, preying on sheep and shepherds. Maybe—

No. That might have been a hope had Berun not found the boot print with the letters scratched into the soil. Those letters—*Kheil*—meant any such hope was in vain.

He looked at his arrow, at the tiny bit of blue hemlock fiber twined through the steel tip. He knew he'd have to hit the tiger with three such arrows to take her down. Unless he could get one shaft into her heart, and from this vantage point, that was almost impossible, even for him. If he hit her from here, the poison would take time to work through her body. It would burn, set her heart to racing, and that would only drive her mad with fear and pain. Steel-tipped spears and poisoned arrows would not be able to stop her then. The blue hemlock would kill her, yes, but not before she killed the man with the spear and then turned to attack Berun.

Berun took his hand off his arrow, nocked tightly against the bowstring, and reached up to the lizard on his shoulder. "Time to go to work, Perch," he said.

The lizard climbed onto the back of his hand and hissed, his jaws distending as he saw the tiger below.

Berun held out his arm, pointing the lizard at the tiger, and said, *"Drassit. Toch gan neth!"* And through their bond—*Strike and lead her away. Strike-strike!*

The lizard leaped and spread his limbs, the thick membrane between his hind and forelegs and the first third of his tail spreading to catch the air. Perch couldn't fly like a bird, but he could glide like some of the squirrels of the Yuirwood, and his light frame helped him to ride the air with a feral grace. He glided almost to the opposite wall of the ravine before turning in a tight spiral, then turned again before the waterfall could take him. Two thirds of the way down, the lizard aimed for the tiger's head and folded his legs. The winglike membranes collapsed and the lizard's claws pointed down, sharp as needles.

Perch hit the tiger just where the base of her skull met neck and shoulders, where the fur was thick but the skin soft.

The tiger let loose a teeth-rattling roar and leaped backward. Berun knew how thick the fur was there, and the tiger was startled, not hurt. As she shook her head to dislodge the lizard, Perch leaped, using the tiger's own momentum to propel him onto the rocks. The tiger resumed her crouch, her fangs bared, her gaze flitting between the spearman and the lizard.

Perch stood on a rock, balancing on the base of his tail, and hissed at the tiger. Enraged, the tiger leaped for him but before she struck Perch was gone, skittering away amongst the rocks. She scrambled after him, reminding Berun of a stablecat hunting a mouse through the straw. But Perch was a treeclaw lizard of the deep Khopet-Dag. He and his kind hunted spiders—some that were as big as a man. Small as he was, Perch possessed extreme quickness and cunning. Amid the cracks and crevices of the rocks, the tiger could not catch him. She came close twice, her claws coming down an instant after the lizard scampered away.

The tiger gave up and turned back to the spearman, but she'd gone no more than a few steps before Perch leaped on her rump and sank in his claws, one quick squeeze, then jumped away again. Snarling, the tiger turned and bounded after him. Perch skittered away, a small brownish streak disappearing into the brush where the stream fell in a series of falls down the valley. The tiger followed.

Berun waited until the sounds of the chase faded and he could see no more trace of the huge beast trampling through the brush. He looked down at the spearman, who was staring after the tiger, his eyes wide as coins and his mouth agape. Berun stood and called down, "Hey!"

The spearman started and looked up, bringing his spear around to point at Berun.

"You hurt?" said Berun.

The man started at the sound of Berun's voice but said nothing.

27

Berun repeated the question in Chondathan, Damaran, and Tuigan. Still nothing. The man clenched his jaw shut, and the hands that held the spear began shaking violently.

Berun looked down the opening of the ravine. No sign of the tiger or Perch. Not even rustling brush. The sound of the waterfall crushed any hope of hearing them. He'd have to be quick.

Holding bow and arrow in one hand, Berun climbed down into the ravine. Plenty of rocks jutted from the cliff, but most were worn smooth by years of falling water, and a fine spray made them slippery. Berun nearly fell twice. After the second near-miss he jumped the final five feet or so, landing with a splash. Though he hit near the edge of the pool, it was deep, and he sank well past his midriff. The pull of the water falling down the ravine was surprisingly strong, and Berun had to fight to cross to the other side.

The spearman hadn't moved, but he kept the point of his weapon trained on Berun. The man's hands no longer trembled, and some of the tension seemed to have left him. An odd spark lit his eyes, and Berun hesitated at the edge of the pool. A warning went off at the base of his skull.

Dripping, Berun stood at the pool's edge, two spearlengths away from the man, and took a long look. Closer, he could see that none of the man's injuries were serious. Scratches only. The blood covering him was in thin streaks, as if it had been smeared, spreading it as far as possible. Closer up, even in the dim light, Berun could see that not all of it was blood. Around his face, much of it was ochre, dampened by water—and by the scent he exuded, probably reddened with berries.

"You should leave," said Berun, his right hand tightening the arrow on his bowstring. "The tiger won't be gone long."

The man straightened, still cautious, ready, but obviously relaxing. A slight smile curved his lips. "No," he said. "She will not."

"What is this?"

The man motioned to the ground with his spear. "Put that bow down. Nice and slow."

In one fluid motion Berun pivoted, facing the man sideways to present a narrow target, and brought the bowstring to his cheek. The steel head of the arrow aimed at the man's torso.

"Easy!" said the man, his eyes widening as he took a quick step back. He brought the spear up, but the look in his eyes said he knew it a futile gesture.

"I save your life and you want to rob me?"

"That isn't how this is!"

"I'm not worth dying over. The poorest shepherd on the steppe has more gold in his croft than I have on me. This bow is the only thing of value I own."

"And a fine weapon it is!" said a voice from above.

Keeping the arrow aimed at the spearman, Berun risked a quick glance up at the rocks. Kneeling on the very boulder from where he had watched the tiger was a massive shape silhouetted by the dying blue of the sky. He knew that voice, and even as he studied the silhouette, other shapes joined it—one man to the right and two to the left. Last of all, the massive form of the steppe tiger joined the group. Berun knew who was above him.

The silhouette stood and sidestepped so that a shaft of sunlight, orange as an ember in the evening dim, fell on him. He was half-orc, nearly seven feet of grayish skin over knotted muscle, his coarse black hair falling in a series of braids over his shoulders and down his back. Two incisors, one yellow and one silver, protruded from his bottom lip. Tattoos that suggested thorned vines decorated his arms and face. A bone-handled knife was sheathed at his waist, and the pommel of a sword protruded above one shoulder.

"Lower the bow," said the half-orc. "We're here to talk, not fight."

Berun hesitated. If he could feather the spearman, he might make it down the ravine. Maybe. But even if he could, he'd never outrun the steppe tiger.

Berun lowered the bow. He let the tension leave the string, but he kept a good grip on the arrow between his fingers.

"Well met, Kheil!" said the half-orc. "Been a long time."

✠

chapter four

The half-orc took his time climbing down the rocks. The other men—and they were all men, as near as Berun could tell—kept watch from above, their hands lingering near their weapons. One had a crossbow, latched and ready. Two others held bows with arrows on the strings. Even though Berun could see no hard details, only suggestions of substance amidst the silhouettes and shadows, he could read the tension in the men's stances. Five stood there at the moment, and Berun worried that more might be on the ridge above him. The tiger lounged with them. She crouched on the boulder the half-orc had left. She looked around, the only one at ease.

The half-orc jumped the last distance into the pool then waded to shore. Dripping from the waist down as he emerged from the water, his eyes never left Berun. He walked near and stopped an arm's length away. The half-orc stood a full head taller than Berun, and where Berun was lean, the half-orc was a mass of muscle. He grabbed Berun by the chin and forced him to look up.

"It is you," said the half-orc, almost in a whisper. "Talieth swore, but I never thought . . ." The half-orc studied Berun's features. "I saw you. Saw you taken. How . . . ?"

Berun jerked his chin out of the half-orc's grasp and looked him in the eyes. "What do you want, Sauk?"

31

The half-orc flinched. Hurt sparked in his eyes, then it kindled and his gaze turned to anger. "What do I *want*? That's all you have to say to me?"

Berun glared at Sauk, holding the half-orc's gaze. "What do you want, Sauk?"

The half-orc glared back, breathing like a bellows, then he swung his fist. It felt like a knotted log as it struck Berun on the side of the face, and he went down hard. Floating orbs were just beginning to leave his vision when the top of Sauk's foot caught him in the ribs, driving all air from his body.

"What do I *want?*" the half-orc shouted.

Berun struggled to take a breath, and what little he managed caught in a ragged cough. The punch had driven the inside of his cheek against his teeth, and blood filled his mouth. Coughing and retching, Berun fought to regain his breath. When he opened his eyes, he saw his bow and arrow on the rocks beside him. He couldn't remember dropping them.

The half-orc grabbed Berun's vest above the shoulders and hauled him to his feet. Stars swirled his vision, but Berun could see that Sauk's rage was spent. Regaining his breath, Berun turned and spat blood onto the rocks, then shook himself free of the half-orc's grip.

"Why are you here, Sauk? How did you find me?"

He glanced up, wondering if he was in for another beating, but the half-orc only looked down at him, a mixture of sorrow and anger playing on his features.

"I thought you dead, you ungrateful bastard. I mourned you a year. I bled for your memory." He pointed to a scar that ran from his forehead to his cheek. It was a *luzal unba* mark, a ritualized scar of Sauk's orc clan, a self-inflicted wound cut down the face in remembrance of a lost brother. "How did I find you? I didn't. Talieth did. Saw you in her scrying pool. Swore to me that you were alive after all these years. I called her a liar."

"You were not wrong. Kheil died in the Yuirwood. I am called Berun now."

"Berun?" Sauk snorted.

"It means 'hope' in the tongue of Aglarond. The druids gave me the name."

"The same druids who killed you?"

"The same druid Kheil was sent to kill."

The two stared at each other, Berun holding the half-orc's gaze, Sauk flexing one fist. Berun knew the half-orc was giving serious consideration to beating him again.

"What happened to you?" said Sauk. The half-orc looked down on him, his gaze hardening with each breath until his gray eyes stared out, hard as flint.

"Kheil died."

"You don't look dead."

"I told you. I am *not* Kheil. I am Berun."

A moment of tense silence, then, "That's how it is, then? After all we shared . . ."

Berun didn't want to antagonize Sauk any further, and mostly he felt . . . not compassion. Not quite. Not for Sauk. But neither did he take any pleasure in deepening another person's pain. Not even Sauk.

He swallowed and said, "Kheil is dead. Nine years dead."

"Let him rest easy," said Sauk. "Is that it?"

"Kheil will never rest easy."

Sauk snorted and looked down on him. He reached into a large pocket of his vest and pulled out what looked like a thin green strip leather. He held it out to Berun, who realized at once what it was. Perch's tail.

"I had to pull your lizard off Taaki," said Sauk. "But the damned thing's tail snapped right off."

"Where is he?"

"Your lizard?" Sauk shrugged. "You tell me. Little bug-eater ran off. You really care that much?"

"You care about Taaki?"

Sauk blinked and his eyes widened. For him, that signified shock. "You have an *arumwon?*"

Berun took the tail. "Something like that."

Among Sauk's orc clan, *arumwon* meant "beast brother," an animal friend meant to serve and protect. Berun suspected it was very much like his own bond with Perch.

Sauk shook his head, a smile threatening to crease his face. "Kheil the assassin turned *zuwar*. Never would've thought." He banged his chest with a tight fist. *"Kumash damun!* Taste the blood! Eh, Kheil?"

Blood had filled Berun's cheek again, but he knew that if he spit now, Sauk would take it as a grave insult. Berun swallowed. "The Beastlord did not call me, Sauk," said Berun. "I serve the Oak Father."

A look that was half smirk and half scowl twisted Sauk's face, as if he'd bitten down on a bitter root. "That explains why you hunt with a lizard instead of a tiger."

"That lizard whipped your tiger."

A dangerous glint lit Sauk's gaze. "Taaki did as she was told. She got you down here. She'd've eaten your little lizard had she wanted. Little thing like that, she probably wouldn't have bothered chewing."

Berun opened his mouth to say, *She'd have had to catch him first, and she was doing a poor job of that,* but good sense took hold of his tongue and he clamped his jaw shut.

"You hungry, old friend?" asked Sauk.

"Not really."

"You always were a master liar, Kheil, but I could always see through you. Me and Talieth, we were the only ones, eh?"

Berun said nothing.

"We have things to discuss," said Sauk. "Many things. And tongues always wag better over a full stomach. Come."

Berun unstrung his bow and carefully slid the arrow back into his quiver. It would be no use against so many. If it came to a fight, it would be bladework.

One of Sauk's men tossed a knotted rope over the rocks so they could climb up. Sauk went first, then Berun, followed by the spearman. When Berun came up over the ledge, the steppe tiger crouched an arm's length away. Taaki looked down at him, her eyes narrowed. Her nostrils flared and the lips pulled back over her teeth. Again the growl seemed to hit the gut more than the ears.

"*Ragh ala,* Taaki," said Sauk, calming her. He looked down on Berun. "She remembers you. Still doesn't like you much."

Berun stepped aside to give the spearman room to get up—and to put the half-orc between him and the tiger. "She never liked Kheil," he said. "She doesn't know me."

"Hunters know their own," said Sauk. He turned away, and the tiger followed.

Berun kept a careful eye on the underbrush and treetops as they walked. Perch was close but keeping himself hidden. In the early evening with the shadows thick, it was easy for Perch to stay out of sight. Not once did he show himself, but Berun knew he was there all the same.

The loss of his tail hadn't really hurt Perch. It was a gift of his species—the tail snapped off to distract a predator long enough to get away. Given proper nourishment, he'd grow a new one soon enough.

They walked less than a quarter mile, to a place where an offshoot of a stream fed a reed-choked pool. Sauk and his men made their camp just where stream met pool, so they were surrounded by water on two sides. Full dark had fallen, and Sauk's men busied themselves building fires.

Taaki padded off into the woods, and Sauk motioned for Berun to sit opposite a small fire from him. The half-orc seemed grim, his brows low and his jaw tight. Berun knew that he had probably spent their walk going over their conversation, getting angrier with each retelling in his mind.

Berun sat and put his unstrung bow across his lap.

Sauk glanced down at it. "A fine weapon. You always hated the bow," said Sauk. "Called it a coward's weapon. You liked to get in close for the kill, see your prey's eyes as the light dimmed. One of the things I liked about you."

Kheil had once said those very words—and meant them. Berun said, "I don't kill for pleasure."

"You seemed ready to kill Gerrell down by the water. And you've been hunting Taaki for days."

"Your man was about to kill me—or so I thought. I was hunting Taaki only because I thought a beast had come out of the Khopet-Dag. She's been killing sheep, you know. Took a shepherd. And the hunters sent after her still haven't been found. Had I known it was Taaki, I—"

"What?" said Sauk, heat rising in his voice. "Turned tail and hid in the woods, hoping I'd go away?"

Berun looked into the fire. The barb struck. He'd been thinking those very thoughts after sending Lewan away.

"I believe you," said Sauk. "You told me Kheil died. I didn't believe you. Didn't want to. Thought perhaps my brother had returned by some miracle. Now I see that I was a fool to hope."

Lifting his gaze from the flames, Berun looked up and said, "Kheil is dead. I am Berun now."

"Berun, sworn of the Oak Father," said Sauk, his upper lip lifted in a sneer. "A damned leaf lover. A blight beater."

The world came into sudden, sharp focus. Even the sounds of the stream and men talking as they went about their business seemed clear, every ripple of the water and companionable jibe distinct. Berun recognized the sudden awareness in him for what it was. Anger. He'd been holding a lid on his fear since seeing those letters scratched in the boot print. Fear that Kheil's old life was catching up to him after nine years of trying to bury it. But Sauk's casual curse of the Oak Father and his servants had lifted that lid off his fear, and here in the nighttime camp, Berun found himself filled with anger. No, not anger. Pure, cold rage. Nine years! Nine years of burying the past, and here it was again, spitting in the face of all he now held precious.

"You never answered me," said Berun, his voice careful and controlled. "What do you want? Why this ruse to draw me out here? 'A fool to hope.' Please. You didn't go through all this for a reunion. You want something. You said Talieth found me. Did she send you? Are you still her father's favorite lapdog?"

The rest of the camp had gone quiet halfway through Berun's speech. Every man now stood watching, some sitting paralyzed with bits of food held before open mouths. Others were caressing the hilts of their weapons. All eyes were on Sauk.

The half-orc's eyes had narrowed to slits, and he was grinding his teeth as he watched Berun.

One of the men standing behind Sauk, a tall man with dirty blond hair who looked as if he hadn't shaved in days, said, "I think we ought to teach this one some courtesy. Eh, Sauk?"

"Val, that you?" said Sauk, not turning around.

"Yes."

"If I want to know what you think, I'll ask you. You want to lead this party? All you have to do is get through me. Understood?"

Much of the boldness went out of the man's gaze, and he looked away from Berun. "Understood. You're the boss."

"Am I?" said Sauk, still not taking his eyes from Berun. "Or am I the Old Man's favorite lapdog?"

Berun said nothing. He forced his muscles to relax. He sat less than five feet from one of the fiercest hunters he'd ever known, and he was surrounded by seven armed men, all watching and ready to kill him, awaiting only their master's word. And there was still the tiger to consider. Hopeless. If he'd had some distance and more cover between him and the men, if his bow were ready, if, if, if . . .

If it came to that, he wasn't going back to the grave alone.

Then Sauk did the last thing Berun expected. He threw back his head and laughed, rocking back and forth on his rump, his hands on his knees. Confused, Berun looked around. A few of the men relaxed, but most still stood tense, hands on weapons. The looks on their faces showed that they were just as confused as he was.

"Oh, Kheil," said Sauk, wiping the tears from his eyes with the back of one hand. "Pardon me. *Berun.* Berun, it must be. Kheil was never such a damned fool."

"Fool or not, Kheil is dead," said Berun. He tried to hold on to his anger, but he could feel it slipping away. "I'm sitting here alive."

Sauk went still again, though the mirth did not leave his countenance. "Well, for now anyway," he said. "You think the Old Man sent us, is that it? Sent his favorite lapdog after his favorite assassin? Bring the naughty boy back home? The little runaway?"

"Isn't it?"

Berun saw several men exchanging amused glances, and the one Sauk had called Val grinned and shook his head, like a favorite uncle amused at his nephew's latest foolishness.

"Not even a little," said Sauk. "Wrong on all counts, in fact. Berun, you are sitting surrounded by conspiracy. Every one of these men, this half-orc included, has sworn to see the Old Man of the Mountain dead. Or die trying. Now sit and listen."

✚

chapter five

You spoke truly about one thing," said Sauk. "I didn't come for a reunion. Gerrell?" The half-orc looked to one of his men, the one who had held the spear on Berun down in the ravine. The man's wounds were all cleaned, though filth still covered his clothes. "Food ready yet?"

"Almost, Sauk."

Sauk returned his attention to Berun. "Not much, I'm afraid. We haven't hunted in days. Bits of smoked venison stewed with whatever else they throw in. Doesn't taste like much, but it'll fill you. There's bread, too, though you might have to pick out the bugs."

"Tell me what you want with me," said Berun, "then I'll decide whether to accept your hospitality."

"What makes you think I'm giving you a choice?"

"There's always a choice, Sauk."

"Not always a good one."

Sauk rummaged through the leather satchel at his belt and pulled out a half-eaten hunk of brown bread. Seeing that, a flood of memories hit Berun. He knew that no matter how hungry Sauk became, if anyone offered the half-orc meat, he would not eat it. Sauk served Malar, the Beast-lord, and he would eat no flesh that he himself had not hunted and killed. He'd choke on moldy, maggot-infested bread first.

39

Sauk bit into the loaf and spoke as he chewed. "That druid. The one the Old Man sent us to kill nine years ago."

"Chereth," said Berun.

"Yes," said Sauk. "Or as we in the Fortress have come to call him: 'The one who got away.' "

A few of the men, listening in, laughed at this.

"He the one who killed y—uh, killed Kheil, that is?"

"No," said Berun. "The rangers executed Kheil. Chereth called me back to serve the Oak Father."

Sauk nodded and swallowed, and Berun caught a glimpse of a strange look that the half-orc quickly hid. A knowing, pleased expression. Another memory hit Berun. Something Talieth used to say. *The best way to catch a liar is to ask him questions to which you already know the answer.* Was that Sauk's game here?

"And then?" asked Sauk.

"Then?"

"After you were . . . 'called back to serve?' "

"Chereth brought me to the Oak Father and taught me the ways of the wild."

"His ways," said Sauk.

Berun knew that Sauk was thinking of Malar. Sauk was *zuwar,* a hunter sworn to the service of Malar the Beastlord. The Beastlord was also of the wild, but only of its more bestial aspects—the hunt, the kill, survival of the strong. The Oak Father did not deny those aspects, but Chereth had taught him that these were only one leaf on a tree that grew many branches.

"You knew Chereth well, then?" asked Sauk.

"He was my master," said Berun, and left it at that. In truth, he had known the old half-elf as well as anyone, which was to say he'd seen only the surface of a pool that ran very deep.

"Did you know that five years ago Chereth came to Sentinelspire?"

"I . . . suspected."

Sauk's eyebrows shot up. "And you let your beloved master go? Knowing what you know? Knowing us?"

Berun clamped his jaw shut and stared into the fire.

"Your Oak Father breeds odd disciples," said Sauk. "Your master walks headlong into death, and you don't so much as go after his body, much less vengeance."

Berun said nothing. He knew that Sauk was trying to provoke him, partially to see what information another torrent of angry words might reveal and partly out of his own personal disgust for the so-called "leaf lovers" and "blight beaters"—druids and their ilk who did not embrace the savagery of the wild.

"Do you know why your master came to Sentinelspire?" said Sauk.

"He"—Berun swallowed to keep his voice from breaking—"wouldn't tell me."

"Ah," said Sauk. "Old leaf lover wanted to protect his precious disciple. That it? Well, you know more than I thought. But this I'll bet you don't know." The half-orc smiled and took another bite of bread. He chewed, swallowed, and took a sip from a waterskin. "Your old druid came to Sentinelspire to kill the Old Man of the Mountain." Sauk paused, giving the words time to sink in—or perhaps letting the hook dangle before the fish. "Imagine that. An old leaf lover coming to the most impregnable citadel east of Thay and hoping to kill the king of killers. Now *there* is a tale!"

Sauk's words didn't really surprise Berun. He'd long known that there was some sort of history between Chereth, Master of the Yuirwood, and Alaodin, Old Man of the Mountain. What exactly that history had been, he had no idea. But nine years ago, Alaodin had sent Kheil, the best assassin in his arsenal, to kill Chereth in his homeland, surrounded by hundreds of allies. Such a desperate mission could not have been a random act, nor even a job bought and paid for by some western lord or lady. It had to be grave and personal for the Old Man to have sent Kheil. In the five years since Chereth had left him, Berun had not passed a day without wondering of his master's fate. All those days of wandering through villages, seeking other druid Circles, looking for word from the old half-elf, hoping for any rumor but finding none. To now have it confirmed . . .

Berun felt . . . what? Tired. That was it. All those years of hoping had given him purpose. To have that hope crushed left him feeling lost and weary.

"But," said Sauk, his voice going quiet, scarcely more than a whisper, "here's the thing I bet you didn't know." He smiled. "Chereth is still alive."

Breath caught in Berun's throat. "Alive?"

"As you and me."

"But . . . the Old Man?"

Sauk smiled. "Hale as ever."

"But you said that you and your men have sworn to kill him. I don't understand."

"You want to know about your master or about the Old Man?"

Both, Berun realized, and he didn't like that.

"Truth be told," Sauk continued, "you need to hear both. That's why we came for you. Your master made the same mistake the Old Man did—he hunted prey in its own den. Nothing is more dangerous than a wild animal cornered in its home. Long tale cut short, the Old Man captured your master and has held him prisoner all these years."

"Prisoner?" said Berun. The thought of old Chereth locked in the stony cells of Sentinelspire . . .

"At times," said Sauk, "the Old Man spends half the day and night talking to the old leaf lover. Enjoys his company like a favorite uncle. Other times, the Old Man questions him. Questions him hard."

Sauk didn't have to explain. Berun knew all too well what an interrogation by the Old Man of the Mountain entailed.

"Sometimes," said Sauk, "the Old Man uses his . . . arts"— the half-orc scowled as if he'd tasted something sour —"to leech power from the leaf lover."

Berun's anger turned cold. The Old Man had once been a devoted follower of Bhaal. The death of his god had hit him hard, made him desperate in his search for a new source of power. He'd never been too particular about where the power came from.

"Other times," Sauk continued, his voice dropping low, "the Old Man hurts your master. Hurts him just for the pleasure of it."

"What?" said Berun. "Why?"

" 'Cause that's what the Old Man does."

"No," said Berun. "Not Alaodin. He's a killer, but it's . . . business. Even the Old Man never hurt just to hurt."

"You've been gone a long time," said Sauk. "Almost nine years. Things have changed at the Fortress. Things happen now that . . ." The half-orc's voice faltered and he shook his head. "Dark things. Vile."

"What kind of things?"

Sauk scowled into the fire and made the sign of the Beastlord—three fingers hooked like claws, which he dragged down his face and heart. "Not here," he said. "Not in the dark."

"You? Afraid?"

"Afraid?" said Sauk, thinking as he chewed a large hunk of bread. He swallowed. "If you mean am I made weak at the thought of dying, then no. I don't know that kind of fear. Not anymore. But there are worse things than death, and I have hunted enough prey—many stronger than me—to know when it is time to strike and kill and boast, and when it is best not to draw attention to yourself. Besting those stronger than you . . . that is honor. Calling down doom . . . that's just foolish."

Sauk chewed his lip and stared into the fire. The rest of the camp had gone quiet, caught up in Sauk's tale.

The half-orc broke the silence. "But that's not why we came for you. This is about that old druid locked in the Fortress."

"His name is Chereth," said Berun. "And why do you care?"

Sauk looked down at his bread, as if considering another bite, but he grimaced and put it away. "About the half-elf?" he said. "I don't. Old leaf lover means nothing to me. But the Old Man . . . he's gone mad. You know me, Kheil. I have no qualms about killing when there is profit in it, or a fair fight. But a bloodlust has seized the Old Man. He's gone beyond simple murder-for-hire to massacres. The old fool is killing for pleasure or just plain meanness. He's put our entire operation in jeopardy. Last winter, he killed three of our best clients—western nobles who paid well. But Talieth . . ."

"What?" Berun cursed the eager tone in his voice. Very few days had gone by over the years that her face, her scent, the feel of her skin did not come to his mind, but every time he thrust them away. Kheil had loved her. And Kheil was dead.

"Talieth suspects something darker is at work. She fears her father is on the verge of doing something . . . irreversible." Sauk ground his jaw and looked away. His nostrils flared and he slapped the ground. "Damn it all, we want him dead."

Berun held Sauk's gaze. The half-orc looked back, unflinching.

"We?" said Berun.

"Me, Talieth, and every man here. A few others at the Mountain."

"So kill him," said Berun, his voice hard.

Sauk snorted, but there was no humor in it. Only disgust. "We tried," he said. "Talieth sent her best blades but the Old

Man killed 'em all. The Old Man has been using your master's power to set new guardians. Things I've never seen before. Things that haunt the dark places of the mountain. Things that scare even Talieth, and I've never seen anything frighten that woman."

A smile threatened to break over Berun's face but he held it back.

"But it doesn't end there," said Sauk. "The Old Man rooted out any who had colluded with the assassins. Didn't just kill them. He tortured them. Till they begged for death. When we left the Fortress, their bodies were still on the walls. Some dead and rotting. Even the crows won't touch them. But some . . . some were still alive." He took a long swig from the waterskin and swallowed with a wince. "Wrapped in thorns and vines, bleeding, their skin rotting away even as they begged for someone to end their pain."

Berun shuddered. "Talieth . . . ?"

"The Old Man suspects her. He's no fool. But she is his daughter. She's still alive—or was when we left—but she walks the razor's edge. She's all but a captive in the Fortress, and the Old Man might kill her any time the whim hits him."

"How did you get away?"

Sauk spared a glance at his men and a smile, sly and pleased, crossed his face. "Well, I said the Old Man rooted out the assassins. I should have said 'any he could find.' He found several. Too damned many. But not all."

"As far as you know," said Berun.

The grin froze on Sauk's face, faltered, then fell. "Yes, as far as we know."

"So the Old Man could just be biding his time. Playing you like a cat pawing at a mouse."

Sauk's eyes narrowed. "I'm no mouse."

"What about your men?"

The tall blond man behind Sauk bristled and scowled at this, but he held his tongue.

"You aren't half as smart as you think you are," said Sauk. "Talieth's always had a gift for magic—more than a little touch of the seer's gift."

"Don't tell me what I already know," said Berun.

"Really?" Sauk's eyebrows rose, but Berun saw the mockery in the expression. "*Kheil* knew Talieth well—in many senses of the word. Seems that Berun remembers. Maybe Kheil isn't so dead after all, eh?"

Berun didn't respond.

"Using her . . . gift, Talieth found you, whatever you choose to call yourself. She knew you were alive. But . . . well, it seems that leaf-loving master of yours doesn't know how to hold his tongue."

"What do you mean?"

"I mean your old master talked. Sang like a damned minstrel for his supper. Mad the Old Man may be, but he's no fool. He figured out who this 'Berun' was . . . is . . . whatever. There are still blades in the Fortress loyal to the Old Man. Had it not been for Talieth's particular gifts, they might have found you first."

"Found me?" Berun's heart hammered, and he suddenly felt as if his breathing were too loud and quick. "What does the Old Man want with me?"

"You have something he wants."

"Something he wants?" said Berun. "What—?"

"Air eye lin, or something like that."

"Erael'len?"

"As you say," said Sauk. "Never could wrap my tongue around the damned elfspeak."

"It's Aglarondan. It means—" Berun stopped, cursing himself.

"Means what?"

"Three Hearts."

"Three Hearts," said Sauk. "How sweet. Damned leaf lovers. No teeth in their jaws. When your old master talked, the Old

Man became interested. *Very* interested. Seems he not only misses his favorite assassin, but he's hungry for this thing you carry, the Three Hearts.

"Which is why Talieth sent me after it," said Sauk. "After you. So what do you say? Kill the Old Man and help save your old master. Are you with us?"

"No." The word slipped out before Berun could stop it. But he didn't regret it.

"No?" said Sauk, his tone equal parts shock and outrage.

"I . . . can't," said Berun. "Things are different now."

Lewan. That's what it all came down to. The boy wasn't everything. There was the Old Man, Talieth, Sauk, and Sentinelspire itself, all facets of Kheil's old life that Berun had hoped were dead and buried forever. Going back to them . . . it would be too much like stepping back into Kheil's skin. There was the thought of Chereth, his beloved master, a prisoner, possibly being tortured or worse, but every thought of the old druid only reminded Berun of his oath. *I swear I will not come after you, save on your word alone. By my blood upon thorn I swear it.* By blood and thorn had he been given life, a second chance. He couldn't defile that. But beyond all that was Lewan. He couldn't forsake the boy. Like Berun, Lewan was alone in the world. All they had was each other.

Sauk held his scowl a good long while, but then he smiled and shook his head. "Nothing I can say to change your mind, old friend?"

"Sauk, you must understand, I have . . . other responsibilities now." He took a deep breath and offered up a silent prayer. "I will help, if I can. But you must allow me to do it *my* way."

Sauk's smile went feral. "Now there's the Kheil I remember."

"You said it yourself," said Berun. "The Old Man has new guardians, things none of us understand. If he's somehow

47

leeching power off Chereth, then I need to find others who understand such powers better than I do."

"You mean druids."

"Yes."

"But you—"

"I'm no druid, Sauk. Chereth was my master, and he taught me many things. Had he continued to teach me . . . someday, perhaps. But now I am simply a servant of the wild. I'll be no help to you. But perhaps I can find those who will be."

"There's no time for that."

"If I can find a grove, there are rites I can perform to contact help."

"I can't allow that."

"Why?"

"Make no mistake here," said Sauk. "We're out to kill the Old Man. Kill him dead and put him on a pyre. But the Fortress of the Old Man, the blades—those will live on. And you know our ways. Invitation only, and only those wishing for our . . . services. You think I'm going to allow you to bring a flock of tree lovers into a fortress that has stood undiscovered by outsiders for generations? You know us better than that, Kheil."

"Berun."

"*Berun,* then! I don't care what you call yourself. We must stop him, and we need you—and what you carry—to do that." The earnestness in Sauk's eyes hit Berun. "Don't you want to help your old master?"

"I do. But rushing to my own death won't help him. If half of what you say is true, if the Old Man's powers are beyond Chereth's, then I can do nothing against him. I'll need help."

Sauk's gaze hardened again. "That the way it is, then? Despite what you call yourself now, you have to remember that we were once as brothers. I come to you asking for help and you turn me away?"

That felt like a slap. Something tingled deep in Berun's mind. Not shame, exactly. More like confusion and a niggling fear that there was some truth to the half-orc's words. Still, his mind was made up. The only sure way of getting Chereth out alive was to find help. And there was Lewan to think about.

"My mind is made up, Sauk."

The half-orc's shoulders slumped, just for a moment, then he stiffened again. "I was afraid you'd say that. Have it your way."

Sauk whistled, a harsh shriek between his bottom lip and top teeth that cut through the darkness. For several moments nothing happened, and then he heard it. Something approached through the woods. Not Taaki. The tiger would never make so much noise, even in the dark.

Two more of Sauk's men emerged from the wood, and between them walked Lewan. The boy's bow was gone, and his quiver and sheath hung empty from his belt. His left sleeve had been ripped halfway off his shirt, dirt and mud smeared him, and he had grass and twigs in his hair. He seemed unhurt, but his eyes had the look of a deer that had been outrunning a wolf pack and knew it could run no more.

Berun leaped to his feet, his unstrung bow clutched in one hand. "What is this?"

The half-orc rose and put out a placating hand. "Easy. Calm yourself. We need you—and what you carry. The boy will be safe as long as you come with us and behave yourself."

Berun stared spears at Sauk for several long breaths. It didn't seem to bother the half-orc.

"Lewan," said Berun, looking to his disciple, "are you hurt?"

The boy blinked and looked at Berun. His jaw started to quiver, but he clenched it and swallowed. "I'm fine, master."

"He just had a good long run that didn't end well," said the man to Lewan's left. "We did him no harm."

Berun returned his attention to Sauk. "Free the boy, and I'll come with you."

"You will come with us anyway," said Sauk. "And so will the boy."

Berun ground his teeth, looked off into the dark, and took a deep, controlled breath. He'd have to play this just right. He'd done this before, but never against so many, and never against a hunter like Sauk.

Closing his eyes, Berun let out the breath, nice and slow. Still standing, he relaxed his muscles and took another breath, this time through his nose, drawing in strength. Keeping his gaze set on the dark, Berun reached out with his other senses.

Scent. He smelled the wood smoke of the campfires, the thin stew bubbling in a cast iron cauldron, the damp of the streamside mud, the slight musky tang of sweat, leather, and unwashed clothes from Sauk and his men.

Sounds. The crackling of the nearby fire, loudest of all. The shuffle of men beside their fires, their low conversation, the scrape of their boots over ground. A slight breeze rattling the tops of the trees. Crickets, frogs, a night bird or two. The flutter of a moth past his ear.

Feeling. The air, tinged by smoke, passing in and out of his throat, filling his lungs. The soft scrape of his clothes against his skin. Cool air along his left cheek, warmer air on the right side that faced the fire. And deeper down, deep behind his eyes where men could only see in dreams, Berun sensed Perch, the edge of the little animal's mind touching his own. Berun knew that the treeclaw lizard crouched above them somewhere in the darkness amongst the branches, watching. Perch could sense the tiger in the area, taste her scent on the air, but he couldn't see her.

Returning his gaze to the half-orc, Berun said, "Nothing I can say to change your mind?"

Sauk stood, slowly, watching Berun, perhaps sensing

something out of the ordinary. He returned Berun's stare, eye to eye. "No," he said.

"That's what I thought you'd say." Keeping his face turned to the half-orc, Berun fixed his gaze on the man on Lewan's left. *That one,* he told Perch. *Strike. Tooth and claw. Tooth and claw!*

Perch's excitement lit up. *Fight-fight-fight! Strike-tooth-and-claw!*

A shadow fell from the darkness overhead. . . .

✠
chapter six

And hit the man next to Lewan in the face. The man went down screaming, the lizard hanging on.

Berun shouted, "Lewan, go! Go!"

The man on Lewan's left thrashed on the ground and slapped at the leathery shape clawing at his face. The other man had hold of Lewan's forearm. The boy twisted and brought his knee into the man's crotch. The man's eyes squeezed shut and he crumpled to the ground.

Lewan, eyes wide, cast one quick glance at Berun.

"Go, Lewan!" shouted Berun, just as Sauk screamed, "Get that boy!"

Seeing five men coming for him, Lewan turned and ran for the woods. Sauk's men leaped after him. Berun let his bow slide down his grasp so he held it only a foot or so from the end. The bow was only thick in the middle and wouldn't make much of a staff, much less a club, but it might serve to distract the half-orc if nothing else. These men, if they were from Sentinelspire, were most likely trained killers. The best at what they did, surely. But Berun was willing to bet that Sauk was the only true woodsman in the group.

Berun turned, cocked his arm, and swiped the bow outward, aiming for Sauk's face.

The half-orc sidestepped and ducked. He turned and

looked at Berun, his lips curling in a snarl over his incisors. "That's how it is, then?"

Seeing their master facing off against Berun, two of Sauk's men—Val and Gerrell, if Berun remembered right—stopped just inside the reach of the firelight and turned around.

"Let him go, Sauk," said Berun. "The boy isn't in this."

"He is now," said Sauk—and lunged, aiming a jab at Berun's face.

Berun sidestepped, brought the bow up, and turned the punch aside—just as Sauk's left fist hit him in the gut. In that last instant, he thought he felt Sauk's knuckles scrape his backbone. All breath burst out of Berun in one gasp. His legs turned to water and he fell. His next thought was plain, stupid pride—he was grateful his bowels had held and he hadn't retched up his last seven meals. Then his thoughts vanished. His vision blurred and his body poured every bit of energy into getting breath back into his lungs.

Lewan used the fall. He'd been running as fast as he dared. But beyond the light of the campfires, all was pitch black, and through the trees he had to cast his arms in front of him and run more by feel than sight, each headlong sprint broken by stumbles over the uneven ground, roots, and rocks. Shouts from behind spurred him on.

Branches scratched his clothes and scraped skin off his face and hands. After a bad stumble that left his shin bloody, Lewan risked a glance back as he pushed himself to his feet. The men had stopped long enough to light torches. He could see two of them amongst the trees, and the distance from them to himself made hope flare in his heart.

Then something roared off to his right. The tiger.

Lewan ran, pumping his arms, heedless of the branches and leaves. He'd run perhaps two dozen steps when the ground fell away beneath him. He hit the downslope, biting his cheek as he did so, and continued a long slide down a hill covered in generations of leaves and fallen branches. When he finally came to rest at the bottom, the avalanche of detritus he'd caused kept coming, burying him.

And so Lewan used it, keeping absolutely motionless, forcing himself to take deep, slow breaths rather than the gasps his body demanded. From somewhere above he heard men crashing through the brush.

"Here!" one shouted. "This way!"

"No." This voice fainter. "He'd keep to the ridges where the ground is surer. Can't you see?"

"I can see. But he can't. He's got no light, and look how all the leaves are disturbed."

Lewan's heart hammered, and he tensed, preparing to run again.

"A tracker now, are you? Just 'cause you follow Sauk don't mean—"

"Move, you idiots," said a third voice, and Lewan heard something coming down the hill.

Close now. Lewan could feel the vibration through the ground. The man stopped, probably no more than a pace or two above him, then began moving again.

A toe struck Lewan's shoulder.

"Got him!"

Lewan erupted from cover, put all his strength behind one fist, and brought it up into the fork of the man's legs. A pained gasp escaped the man, then he folded in on himself, dropping the torch.

"Ha!" said a voice from above. "That whelp got him again. Same damned place!"

The man lurched onto his knees as his companions started their way down. Lewan snatched the torch from the fallen leaves and thrust it at the man's face. The man saw it coming and slapped at the fire, then began to fall forward. He screamed in agony as the burning pitch stuck to his fingers, but the thrust had swiped the brand from Lewan's grip.

Lewan turned and ran, following the course of the valley between the two hills.

"After him!"

"My—hand!" said a voice that was half sob.

A harsh laugh, then, "That ain't the part *I'd* be worried about. I'd—holy gods!"

Lewan heard a rustle of leaves on the slope above him, then a mammoth weight hit his back and crushed him onto the leaf-covered ground.

When awareness began to seep back in, Berun saw the blond man—the one Sauk had called Val—standing over him, holding his bow and quiver. The man wore an insolent, almost pleased smile. Another man, shorter and darker, stood behind him. Sauk was crouched beside him, one fist clutching Berun's torn shirt. The other fist jerked back, and Berun felt fingers scrape the back of his neck just before he heard a snap. His necklace!

Sauk stood, a broken leather braid dangling from one fist. On the end of the braid was tied an intricate knotwork of hardened vines. Something in the midst of the vines caught the firelight and sparkled, almost as if an ember burned there. *Erael'len.*

"No!" said Berun as he lunged for it.

Sauk stepped back, almost casually, as Berun's hand swiped at empty air. Then the half-orc stepped forward again and brought the toe of his boot into Berun's side, just below the bottom rib. Biting back pain, Berun swiped at the necklace again, but Sauk caught his wrist and twisted. Berun struggled, but it was no use. His free hand reached for his knife—

The half-orc twisted harder, tough nails breaking through

Berun's sleeve and piercing skin. Bones in his wrist scraped together, then Sauk wrenched, bringing the entire arm around behind Berun's back.

Sauk planted one foot in the middle of Berun's back and said, "You draw steel on me and I'll tear your arm off. Understood?"

Berun poured the rest of his strength into a final attempt to pull his arm free.

Straightening the leg planted on Berun's back, Sauk pulled the arm tighter. Though he tried to hold it in, tried to clench his jaws shut, a scream escaped Berun.

"Understand now?" said Sauk.

The tension in the arm loosened. Not enough that he could move it, but just enough that Berun no longer felt as if muscles were tearing.

"Don't think he heard you." That was Val's voice. Berun couldn't turn his head enough to see, but he felt someone yank his knife out of the sheath.

Sauk let the arm go and put his full weight into the foot on Berun's back. His ribs creaked and he could only take shallow breaths.

"Just remember," said the half-orc, "*you* brought this on. If you'd behaved yourself, you and the boy would be sitting round the fire sharing some soup. Now—"

Shouts of men out in the woods. Berun could hear them. But beyond that, he heard the deep thunder of the tiger's roar, more shouting from the men, and then screaming. A boy screaming.

"Lewan!" gasped Berun, and he tried to push himself up. It was like pushing against a mountain root.

"You just stay down," said Sauk. "Taaki isn't going to kill the boy. But she *will* catch him, and she's not nearly as gentle as my men."

"Let"—Berun could barely take in enough air to speak —"boy—go."

"No," said Sauk.

"Why?" He wanted to ask, *What is he to you? He isn't involved. Let him go and I'll come along, do whatever you say,* and a dozen other things, but he couldn't find the breath to form any words.

"Right now? 'Cause you caused me a lot of trouble. Put my men to a lot of trouble. And you tried to hit me with your bow." Sauk stepped away, turned his head, and spat. "That wasn't nice, Kheil."

Sweet air filled Berun's lungs, and he rolled over onto his back. Breath was coming easier now, but his gut still hurt—a little higher with that first punch, and Berun knew he'd be holding broken ribs right now—and his arm felt like splinters were tumbling through his veins. Sauk stood a few paces away, arms across his chest. What he'd done with *Erael'len,* Berun couldn't see. Val stood beside the half-orc, Berun's bow and quiver cradled in his arms, the knife in one hand, and the insolent smile on his face. Gerrell stood behind them, spear in one hand, looking as if he didn't quite know what to do.

"Berun," said Berun.

"Berun," said Sauk. "Kheil. Leaf-lovin' blight-beater, I don't care what you call yourself. Keep this up and Berun might join Kheil, and they can bicker over who is who in the after-life. But to finish my answer—even if I weren't annoyed with you, I'd still keep the boy. It'll give you incentive to behave yourself. I have nothing against the boy. But understand, I've got no love for him either. You play nice—no more flyin' lizards in anyone's face, no more trying to slap me with your twig-tosser—and you and the boy can go your way once our business is done. You try any more of this nonsense, and I'll let Taaki have her way with little Lewan. Might even make you watch."

Berun stayed on the ground. He didn't want another boot on him just then, but he looked up and glared at the half-orc. *"Dukhal."*

Berun had never been fluent in the language of Sauk's orc tribe, but he knew enough to give a good curse. *Dukhal.* A bastard whelp. A vile enough insult to any orc, but for Sauk it held a particular barb. He was the son of the clan's chief and a human slave. His mother had died before Sauk could walk, and he'd spent his childhood competing for—and never winning—his father's affection and respect among the chieftain's legitimate sons.

Sauk's eyes went cold and hard. "There you go hurting my feelings again," he said. Then his visage seemed to soften a bit and something happened Berun would never have predicted. The half-orc looked almost . . . sad. Truly hurt. "I see now that Kheil my brother is dead indeed. I was not wrong to bleed for him. Still, we need you. I didn't lie. Help us with this . . . Berun. Help us, and you and the boy can go wherever your new god takes you." He turned to Val. "No need to tie him, but don't give his weapons back. As soon as he can sit up, put him by a fire and feed him. And keep an eye out for that lizard. Don't know where it got off to."

"The lizard?" said Val, looking annoyed. "What do you want me to do with a damned lizard?"

"Give it to him," said Sauk. "If he can get it to behave, fine. If not, throw it in the soup." He turned to walk away.

"Where are you going?" asked Val.

"Taaki can catch the boy," said Sauk over his shoulder. "But I don't know if she can bring him in without hurting him. I don't want to be up all damned night stitching up a mewling boy."

The half-orc sauntered off, and the dark of the wood soon swallowed him.

The blond man tossed away the unstrung bow and quiver, then held the knife up and knelt next to Berun. His insolent grin widened. "Name's Valmir," he said. "You can call me Val. Most around here do. You just listen to Sauk and behave yourself, and you and me'll get along just fine."

Berun considered bringing his leg up and jamming his boot in Valmir's face—the man was close enough—but he knew that even if that worked, he stood little chance of finding Lewan in the dark before Taaki and Sauk. This wasn't over. But something Sauk had told him earlier came to him—*I have hunted enough prey to know when it is time to strike and kill and boast, and when it is best not to draw attention to yourself. Calling down doom . . . that's just foolish.* And so Berun let his head fall back into the cushioning grass. He could still hear the tiger roaring, but the screams had stopped.

✚

chapter seven

15 Tarsakh, the Year of Lightning Storms (1374 DR)
The northern Shalhoond

They walked. Sauk roused the camp when dawn was no more than a pale shade of gray in the east. Lewan had barely slept. The events of the previous night had hit him hard. The tiger had not harmed him—at least not physically. Master hunter that she was, she'd forced him to the ground, much as she would a deer, but she'd kept her claws in, and her teeth had held his neck without piercing the skin. That had been the worst. In his travels with Berun, Lewan had seen cats hunt. Once the prey was subdued, they took it by the neck, and with a quick snap, it was all over.

He had lain there, crushed leaves filling his mouth, the breath of the tiger filling his ear and rushing all the way down his shirt, and had waited for those jaws to end him. He'd wondered if there would be pain, wondered if he'd be able to hear his own neck snap, or feel his throat cave in, or the teeth tear through the blood vessels of his neck.

But the snap hadn't come. The tiger had held him there, her massive paws pinning his back while her jaws gripped his neck. He had no idea how long he'd lain there. He thought he might have screamed, but afterward he couldn't remember. His first clear memory after the initial attack was the jaws loosening, moving away, then the great weight of the tiger was gone. Lewan had looked up, leaves clinging to his face, and the half-orc and his men were standing around him.

"Don't try that again," said the half-orc.

And that was it. No beating. No warning. No threats of punishment.

Except from one man, the one whom Lewan had hit with the torch. He came at Lewan, one hand clenched tight and trembling at his side, but the other holding a torch. In pain as he was, still he was quick, and he lunged with the flaming torch.

"Burn me, whelp? I'll—!"

Sauk's boot took the man in the gut, doubling him over, and the half-orc snatched the torch.

"You'll do nothing," said the half-orc. He looked down on the man, who lay near where the tiger had pinned Lewan. "Dren, see to his hand. Kerlis, you'd do well to stay away from the boy. I'm setting Taaki to watch him. You come at him, and Taaki will take you. And I won't stop her."

And that had been it. The half-orc had made sure Lewan wasn't hurt, even brushed off the clinging leaves and twigs, then brought him back to camp where he was fed, allowed to clean up, and given warm blankets by the fire. Still, after the events of the day, he'd lain awake long into the night, unable to stop his trembling. The only thing resembling punishment was that he was not allowed near Berun. He'd seen him, huddled near a fire on the far side of the camp. The way his master sat—hunched over, stiff, and favoring one side—Lewan knew he was hurting, but the two times Lewan rose and tried to walk over, the tiger came and stood in front of him with a growl so low that Lewan felt it in his boots.

And so it was the following day. As they walked deeper into the wood, the country becoming rougher and climbing with every mile, Lewan walked near the front of their procession, Sauk beside him or just ahead, the tiger following. In the few places where the forest paths broke through clearings, Lewan caught sight of Berun, walking at the very rear of the line, surrounded by three men, two of whom held naked blades. The third, the blond one Sauk had called Val, kept a wary eye on their surroundings and seemed to be trying to engage Berun in conversation, but to no success.

"Thirsty?"

Lewan turned around. Still walking at the easy pace he set, the half-orc held out an open waterskin.

When Lewan just stared at it, Sauk said, "Just water. Won't bite you."

Lewan took the skin and squeezed a few sips into his mouth. Just enough to keep him going. He tied it shut and handed it back to the half-orc.

"Keep it," said Sauk.

Lewan nodded thanks and tied the skin's cord round his belt.

"Feeling sick?" asked Sauk.

"No. Why?"

"Your color's no good. You look pale, and you've been jumping at every noise all morning."

They left the clearing and plunged back into the cool of the wood. In the brush off the path, spider webs hung heavy with morning dew. A few even crossed the path, but Sauk used his scabbard to clear them out of the way.

"I'm well enough," said Lewan.

"Not afraid of spiders, are you?"

"No."

"Don't let the webs worry you," said Sauk. "Nothing too dangerous in the lowlands. The big monsters stick mostly to the mountains, especially this early in the year."

"I've been living here for several seasons," said Lewan.

The half-orc grinned. "You know this country better than me. That what you're saying?"

Lewan shrugged. "I don't know you."

Another fit of trembling hit Lewan. He clenched his jaw and fists to quell it. The half-orc laid a palm against his face. Lewan flinched back.

"Just checking for fever," said the half-orc. "I mean you no harm."

Lewan snorted despite himself.

"Truly," said the half-orc. "You have nothing to fear from me."

"Then let us go."

"Us?"

"My master and I."

"Can't do that," said the half-orc. "You and Kheil are needed, whether he'll admit it or not."

"His name is Berun."

The half-orc rolled his eyes, then returned his attention to their path. "He never told you?"

"Told me what?"

"Your master . . . Berun"—Lewan heard the sneer in the word, though he couldn't see the half-orc's face —"used to go by the name Kheil. Kheil was once the best assassin west of Kora Shan. Some of the most powerful houses in Faerûn paid vast amounts of gold or favors for Kheil's services. Our master, the Old Man of the Mountain, most often specialized in quiet killing. Trained most of his men to make murder look like an accident. But Kheil was . . . special. Kheil was used when a message needed to be sent. Kheil didn't just kill. He *slaughtered*—and liked it."

"I don't believe you."

The half-orc chuckled and brushed a thick web from across the path before plunging onward. "Believe what you want. Kheil and I were more than comrades in arms. We were brothers."

"You're a half-orc."

"Dam yeluk ufrum kahutat naw."

"What?"

"A saying of the orc tribe where I grew up. It means, 'Blood is thicker than milk.' Means that brothers in blood"—the half-orc raised his right arm and flexed so the muscles of his forearm pushed up an old scar across his wrist —"are closer than brothers who shared the same mother's milk. That was Kheil and me."

Lewan scowled and looked away. Just off the path, a fat brown spider sat on a magnificent web larger than a knight's shield. Even as he watched, a moth hit the web, stuck, and began to struggle frantically. The spider skittered down, stopped, and watched a moment as the moth's struggles tangled it further, then it struck. It didn't bother Lewan. Killing was part of life. The moth would nourish the spider. In a few more tendays, her eggs would hatch, and her body would nourish her young. Struggle and death was part of living, but what Sauk was talking about—no other way to say it. It was murder, plain and simple.

"When I was fifteen," the half-orc continued, "about your age, eh? I killed my father's son. A good fight. He died well. But I did not mourn him. Hated him, in fact. Might have even danced on the ashes of his pyre had I not left him to rot by the river. But Kheil, I would have died for. I did kill for him. More than once. When I saw him taken that night in the Yuirwood, it was the blackest night of my life."

"My master," said Lewan, "isn't like that. He's not a . . . a *murderer.*"

The half-orc laughed, but kept it low and quiet. The wood pressing in on them seemed to call for silence. "Not now, maybe," said the half-orc. "This . . . Berun isn't the brother I knew. What do you know of him?"

"Know of him?"

"You seem damned determined not to believe me," said the half-orc. "Right now, I could tell you the sky is blue and we're walking in the woods, and you wouldn't believe me—because you don't *want* to. Even though in your heart you know it's true. So if you're so sure your precious master isn't the killer I know him to be, tell me why. You can't have known him more than nine years. I knew him far longer than that."

Lewan looked over his shoulder. The path had gone straight for a while, and he could just catch sight of Berun, still at the end of the line between the three men.

"Berun saved my life," said Lewan.

"Now there's a tale," said the half-orc. "Do tell."

Lewan took a deep breath. Years had dulled the edge of the pain, but these were memories he still didn't like to dredge up. "Raiders—outlaws out of the Ganathwood—hit my village. Killed my parents. Took me captive. They were almost back into their territory when Master Berun and his own master came upon them. They attacked the raiders. Saved my life."

"Your master and one other killed a whole band of raiders?" The half-orc smiled. "Sounds like a killer to me."

"That was justice—those bastards had it coming!" said Lewan, a bit of heat rising in his voice. "Not murder. The raiders deserved death. Deserved worse! Berun and his master didn't kill for pleasure or profit. They killed to save me."

"Killing is killing. The why . . . now that is something else."

The only other time Lewan had seen his master kill another person—a Tuigan outcast from his tribe who'd turned to banditry—Berun had taken no pleasure in it.

"It's the why that makes a murderer," said Lewan.

The half-orc turned and smiled down on him. "Like me?"

Yes, Lewan started to say, his mouth open, but instead he said, "I don't know you."

65

"I have killed for coins, boy," said the half-orc. "More times than I can remember. And I've killed for pleasure, hunting and slaying those stronger than me, more powerful. But my cunning won out, and I'm still breathing while they're rotting. Killing's part of life. Shy away from it, and you stand a good chance of being one of the rotters."

Lewan looked away.

"You ever killed anyone?" said the half-orc.

Lewan was silent a long time. Again, the pain of memories drained the color from his face. When he was sure he had control of his voice, he said, "I'm a hunter. My master taught me well."

"Meaning you've killed deer and rabbits. Maybe even a bear."

"I've killed three bears."

"But never a man? Never prey with weapon in hand and cunning in heart?"

Lewan scowled and looked away.

"I'll take that as a no," said the half-orc.

Walking at the rear of the column through the woods, Berun only caught occasional glimpses of Lewan. But each time he did, the boy was listening to Sauk. Berun scowled.

"Your boy is fine," said Val, who walked beside him.

Berun turned his scowl on the blond man.

"You look ready to chew rocks," said Val. That insolent smile again.

What Berun would have given to remove that smile with a few punches. Barring that, he'd have given his next three meals for the path to narrow again so that Val would walk behind him and not be so eager for conversation. The man's incessant chattering was bad enough. Combined with the raw pain in Berun's ribs and the dull fire in his shoulder from the beating he'd endured last night, Berun felt ready to kill. He hadn't hurt this bad in a long, long time, and he hadn't been another's prisoner since . . . never. Berun had *never* been a prisoner. Kheil had died a prisoner, and Berun had been reborn a free man.

And here he was held captive by Kheil's old life.

"The boy your son?" said Val.

Berun looked away.

" 'Cause he don't look like you," Val continued. "Looks like a Murghôm. Mulhorandi, maybe. His mother a Murghôm?"

Berun slowed down, hoping Val would walk ahead, but one of the two men walking behind them jabbed his short sword into Berun's back. "Move it! No lagging."

Val's smile widened. Berun knew he could have easily bested these three, even snatched one of their blades and disappeared into the forest before the other men could do anything about it. But Sauk not only had *Erael'len,* he had Lewan. And there was the tiger. Berun knew that to beat the tiger, he'd have to think like a tiger. Don't rush. Wait and let your prey give you the best chance to attack. Conserve your strength and wait.

"I don't think he's your boy," Val said. "Too old. If the stories I heard are true, that boy had to have been at least five or six years old when you left Sentinelspire. Unless you sowed some foreign fields while you were working for the Old Man . . ."

Their path narrowed, the trees and brush closing in, and Val fell behind. But it didn't deter him.

"Not much of a talker, are you?" he said. "Talieth said that was one of your better qualities."

"What about Talieth?" Berun slowed and half turned before he caught himself.

"Weh-hell!" said Val, beaming. "He *does* speak! A little salt in an old wound there, eh?"

Berun turned his eyes back to the path and kept walking.

He was glad Val was behind him and couldn't see the heat filling his face.

"It true what they say about you and Talieth?" Val said.

"Aren't you tired of talking yet, Val?" said one of the men behind them.

"Just trying to pass the miles."

"Well, we're tired of listening to you," said the other man.

"Then fall back," said Val, a sharp edge in his voice. "You don't have to hold my hand."

"Sauk told us to guard him. Told you that too. Didn't say nothing about sharing our life stories."

"He's not going anywhere," said Val. "Not while Sauk's got his necklace and his boy."

Berun glanced back. The two men didn't fall back, but their scowls now matched his own.

Val grinned and looked at Berun. "Isn't that right?"

Berun turned forward. He pushed aside a branch, thick with broken cobwebs, then let it fly back at Val.

"Don't want to talk about the boy," said Val as he ducked under the branch, "and Talieth seems to be a sore spot. What *do* you want to talk about?"

"I agree with your friends," said Berun. "You talk too much."

"Friends?" said Val. "These two camel humps aren't my friends."

"Lick my—" one of the men started, but Val ignored him and kept talking.

"See. They don't like me twice as much as I don't like them. We just work together."

"We'll remember that next time we're in a fight," said one of the men.

"Kerlis, you couldn't catch one boy in the woods without burning your hand and crushing your little manhood. Twice. I'm not really counting on you in a fight. Unless we're up against a bunch of little girls."

"You—!"

"Leave it," said the other man. "Sauk's already threatened to feed you to Taaki. Don't let this blond pretty boy drive you into the tiger's jaws."

Berun glanced back. Kerlis looked ready to tear logs with his bare hands. The other man just looked weary.

"Wonderful company, aren't they?" said Val, his smile undiminished.

Berun turned around in time to see something flit off the path and into the brush. For a moment, he hoped it was Perch, whom he hadn't seen since last night, but a closer look showed it was just a spider. A big one. A bark spider. Nasty bite, but the venom did no more than cause a rash and make you thirsty.

"Something tells me you don't have many friends," Berun said to Val.

He heard the man chuckle. "I didn't come to Sentinelspire to make friends. Besides, working for the Old Man provides the only kind of companionship I'm interested in."

Thinking of Perch brought a twinge of worry. Berun felt sure Sauk would have said something had he found—or harmed—the lizard, but he didn't know these other men. They killed people without hesitation. Most of them probably enjoyed it. They likely wouldn't give a moment's thought to harming a treeclaw lizard. Berun kept his eye on the path, let his body do the walking, and tried to relax his mind, to quiet his thoughts, and stretch his senses.

"It true what they say," said Val, "that you and Sauk used to be friends?"

Berun ignored him.

"Word around the campfire is that you used to be the best cold-blooded damned butcher Sauk ever knew—and that's something, coming from Sauk."

"Valmir," said Berun, "I don't share your campfire, so I don't care what is said around it."

Val laughed, the chuckle of a mischievous little boy pulling his sister's hair. "Like it or not, you're going to be sharing lots of our campfires. Talk or don't. But you don't tell your tale, and others'll tell it for you."

It wasn't working. Perhaps it was the pain. More likely the constant chatter. But Berun could not sense Perch in the area. He knew the lizard was likely following them, staying out of sight, but even a slight reassurance would have done much to ease Berun's mind.

"The villages," said Berun.

"What villages?"

"Out on the steppes. Hubadai Khahan's new settlements. The attacks on the flocks, the attacks on the shepherds, the dead man . . . that was you?"

"Me?" said Val.

"This band," said Berun, motioning wide with his hands at their procession, and regretting it. He winced at the pain it brought to his shoulder.

"Nah," said Val. "Not me. Nor any of the others. That was Sauk's doing. Sent that tiger of his. He and Taaki . . . not natural, if you ask me, but that damned creature will do whatever Sauk wants her to."

"And Sauk wanted Taaki to kill that shepherd?"

"Kill?" said Val. "Don't know that he put that much thought into it. You'd have to ask him. But Sauk knew that the locals'd hire you once they thought some beast had come hunting them. Knew it'd draw you out. Swore it. Said he knew you like a brother. That true? You and him blood brothers?"

Berun ignored the question and sidled around a thorn bush that crowded the path. Broken spider webs clung to its waxy leaves where Sauk had cleared the path. Dozens of spiders— little budbacks no longer than Berun's thumbnail—crawled over the brush in an agitated swarm. The budbacks' venom wouldn't hurt a man—not even so many—but they liked to bite when annoyed.

"Can't stand all these cursed spiders," said Kerlis as he sidled around the bush. "Damned woods are full of 'em. Makes my skin crawl."

The man slapped at the bush with his sword, then hurried away.

Wait, and let your prey give you the chance to attack. Berun smiled.

✛
chapter Eight

Sauk pushed them hard. They ate and drank while they walked, and by mid afternoon they began their climb into the broken foothills of the Khopet-Dag. The trees in this region were small, but their branches and leaves were thick, darkening the forest floor beneath them. Birdsong ceased, but the air was alive with newly-hatched insects, and spider webs of every sort festooned the wood.

Some of the trees, long dead from blight or drought, were completely enshrouded in webs. Others were entirely free of the sticky strands, and Berun knew that treeclaw lizards were near. Part of Berun was glad, knowing that Perch would feel right at home, but part of him worried that his little friend might become distracted by the abundance of food. Most of the spiders were no larger than a man's knuckle, but Berun saw a few larger than his hand, and he knew that Sauk's men saw them too. Everyone walked with weapons in hand, and they scanned the forest canopy as often as they watched the path. Kerlis had gone pale as a dead fish's eye, and the fist that gripped his short sword trembled.

Even Valmir had gone silent. Whether it was because the forest seemed to call for silence, his wariness of the spiders, or the exertion from walking the steep hills, Berun neither knew nor cared. He simply thanked the Oak Father and every benevolent deity that the man had finally ceased flapping his jaw.

As the sun fell behind distant peaks, their procession topped a small rise where the rocky ground gave only enough soil for stubborn grasses and thorny bushes, giving them a view of the sky for the first time since late morning. Larger foothills stood before them, and the canopy of the great Shalhoond lay behind and to either side. The southern horizon was dark—a storm building over the Ghor Nor. Looking eastward, Berun could see all the forest laid out beneath them, and the Amber Steppes painted a deep gold out of the mountains' shadow. Beyond the grasslands, jutting from the horizon like a broken tooth, stood a mountain. Sentinelspire.

"Keep moving," whispered Valmir. "We don't want to get separated from the others."

"Spiders bother you?"

No grin from Valmir this time. In fact, his face was downright grim. "There's worse than spiders in the Khopet-Dag these days," he said. "Now move. We're out in the open."

Berun quickened his pace until they were just behind the next man in line. When they descended the opposite side of the hill and were once again beneath the trees, Berun turned to Val and said, "Sentinelspire is east. Why are we walking west?"

"Sentinelspire's *two hundred miles* east," said Val. "You really want to walk all that way?"

"Beats all these damned spiders," Kerlis muttered.

"We aren't walking?" asked Berun.

For once, Val seemed annoyed at the chatter, his scowl deepening. "There's a portal in the foothills," he said.

"I never knew of a portal in the Khopet-Dag."

"There's lots of things you don't know," said Val.

"Meaning what?"

"Meaning you've been away a long time. Things have changed at the Fortress. Lots of things."

✦ ✦ ✢ ✦ ✦

Night hit the woods fast. Though it was still dusk above the tree canopy, the thick leaves blocked out what little light bled down from the sky. Wind from the south had picked up, thunder rumbled in the distance, and Berun could smell the storm coming. Sauk stopped and ordered them to camp at the first sizeable stream they found—a small rivulet that cut its way through steep banks and over the black rocks of the hill before them.

The men set to work, building a few fires and preparing their meager meals. No tents. Each man carried blankets, and they would sleep beside the fires. Berun was thankful for his oilskin cloak. By the sound of the thunder and the smell of the wind, they would have a significant rain before midnight.

Seeing the work well underway, Sauk called out to a man to whom Berun had not yet spoken. Tall and swarthy, he had the build and complexion of a Thayan, but he wore the fine clothes of a westerner. Although he was in need of washing, it was evident he took pride in his appearance; his beard was well trimmed, and his hair was just growing out of what was obviously a carefully chosen cut.

"Merzan," said Sauk. "Me and Benjar and Hama are going out to scout. You're in charge." He looked at Lewan and Berun. "You two just sit by the fire and rest. No talking. Merzan, take appropriate action if they try to speak to each other."

"As you say, Sauk," said Merzan. He gave Lewan and Berun a look of complete indifference. That bothered Berun. A grin might have shown overconfidence—something Berun could use. A bluster or boast might have meant he was dealing with someone too keen on who was in charge—something else Berun could use. But the complete lack of emotion likely meant that Merzan was an iron-cold killer, who didn't care one way or the other whether Lewan and Berun lived or died. That meant trouble.

Berun settled himself beside the fire that Benjar and Hama—Vaasans, by the looks of them—had left. His shoulder felt better. Perhaps all the walking had helped to stretch it. But his side where Sauk had kicked him still throbbed with pain.

Valmir sat across from him. The blond man looked tired, but the easy grin was back. "Hungry?"

"A little," said Berun.

Val rummaged through a heavy canvas pack. "No servants out here. We'll have to make our own."

"Sauk took my pack."

"No worries," said Val. "I got you."

"Very kind."

"You haven't tasted my cooking yet. May not think me so kind after."

Berun shrugged out of his cloak and loosened his belt a notch. He winced at the pain in his ribs.

"Still hurting?" asked Val.

"I'm fine."

"Have it your way. Tea'll be ready soon."

Berun watched Val set a small iron kettle near the fire and rummage through his foodstuffs.

"What kind of changes?" asked Berun.

"What?"

"Back on the hill. You said there've been lots of changes at Sentinelspire. What kind of changes?"

Val's smile widened. "So you admit that you used to live there?"

"I never denied it."

"Never admitted it, either."

"Why give you answers you already know?"

Valmir nodded. "Fair enough, I suppose. Let's just say the Old Man's been busy all these years. And not always in good ways. That man could give Sauk lessons in cunning."

"Then won't he know we're coming?"

"Don't you worry about that," said Val. "Sauk is still as much a cunning hunter as he ever was, and the Old Man still trusts him. We might have to disguise you a bit, though I'd wager that you look nothing like you used to. Am I right?"

"I'm . . . not the man I used to be."

Val laughed. "Who is?"

Berun glanced to the other side of the camp. Lewan was sitting beside a fire. He accepted a bit of food and a small tin cup of water from one of the men. It bothered Berun that the boy seemed so at ease.

"Don't underestimate your old friend Sauk," Val continued. "He could get King Haedrak into Sentinelspire if he wanted to."

"But you said the Old Man was even smarter. 'Could give Sauk lessons in cunning,' you said."

"True enough," said Val as he continued to prepare the tea. "But I also said that the Old Man still trusts him—and we aren't on our own. We got us some . . . what you might call 'inside help.' "

"You mean Talieth."

Valmir's movements suddenly became very careful and precise. Very intentional. "What do you know about Talieth?"

"Another one of those questions to which you already know the answer?"

Val's grin didn't falter, but the good humor left his eyes. He shrugged and said, "People talk."

Berun knew that was enough on this subject. Kheil and Talieth . . . to say they had a history together would be only the beginning of a long tale, and it was not a happy one. And this was obviously a sensitive point for Val. That intrigued Berun.

"How long have you been at the Mountain?" said Berun.

"A few years."

"Where before that?"

"Why are you so interested in talking all of a sudden? Couldn't get a damned word out of you all day."

Berun shrugged. "When I walk, I walk. But fireside is good for talk."

The glint of mischief lit Val's eyes again. "And there's one thing you don't like to talk about. Am I right?"

"That's true of everyone," said Berun. "You don't want to tell me where you're from, then?"

"Not much to tell," said Val as he inspected the insides of two tin cups. Apparently satisfied, he took the kettle from the coals and poured the tea. He looked at Berun through the steam rising from the cup as he handed it to him. "I was a thief in Darromar. A moderately successful one. Enough that I began to get a bit of a reputation. I had an . . . incident with the local guild and had to ply my skills elsewhere. Went to Tethyr, where I took in with a fellow who started teaching me a bit of the Art."

"Magic?"

"Nothing special. Just a few spells here and there that help in my line of work. But that line of work proved a bit too successful again. I was hiding from a local noble's hired men when worse trouble came knocking at the noble's door. Turns out he'd angered some of the wrong people, and the Old Man was hired to take care of the problem. One thing led to another, and I ended up impressing Merzan, who offered me . . . what you might call an audition."

"One thing led to another?" said Berun. "What's that mean?"

"It means things got ugly with the nobleman, and Merzan was impressed with how I handled the situation."

"Care to elaborate?"

"Care to talk about Talieth?" said Val as he took a careful sip of the tea.

Berun sipped the tea and scowled.

Valmir chuckled, but Berun didn't hear much humor in it.

✛ ✛ ✛ ✛ ✛

The dregs of Berun's thin soup were just beginning to cool when Sauk and the scouts returned. One glance at the eagerness in the half-orc's gaze and the confidence in his gait told Berun that something was happening.

"Any problems?" Sauk asked Merzan.

"None," said Merzan, still displaying no emotion.

The steppe tiger emerged from the shadows, skirting the scouts to stand beside her master. She fixed her gaze on Berun. She didn't growl, but Berun could feel the weight of her stare. Taaki had never liked Kheil, and she seemed to like Berun even less.

"Good," said Sauk, " 'cause we've got news. Good news."

"What is it?" said the man sitting across from Lewan. The boy looked tired, but the fear and shock were largely gone from his eyes.

"*Yaqubi,*" said Sauk, "bedded down in the next valley. Most likely headed back into the mountains after trading on the steppe."

"Which means they're likely fat with gold," said Merzan.

"How many?" asked the man near Lewan.

"Seven."

"Easy pickings," said Kerlis.

"Yeah, your favorite kind," said one of the men who had gone scouting with Sauk.

Kerlis spat and scowled at the man, but he held his tongue.

Sauk looked to Kerlis and said, "If you think *yaqubi* are easy pickings, you've never fought them. They know these woods better'n your finger knows your nose. They may seem small and shy, but they're the best hunters around the Khopet-Dag. In the mountain valleys where some of the spiders are big as horses, the *yaqubi* thrive." He swept his gaze over the rest of his men. "We'll take them. Don't doubt it. But this will be a good hunt. We'll earn their blood."

Laughter and a quiet cheer went up throughout the camp. All except for Kerlis. Watching him, Berun was reminded of the wolf packs that roamed the Amber Steppes. Every pack had its leaders, the mated male and female, and a precise order down from there. In every pack was the lowest wolf, always the last to eat, the last to drink, and the recipient of the leader's bad temper. If this band had been wolves, Kerlis definitely would have been the lowest wolf in the pack, and Lewan's recent escape and Kerlis's mishandling of it seemed to have roused Sauk's anger toward the man. Berun felt a small twang of pity for Kerlis, but mostly he knew he'd have to watch the man. Kerlis would know better than to take out his anger on Sauk or any of his men. If he felt that the boy was the source of his recent woes—and Berun knew he did—then he would be the focus of Kerlis's ire.

"Kerlis," said Sauk, "you and Dren will stay here with the boy. Berun"—the half-orc's lips twisted around the name — "care to join the hunt? A good fight. Just like old times, eh?"

"No," said Berun. "I won't murder innocents."

Sauk snorted. "In that case, you better stay here, too, lover boy."

A few of the men laughed. Berun looked around to see who was "lover boy," and was surprised to see Valmir blushing. The blond man's interest in discussing Talieth suddenly became clear.

✠

chapter nine

The raiding party had been gone a while. The wind had picked up, though their camp was deep enough in the valley that the surrounding hills and trees kept off the worst of it. The occasional thunder off the mountains was getting closer. Still no rain, but it was only a matter of time.

Valmir had washed the iron kettle, refilled it, and it was just now beginning to bubble over the fire. For washing and shaving, he'd explained.

"Something wrong?" Valmir asked Berun.

"No," Berun replied.

"You been quiet since Sauk and the others left."

Berun rubbed his temples to clear his head. One bit of good news, at least. Perch was back. While Val washed the kettle and cups, Berun had taken the opportunity to reach out to his friend. The little lizard was up in the trees, watching them. The approaching storm had made him skittish, and he was worrying over the absence of his tail. But he'd found a comfortable place in the canopy to watch. His feelings came through, touching the edge of Berun's consciousness—*Come down? Warm sleep?*

Berun sent out a call—not words, but the intent was clear: *Not yet. Fight coming. Be ready.*

The wind had the trees swaying in a chorus racket, but Berun's sharp ears picked up something rattling in the branches overhead.

Not yet, he told the lizard. *Sit-sit-sit. Be ready.*

—ready-ready-ready. Fight-fight-fight! Tooth-and-claw-and-fight!

Berun concentrated, sending forth one image, one thought wrapped in a question—*Tiger . . . ?*

Gone-gone. Over hill with the big-big one. Big one grab-grabbed my tail. My-tail-my-tail-my-tail!

New tail soon, Perch. Be ready. Fight coming.

Fight-fight-fight!

Berun smiled and called out to Valmir. "The soup all you have to eat?"

The blond man had just finished stowing the cleaned cups in his pack. "Still hungry? I warned you not to expect too much from my cooking."

"It isn't that."

"Then what?"

Berun shrugged and said, "Just . . . Sauk's mention of 'old times' reminded me of something."

"And what's that have to do with my soup?" asked Val.

Berun poked at the fire with a stick, sending a torrent of sparks into the air and stirring the flames to new life. "Back when I used to live at the Fortress," he said, "I did more than work for the Old Man. Besides . . . doing what I did, I was also the best cook between Teylan Shan and Yal Tengri."

"That's not saying much," said Val, "considering that half the tribes out here drink rotten horse milk."

"Ah, have a little faith," said Berun. "Let me prove it to you."

"You want to cook for us?"

"I do."

Val tilted his head and looked at Berun through narrowed eyes. "Why?"

"Why not? I'm not tired, but I am still hungry, and if all we have are supplies for soup, I could show you some spices that you might not have tried before. You have anything better to do?"

Val's gaze did not soften. "Spices?"

"In my pack."

"And there wouldn't be anything else in your pack that we should worry about?"

Berun sighed. "If you don't trust me, you could keep the pack and hand me what I need."

Valmir looked to Kerlis, who was sitting, morose, by his own fire, and Dren, who was sitting beside Lewan and honing his dagger over a whetstone. "You two have any objections?"

Dren just shrugged. Kerlis scowled and spat into the fire.

"You sit still," Valmir told Berun, and he walked over to where most of the camp's supplies were piled. He found Berun's large leather satchel and returned to the fire. He sat, opened the flap, and turned the open satchel into the firelight. "Let's see if we can get this over with before the rain hits."

"See the roll of felt wrapped in twine?" said Berun.

"Yeah."

"Those are needles and spare arrowheads," said Berun. "Quite sharp, so don't unwrap them. On the other side of the spare clothes is an inner pocket. See it?"

"Yes."

"In that pocket is a small leather bag stitched with a red thread. Make sure it's the pocket on the opposite side from the needles. The other pocket is poisons."

"Poisons?"

"I live most of the year in the wild. I sometimes have to hunt things larger than me, and it takes a bit more than an arrow to bring them down."

Val removed a leather bag slightly larger than his hand. "This it?"

"The very one." Berun reached for it.

But Val drew it back, untied the drawstring, and looked inside. "How about you tell me what you want and I'll pass it over?"

"You have salt already, so try to find a white doeskin bag. It should have a brass hinge on top rather than a drawstring."

Val rummaged a moment, then produced the bag. "What is it?"

"Just sage."

Valmir opened the little hinge and sniffed at it. Satisfied, he closed the latch and tossed it to Berun.

"Now, a larger oilskin pouch with black stitching."

Val found it, sniffed the contents, and his brows rose appreciatively. "What's this?"

"It's called lingale," said Berun. "It will help to bring out more flavor in the meat, and if we let it simmer, it will thicken the broth nicely."

"Nice," said Val. "What next?"

"This one is my little secret," said Berun. "The *yaqubi* call it yellow safre. Quite good. You'll find it in a similar oilskin pouch, only this one has lighter stitching."

"Not much of a secret anymore." Valmir grinned as he looked for the pouch.

"This is just cooking," said Berun. "I don't guard these secrets that closely."

Valmir tossed him the pouch.

"One more, I think," said Berun. "It's probably near the bottom. Been a while since I used it. This one is a bottle made from bone. Should have a thick wad of felt stuffed in the top for a cap."

"Why bone?" asked Val as he rummaged through the satchel.

"Clay or glass might break, and leather tends to soak up the flavor of this particular spice."

Valmir produced the bottle and tossed it to Berun. "What is this one?"

Berun twisted the felt out of the bottle and gave the contents a careful sniff. "This one is most special. I trade for it with Shou merchants in Almorel." He shook a generous pile into the palm of one hand.

"What's it called?"

"They call it *tep yen*," said Berun. "I suspect it's some sort of fruit, but these are the seeds, dried and crushed." He leaned over the fire and extended his hand. "Here. Smell. It's quite good."

Careful of the fire between them, Valmir leaned toward Berun's open palm. He inhaled through his nose, and his brows rose in appreciation. "Good," he said. "Smells hot."

"It is," said Berun—and blew the *tep yen* into Valmir's eyes.

Valmir shrieked—a high-pitched scream so loud that Berun thought the man might tear his throat. Val fell back, his hands scrabbling at his eyes and his feet kicking the fire.

Kerlis and Dren leaped to their feet. Kerlis, eyes wide and a snarl on his lips, already had a short sword in hand. Dren was calmer. A small smile played across his lips as he glanced at Valmir, who was still thrashing and screaming. Dren would be the problem, then.

Dren reached behind his back, and his hand reappeared with a knife. But the other hand he held open and outward in a sign of peace. He stepped around the fire and took three steps toward Berun.

Relief swept through Berun. If Dren had stayed by his fire and held Lewan hostage, this little plan would have fallen apart right away.

Fight-fight-fight? The feeling—the eagerness—touched the edge of Berun's mind.

Not yet, he answered. *Hold. Be ready.*

Ready-ready. Fight-fight-fight!

"On your belly!" Kerlis shouted to Berun. He'd stopped a

few paces away, and his eyes flitted back and forth from Berun to Dren.

"Not for you," said Berun. He crouched near the fire and motioned the men forward.

"Just sit down," said Dren. "Don't make us hurt you."

"You won't hurt me."

"Have it your way." Dren's open hand tightened into a fist.

The two men advanced. Berun figured Kerlis would strike first. After the events of the day, the man had a lot to make up for. Berun waited until Kerlis was only a few paces away, then he lifted the near end of the spit over the fire—kettle of boiling water still dangling from the middle—and hurled it at Kerlis. The kettle struck him and the boiling water splashed over him.

Kerlis went down thrashing, and his screams drowned out Valmir's.

Fight-fight-now? Perch was tense.

Not yet, answered Berun. *I have this one.*

Berun turned his full attention to Dren, brandished one fist, and said, "You'd do best to go after Sauk and get help. You're going to need it."

The larger man smiled and waved his dagger. "You'd do well to sit your arse down. You're all out of boiling water, and I have the steel."

"Have it your way," said Berun, and he feinted forward.

Dren's smile turned into a snarl and he lunged, sweeping the dagger before him. Berun jumped back, raised the thumb of his fist, and shook the open bottle of *tep yen* in the man's face. The red powder burst out in a cloud and enveloped Dren's head and shoulders.

"Try—" began Berun, but Dren's shrieks cut him off. The man dropped his dagger and clutched at his face, but he kept his feet. Berun waited for the heavy cloud to dissipate, then stepped forward and punched Dren squarely in the temple. The man went down like a sack of stones.

"—not to breathe it in," Berun finished. "That hurts even worse."

Berun looked to Lewan. The boy stood a few paces away, wide-eyed and holding a burning brand in one hand.

"Come," said Berun over the screams of the three men. "Gather your things. Find my bow."

Kneeling beside Val, who was still thrashing and whimpering, Berun reached for the buckle of the man's belt. Val cried out and punched blindly in Berun's direction.

Berun slapped the punch away and brought his elbow down hard into Val's gut. The man's cries cut off in a choke. "Enough of that," said Berun. "Just getting my knife back."

He removed Val's belt and retrieved his knife and sheath. He held Val's belt and knife in his hand a moment, considering. It was a fine blade. Not too ostentatious, but well crafted. The belt was well made but had seen a lot of use. Berun tossed both into the fire. His pouch still lay where Val had dropped it. Berun picked it up and cinched the flap shut.

Val had stopped his full-throated screaming, but he still rubbed at his eyes and rolled back and forth on the ground. "I'll kill you," he said between sobs. "You godsdamned bastard. Don't care what Tali says. I'll kill you."

Berun looked down at the blond man. "First thing the Old Man ever taught me," he said. "The assassin's greatest weapon is not dagger or dart or poison. The assassin's greatest weapon is the weapon at hand and the willingness to act. I just bested the three of you with spices and boiling water."

"I'll kill you!" Valmir lashed at Berun with one foot, but Berun sidestepped.

"Listen to me," said Berun. "Listen closely. You leave me alone. You leave the boy alone. You come after either of us, and I'll teach you the second thing the Old Man taught me."

Berun lunged down and punched Val in the gut. All the air shot out of the blond man, and he clutched at his midsection. His eyes, still clenched shut, were red and swollen. Berun punched him again across the side of the face.

"I'll—!" Valmir swiped at Berun and tried to sit up.

Berun punched him again, and Val went down, out cold. For a moment, Berun considered kicking him a few times, maybe cracking a few ribs. Might make up for the chattering Berun had been forced to endure all day. And that smug smile. It would feel good to knock that smile off his face for a long while.

"Another time," Berun said, and turned away.

The boy still hadn't moved.

"Lewan," said Berun.

The boy started.

"Listen carefully," said Berun. He walked over and lowered his voice. It was doubtful that the men would be able to hear him over their own shrieking, but it never hurt to be careful. "I must take care of Sauk and his men or we won't make it out of these woods alive. You remember the lightning-blasted tree where we cleaned the deer last spring?"

Lewan thought a moment, then nodded, but the fear did not leave his eyes.

"Get as far from here as you can. Sauk and the others went west after the *yaqubi*. You go east. Find that tree. I'll meet you there tomorrow. You understand?"

"Yes, Master."

"Good. We don't have much time."

"Master?"

"Yes?"

"What about the tiger? You can't take her on your own."

"Taaki and I have . . . crossed purposes before. Leave her to me. Now move."

Berun watched while Lewan gathered a few supplies, gave his master a final questioning look, and disappeared into the dark. In moments the darkness and swaying boughs of the storm-tossed woods swallowed him.

A small form emerged from the flickering shadows and scuttled up to Berun. Perch stopped, looked up at his master, and let loose a series of excited chitters.

"Yes," said Berun. "Now it's time." *Fight-fight-fight.*

✝

chapter ten

We wait for the storm," said Sauk.

The half-orc had gathered his raiding party on a small shelf of rock about halfway down the hill. The assassins huddled in the darkness, each no more than a dim shape against the rock. The wind from the oncoming storm cut through the trees so they swayed and tossed like a Shou feather dancer. Through the occasional break in the tossing boughs, Hama could see the *yaqubi*'s tiny campfire several hundred paces below them.

"Once the rain starts," said Sauk, "listen for Taaki."

"Where has she got off to?" asked Hama.

"She's a ways up the hill on the other side of their camp. Listen for her. She's the signal. Once your hear her, get in the camp and kill 'em all."

"Will we be able to hear her over the storm?" Sauk was less than a few feet away, and Hama could barely hear him over the wind in the trees. The sky flickered, and thunder crashed on the mountains to the west, as if to emphasize the point.

"You'll hear her," said Sauk.

"Why wait?" asked Merzan.

"What?"

"For the storm."

"You know that little lizard our captive keeps setting loose on us?" said Sauk.

"Yes."

89

"That's a treeclaw lizard, and Berun"—Hama could hear Sauk's lips twisting around the name —"learned to train it from the *yaqubi*. They use the damned things like hunting dogs against the spiders in the deep woods. And like dogs, the little beasts make great guards. Only these little hounds can hide in the trees so that they're near invisible. No telling how many are nestled in the brush around the camp. But they'll hole up once the rain starts. That's when we hit them."

"Those lizards," said Benjar, "are they poisonous?"

"Nah," said Sauk. "But you'll feel their claws and teeth if one gets on you. But they're just lizards. If one gets you, just grab and squeeze."

"It's the spiders we need to be worried about," said Merzan.

"Spiders?" said Hama.

"This is the Khopet-Dag," said Merzan. "The *Spider*haunt Peaks. You and Kerlis nearly wet yourselves all day worrying about them on the trail."

"You said most of them weren't dangerous."

"Most," said Sauk. "We're nearer the mountains now. The big ones don't usually come down this far. And the smaller ones—the rain will drive them into their holes. Don't worry about the spiders."

"But what if we run into one of the dangerous ones?" said Benjar.

"Damn it," said Sauk. "Did you see a single spider all day that you couldn't squash with your heel? No? You see a spider you don't like? Kill it. Spiders aren't bees or flies. They don't swarm."

Berun found what he was looking for near the top of the hill—a small swath of forest where seedlings no more than a season or two old were growing in the remains of an ancient tree. The old tree had fallen several seasons ago and gone to rot. Softened by melting frost and spring rains, it was now a hive of thousands of spiders. The treeclaw lizards preferred the fertile valleys between the hills where water was more plentiful, so the many spiders that made this part of the wood their home laid their eggs along the hilltops, and rotted logs were a favorite haunt.

It was late enough in the year that most of the egg sacs had hatched, but early enough that most of the spiderlings were still lurking in the immediate area. They'd had at least a couple of tendays to feast on flies, moths, and the young fangflies newly hatched from the thick mud along the valley streams. They'd grown nice and fat, and their fangs were full of new venom. But they were still growing and hungry. Ravenous, in fact. Still, there were not enough of them to suit Berun's purpose. Not here. But if his scheme went as planned, more would gather from the surrounding hills and valleys as his spell surged.

Berun settled himself near the base of the old log. He could smell the rot, thick and musky even in the strong rain-scented breeze. In his trek up the hill he'd barreled through a fair number of spider webs, and the tiny fibers fluttered about him like wisps of down, tickling his skin.

Perch, rummaging inside the log, swallowed the last of a spiderling he'd happened across. Running through the wood, Berun had opened the link he and Perch shared, tearing it wide, opening himself to the mind of the little lizard. He could feel the lizard's metabolism quickening, already growing a new tail, needing nourishment, and his friend was *hungry*. The dozens of spiders hiding in the crevices of the old log were too much temptation to ignore. The incessant messages of *fight-fight-fight* that had whispered along the link Berun shared with the lizard had changed to *hunt-hunt-hungry-hungry-SPIDER!*

Berun closed his eyes, took a deep breath, and sent a feeling of urgency, of need, to Perch. *Hunt spiders later. Time to fight. Now, Perch.*

Fight-fight? Perch stopped in his attempt to chase a young spider out of a moist crevice where the log met the ground.

Fight, yes, Berun answered. *Fight now. The tiger. Find the tiger.*

Wariness and a tingle of fear wafted into Berun's mind. *Fight . . . tiger?*

Anger the tiger, said Berun. *Make her growling-mad—then lead her away. Far away. Understand?*

Growling-mad tiger means eating scared-me. Perch emerged from the log. Berun could feel his little friend watching him, though it was too dark to see him.

You are fast, Berun told him. *In-the-shadows in-the-tight-places fast. Get the tiger chasing-you-mad, then run-run-run.*

Chasing-me-mad run-run-run. Perch hissed and chattered. *Fun-fun fight-chase-run-fun!*

Go, my friend.

Perch ran, unseen in the dark and unheard under the storm-swaying trees. In moments, he was gone. Berun relaxed his mind, seeking the rhythm of the storm, of the wood, of the world around him. In the gusts of wind, the wisps of spider web tickled his skin.

"Now," said Berun. "Now, Sauk. Here it comes. You should've stayed in your mountain."

He began his chant.

The tiger crouched a prudent distance from the camp. Her heart-brother had warned her about the lizards, biters and scratchers who hid in the trees. The little nuisance earlier today had angered her, but her coat was far too thick for such a creature's claws to be a real threat. No. The real threat was that the beasts would warn their masters below, and that would displease Taaki's heart-brother. So she kept to the thick brush, becoming a part of the darkness itself. She couldn't even see the distant twinkling of the campfire, but the smell of their fire was thick in her nostrils. She knew exactly where they were. At the signal from her heart-brother, she would roar to put fear in her prey then rush down the slope, making less sound than the wind in the trees.

Something rustled to her right, a furtive movement over the old leaves and twigs that littered the forest floor. Every part of the tiger went still as stone, save for her ears, which pivoted toward the sound.

The sky above the forest flashed, painting the wood in sharp contrasts of light and shadow, and thunder followed a moment later. The storm was close now, the scent of rain heavy on the wind. The last of the thunder faded, first from the ground, then the air as it rebounded off the mountain. Only the wind through the leaves and branches made any sound—

There.

Again, something skittered through the brush, but it was closer now. Very close.

A rumble gathered deep in the tiger's chest, and the skittering sound stopped.

The tiger waited.

A sharp patter joined the hissing of the leaves and creak of branches, but it was only the first drops of rain.

Soon . . . Her heart-brother, warning her.

Leaves rustled nearby, stopped, and the tiger heard a small hiss.

A lizard.

The tiger knew it, and the knowledge sang through the link she shared with her heart-brother.

Kill it!

The tiger lunged.

Hama sat, his legs crossed under him and his back against a tree. He dared go no closer, not if the *yaqubi* had who-knew-how-many of those little lizards lurking in the trees. He was close enough that he could charge the camp quick enough.

The first drops of rain, fat and falling hard, began striking the forest canopy. The leaves provided a barrier—so far—but they struck with enough force to be heard over the wind.

Any time, now.

Hama rose to a crouch and drew his knife.

The patter of the rain came stronger, and drops began to reach the ground. Something about the drops sounded . . . wrong. Just off slightly. The wind had been skittering through the leaves all evening, but Hama swore the sound had changed, just slightly.

As Hama stepped round the bole of the tree, something struck his hand. He ignored it, thinking it was only a raindrop, but when another struck his forehead, he brushed it aside.

Something bit his finger, and he hissed. Reflex took over. He flapped his hand and in half a heartbeat, felt tiny legs lose contact with his skin.

Lightning flashed over the mountain. In the flicker, Hama could see the wind-tossed boughs, stirred by the storm. But he'd been wrong about the raindrops. The rain had not yet come. Other things were dropping from the trees. Some were no larger than his thumbnail, but some were larger than his hand. A hundred or more shadows moved along the forest floor—moved against the wind. The nearest were only a few feet away.

Hama looked up. The last of the lightning died, and in the instant before complete darkness surrounded him, Hama saw dozens of spiders crawling around the tree. Crawling right for him.

Thunder shook the ground as the first of the spiders crawled over his boots.

Hama turned to run, but on the dark hillside his haste

betrayed him. Three steps and his feet went out from under him. He fell into a bush thick with new spring leaves. His heart hammered in his chest, and his breath was coming in quick gasps. In the brush he could not tell the difference between the leaves, branches, and hundreds of tiny legs crawling over him.

Hama screamed.

Sauk heard the first wave of rain washing over the valley. Fitful at first, it gained strength with each gust of wind.

Most of his attention was fixed on the tiny glow of campfire twinkling in the valley below him, but a small sliver of his mind was with the tiger—every beat of her heart, every breath and careful, considered movement. He could not see what she saw or hear what she heard, but his mind registered her reactions to sight, sound, even smell.

Lightning lit the mountain along the western sky. Thunder followed, and with it came the torrent, like a wave washing over a shore.

He told the tiger, *Soon . . .*

Lizard! It came through not in a word, but in the awareness that one of the little creatures had found her.

Kill it! he told the tiger.

He felt her lunge. Then a scream—a man's scream, but not on the opposite hillside where Taaki waited. This came from off to Sauk's right. A shriek of utter terror.

"Damn!"

Sauk would kill whoever it was. Break his neck with his bare hands. Hama, by the sound of it. The fool had just ruined their element of surprise. The *yaqubi* were a skittish lot, and they might well be gone before the assassins even hit the valley.

The rain came harder, rattling the leaves overhead, but Sauk's sharp ears caught something else. Even over the sound of the wind-tossed trees and falling rain, Sauk heard a skittering like . . . tiny feet. Or claws. Hundreds of them.

Sauk turned his back on the valley and looked up the hillside. His half-orc eyes could see far better in the dark than any human's. He could see the forest floor *moving*.

Lightning cracked the sky over the valley, and in the sudden harsh light Sauk saw that he was about to be overtaken by a tide of hundreds—hundreds of *thousands*—of spiders.

"Damn you, Berun," he said. "Damn you, you clever—"

And then the spiders were on him.

The storm washed over the foothills of the Khopet-Dag. Wind and rain pummeled the forest while lightning lashed from cloud to cloud overhead, and thunder followed all. The thick canopy of the forest caught the rain and funneled it downward in thousands of tiny waterfalls so that by the time the fury of the storm had passed, and the rain settled in for a long, steady deluge, all the forest floor was a muddy, sodden mess.

It took Berun longer than he'd hoped to find Sauk. The little starstone he held gave off only a faint glow, and the storm had washed away any sign of the half-orc's trail. If only Perch could keep the tiger busy a little longer, this just might work.

Sauk lay in the mud at the bole of a tree. The spiders were gone. The effects of Berun's spell were long spent, and the spiders had either drowned or taken refuge from the storm wherever they could find it.

The half-orc was doubled over and shivering. The tree's thick, waxy leaves kept the worst of the rain off him. In the dim silver glow of his starstone, Berun could see dozens of swollen bites across Sauk's exposed skin. His eyes were squeezed shut, and tiny convulsions rippled through his muscles.

Berun touched Sauk's temple with the back of his hand. The half-orc burned with fever. At the touch, Sauk's eyes fluttered open. He tried to snarl, but it turned into a tooth-chattering grimace.

"D-d-damn you," Sauk rasped.

"Damn me later," said Berun. "Right now, I only want what's mine."

He opened the pouch at Sauk's belt and rummaged through it. It wasn't there.

"Where is it, Sauk?"

"Puh-p-piss on you." Sauk grimaced and doubled over further as a stronger convulsion hit him.

"Don't worry," said Berun. "The venom from most of those spiders isn't fatal. Not even from so many. Not for a big, strong hunter like you. Now where is it?"

Berun set the starstone on the ground, grabbed the collar of Sauk's tunic, and ripped. Several necklaces hung round the half-orc's neck. Some bore symbols of his faith, others were trophies of past kills, and the brass chain seemed plain jewelry. But around one particularly fine leather thong was what Berun was searching for: *Erael'len*.

Sauk tried to bat Berun's hands away, but he was fever weak, and Berun ignored him. He eased Sauk's head up, pulled off the necklace, dropped it over his own head, and tucked the talisman under his shirt.

"Th-this is-s-sn't . . . over," said Sauk.

"I know," said Berun. "Listen to me, Sauk. Your plan is too risky. If you think you can sneak me in under the Old Man's nose, you've grown soft. He's using you to get to me. You're only going to get us all killed. If it were just me, I might let you try, but I won't let you pull the boy into this. I'll help. *My* way. But only after I see Lewan safely away."

Sauk growled something unintelligible.

"Leave the boy out of this," said Berun. "Let me handle this my way. I'll get my master out of the Fortress and take care of the Old Man. *My way.* But if you come at the boy again, Sauk, I swear I'll kill you."

"Muh-m-m—" Sauk gasped, then said, "*Mal karash!* Oath breaker!"

Berun retrieved his starstone and looked down on the half-orc who had once been his closest friend. Lightning flashed, painting the half-orc's face in sharp contrast.

"Kheil swore brotherhood to you until death," Berun said. "He kept his oath. I owe you nothing."

Thunder shook the world around them, and before it faded, Berun left the half-orc lying in the mud.

✛

chapter Eleven

Lewan laid his hand against the bole of the tree, dead from a lightning strike in a long-ago storm. His hand trembled like an old man's.

It had taken him much longer to find the tree than he'd hoped. Running at night, through the storm, even with the small starstone to light his way, Lewan had been forced to go the long way round the hill. The way he and his master usually took up the southwestern face had been far too slick—mud running down in tiny rivulets over the slick rocks. Desperate to be away from the assassins, he'd tried two different ascents and fallen both times. The second time, a broken branch had opened a wicked gash along his right arm, almost from wrist to elbow, and he'd bled most of the way to the tree.

The pain, the blood loss, the wet, and the miles-long run through rough country had left him more weary than he could ever remember being. He was soaked down to his smallclothes, and moving had been the only thing keeping him warm. No help for it. Even if he could find dry kindling in this mess, lighting a fire on a hilltop would be beyond foolish. He'd simply suffer through the storm. Once the rain stopped, he'd don his dry clothes.

Lewan turned away from the tree and opened his left palm to allow the blue-silver light from the starstone to give him a better view of his surroundings. The lightning strike that had killed the tree had also started a fire, and most of the brush around the tree was stunted and no more than a few seasons old. To get out of the rain, he'd have to go back into the forest.

It didn't take him long to find a suitable spot—an old pine that had fallen under its own weight in ages past. It hadn't made it all the way to the ground but lodged in a tight grove of aspens, and the aspens had continued to grow, unperturbed by the old cousin who had fallen into their midst. Through season after season the dead pine gathered more and more deadfall, leaves, mud, and the dwellings of various forest creatures. It formed a sort of roof. Once Lewan had cleared out several years' worth of dead leaves and pine needles, he had a nice hollowed-out spot that, while not exactly dry, was at least not sodden. There he settled in to wait.

Down the hillside several dozen yards into the forest, he could no longer see the lightning-blasted tree, but he knew his master would come. If he didn't find Lewan right away, he'd look around, even call out if he'd managed to fend off pursuit. Right now, Lewan needed rest.

He dampened the light of the starstone, huddled into his cloak, and lay down. Exhaustion claimed him, and he was asleep in moments.

Cold woke him. With his body no longer on the move, the chill had settled into his sodden clothes. His body was shivering, his teeth chattering.

Lewan sat up and gasped at the sudden pain that flashed along his arm. He could no longer feel his right hand, and the arm throbbed. Whether it was from the cold or from infection trying to settle in, he'd have to do something about it soon.

He grabbed the starstone with his left hand and rubbed it between thumb and fingers, stirring the light back to life. He peeled the remains of his right sleeve back with his left hand and teeth. He gasped and winced as bits of thread and cloth pulled out of the wound. A wet, puffy scab ran down most of the length of his arm. He suspected it looked worse than it really was. Once he cleaned it and applied a salve—he prayed it was still in the pack he'd retrieved from the assassins' camp—it would likely hurt for a tenday, then be nothing more than a bothersome itch for the rest of the month.

As he sat worrying over his arm, Lewan heard something moving through the brush not far up the hill. Even over the roar of the downpour he could hear it. He squeezed his left hand into a fist, shutting out most of the starstone's light. He held his breath, listened, and peered into the dark. Even after his eyes adjusted to the darkness, he could see nothing beyond his meager shelter. The forest was a patch of utter blackness.

There it was again—something making its way through the brush and mud. It wouldn't be an animal. The beasts were smart enough to find shelter and stay there until the storm was over.

Lewan considered calling out. More than likely, it was Berun come at last. Not finding Lewan at the lightning-blasted tree, he would've started searching. But if it wasn't Berun . . .

It was either his master, Lewan knew, or one of the assassins, and they could not have known where Lewan was going unless Berun told them. Except for maybe Sauk and his tiger. Lewan knew that of the band, only those two would stand any chance of tracking him. So . . . either Berun or Sauk.

Lewan stuffed the starstone into his shirt pocket and reached for the knife at his belt. He drew it—a wicked, ugly thing that he'd taken off one of Sauk's men back in the camp. Lewan had carried a knife for years—as a tool. This blade was a weapon crafted for one purpose: murder. It felt heavy in his hand.

Whatever was moving on the hill was getting closer. Had the sun been up, Lewan could have seen whatever it was.

A voice came out of the roaring rain. "Lewan?"

Lewan let out his breath. It was Berun's voice.

"Here, master!" he called out as he made his way out of the shelter. He stood and removed the starstone from his pocket. As it warmed next to his hand, the light grew, catching and sparking in the droplets of rain so that Berun seemed to emerge from a thin curtain of crystal. His master had his hood down, and his long hair lay heavy and dripping over his face and down his shoulders. He held his unstrung bow in one hand.

"Lewan!" Relief flooded Berun's face, but it lasted only a moment. He looked worried as his eyes took in the sight before him. "I've been scouring the hill. When I didn't find you . . . you're hurt!"

"Just a scratch." Lewan managed a grin over his chattering teeth. "I took a bad fall trying to get up the hill."

The concern didn't leave Berun's gaze. "Why the knife?"

"Until you called out, I thought you might have been one of them."

"I took care of them."

Lewan remembered everything Sauk had told him on their walk yesterday, of Kheil the assassin, one of the most feared murderers in the East. "Took care of them?" he asked.

"They'll live," said Berun. "Though if Sauk ever catches up to us, we might not. He's never been one to forgive a slight."

"So it's all true, then? You *do* know him."

Berun looked at him, and in the meager light of the starstone, the shadows under his brows seemed very deep. Lewan swallowed and held his master's stare.

"We'll speak of this later," said Berun. "Let's get you cleaned up and warm."

✦ ✦ ✦ ✦ ✦

They returned to Lewan's makeshift shelter. Berun cleared out more leaves and deadfall to make room for them both, then hung both their starstones from the branches overhead. By their light he had a look at the cut along the inside of Lewan's arm. He cleaned off the worst of the dirt and half-dried blood with his fingers, then dabbed at the wound with a clean cloth that he'd soaked in the rain.

"More of a deep scrape than a cut," he said. "Still, it bled quite a bit. A branch, you said?"

"I slipped in the mud and came down on a log."

"Fortunate it wasn't worse."

Lewan winced and sucked in a sharp breath. He was still freezing, and his arm was almost numb, but his master's ministrations were working feeling back into the skin, and with the sharp tingling came pain. Fresh blood seeped out of the wound.

"Let me salve and bandage this," said Berun, "then we'll get you into warm clothes. We'll rest 'til first light, then we need to move. I bought us some time, but we need to be leagues from here by midday."

"Where is Perch?"

"He led the tiger away."

"Is he . . . ?" Lewan couldn't bring himself to finish.

"He's alive," said Berun. "He's frightened and cold, but he's alive. That much I know. Beyond that . . ."

"Master," said Lewan, "what . . . what did you do? To them. To Sauk and his band."

Berun turned to rummage through the largest of their packs. He found the small wad of clean linen they used for bandages and a polished wood vial of salve. He opened the vial and began to smear a thick, pungent paste into the wound.

"They're alive," he said. "I used an old trick Chereth taught me. Used the wild against them."

"The wild?"

"I roused every spider in the valley and surrounding hills and set them on Sauk and his men. They'll live, though I doubt they'll feel much like chasing us for a few days. Still . . . Sauk is not one to underestimate. I want to be well into the mountains by dark tomorrow."

"You do know him, then?"

"I told you we'd speak of this later."

"We'll be on the run at first light," said Lewan. "Why not talk now?"

Berun looked up from his work and scowled, obviously displeased at Lewan's impudence. "What do you want to know?"

"You do know the half-orc?"

"Did."

"You are Kheil, then?" said Lewan. "Sauk spoke truly? You're a . . . a killer? A murderer for hire?"

Berun put the stopper back into the vial and wiped his fingers on his shirt. He stuck his chin out and was breathing heavily through his nose. Lewan knew his master well enough to recognize that Berun was upset. Pensive. Usually when this mood hit, it was wise to leave and let Berun brood on his own. But not now.

"Is it true, master?"

Berun sighed and began wrapping Lewan's arm in a bandage. "Not any more," he said. "Years before Chereth and I found you, before you came to live with me, I . . . I was . . . reborn."

"Reborn?"

"In my past life, the man I used to be—Kheil—was a killer, a murderer. Kheil served Alaodin, the Old Man of the Mountain who dwells in his fortress on the side of Sentinelspire. Four years before I met you, Kheil was sent to kill an old druid in the Yuirwood."

"Chereth?" said Lewan. "Your master?"

"Yes. Kheil led Sauk and a dozen assassins into the Yuirwood. Why? Didn't much matter. They were there to do a job.

But . . . the job did them." Berun finished wrapping the arm and tied the bandage. "How's that?"

"Tight."

"Good. It'll loosen as we're on the move. Now, let's get you into some dry clothes so you can warm up."

Lewan unhooked the clasp of his cloak and shrugged it off. "What do you mean, 'the job did them?' "

As Lewan got out of his wet clothes and put on dry ones, Berun told his tale. He spoke in a lifeless tone, without detail, of how the Masters of the Yuirwood had killed Kheil upon the Tree of Dhaerow, how Chereth had used *Erael'len,* calling upon the Oak Father, and raised Kheil to life. The old druid had named him *Berun,* which meant "hope" in the tongue of Aglarond.

"Why . . . ?" Lewan struggled to find the words. "Why have you never told me this before?"

Berun looked down, and in the dim light cast by their starstones, his face was hidden in shadow. "I am Berun now. Kheil is dead. Best to let the dead rest. Kheil's life is in the past."

Lewan watched as his master wrapped all of his wet clothes into a tight bundle, tying them with a cord from their supplies. The shirt was probably a loss, but they could use the scraps for other purposes.

"Kheil's past just came hunting us," said Lewan. "Something tells me that half-orc won't give up so easily. What do we do now?"

Berun rubbed his fingers through his beard. "We go into the mountains. Deep into the Khopet-Dag. Sauk might follow us there, but his men won't. Leading so many into the mountains would attract unwelcome attention. He knows that."

"And we won't?" asked Lewan.

"I'll be careful," said Berun. "We're going to the *yaqubi.*"

"The *yaqubi?* Why?"

"Chereth and I lived with them for a couple of seasons." The ghost of a smile flickered over Berun's lips. "It's where I found and bonded Perch. The *yaqubi* are good people. You'll be safe there."

"Safe?" said Lewan. His heart skipped a beat and started hammering in his chest. "You mean . . . you're leaving me?"

"Lewan—"

"You can't! Please! I—"

"Lewan!" Berun grabbed Lewan's shoulders and shook him.

Lewan closed his mouth with an audible *snap*. He blinked and stared at Berun, trying to find the words that would convince his master. Berun was the only father he had known since his own father . . . Lewan clenched his eyes shut and turned away. He could feel a sob building in the back of his throat. I will *not* cry, he told himself, and he took a deep breath to calm himself.

"Listen to me, Lewan," said Berun. "What Sauk told me . . . I don't know if any of it is true or not. Chereth, the Old Man . . . any of it. But I have to know. I have to be *sure*. If there is even a chance that my master is alive . . ."

"I'll come with you."

"No."

"I'm ready, master. I am! I can help. I—"

"No, Lewan." Berun did not shout. His voice was low, almost gruff, but there was no room for argument in it. "No. Not to Sentinelspire. You don't know that place. It is . . ."

"What?"

"It's . . . hard to see clearly there."

"I don't understand."

"I know." Berun offered a smile, but it never touched his eyes, and in the gloom of the forest the expression seemed almost obscene. "You must understand, Lewan. Sentinelspire is a realm built on blood. Murder. Despite what the bards may tell you, murder doesn't come easy. At least not to most people. Killing a man is a hard thing. Killing for no good reason save that you're told to do so . . . that's . . . damn. I don't have the words. It's not natural, is what it is. You have to convince a man not only that he can kill, but that he *wants* to. To do that . . ." Berun shook his head. "I don't want you anywhere near that place."

"I'm strong, master," said Lewan. "You've taught me well. I'm not afraid."

"That's what worries me. That's how the Old Man gets to you."

"But—"

"No, Lewan." Berun's voice was hard. Cold. "My mind is set as stone. I'm going alone. When I'm done, I'll come for you."

"And if you don't come back?" Even Lewan could hear the petulance in his voice. Like a child. A scared little boy. But he didn't care. "What then? What about me?"

Berun held the silence a moment, looking him eye to eye, then said, "Get some rest. We move at first light."

✠
chapter twelve

16 Tarsakh, the Year of Lightning Storms (1374 DR)
The foothills of the Khopet-Dag

Morning dawned no drier. Lewan woke to the sound of the rain roaring outside their shelter. Sitting across from him, his head resting against the remains of a long dead waxleaf shrub, Berun slept, his lips open slightly. Sometime during the night Berun had changed into dry clothes and braided his hair to keep it out of his face.

Lewan sat up. His muscles were stiff, and though his injured arm still hurt, the pain was good. Pain was feeling; the numbness was gone. Lewan leaned over and shook Berun.

"Master, wake up. It's morning."

Berun's eyes snapped open. He looked around and groaned. "I didn't mean to sleep."

"You can't exhaust yourself," said Lewan. "Yesterday was hard."

"Today will be harder," said Berun. "We must go far and fast. The rain will help to hide us. All but the biggest spiders will stay under cover. But it won't make traveling pleasant."

Lewan looked outside. Above the trees, the rain still came down in sheets, and millions of tiny waterfalls fell from leaves and branches. Water had begun to seep into Lewan and

Berun's shelter, and a tiny river was running down the hill just beyond the pile of leaves near the entrance.

"Should we not wait out the storm?" asked Lewan.

"We dare not risk it. Sauk and his band are still too close for my liking."

"You said the venom would take a few days to work through their blood."

"I also said we shouldn't underestimate Sauk. We need to have leagues behind us come nightfall."

They shared a light meal and washed it down with rainwater, then set about securing their packs and tightening their bootlaces. Berun hesitated at the entrance.

"What's wrong, master?"

"Help me," said Berun, and he began stringing his bow. It was no easy task in the cramped confines of their shelter. But wedging it between them, Lewan holding one end while Berun secured the string on the other, they managed.

"The rain will ruin your string," said Lewan.

"I have a spare," said Berun. "But until we're deep in the mountains, I'll feel better with it." Berun looked out at the wet morning gloom. "I'd feel a great deal better if I knew where Perch and the tiger had gone."

"Still nothing from Perch?"

Berun shook his head. Lewan could see the worry on his face.

"In this weather," said Lewan, "I'm sure he holed up somewhere."

"Under normal circumstances," said Berun, "so would a tiger. But . . ."

"These are hardly normal circumstances." Lewan tried to force a smile.

"And that's hardly a normal tiger. So I'll walk with the bow, rain be damned."

They left their shelter, huddled in their damp cloaks. Their breath steamed in the cool morning air.

"Walking will warm us," said Berun. "I'll risk a fire tonight to dry our things."

Lewan looked around. It almost seemed as if the gods had lifted the ocean and decided to dump it onto the Shalhoond. This was an unusually fierce storm, even for the mountain lowlands in early spring.

"You're certain we must travel in this?" Lewan had to raise his voice to be heard over the roar of the rain.

"We must," said Berun. "At best, it will be a couple of days before Sauk's men are eager to travel. But I warrant Sauk will not wait that long. He'll be after us sooner than I'd like."

"Much sooner, I'd wager," said a familiar voice, and Sauk rose from the nearby brush.

Berun pushed Lewan behind him, threw back his cloak, dropped to a crouch, and reached for an arrow.

"Easy!" said Sauk.

The rest of Sauk's men rose from their hiding places, and somewhere in the forest behind them the tiger roared.

"I was hoping you wouldn't have the bow ready. That . . . *complicates* matters." Sauk smiled and thrust out his chest, obviously reveling in Berun's shock. "Oh-ho, I bet you have questions."

Berun's fingers flexed over the bow. His other hand fingered the nock of an arrow in his quiver. "How . . . ?"

"You thought we'd venture into the Khopet-Dag without antidotes for spider venom?" Sauk laughed. "You *have* been gone a long time. The Old Man's blades may not all be men of the wilderness, but we aren't stupid. We came prepared."

Lewan looked around. Every one of Sauk's men was here. None looked happy, and Lewan could see why. Every one of them bore welts on face and hands from spider bites, Val's eyes were still red and puffy from the *tep yen*, and Kerlis's skin was red and had the slick sheen of a recent healing. Every man looked ready to murder. Kerlis, in particular, was staring daggers at Berun.

A show of force, then. Every man in Sauk's band stood before them. That gave Lewan a small amount of hope. If the half-orc had meant to kill them, he would have kept some of his men in hiding and made this an ambush.

The tiger roared again from somewhere behind them. The sound reverberated off the hillside, but Lewan could tell that she was not in the same place she'd been the last time she'd roared. She was on the move. Tigers were not like most other predators. Ambush hunters, they did not roar to frighten their prey. A tiger roared for one reason: to communicate. She was letting Sauk know that she had their prey covered. One way or another, Lewan and Berun were surrounded.

Lewan looked to the half-orc. Sauk dropped his smile. His face hardened, and his eyes glinted cold. "Throw down your weapons," he said. "Give me back that relic you took. After your stunt last night, you and the boy will walk with your arms bound today, but you'll go alive. *If* you do as I say."

Lewan looked to his master. Berun had gone very still—everything except his eyes, which went from man to man, never resting upon one for long. This wasn't lost on Sauk.

"Don't be a fool," said the half-orc, and Lewan heard genuine concern in his voice. "Even if you get away, you'll never get past Taaki. Even that bow of yours will only annoy her before she gets you."

Berun stood, looking at the assassins gathered round them. Lewan's gaze flicked between his master and the assassins, waiting for a cue. All eyes were on Berun. His move.

Berun's shoulders slumped, he looked to the ground, and a great sigh went out of him. A look of utter relief washed over Sauk.

"Master . . . ?" said Lewan.

Still keeping the width of his body between the band of assassins and his disciple, Berun turned and looked at Lewan. Nothing Lewan had seen in all their years together, not even the terrifying events of the past day, had ever frightened him like the look he saw on his master's face. Lewan had known that Berun had been deeply afraid yesterday on the trail upon finding the name *Kheil* scratched into that print. His master had been worried after their capture, but even then, Lewan had seen the careful calculations, the scheming, going on behind his master's eyes. But the look he saw just then was complete and utter despair. That look in Berun's eyes drained Lewan of all strength. It was a feeling he had not felt since . . . since that day in his village when he'd heard the raiders, listened to the screams of the dying, smelled the smoke in the thatch of the house where he lived with his parents, found his mother . . .

"Mas—?" Lewan began, his voice trembling.

Something lit in his master's eyes. A defiant fire. The corner of Berun's mouth twitched in the beginning of a smile. *Watch this,* it said.

Sauk must have sensed something too, for the look of relief froze on his face, the words he had been about to say caught in his throat, and surprise—and more than a little fear—lit his gaze.

"Spears!" shouted Sauk, reaching for his sword.

"Lewan, run!" Berun's right hand rose, an arrow balanced between the fingers. He laid the shaft across the bow and shouted, "Down the hill! *Run!*"

Shocked and confused, Lewan froze. Sauk's men fanned out, each holding a spear in hand. They moved with practiced ease. Trained killers, every one.

"Master, I—"

"Lewan, run!" Berun cast a glance over his shoulder, then pulled the arrow to his cheek, bending the bow taut, and pointed the steel tip at Sauk. "The boy leaves. As soon as he's safely away, I'll come in peace."

Kerlis stepped forward. "There's twelve of us. You can't get us all before we get you."

Berun pivoted, his left arm with the bow coming round. He aimed for only an instant, and the fingers holding the string opened. The bow twanged, and the arrow took Kerlis in his left eye. By the time his body hit the ground, Berun already had another arrow across the bow and the shaft against his cheek.

"Eleven now," said Berun. "Next one who makes a move is the next one to die."

No one moved. The Vaasans were grinning and flexing their hands around their spears. Merzan's face held no expression whatsoever, but his eyes were trained on Berun, and he stood ready. Valmir had one hand firmly around his spear, but the other was hovering near an open pouch at his belt. Ready to reach for spell components most likely. The other assassins all stood ready. Except for Sauk, all had spears, but like none Lewan had ever seen. The shafts were plain and unadorned, but rather than a head or barb, they ended in a sharp spike, no larger than a horseshoe nail. An oily paste coated each spike. Poison.

Sauk shook his head, then smiled and swiped his blade in front of him, cutting the air with a harsh *swish*. "Spear 'em, boys!" he shouted, and leaped forward, low and ready.

Berun pivoted again and loosed at the half-orc. Sauk swung his sword down in front of him, swiping the arrow aside in midair, snapping it in the middle. The fletched half slapped into his shoulder, but it didn't even slow him. He came at Berun like a bull, his grin twisted into a snarl, muddy water spraying around each step.

Lewan knew his master would never have time to nock another arrow. Berun knew it too. He stepped back and flung his bow at Sauk's legs. The half-orc tried to leap aside, but he slipped on the slick ground and went down in a great splash of mud and water, giving Berun time to back away.

Berun tore his cloak off, dropped it on the ground, and drew his knife. "Lewan, I said run!"

Lewan drew his own knife. "I'm not leaving you, master."

Sauk rolled to his feet. Merzan and one of the Vaasans were closing on Berun with their spears raised.

"I can handle them if you'll—"

The Vaasan threw. Berun twisted to the side and his left hand shot out to grab the spear as it passed where his chest had been only an instant before. He regained his posture and brought the spear around in guard position. The Vaasan drew his knife and backed away to make room for the other spearmen.

Sauk swiped his hand across his face to clear away the mud. "Damn it, Kheil, stop this! I don't want to hurt you."

"My name is Berun." He feinted with the spear, causing Merzan to back up a step.

The others were closing in. In moments, Berun and Lewan would be encircled. The other Vaasan, still holding a spear, was only a half-dozen paces from Lewan.

"Val?" called Sauk, though he never took his eyes off Berun. "You got your spell ready?"

Val reached into his pouch and grinned. "Ready and waiting, boss."

"Then do—"

Berun stepped forward and thrust as if to throw at Valmir. It was a feint, but the assassin fell for it. He tried to sidestep but slipped in the mud and went down cursing. Berun followed through with the feint, and brought the spear round in a throw. This one he let fly. It took the second Vaasan just below the ribs. The man screamed and fell back, but he kept hold of his spear.

The assassins charged, Sauk leading them, but Berun was already on the move, running for Lewan. He grabbed his disciple by the clasp of his cloak and pulled him along, running downhill and away from the assassins.

Lewan felt a spear catch in his cloak, but in three strides it pulled loose. He and Berun didn't slow. They ducked around the grove of aspens that formed their shelter. Lewan's foot slipped in a pile of rain-slicked leaves and he started to go down, but Berun hauled him up and pushed Lewan onward with a whispered, "Go!" Berun hugged the edge of the aspens with his knife held low.

Lewan stopped, holding his own knife ready. He saw a look of anger cross his master's face at the disobedience, but there was no time to argue. Gerrell, the man whom Sauk had used to bait Berun into the ravine, came round the aspens. He had a spear in one hand and a knife in the other. He caught sight of Lewan, his eyes lit with success, then Berun brought his own knife up. The strength of the strike combined with Gerrell's own momentum doomed him. Four inches or more of sharp steel passed through his throat. Blood sprayed across Berun and the white aspen bark, and a great fountain of it drenched Lewan as the man crashed to the ground. Gerrell punched and kicked, splashing mud and red-tinged water as his lungs filled with his own blood.

Berun jumped over the man and grabbed the clasp of Lewan's cloak. He ripped it off and turned to face Dren. Sauk and the others were right behind him. Berun held his knife in guard position and whipped the heavy wet cloak before him. It wouldn't stop a spear, but it might tangle and deflect it.

A shadow moving at the edge of his vision was the only warning Lewan had. He turned in time to see one of the assassins—he must have come round the other side of the aspens—a malicious grin on his face and the spear coming forward.

Lewan tried to fall away, but it was too late. The poison-coated spike plunged into the muscle between his left shoulder and chest. Through skin and flesh, he felt it scrape along the bone then plunge deep. He screamed, more in shock than pain, for his left side around the wound went suddenly numb.

Without thinking, his other hand with the knife lashed out. His blade opened a deep gash up the left side of his attacker's face. The man shrieked and backed away, but the spear remained lodged in place.

Screams came from behind him, but he couldn't make out their meaning. The numbness was spreading up his neck and into his face, and a loud hum was growing in his ears.

"Masss . . . " he called out, but it faded into a groan as his knees buckled.

His master came into his field of vision. Lewan's cloak was gone, and Berun's right hand was a mass of wet redness from his elbow down to the tip of his knife. He yanked the spear out of Lewan, tossed it in the direction of their attackers, and pulled Lewan after him down the hill.

Something hit him. Lewan didn't see it coming, but he felt a massive weight smash into them, and even as his master's grip broke and he went down, the thick scent of the tiger hit him. The world spun round Lewan, but he managed to push himself to his hands and knees and look up. Only a few paces away, his master held the tiger at bay with his knife. Sauk and his assassins were just beyond the great cat.

The tiger snarled and swiped at the knife with one paw. Berun avoided the blow and stepped back.

Lewan could see Sauk shouting something, but he couldn't hear the words. The roaring in his ears had drowned out all other sound. He could no longer feel his left arm. His jaw hung open, and try as he might, he could not close it.

The tiger backed away a step and crouched, flexing her muscles to pounce. Her lips curled back over her teeth, her haunches lifted in preparation to launch her massive body at Berun—

And a small missile hit her on the head. Perch, biting and clawing. The tiger roared—Lewan could feel it in his chest and the ground beneath him even though he could not hear it—and shook her head back and forth. But the little lizard held tight. The tiger only managed to shake him down onto her face.

The tiger ceased shaking and swiped her right paw, claws extended, at the lizard. Perch leaped at the last possible instant, and the tiger's claws raked through her own eyelid and gouged the eye beneath. She screamed, and Lewan saw Sauk's eyes go wide, first in shock, then in fury.

Maddened by pain, the tiger barreled away, plowing right into Valmir and sending him crashing into a thorn bush.

Sauk descended on Berun. Lewan saw that all mercy and all remembrance of their friendship was gone, replaced by complete rage. The half-orc brought his sword around in a backhand sweep that would have beheaded his master had Berun not thrown himself back. But the move cost him. On the slope in the slick mud, Berun slipped and fell. He hit a carpet of leaves made slick by the rain and seasons of rot. He slid several paces down the hill and might have gone all the way to the bottom had a large brake of holly not caught him.

Color was fading from the world, and shadows were closing in round the edges of Lewan's vision. Still the roaring filled his ears, but in those last moments he thought he heard a voice behind the roaring—a raspy, smoky voice chanting a rough sing-song. An incantation, almost.

Lewan's left arm collapsed under him and he rolled to one side. But he kept his eyes open, fixed on his master, who was rising from the holly, covered in mud, leaves, ages-old pine needles, and blood. Sauk was still coming down the hill, right for him.

A huge patch of ground erupted before Berun, scattering leaves, branches, and the rotted remains of an old tree. The ground rose up, almost three times taller than Sauk. Shaped almost like a man it was—or a half-formed shape of a man, like the beginning of a sculptor's statue. It dripped mud and leaves, and branches protruded from its torso and head.

Stunned, mouth agape, Sauk slid to a stop only a couple of paces from the shambling mound of man-shaped earth. But the thing fell upon Berun. In the final instant before it struck, Lewan could have sworn he saw a mouth open at the crown of the man-shaped earth. It grew and grew until the mouth took up most of its torso. It closed over Berun, and the mound lost all shape, becoming nothing more than a wave of undulating earth and detritus.

The earth settled again, but Berun was gone. Blackness closed over Lewan, and he didn't feel his face strike the wet ground.

Part Two

✚

THE FORTRESS OF THE OLD MAN

✠
chapter Thirteen

19 Tarsakh, the Year of Lightning Storms (1374 DR)
Sentinelspire

Awareness returned little by little. First the sensation of warmth. Not like fire, nor even sunshine. A soft warmness. Then sound, though it was no more than a breeze sighing over stone. Then scent. Many subtle aromas—fire, both wood smoke and the spicy aroma of candles, clean water, the particular thin scent air takes at high altitudes, and the sweet smell of spring blossoms—all blending in a pleasant whole. Last of all came true awareness.

Lewan opened his eyes. He lay in a soft bed wide enough for five people, his head nestled on goose down pillows, his body wrapped in silk sheets over which had been laid a soft coverlet sewn of rabbit skins.

The room around him was ... luxurious. Lewan knew the word, though he had only been able to ascribe meaning to it from bard's tales. Never had he seen such opulence. A massive stone fireplace centered the wall opposite his bed. A fire was burning to embers in it. The bed itself lay under a canopy around which a netting of sheer red fabric had been pulled up. Tiles the color of rich cream lined the floor, over which lay thick rugs. A door of some wood the hue of burnt cinnamon centered the wall to the right of his bed. Scented candles burned throughout the room. The wall to the left of his bed opened onto a balcony, beyond which Lewan could see blue sky interspersed with high, thin clouds, fine as gossamer strands. Even through the scent of wood smoke and candle wax, he could tell that the air was thinner, crisper, yet a scent of many growing things pervaded all. Mountain air—but *lush* mountain air.

Lewan sat up, and a tiny spark of pain ran through his left shoulder. He looked down and realized two things. First, he was naked and completely clean. Even his hair had been washed and trimmed, his face freshly shaved. Second, the wound near his shoulder was no more than a pale blotch of skin with the slick-smooth sheen of magical healing. His last memory was the morning on the hillside in the Khopet-Dag. The assassin had sneaked up on him and plunged the poisoned spear into his shoulder. Obviously the poison had been meant to subdue him, not kill him. The earth had risen up and swallowed his master. Or had it? Lewan had been unable to hear anything, save for a strange chanting, and his vision had not been clear. Had that been a dream?

The door opened, and in walked a girl. She seemed close to Lewan's age, perhaps a bit older. The slight cant to her eyes, the long hair the color of a raven's eye, and skin the color of honeyed wax gave her the look of one of the Shou. She carried a bundle of folded cloth before her.

Her eyes widened at the sight of Lewan sitting up in bed. She nudged the door closed with one foot, then bowed. "I am Ulaan, your servant. I have brought you clean clothes."

"My . . . servant?" She was dressed like no servant he had ever seen. Her dress, the color of sunset on the clouds and of a simple cut, was made from silk that would have befitted the daughter of the wealthiest merchant trading along the Golden Way.

"I serve the Old Man," she said, "Lord of Sentinelspire. You are his honored guest. I am to see to your every need. Should I displease, another servant will be provided for you."

Lewan swallowed. His eyes stayed on the girl, but his attention focused inward. Servant? Honored guest? None of this made any sense.

"You wish for me to send for another?" Ulaan still had not risen from her bow. Her gaze was fixed on the fine rug before her, and as Lewan's attention returned to her, he noticed that her posture offered a generous gaze down the front of her dress.

Lewan blushed and averted his gaze. "Uh, no. That . . . that's won't be necessary, thank you."

"Thank me for what?" Ulaan rose and looked at Lewan. Her expression was one of complete deference, but there was a coy spark in her eye.

"Where am I?" asked Lewan. "How did I get here?"

"You are the guest of the Old Man of the Mountain," said Ulaan. "Others will tell you the tale in full, I am sure. It is my task to see that your needs are met." She lifted the folded bundles of cloth. "I have brought you clean clothes. Yours could not be saved. Shall I dress you?"

Lewan's blush deepened. "No! That, uh . . . that won't be necessary, thank you."

"Young master, my sister Bataar and I bathed and shaved you, and I have tended you since your arrival. You have nothing that I have not seen and touched."

✚
chapter fourteen

Talieth found Sauk where she thought she would—on the mountainside, sitting cross-legged before a small fire. He often came up here when he wanted to be alone. The large outcropping of bare rock was around the north face of Sentinelspire, well out of sight of the Fortress in its secluded canyon. The broken cone of the mountain rose behind, and before them spread the Endless Wastes. Hundreds of miles of steppe.

The wind off the mountain whipped her heavy cloak in front of her and tossed her hair in front of her face. She was glad for the cloak. Early spring as it was, the wind at this height still held a chill, and her cheeks were soon raw and flushed.

The chill did not seem to bother Sauk. The half-orc sat naked except for a loincloth. His long hair was unbound, and the breeze tossed it over his shoulders. The stiff wind made the fire's meager flames struggle for life, but Sauk was close enough to the fire that his broad back kept off the worst of the breeze. As she came around to stand before him, she saw that the druid's relic, the Three Hearts, lay discarded on the dusty stone beside him. A huge knife lay upon his lap, and blood tinged its edge. The old scar that ran from his hairline down his forehead and left cheek oozed fresh blood. Some of it had dripped and dried on his chest. She knew he was aware of her, had been so for some time, but his gaze never shifted off the horizon.

"Where is Taaki?" she asked.

"And a good morning to you, too," said Sauk, still not looking at her.

"How is she?"

"Her eye is gone. How do you think she is?"

"I am sorry, Sauk. We will find a healer for her. I swear it. Once this business is done, Taaki will have both her eyes again."

Sauk sat in silence, still not looking at her. She let him brood. When he had brought his band and their sole captive back to the Fortress two nights ago, she had never seen him in such a mood. He had beaten one of her personal guards and would have likely killed the man had she not stopped him. All because the man had looked at him in a way Sauk didn't like.

"Why are you here, Talieth?" said Sauk.

"Our captive is being dealt with."

"You came all this way to tell me something I already know?"

Talieth's jaw clenched. She hugged her cloak about her and followed Sauk's gaze out to the horizon. On a clear day, one could see the Firepeaks some two hundred miles to the north. But today they were nothing more than a smudge of dark haze on the horizon. The remains of the storm, most likely. Or perhaps the Firepeaks were oozing steam again.

"I need to hear the words from your mouth," she said at last.

"Kheil is dead," said Sauk, and the flatness of his tone, the utter lack of any emotion, shocked her.

"You said that once before." She looked at Sauk, all the weight of her station bearing down upon him. But it didn't seem to bother him.

"My brother died in the Yuirwood nine years ago," said Sauk. "Your vision dared me to hope otherwise. I now know that hope was false. Kheil is dead."

She pointed at the naked blade on his lap. "Then why this? Why cut your *luzal unba?*"

Talieth knew of this particular tradition of Sauk's orc clan. She'd been there nine years ago when he'd cut it the first time. When a warrior lost a family member, he cut a scar over his

125

face in remembrance, from the crown of his head to his cheek. The wound bled profusely, even running into the eye like tears, symbolizing both death and grief. Ever afterward, the mourner would gaze through the scar of his grief.

"The first cut was for my brother's death," said Sauk. "This one is to remind me."

"My scrying does not lie," said Talieth. "I saw Kheil. Older and changed, but it was him."

"You saw the body, the face. The spirit we knew and loved is gone. Nine years gone. The one you saw calls himself Berun now. He killed two of my blades and tried to kill me. That was not my brother."

"And this . . . Berun. You saw him die. You are certain?"

A look of annoyance passed over Sauk's face, but he still did not lift his gaze from the horizon. "I saw the earth rise and take form. A great earth spirit swallowed Berun before going back into the ground. Unless the bastard found a way to breathe mud, he's dead."

"So you said nine years ago."

Sauk looked up then, only his eyes moving, but she saw every muscle in his body tense. "Tell me, Talieth. Are you calling me a liar or a fool?"

"Neither," said Talieth, holding his gaze. "I am telling you that Kheil—"

"Berun."

"*Kheil* escaped death once before. You said the earth rose to swallow him. A strange thing. A rogue earth spirit? Perhaps. They dwell in the Shalhoond. And far worse things haunt the Khopet-Dag. But I wonder . . ."

"What?" said Sauk. His eyes narrowed. The fury he held in check, and Talieth could see curiosity burning in his eyes.

"I have heard it said that druids can accomplish such things," said Talieth. "You wouldn't know of any meddlesome druids about, would you, Sauk? Any who might have reason to keep . . . *Berun* alive?"

Sauk blinked and dropped his gaze. In his present mood, that was an expression of true shock. "You're saying—"

"I'm saying it would be foolish to underestimate our opponent. This is not a game we can afford to lose."

"If . . . *if* he survived, why can't you scry him? Use your . . . whatever you do, to find him?"

Talieth looked to the horizon. "Don't think I haven't tried. If he is out there, his presence is hidden from me."

"Perhaps because he is dead?"

"Or perhaps because whatever—or whomever—came to his aid is able to hide him from me."

Sauk thought a moment, then said, "This is possible?"

"Possible?" said Talieth. "Yes. Likely? No. But many damned unlikely things have happened of late, have they not?"

Sauk nodded and sighed. "I will be ready."

"Speaking of which, have you been able to glean anything?" She gestured toward the Three Hearts.

"Nothing," said Sauk. "I serve the Beastlord. My communion is the hunt. This relic"—Sauk shuddered, and a hint of sneer passed over his face —"it sings of growing things and deep secrets. I do not like it. I will continue to pry at it if you wish, but I don't hold much hope."

A tremor shook the mountain. Nothing more than a slight vibration at their feet, but it was enough to set stones rattling down the mountain and bring a shower of dirt and grit down upon them.

Talieth wiped the dust from her eyes and picked up the relic. "We have no time for you to fumble your way through the relic's secrets."

"Where are you taking it?" Sauk called after her.

"To someone else," she said, and strode away.

chapter Fifteen

On the balcony outside his room, Lewan stood dumb-struck. Never had he seen such utter beauty. He'd been on mountainsides many times. More than he could remember. He'd lived in forests entire seasons during his sixteen years. The largest city he'd ever visited was Almorel by the Lake of Mists. It was probably a small city as many in the world would count such things. Perhaps even rustic compared to the grand cities of the West or in distant Shou. But to Lewan, who spent most of his days in the wild, it was a city nonetheless. Mountains, forests, and cities . . . these things were not new to him. But never had he seen all three come together in such splendor.

His balcony was one of several jutting out from the upper floors of a tower, and it offered a view of the entire fortress. The fortress itself had no walls, for the canyon in which it had been built—or in some places apparently carved—served as a natural and seemingly impregnable wall. Although Lewan had no training in the ways of war, even he could see that the only hope of taking this fortress would be through stealth or the air—and no realm in the Endless Wastes commanded an army capable of such an air assault.

The tower in which he'd been housed was one of several in the fortress—and far from the tallest. The tallest—a massive structure in the center of the fortress—was at least six hundred feet high, perhaps more, and its upper stories looked out over the upper rims of the canyon. From the top of that tower, one surely could have seen beyond the canyon and well into the steppe for hundreds of miles.

All the buildings were of a style strange to Lewan's eyes—one he'd never seen before, all odd angles and interlocking designs of stone, many of which had a decidedly purple tinge. The great tower in the center was strangest of all, for it seemed that great pillars of stone had been twisted braidlike around the entire shaft. They disappeared into the upper stories, and the top of the tower itself seemed a garden or small park, open to the winds on every side. And around the entire tower—indeed around most of the buildings in the fortress—grew vines, trees, flowers, and vegetation of every sort. Some of the flowers ringing the great tower seemed big as shields.

Strangest and most wondrous of all were the statues. Pillars—mostly stone, but there were at least two forged of some silvery metal—rose above many of the buildings, and atop them were great statues. Some were in the form of beautiful men and women. One woman, sculpted entirely from black stone, stood poised on one foot, her long hair and robes seeming to flow out behind her, and one hand held aloft a metal rod at least twenty feet long. Other statues were of creatures that ranged from the beautifully strange—a griffon, a winged deer, a feathered serpent—to the grotesque—a batwinged gargoyle with the horns of a ram, a wolf with three heads, a bearded old man with antlers, and a hugely muscular man with the head of a camel.

Green grew over everything—climbing buildings, winding through the streets, ringing towers. In places it was hard to see the stone. Blossoms were everywhere as spring took hold. Their sweet smell mingled with the crisp scent of the high mountain air and the loamy aroma of the greenery.

A large waterfall fell over the western canyon wall to feed a great pool, out of which flowed dozens of waterways that wound throughout the fortress. Lewan counted no less than eight fountains within the fortress, and he thought he could even see the sparkle of water on the roof of the great tower. How could water flow up so high? People lounged by some of the fountains—men in robes or loose-fitting garb, women in colors to rival the flowers and blossoms.

And over all this—buildings, towers, statues on pedestals, the great dome near the western canyon wall—flew birds of every color. Black ravens, white doves, and songbirds ranging from deepest blue to brightest yellow and every shade between. Lewan, who had lived most of his life in the wild and could name every bird of the Amber Steppes and Shalhoond in at least two languages, had never seen at least a dozen of these birds.

Lewan had never really considered the meaning of the word paradise. But standing there in the late morning air, clean and dressed in the loose-fitting linen clothes Ulaan had brought him, he knew that he could not imagine anything more fitting than the scene before him. This was paradise.

But then his master's voice rose up in his memory. *Sentinelspire . . . you don't know that place. It's . . . hard to see clearly there. Sentinelspire is a realm built on blood. Murder. I don't want you anywhere near that place.*

How could his master have been so wrong?

Lewan winced at the thought. The bright mood that had grown in him darkened. He could still remember a great shambling mound of earth and mud rising, almost in the shape of a man, and burying his master. Had it been real? Or part of a dream brought on by the poison in his veins?

Ulaan had been unable to tell him, only said that all would be made clear in time and that he should not leave his room.

He heard the door to his room open, then footsteps. He walked back through the double doors of his balcony and through the filmy curtains fluttering in the morning breeze.

Ulaan had returned, bearing a large platter of food and

drink. Behind her, coming into the room, was the most striking woman Lewan had ever seen. She stood a bit taller than Lewan, and she walked with the bearing of a queen. Her black hair hung in dozens of braids well past her waist, and tiny rings of gold and jewels sparkled among them. A circlet of fine chain ringed her head, and tiny rubies dangled from finer chains on her forehead. Her dress, fitted tightly from wrist to neck and down her torso, flowed out in a loose skirt beneath her waist. Tiny red jewels were sewn into the seams, complementing the silky fabric that flowed between deepest red and the warm yellow of a dusty-sky sunset. Her skin was darker than Lewan's, but where his was weathered from years of sun, wind, and rain, hers was flawless and smooth. Her dark eyes looked out beneath sharp eyebrows, arched in what was something between amusement and offense. With dawning horror, Lewan realized he'd been staring. No, not staring. Gawking.

He snapped his mouth shut, averted his eyes, and bowed.

Ulaan set the platter on the table by his bedside, bowed to them both, and fled the room, closing the door behind her.

"I am Talieth, Lady of the Fortress," said the woman.

Talieth. He'd heard that name before, when Sauk's men had dragged him into the camp. The half-orc had tried to calm his master by saying, *Talieth will explain everything when we get to the Fortress.*

"Please take your eyes off the floor," said the woman.

Lewan obeyed, but he could find nowhere to look. He could not hold the woman's gaze, and anything lower than her face put him in even more dangerous territory. She had ordered him to look up, so he settled for a spot just over her left shoulder.

"I don't know where you are from, young man," she said. "But here, it is considered polite to give your name when introducing yourself to the lady of the house."

"I, uh, I—" Lewan swallowed hard and took a breath to calm himself. "I am called Lewan."

"Called by whom?"

"My . . . my master. Berun."

Lewan risked a glance at her face and was surprised to see a look of genuine sorrow there.

"That is part of what we must speak about, Lewan. But first"—she spread her hands, as if presenting a gift —"I bid you welcome to Sentinelspire. I hope Ulaan has fulfilled her duties in making you comfortable."

"Uh, she has, my lady. She brought me these clothes. I told her how hungry I am and she, uh—" Lewan gestured at the platter of food.

"Forgive me, Lewan," said Talieth. "You've been through quite an ordeal the past few days. Please. Sit. I will speak while you refresh yourself."

Quite an ordeal. Lewan had to force himself not to grit his teeth as he walked to the table and sat upon the stool. He looked to the platter—anything to keep his eyes off Talieth. Beside a large metal pitcher of water and a silver bowl of wine was a plate of meat sliced almost parchment thin. Rare beef, he thought, though he couldn't be certain. Beside that was a small loaf of dark bread and various raw vegetables and fruits—most of them out of season, yet they seemed fresh off the vine. He poured water into the empty cup, drained it, then set about devouring the food.

An ordeal. Those words reminded Lewan exactly why he was here. These people had hunted him and his master, bound them, speared and poisoned him, and . . . and Berun was dead. The grapes he'd been chewing seemed to turn to ashes in his mouth. His spirit, which had been lifted at the wondrous sight of the fortress, sank, and in its place a hot anger filled him. It didn't banish his fear, but his desire to defer and mind his manners before this "lady" was suddenly gone.

Lewan forced himself to swallow, then asked, "Why am I here?"

"You are here to rest. After what happened, you need it."

"What . . . happened? What *happened* . . . happened because of you."

Lewan risked a glance up. Talieth stood beside the foot of his bed, looking down on him. He could not tell if she was angry or shocked at his boldness. Her lips pursed as she considered his words, then broke into a very unladylike grin.

"Bold," she said. "I admire boldness in a man." She sat on the stool next to him and smoothed her skirt as she gathered her thoughts. "What happened out there was . . . unfortunate. Sauk had orders to bring your master here. It grieves me that Sauk had to resort to violence—gods know he probably didn't hesitate—but you must understand, Lewan. We are in *desperate* need. Your master was our best hope."

"Not anymore," said Lewan. He managed to hold her gaze for a moment, but he dropped it and looked back to his food. Still, his voice did not tremble when he said, "My master is dead because of Sauk."

"I'm sorry, Lewan," said Talieth. Lewan looked up in shock at the tone in her words. Her voice seemed on the edge of breaking. Tears welled in her eyes. "So sorry. I . . . loved him, too. Once. Did he ever speak of me to you?"

Lewan tried to hold on to his anger, but seeing the lady's sorrow, he could not. He even felt a twinge of guilt for telling her the truth. "No, lady. No. My master . . . I never knew him as anything but Berun, a servant of the Oak Father. His life before . . . I'm sorry, lady, but it's all very new to me. He never spoke of it."

"Well, then"—she wiped at her tears and took a deep breath through her nose, forcing herself back into the calm composure of the lady of the manor —"it seems that you and I have many things to tell one another. I would very much like to speak with you of your master. I . . . miss him. Very much."

Much to his horror, Lewan felt tears rising in his own eyes. His throat felt suddenly thick. He would *not* cry in front of this woman. His rising tears made him angry.

"Berun would be here now," he said through clenched teeth, "if not for you. You and your cursed half-orc and his band of murderers."

"Really?" Lewan heard the ice in Talieth's voice, but when he looked up there was fire in her eyes. "Was it I who killed your master? No. Or was it the half-orc and his men? No again. According to every man there, including the 'cursed half-orc,' the earth rose up and swallowed your master. You dispute this?"

Lewan scrubbed the back of his sleeve across his eyes before the tears could fall.

"Well?"

"No," he said, and the petulance in his voice only made him angrier.

Talieth wiped her own tears, then stood and paced the floor before the cold fireplace. "Believe me or not," she said, "I do miss him. But you saw it yourself. It was not me or anyone I sent who killed your master. Sauk and his men are hunters, the fiercest and most cunning in thousands of miles, and there was nothing they could do to save him. You saw it yourself."

Lewan's head felt thick with unshed tears. He reached for the pitcher of water, but his hand shook so badly that he simply grabbed the handle and squeezed. "My master would not have been there were it not for you. Do you dispute *that?*"

"And he would not have been there had he not tried to escape," she said. "Had he come as I asked. As I *begged*. Lewan. If we are going to go through all the what-ifs and what-might-have-beens, this will take a very, very long time. Time, I'm afraid, we do not have. You know why we needed your master?"

"He . . . he never had the chance to tell me." Lewan released his grip on the pitcher and put both hands in his lap. They curled into fists, and he fixed his eyes on them as he struggled to keep his voice from breaking. "He and Sauk talked in camp. Quite a lot. But I was kept apart. I—"

Talieth stopped her pacing and looked at him. "Yes? You what?"

"I don't think I was supposed to be there," said Lewan. "I think Sauk was surprised to find me with Berun, and he . . . had to improvise. He kept us apart, I think, to try to control my master."

Talieth said nothing at first, and when the silence grew uncomfortable, Lewan dared to look up. Talieth was standing before the darkened hearth, one arm cradling the other while she tapped her lips with one finger. She was watching him, and with most of the light coming from the open balcony behind her, her eyes seemed twin wells of shadow.

"Do you pray to the gods, Lewan?" she asked.

Lewan frowned, surprised at such an odd question. "I, uh . . . I serve the Oak Father, as Master Berun taught me."

"I am no priestess," said Talieth, "but even I can recognize a gift from the gods when I see it."

"What?"

"Think about it, Lewan," she said, and she stepped forward again until she stood at the foot of his bed. "We are in desperate, dire need. I had hoped that your master and the relic he carried could save us, could save all of Faerûn. But your master has been taken from us. Were it not for one thing, I would despair."

"What thing?"

Talieth came closer. She placed a hand on his shoulder and said, "You."

✚
chapter sixteen

Sauk's quarters—he didn't consider it a home so much as a place to store his meager possessions; his home was the wild—were in the smallest of the Fortress's many towers, a squat stone cylinder that overlooked the gardens and pools round the western falls. This meant he had to walk through most of the Fortress from the main gate, and the most direct path took him past the Tower of the Sun, which dominated the center of the Fortress.

His hunter's nature—the part of him in tune with the pulse of the wild—did not like the Tower. He'd never liked it. Even before the Old Man's madness, it had been little more than a crumbling relic of the long-dead Imaskari Empire. Now, covered in vines, flowers, and foliage of every sort, it ought to have appealed to him. It was, after all, the wild taken root and flourishing in the midst of a citadel of stone. Still, there was something . . . *wrong* about it, something that made Sauk's skin crawl and made him want to grind his teeth and look away.

Still, it was that very wrongness that brought him by the Tower whenever he was about. He would often go far out of his way to pass the Tower's main gate that led into the overgrown courtyard. As much as the place raised his hackles, his hunter's nature also knew that the best thing to do with an enemy was to keep a careful watch.

Returning from his vigil on the mountain, still bare-chested with his shirt thrown over one shoulder and the dust of the mountain covering him, Sauk strolled past the main gate of the Tower of the Sun. The walls of purple stone surrounding the massive cylinder of the Tower could scarcely be seen through the riot of vines, leaves, and flowers that had grown over the wall and spilled into the street. Only the main gate remained clear, and as Sauk approached it, four men—veteran blades, every one—walked out and onto the pathway. Sauk knew them. Every one was loyal to the Old Man and had not been brought into Talieth's plot. But if they had any suspicion of the conspiracy, they'd never given any sign.

"Vasilik!" Sauk called out.

Vasilik, a blond and bearded Illuskan, was the only blade in the Fortress who could look Sauk eye to eye, though he lacked the half-orc's bulk. With his pale skin and long hair, the man looked like the famed barbarians from so many bard's tales, but Vasilik had been no more than muscle for one of the guilds in Waterdeep before joining the blades of Sentinelspire.

"Well met, Sauk," he said. The other three stopped at his side.

"How fares the Old Man?" asked Sauk.

A look of reverence—almost of *awe*—passed over the men's faces. One even lowered his eyes, almost as if in prayer. Fools, thought Sauk.

"Hale as ever," said Vasilik. "He has ordered all the blades and servants from his Tower, for tonight is a holy night. A night of preparation and contemplation. Would you care to join us?"

"Where will you take your vigil?"

"Under the oaks in the Garden of Winged Horses," said Vasilik. "We would be honored if you would join us."

"I will consider it."

Draalim, a small Calishite whom Sauk knew often posed as a merchant throughout the Sword Coast, spoke up. "All the faithful must prepare, Sauk. The day draws close."

"It does indeed," said Sauk, and he walked around them.

Valmir watched the last of the bright green tail disappear into the foliage of the tree. He'd been watching the snake for some time. First as it crawled out from the bushes that lined the pathway to the fountain, then over the lawn. It had come within spitting distance of his bare feet before sliding through the grass to begin winding its way up the tree. Probably hunting birds' eggs. Gods knew, this time of year the trees would be full of them.

Valmir'd been lounging under the tree since finishing his exercises. He'd been teaching himself a few spells here and there—mostly little cantrips or invocations to help in his line of work. But since becoming one of the blades of Sentinelspire—or more correctly, since charming his way into Talieth's bed—she had begun teaching him more powerful spells. Beyond moving silently, unlocking a door, or covering his scent from hounds, Talieth's spells had true power. He'd mastered only one so far, but he'd been practicing the rest. Still didn't quite have the fourth order of finger movements down, but he was getting close. A nearby boulder still bore the scorch marks from his few near successes. But doing the damned finger motions tired him out, and Valmir had never been one to hesitate from a good rest.

The Star Fountain—so named because of the star blossoms that dominated the surrounding foliage and dropped their petals into the singing water beneath the fountain—was his favorite place to spend the morning doing absolutely nothing. Here, under the shade of the massive old oak whose roots sank into the fountain's pool, there was plenty of shade, and most of the bees left him alone, preferring the sunlight amongst the star blossoms.

Birds overhead began making a terrible racket. That snake must be getting close to a late breakfast, thought Val. The birds were so noisy that Val saw Sauk passing by on his right before he heard him. The half-orc was bare above the waist. He carried his shirt and a big leather satchel in one hand.

Valmir started to call out, but he thought better of it and closed his mouth. Sauk seemed very deep into his own thoughts. Valmir had been with the band when one of Talieth's personal guards had made the stupid mistake of looking at Sauk at the wrong moment. Val had stood with the others and watched while Sauk beat the man nearly to death. Chiganis had survived, which Val couldn't quite make up his mind about. He didn't like the bastard, but he wasn't sure if the man deserved to die that way just because of a look the half-orc had deemed disrespectful.

Sauk happened to glance Val's way as he passed. He stopped. "What are you doing here?"

"Nothing at all," said Val, and he did his best to keep the insolence out of his voice. No easy task for him. "You?"

"Been out."

"On the mountain?"

Sauk nodded. His black mood seemed to be gone, but one could never be too sure. He nodded a farewell and turned to leave.

"Sauk?"

The half-orc stopped and turned.

"How's Taaki?"

Sauk's eyes narrowed. "She'll live. Why do you ask?"

Val feared he'd trod onto thin ice. "Just concerned is all. She healed up yet?"

"If I were you," said Sauk, "I'd concern myself with other things. But then, I suspect you're nothing but relieved now. Am I right?"

"I don't get your meaning."

"Our quarry didn't make it back."

"And why would that relieve me?" said Val. "I'll admit I didn't much like it when the bastard tried to blind me with his cooking, but . . . relief? I don't follow. Relief that he's dead?"

"Yeah," said Sauk. "I think you're relieved he's dead. Or you ought to be, if you're smart."

"What makes you say that? You and Talieth said he was our best hope for . . ." Val looked around. In the fortress, one never knew what ears and eyes might be lurking. "You know. If we're back where we started, why would that relieve me?"

"Because as long as I've known you, Val, you never think of we, of us. You're all about you. And unless you're damned stupid—and I don't think you are—you had to know that Kheil's return might have . . . changed your situation. Looks like *you* are back where *you* want to be. Eh?"

Valmir scowled. "What are you saying?"

"I'm saying, enjoy the bed while you can. Things change." He glanced at the boulder that had been the target of Valmir's earlier attempts at the spells. "And keep practicing the magic. Something tells me you're going to need it."

Sauk smiled—though there was no kindness in it—then tossed his shirt over his shoulder and walked away. Val watched him go, and it occurred to him that he hadn't seen Talieth all morning.

✠
chapter seventeen

Me?" said Lewan. "I don't understand. How can I help you?"

"What I am about to tell you, Lewan, you cannot speak of to anyone else. Not Ulaan." Talieth approached as she spoke, bringing the full bearing of her station down upon Lewan. He had to force himself not to cower. "Not to *any* of the servants or anyone else in Sentinelspire. Do you understand?"

Lewan nodded, too intimidated to speak.

"You have lived in the Endless Wastes most of your life, have you not?" she said.

"Since I was twelve. Before that, I lived in a small village. In Murghôm."

"Murghôm?" Talieth smiled. "I thought you had the look of them. Your master has raised you since . . ."

"Raiders attacked my village," said Lewan, and he left it at that. Those were memories he preferred not to uproot.

"Your parents?" said Talieth.

Lewan looked away and clenched his jaw. His mother's face in that last moment kept trying to come up, but he pushed the image away. He took in a deep breath through his nose, willing himself not to cry, then said, "Berun and his master saved me."

"His master?"

"An old druid from the Yuirwood." Lewan shrugged. "I

met him only that day, and I scarcely remember him. But my master spoke of him often. With great affection."

"Chereth, wasn't it?"

Lewan blinked and looked to her. "How . . . how did you know?"

"That is where our tales come together. But I must start farther back. In all your years, in your village in Murghôm or your life with your master, did you never hear of the Old Man of the Mountain?"

Lewan shrugged.

"Your master never spoke of him? You never heard whispered tales round the campfire or in some bard's tale in a tavern?"

"I've never been in a tavern."

Talieth tilted her head to one side. "Really? Why is that?"

"My master disapproved of cities. He said that anything bigger than a village made him . . . itch. I've been to Almorel a handful of times. But never for more than a day, and we never stayed the night."

Talieth looked away, seemingly lost in thought. Confused, almost. But then she shook her head and said, "No matter. So you have never heard of the Old Man of the Mountain?"

"Never, lady. That is . . . not until . . ."

"Until when?"

"Walking through the Shalhoond with Sauk and his men. The half-orc told me of the Old Man of the Mountain. He said that my master had once been known as Kheil, that he worked for the Old Man."

"As an assassin," said Talieth.

"I . . . I didn't believe Sauk then."

"And now?"

A tiny voice in the back of Lewan's mind warned him to say nothing, to plead ignorance. But what could it hurt? Sauk knew the truth already. If he and Talieth both served this Old Man, surely she knew as well.

"The night after we . . . after escaping Sauk and his men, my master told me the truth."

"And you believed him?"

"Of course."

"Good," said Talieth. "Then this will make the rest of my tale easier. You know your master once served Alaodin, the Old Man of the Mountain, as an assassin. What you might not know is that Alaodin is my father, and he has gone completely mad."

"Mad?"

"Oh, he's not gibbering and drooling and talking to the walls." Talieth's brow knotted up, and her attention seemed focused entirely inward, a mixture of sorrow and contemplation. "Suffice to say he was not born into the exalted position he holds. My father grew up hard. Early life for him was not so much living as surviving, and he did not have the benefit of a master who loved him."

A master who loved him. A sob rose in the back of Lewan's throat, but he took a deep breath and choked it down. Ignoring his trembling hands, he poured himself more water and took a long drink while Talieth gathered her thoughts.

"My father learned that to survive—and later, to protect those he loved—required power. No matter how rich, powerful, and influential he became, he never forgot the hard lessons of his childhood. They . . . haunted him. And perhaps he was not as careful as he should have been in where he sought power. He became a devoted servant of Bhaal, and when his god died . . . I think that was the beginning of my father's madness."

Lewan thought that anyone who would willingly serve Bhaal was well on their way to madness already, but he held his tongue.

"The death of his god reawakened something my father had not known in many years," said Talieth. "Desperation. And fear. He began seeking new paths to power—lore, relics, allies. Although I cannot be certain, I believe it was during this time that my father first came into contact with your master's master, Chereth."

"Chereth would have never allied himself with assassins!" said Lewan. He looked up and forced himself to hold Talieth's gaze.

If anything, she seemed amused by his effrontery. "I thought you said you never knew Chereth?"

"My master spoke of him often. He—"

"And your master never hid anything from you?" said Talieth, her voice sharp. "Never, perhaps, chose to withhold certain truths in order to protect you from . . . harsh realities?"

Lewan held his glare a few moments longer before dropping his eyes to his half-eaten meal.

"In truth," Talieth continued, "I could be wrong on this point. I don't know when my father first had dealings with Chereth. And it's entirely possible that Chereth never told your master of this. You Oak Children do seem rather adept at keeping secrets from one another. But I *do* know that they . . ." She thought a moment. ". . . crossed purposes."

Rather adept at keeping secrets from one another. That stung. Mostly because Lewan knew it to be true. How could his master have hidden so much from him? And why? Did he not trust him? Did he think him some fragile little boy incapable of knowing the truth? Or was it simply shame at his past life? And how much had he truly known about his own master?

"My father and Chereth . . . I wouldn't call them allies," continued Talieth. "Certainly not friends. But they aided one another from time to time when it suited their purposes."

"A servant of the Oak Father does not aid assassins," said Lewan, though that particular truth, as much as he wanted to believe it, suddenly felt like trying to hold water with an open hand.

Talieth chuckled, a low throaty laugh with little kindness

or humor in it. "Do you hate us so much, Lewan? You don't know us."

"I know you kill for profit."

"So do kings and khans," said Talieth. "You are too young to remember when Yamun Khahan's horde invaded the west. You think he killed all those thousands of people out of kindness? Kings kill by the thousands. They'll cloak it in glory or some righteous cause, but make no mistake. Profit is the oldest reason for killing, yet it's alive and well. None are better at it than kings. And in his own way, my father was a king."

"It's . . ." Lewan struggled to find the right word, then decided simple was best. "Evil."

Talieth threw back her head and laughed. "Evil? Your dear master never killed?"

"Never for coins!"

"Never?" She gave him a hard look, the demeanor of a queen displeased at an errant servant.

"You mean Kheil," said Lewan. He chose his words carefully so his voice would not tremble under Talieth's gaze. "You—"

"I *know* Kheil killed for coins," said Talieth, her voice rising to cut him off. "And many times for far less than that. That man loved blood like some men love wine. No, I am speaking of your Master *Berun*. He never killed? Not once?"

Lewan scowled. "Not for coins."

"Then for what?"

"To protect himself," said Lewan. "To protect others. He—"

"Others? What others?"

"Villagers sometimes hired him to track bandits," said Lewan. "He guarded caravans on the Golden Way a few times."

"And he did this for free?" said Talieth. "Out of the kindness of his heart? Or did he do it for coins?"

Lewan turned his gaze away, unable to stomach her smug expression.

Talieth's voice softened. Not all the way to kindness, certainly, but she no longer seemed on the edge of anger. "Don't misunderstand me, Lewan. You have a code by which you live. Which you honor. I respect that. But we, too, have our code. Do not despise us. Do not judge what you do not know. Would not even your master say such behavior is foolish?"

Lewan could sense the *wrongness* of her words, but he couldn't reason his way around them. The seed of doubt was not yet sprouted, but it had been planted in fertile soil.

"Chereth," Talieth continued, "what interest he and my father shared . . . I have no idea. But I do know that something happened between them. Again, here my knowledge is incomplete. All I know is that whatever happened was bad enough that my father sent men to kill the druid. Sent"—Lewan caught the faintest hint of a break in her voice —"Kheil. And you didn't send Kheil for a quiet kill. No. You sent Kheil when you wanted a message sent. When you wanted bloody murder and everyone to know about it. My father sent Kheil and a band to the Yuirwood. They . . . did not succeed."

"Kheil was killed."

"Yes," said Talieth, her voice carefully controlled. "And I thought him truly dead. I went nearly mad with grief myself. Had I known . . ." She stopped long enough to compose herself, then continued. "But several years ago, Chereth came here. To the Fortress. He came to kill my father, and it says something about the old druid's power—and perhaps my father's early madness—that he came so close to succeeding. Many of our people died. More than a few of Sauk's scars were earned that night. But my father finally managed to subdue the old druid, and he has held him captive all these years. I only knew that Chereth was the man responsible for the death of the only man I ever loved."

146

Despite his anger and confusion, Lewan kept his face carefully neutral. It seemed obvious to him that her father was mostly to blame for Kheil's death, but she was well into her tale—telling Lewan things he'd never heard—so he did nothing to contradict her prejudiced view.

"Having the druid here in the fortress only reawakened my grief. I might have killed Chereth myself had my father not protected him. Make no mistake. The old druid was a prisoner. Never unguarded. But as long as he behaved himself, my father would allow no one to harm him. No one except my father. I told you that my father's hunger for power often knew no caution. Though he was once a devoted priest of Bhaal, after the death of his god, he . . . broadened his interests, studying the arcane, searching lore wherever he could find it. Even this fortress, the place you now sit, is ancient. Built by the Imaskari thousands of years ago, and it holds many of their secrets still."

"And your father," said Lewan, "he used these powers on Chereth?"

"Used them on him, with him—perhaps even *for* him," said Talieth. "As I said, my father's hunger for power knew no bounds. He coerced knowledge from the old druid, by kindness or by torture. My father is an expert at both. But he also found ways to use the druid to leech the powers of the earth itself to serve him. This, I believe, is when his madness fully bloomed."

"I still don't understand," said Lewan. And he wasn't sure he wanted to. None of this had anything to do with him. His master was dead. If Chereth truly were alive, the best Lewan could do for him was to escape himself, perhaps seek a circle of druids somewhere, and tell them of the old half-elf's plight. One half-trained novice could do nothing against such powers.

"Tell me," said Talieth. "Did you feel the earth tremble not long ago?"

"Yes," said Lewan. "It's why I went out on the balcony. I thought it might have been a landslide."

"No, Lewan. You've lived in the Endless Wastes most of your life. You do know that Sentinelspire is a volcano?"

"Yes. But she hasn't erupted for thousands of years. The Firepeaks—"

"Are nothing compared to Sentinelspire," said Talieth. "Yes, the mountain has slept for untold thousands of years. My father believed that the Imaskari found a way to put her to sleep, to channel her energies elsewhere."

"Elsewhere? I . . . I don't understand."

"The Imaskari were masters of magic. But they were particularly knowledgeable about the other worlds beyond our own, and their wizards found ways to open doors to those worlds."

"You mean portals."

"You know of them?" said Talieth, sounding both surprised and pleased.

"My master told me of them. Sauk said that we were to take one here, before . . ." Lewan's voice caught in his throat.

"Yes, let's not get off on that path again," said Talieth. "The portals. Some can take a traveler hundreds or thousands of miles as if walking from one room to another. But others . . . others can lead to other worlds altogether, some so deadly that the very air is poison, the seas fire."

Lewan could not imagine why anyone, even a wizard, would wish to go to such places.

"The Imaskari," Talieth continued, "found ways to use this art for their benefit. This fortress is perhaps one of their greatest achievements. You've seen the greenery throughout our home? The fountains? The great fall over the western wall?"

"Yes."

Talieth gave him a self-satisfied smile. "We're in the Endless Wastes, Lewan. Where does all this water come from? Snowmelt off one mountain? You say you've lived in the wild for years. Surely you can see that no amount of snowmelt could account for such abundance of water in the Wastes."

"I hadn't really thought about it," said Lewan.

"No? Well, I can tell you that no amount of melting snow could provide enough water for that fall year round. The water all around you, feeding the vines and flowers and greenery, growing our food, filling that pitcher before you . . . very little of it came from rain or snowmelt. No. Deep beneath the fortress, and in hidden caves farther up the mountain, are the Wells."

"Wells? Like water?"

"Some, yes. The Wells are simply what my father named them, but in truth, they are portals to other worlds. Some are portals to realms of purest water, and the Imaskari found ways to channel that for their benefit. But not just water, Lewan. Have you noticed these slots throughout your room?"

She walked to the nearest wall and pointed where the wall met the ceiling and the floor. Horizontal slots were cut in the stone. Very narrow—even a mouse would have trouble squeezing through. Lewan could not guess their purpose.

"I hadn't noticed them," said Lewan. "I woke only moments before Ulaan came with my clothes."

"Ah," said Talieth, and her smile turned mischievous. "And she does command one's attention, does she not?"

Lewan blushed. "I dressed myself *after* she left the room. She returned long enough to offer food. When she left, I dozed some before the earthquake woke me. I went out to the balcony. I . . . I never spent time examining the room."

"And a young man of the wild such as yourself is surely unused to such splendor. True?"

Her words might have seemed condescending—especially from a lady of her bearing—but Lewan heard no such thing in her tone.

He shrugged. "I'm sure I would have noticed them eventually. What are they?"

"Another of the fortress's wonders—if perhaps one of its more indulgent," said Talieth. "In high summer, the Wastes are damnably hot, even here on the mountain. But these slots are openings for a series of tubes that wind throughout the fortress. Far beneath us, they connect to a portal, a doorway to a world of endless cold, where the winds could flay the flesh from your bones. This air is channeled throughout the fortress in high summer, so that even on the hottest day, our rooms are pleasantly cool. And there are more wonders. You've lived through the winters here, yes? On the coldest days, your breath turns to snow. Not here. Other portals connect to a world of fire, so we never lack for heat. The Dome of Fire near the southern wall has many of these channels, and we can funnel fire into wondrous shapes through crystal as old as the Imaskari."

Lewan took it all in. Much of it seemed too strange to believe, but Talieth spoke with such candor.

"What does all this have to do with me?" asked Lewan.

"Ah, my point, yes," said Talieth. "I said that my father believed that the Imaskari put Sentinelspire to sleep by channeling her fire and fury elsewhere."

"Yes?"

"What do you think would happen if those channels were closed?" said Talieth, her voice going very quiet. "Or worse, what if they were reversed?"

"You mean," said Lewan, with dawning horror, "the mountain might . . ."

"Wake up? Oh, yes. With a vengeance. But it's far worse than that, Lewan. I have only the faintest understanding of the arts my father has bent to his will. He not only plans to reverse the channels, but he has been building the mountain's power—and power from other worlds as well—so that this eruption will be like no other in all the history of the world. You've seen the Firepeaks to the north?"

"Yes," said Lewan. "I've been there."

"Even at their fiercest, they are guttering candles compared to what will happen if my father wakens Sentinelspire. Sentinelspire will be a lightning bolt. A hundred lightning bolts. The destruction will be . . . catastrophic. Not just for Sentinelspire, but for all Faerûn."

"Why?" Lewan asked. "Why do such a thing? That's—"

"Madness," said Talieth, her voice low, almost a whisper so that she had to lean close to be heard. "Yes. My father has gone quite mad. I can only guess at his reasoning. Revenge? Perhaps he wishes to strike back at a world that slew his god and robbed him of power? Perhaps he has some plan I cannot see. I don't know. But I know that he must be stopped."

"That . . . makes no sense," said Lewan. "If he destroys the mountain and all the lands around . . ."

"Oh, he isn't planning to kill himself," said Talieth. "He plans to use the portals to be far away. He and anyone he deems worthy."

"So what is he waiting for? Why not tomorrow? Why not today or right now?"

"Such power isn't like clapping your hands, Lewan. I know only a little of the Imaskari magics, and I know less of the ways of the druids. But I know that much power is tied to the seasons, the path of Selûne, the stars, and any number of things. Is it not so?"

"Yes," said Lewan.

"Portals, like doors, require keys. And very special doors require very special keys. I think my father has been searching for one particular key for many years. Perhaps it explains his contact with Chereth."

"A . . . a key?" said Lewan. "I don't understand."

Talieth reached into the folds of her skirt, her hand disappearing into a deep pocket, and what she pulled out Lewan recognized immediately.

"Erael'len!"

"The Three Hearts. So named because of the holy objects concealed within." Talieth held up the relic so it caught the light from the open balcony. Inside the latticework of twisted wood, something caught the light and sparkled. "Stoneblood," she said. "The hardened sap of the three trees most holy to Silvanus."

"Oak, Ash, and Thorn," said Lewan. All were bound within an intricate web of wood that was itself almost as hard as stone. "But . . . how did you . . . ?"

"How did I come by it?"

Lewan nodded.

"Sauk," she said.

"But . . . but my master took it from Sauk."

"So he did. And after . . . what happened, Sauk found it lying in the mud."

Lewan looked away and stared off into nowhere. It didn't seem right. After all they'd risked . . . to have the relic simply cast off, left lying in the mud . . .

"You see what I meant, don't you, Lewan?"

"What?"

"A gift from the gods," said Talieth. "That . . . thing taking your master. Had it taken *Erael'len* as well, all might be lost. Do you think it mere chance that the relic was left behind? I have lived too long and seen too much to believe in mere chance. You came to us for a reason, and *Erael'len* was given to us for a reason."

"So *Erael'len* is the key your father needs?"

"I think so, yes," said Talieth.

"Then why bring it here? You should be carrying it across the mountains or giving it to druids to guard and protect."

"You understand keys, yes, Lewan?"

"Yes. Just because I live in the wild doesn't mean—"

"Then you understand that a key can not only open a door, it can lock it as well."

"Oh," said Lewan, as the realization hit him.

"Yes," said Talieth. "And this particular key will lock the most important portal. For I think that this portal—ancient beyond any recorded histories—predates even the Imaskari. Its original users were not those wizards, I think."

"Druids?"

Talieth lowered the Three Hearts, letting it dangle from its necklace of leather by her side. She shrugged. "Who knows? Druids? Perhaps the forerunners of the druids, or even the forerunners of their forerunners. Perhaps Silvanus himself, for all I know."

Lewan closed his eyes. This was too much to take in.

"I hope you see now why we need you," said Talieth.

"Me?"

"Chereth is beyond helping us. Even if I could reach him, he has been my father's prisoner for years. If his mind is still whole . . ." Talieth did not finish the thought. "It was my hope that your master could use the Three Hearts to help us. But that"—the sudden force in her voice told Lewan she was on the verge of crying again —"is no longer a path open to us. That leaves us with you. So tell me, Lewan, will you help us? Help us stop my father before it is too late?"

"That's why you captured me? To help you stop a madman? I'm only a novice!"

"Captured?" said Talieth. "Lewan, please understand. You are our honored guest. If Sauk and his men were . . . a bit rough getting you here, well, I beg your forgiveness for that. But I must say that it was due mostly to your master's refusal to come. If he had come as we asked, Sauk wouldn't have forced him."

Lewan opened his mouth to protest, but Talieth cut him off.

"Still," she said, "honored guest as you are, you must understand that the Fortress is a place of many dangers, especially now that my father has gone completely mad. He sees enemies at every corner, and many of the people who live here still serve him. We must keep your presence hidden from him at all costs. You must go nowhere unattended. Especially tonight! Do you understand?"

"Tonight? Why?"

"Tonight is a holy night for the druids, and my father intends to harness more of Chereth's power for his own purposes. I have reason to believe we are in our final days here at Sentinelspire."

"Wait!" said Lewan. "A holy night? What night is this? How long was I asleep?"

Talieth looked taken aback at his question. "You slept in a fever here for two days, but Sauk said you'd been sleeping a full day before your arrival. Today is the third tenday after the spring equinox. Lewan . . . ? Is something wrong?"

✠
chapter Eighteen

Lewan spent the rest of the morning and most of the early afternoon on his balcony, taking in the clear air, the scents of flowers, and the sounds of the birds. He watched a lizard hunting the tiny blue butterflies in the vines that clung to the stone next to his balcony. It made him think of Perch, and his already dark mood darkened further, a reflection of the growing gloom in the canyon. This night of all nights, surrounded by so much stone, cut off from the natural world that had so defined his life for the past several years, Lewan felt very alone.

Another storm had climbed up the mountain—a fierce one, by the look of it. Lewan could see the lightning flashing in the clouds, and the thunder came deep and low down the slopes. It would fall on the fortress before sunset.

He returned to his room, grateful for the warm light of the candles. The ashes in the hearth were cold, but more wood lay stacked in an iron rack next to the fireplace. He knelt beside it, and for the first time noticed that each of the four curves of black iron ended in the shape of a leering face, eyes wide and lips open in an almost feral grin. Who would craft such an awful thing?

The tin bucket of kindling next to the firewood was filled with shavings from apple wood. Lewan breathed in their scent as he scattered the kindling over the ashes. He chose the small birch logs next. They would burn hot and fast. Once the fire was going, he would add the cherry wood. It would burn warm and slow, and he loved the scent.

The flames were just beginning to catch in the birch logs when the door opened and Ulaan entered, carrying a platter of food. Behind her came another girl, slightly taller and dressed in a loose silk robe of blue and green. She was so like Ulaan that they could have been sisters. A bundle of fresh candles dangled from one hand, and she bore a large brass wash basin.

Seeing the platter of half-eaten food still filling the small table, Ulaan placed the new platter on the bed and turned to face Lewan. She motioned to the other girl. "This is my sister, Bataar."

Bataar rose from where she had placed the wash basin on the floor, then gave him a small bow, never meeting his eyes.

"The Lady Talieth said that you are feeling unhappy," said Bataar. "She ordered these brought to you in hopes of lifting your mood."

She turned and clapped her hands. Thunder rumbled outside, putting a slight vibration in the floor, and four servants, each muscled as thick as a seasoned warrior, entered the room. Each pair bore a large clay pot between them. In the first pot grew a tree, a mature oak, though it was no more than the half-height of a man. In the second pot grew a full bloom of holly, a mass of dark green leaves and bright red berries. The servants placed each at the foot of the bed, bowed to Lewan and the women, then fled the room.

"Do they please you?" said Bataar.

A laugh—more exasperation than humor—escaped Lewan. Talieth had him shut in this tower, surrounded by cut and crafted stone, cut off from the natural world, and as recompense she sent him two potted plants. Was it some sort of cruel joke? When he felt his laugh turning to a sob, he clamped his jaw shut and turned his back on the women.

"The trees displease you, master?" said Bataar.

"No," said Lewan. More thunder shook the tower, and he could smell rain on the breeze through the balcony curtains. "No, they're fine. But I want to be alone, if you don't mind."

"As you wish," said Bataar. "Lady Talieth, she warned you about tonight? About staying in your room?"

"Yes," said Lewan, his back still to them.

He heard the women shuffle out, but one of them stopped in the doorway and said, "Lewan?" It was Ulaan's voice.

"Yes?"

"Tonight, it would be wise to lock the door as well."

The door closed, the first heavy drops of rain began to spatter the balcony outside, and Lewan could control his sobbing no longer.

✛
chapter nineteen

When the forebears of the Tuigan first wandered into the steppes, Sentinelspire was old. It stood alone and unchallenged, a great sentinel indeed amidst borderless leagues of grassland. The mountain's true origins had been lost to even the wisest of loremasters. Some who lived in the wild and knew well the ways of the earth believed that the forces that shaped the Firepeaks had also formed Sentinelspire, making the mountain a sort of larger relative to its distant, more active cousins to the north. Others—the Tuigan foremost among them—believed that the mountain was no natural creation, that it had been formed from dark magics that rent the very fabric of Faerûn, opening passageways to realms of fire and destruction.

None living knew the truth. But the mountain had been old even when the Imaskari had claimed it as their own and built the hidden fortress on the southeastern face of the mountain. Many of the buildings and tunnels were crafted from the mountain itself. But some of the towers and the hidden chambers beneath the fortress had been built and decorated with purple stone that came from distant lands. Greatest of these structures was the Tower of the Sun—so named because those standing atop it would be the first in the fortress to see the sun each morning. The Tower—and though there were many towers in the fortress, when the inhabitants spoke of "the Tower," there was only one they meant—stood in the very center of the fortress, its topmost galleries looking over the rim of the canyon wall itself. From the top of the Tower of the Sun, one could see for hundreds of miles into the open steppe, and on clear nights every star and constellation looked down upon the tower, their silver light gathering in the purple stone and crystal statues that ringed the rim of the tower.

The broken peak of Sentinelspire itself dominated the western sky and loomed over the canyon. The storm that had spent the late afternoon gathering strength waited until full dark, then poured its full fury on the canyon. Lightning wreathed Sentinelspire's jagged cone, and thunder rolled down the mountainside, strong enough to rattle the stones of the fortress. Early spring storms were not uncommon in this part of the Wastes. They built over the Great Ice Sea to the north and trampled the hundreds of miles of steppe like the Horde itself.

But on this night, the storm that hit the Fortress of the Old Man came with a power that many within the canyon, even those with no training in the mystic arts, found unnatural. Some thought they could hear whispers under the wind, and there was a rhythm to the thunder shaking the mountain. Lights of no natural hue flickered around the Tower of the Sun. Once a great bolt of lightning struck the tower itself, blasting the vines around the stone to cinders, and the flickering aftereffects seemed to linger too long. Rather than fade away, it looked as if the lightning crawled inside the open windows of the tower, where it continued to flash and burn.

As the world turned to midnight, the storm's fury did not abate or pass, but seemed to settle in over the Fortress of the Old Man. The lamps burning in the streets and pathways of the fortress cast only weak pools of light, and the wind blew out many, deepening the darkness in the fortress.

The unnatural lights around the Tower of the Sun dropped into the gardens below, where they lurked amongst the trees or hugged the stone of the tower. The upper regions of the tower were lost in the darkness of night and storm to any not possessing eyes that penetrated the dark—eyes like those of the half-orc and his tiger, crouching under the storm-wracked trees in a garden a few streets away. Most within the fortress had sought refuge in their rooms, behind locked doors. A few of the most devout of the Old Man gathered in the groves, but their eyes were closed or turned inward, intent on their devotions. And so, in the Fortress of the Old Man, the half-orc was very likely the only one who saw the shadows crawling down the vines and branches that encased the Tower of the Sun. He watched as they disappeared into the overgrown gardens beneath the tower, and he watched still as they scuttled out the gate or crawled over the wall to hunt in the dark.

Lightning flashed overhead, flickering off steel in the half-orc's hand. By the time the thunder answered, he was already on the move, the tiger following.

Lewan was aware of none of this. He stood on the balcony, leaning against the ivy-thick railing in the downpour, unmoving as the statues in the courtyard below. His hair hung heavy over his forehead, and the tears on his cheeks mingled with the rain.

So loud was the roaring of the rain and the recurring thunder that he never heard the door open behind him, nor did he hear Ulaan lock it behind her and call out to him.

She found him on the balcony, hesitated only a moment before stepping into the rain, and placed a hand on his shoulder. He jumped slightly at her touch but did not turn.

"Master Lewan!" She had to shout to be heard over the storm. "Come inside! You're drenched."

He ignored her.

"Master Lewan! Master, can you hear me?"

He turned to her, and she flinched at the pain in his eyes. "Go away," he said.

"Master Lewan, what's wrong?"

"Please. Go."

Ulaan looked back into the room, then cast a quick glance outward, where the great tower dominated the center of the fortress. When she turned back to him, Lewan could see a slight tremble in her bottom lip, and her eyes flicked back and forth like those of a deer who hears wolves in the distance.

"Master, I . . . I'm frightened," she said. She clutched at his sleeve with both hands. "Please, let me stay. Please."

Lewan blinked and looked down at her hands. She was trembling.

"Please come inside, Master Lewan," she said. "Please, I beg you."

Lewan could see no point in doing so, but neither could he see any point in refusing her. He sighed and nodded, allowing her to drag him inside. He stood dripping on a rug that was probably worth more than all the coins he'd ever held in his life. Ulaan scrambled to the balcony doors, pushed them shut against the wind and rain, and threw down all three latches. The sound of the rain hitting the thick wood sounded hard as hail, and the wind whistled in beneath the door. Ulaan pulled the gauzy curtains over the doors. They were soaked and too heavy to flutter at the encroaching wind. As she stretched on her tiptoes to pull the heavier drapes over the balcony doors, shutting out the breeze and dampening the sound, Lewan noticed that her silk dress was soaked and sheer. It clung to her like a second skin. Lewan swallowed hard and averted his eyes.

"We must get you out of those clothes before you freeze," said Ulaan. Her voice held a slight tremble, and her hands shook as she reached for collar of his shirt.

"No," said Lewan, pushing her hands away. "You should leave. I can undress myself."

Her eyes went wide. "You said I could stay."

"No," said Lewan. "I never said that."

"Please, master!" she clutched at him again. "Please don't make me go back out there."

Lewan pushed her away, using more force than necessary. "Why? What has everyone so frightened?"

Ulaan clutched her fists to her mouth. "Not tonight, master, please. Please, don't make me go back out there. I beg you. I'll do anything."

"Then answer me," said Lewan, anger plain in his voice. "What has you so scared?"

Thunder shook the room, rattling even the massive brass candelabra flanking the hearth. Ulaan's voice was barely above a whisper as she replied, "This night . . . something . . . special for that old druid the Old Man keeps locked up. Something . . ." She shuddered. "Things are not like they once were in the Fortress. The shadows have a life to them. There are sometimes eyes in the dark. The great tower, it has always been known as the Tower of the Sun, but since the Old Man began using the druid, it has become a strange and wild place, filled with secrets, shadows, and things that grow in the dark. Sometimes—on this night most especially—the dark things leave the tower. It is not wise to be about. Best to stay behind locked doors. Everyone does. Everyone except that crazed half-orc. He hunts the grounds, and gods help any who cross his path." Ulaan swallowed and wiped the rain out of her eyes. She, too, now stood in a puddle of the rain dripping out of her clothes and hair. "Please, please, Master Lewan. Let me stay."

Even though the room was pleasantly warm—from the low fire in the hearth, the dozen or so candles, and a flow of warm air coming from those odd slots in the walls—a shiver passed through Lewan.

"Very well," he said. "But I undress myself. You can stoke the fire. And avert your eyes. You promise?"

"I promise, Master Lewan. Thank you."

She rushed to the fire, the wet silk of her dress rasping as she passed him.

A single towel lay by the washbasin Bataar had brought. Lewan used it to sop the worst of the rain from his hair, then peeled off his shirt.

"The Lady Talieth," said Ulaan, her voice still fragile, "she said that your . . . order? Is order the right word?"

"Right word for what?" Lewan threw his sodden shirt next to the door. He looked to the girl to make sure she was keeping her word. She crouched in front of the fire, her back to him as she fed wood onto the flames. Standing between him and the light of the fire, Lewan noticed that her dress was very sheer, and the light shone right through it, outlining her every curve. His breath caught in his throat, and he quickly turned his back to her. He kicked off the slippers he'd been wearing and began working at the drawstring of his trousers.

"For your faith," she said. "You and your teacher. Lady Talieth said that tonight was a very special night for you, and that you were saddened by not being able to celebrate it with others of your . . . order?"

"Tonight is the *Jalesh Rudra*," said Lewan. He'd finally managed to loosen the knot, and he pushed his trousers and smallclothes off at the same time. Only then, as he stood naked and shivering, did he realize that he had no dry clothes.

"What is this *Jalesh Rudra?*" Ulaan pronounced it very carefully.

Lewan looked around. The damp towel was small. It wouldn't even serve as a proper loincloth. With nothing to put on, he crawled into his bed, under the silk sheets and thick fur coverlet. He leaned against the wooden headboard and pulled one of the large pillows over his bare torso. The two trees at the foot of his bed stood between him and the fire, so Ulaan was no more than a bit of shadow and light beyond.

"A sacred celebration," said Lewan. He added, in a quieter voice, "Especially for me."

The room brightened. Lewan heard the fire roaring to life as the flames caught the wood.

"May I turn around now?" said Ulaan.

"Uh, yes," said Lewan. "Sorry."

She stood and turned, but with the fire behind her, Lewan could see no more than the dark profile of her head and shoulders between the branches of the oak.

"Why especially for you?" she asked.

"What?"

"You said this . . . *Jalesh Rudra* was a sacred celebration. 'Especially for me,' you said."

Lewan hadn't realized she'd heard him. He hadn't meant for her to. "It's . . . a sort of coming of age ceremony."

"Coming of age?"

Lewan blushed and looked away. "Tonight was the night my master was to perform sacred rites in my honor. If my god found me worthy, tonight I was to become a man. To enter into full communion with the god."

"Rites?" said Ulaan. "What kind of rites? What must you do to become a man?"

Even though he could see no more than her upper profile, he saw that she was trembling.

"Are you still frightened, Ulaan?"

"I am better now, Master," she said. "Thank you."

"Please stop that."

"Stop what, Master?" Her voice seemed frightened again.

"Stop calling me 'master.' I am not your master."

She was silent a moment, then said, "What shall I call you?"

"Lewan," he said. "My name is Lewan. I have—uh, *had* a master. But I am no one's master."

"Very well . . . Lewan." Though he could not see her face, he thought the sound of her voice held the warmth of a smile. A pleased smile. She gave him an odd shrug, but then he realized it was neither a shrug nor meant for him. She was undressing.

Lewan closed his eyes, but he could hear the sound of her silk dress peeling off her bare skin. His heartbeat and breath came faster.

"What are you *doing?*" he said.

"I am wearing a soaked dress in a room of stone," said Ulaan. "I'm cold. I will dry better without the wet fabric."

Lewan thought the room seemed a bit too warm, stone or no stone.

He gathered the fur coverlet into a bundle and tossed it over the holly bush at her. "Here. Wrap yourself in this."

"But Lewan, what will you—?"

"I'm not cold," said Lewan. It was true. Lewan had spent countless hundreds of nights sleeping under the stars with no more than a tent or just his cloak and a blanket between him and the elements. This room, with its huge hearth and warm air flowing in through the walls, felt hot to him. Too close. Had Ulaan not been so frightened and so desperate to close off the balcony, he would have kept the doors open for the fresh air, wind and wet be damned.

He heard her wet dress hit the wall near where he had tossed his own clothes, then listened as her bare feet approached. His heart beat so hard he could feel the blood pounding in his ears.

"Do you mind if I sit while we talk?" Her voice came from the stool beside his bedside table.

He opened his eyes the smallest slit and saw that she was sitting there, wrapped from shoulders to toes in the fur coverlet. Her hair was still sodden, but she had pulled it back over her shoulders. Her forehead and cheeks still held a moist sheen from the rain. He closed his eyes again and laid his head back against the headboard.

"Tell me more of your rites," she said. "What happens in this *Jalesh Rudra?* Sauk, too, serves the god of the wild. During his holy rites, he goes onto the steppe to hunt. I have heard that he kills his prey and drinks their blood under the full moon—and his prey are not always animals. Your god . . . does he do these things?"

"No!" said Lewan, his face twisting in disgust. He opened his eyes and looked at her. "Nothing like that."

"I didn't think so," said Ulaan, and for the first time that night he saw her smile. His breath quickened again, and the blood pounding in his ears began pounding in other places. "What, then? Tell me, Lewan."

Lewan swallowed and took a deep breath, praying that his voice would not shake. "My master and I seek out one of the sacred groves. We paint each other in symbols sacred to the Oak Father and make an offering of the leaves of Oak, Ash, and Thorn. Over running water, if it can be found. Then, when the Moonmaiden is at her height, the master of the ceremony plays the sacred pipes. If the Oak Father finds favor with the offering, he sends his messengers. They dance for us, and if I am found worthy, one of the messengers and I will, uh . . . c-commune."

"Commune?" asked Ulaan, her brow creasing in confusion.

Lewan looked away and hoped that in the warm light of the fire and candles, Ulaan could not see his blush. He closed his eyes and breathed deeply.

"Lewan?"

"Yes?"

"These messengers from your god? They wouldn't happen to be women, would they?"

Lewan's heart skipped a beat and he said in a hoarse voice, "Uh, spirits. Tree spirits. Or water spirits, maybe."

"You mean dryads?" said Ulaan.

Thunder rumbled in the sky outside, but the beating of Lewan's pulse almost drowned out the sound. "Uh, y-yes."

"Dryads take the form of women, don't they, Lewan?" Ulaan's voice seemed lower now. Husky and barely above a whisper. "Young women. Young, *beautiful* women. How do you commune with them?"

"Uh, I . . ." He couldn't bring himself to say it. Didn't know *how* to say it without sounding like a damned fool.

"Lewan?" Ulaan's voice sounded closer. Lewan opened his eyes. She was standing beside his bed, but the coverlet lay in a pile on the floor.

"Ulaan . . . I—"

"Lewan, do you think I am beautiful?"

She crawled into bed beside him, and he answered her.

chapter twenty

When Lewan woke the next morning, he lay in bed with his eyes closed, enjoying the feel of Ulaan nestled in his arms. She was very warm, and he could smell a flowery scent in her hair. He enjoyed a moment of sheer contentment, of wonder almost, and then the realization of what he had done hit him. All his life with Berun, learning from his master, he had prepared for last night, for the *Jalesh Rudra,* when he would become a man and fully enter into communion with the Oak Father. But last night . . .

No, not just last night. Four days ago, his master had died, consumed by the very earth that he had held so sacred. Lewan had been unable to celebrate the *Jalesh Rudra* through no fault of his own. That choice had been taken from him. But did that excuse what he had done? He had sworn his life to the Oak Father—his spirit, his mind, and his body. Those who walked this sacred path swore an oath of chastity, of complete faithfulness to the divine, pledging themselves for the servants of the Oak Father alone. Last night was to have been the final consummation of that oath. Instead, he had chosen a different consummation.

Ulaan moaned softly in her sleep. She snuggled closer, and

he felt the soft smoothness of her skin rubbing against his own, touching him in places that no other person had ever touched.

He opened his eyes, and Talieth was standing at the foot of the bed between the oak and holly. Lewan gasped. Talieth stood with her back straight, arms crossed under her breasts, looking down on Lewan and Ulaan. The green of her dress was just a shade darker than the leaves of the miniature oak.

"Dress yourself," she said. When Lewan showed no sign of obeying, her eyebrows rose slightly and her chin jutted out. "Now."

Lewan scrambled out of bed, too frightened to even care about his nakedness. Ulaan moaned softly in her sleep, turned over, and lay still.

"I—" Lewan began, but Talieth cut him off.

"I said dress yourself." She kept her voice low, though Lewan could not believe it was out of concern for the girl's slumber. "We will speak on the way."

Someone had brought fresh clothes for both him and Ulaan. Who could have—?

Talieth walked across the room, sparing him a sidelong glance, and placed one hand on the doorknob. Quick as he could, Lewan pulled on the fresh clothes—loose-fitting linen trousers, a shirt of black silk, soft fur-lined boots, and a robe with a deep hood. The robe was well crafted, but of plain soft wool and unadorned. It seemed entirely out of place over such finery. When he was finished, Talieth looked him over, gave a curt nod, then led him out of the room.

It was the first time he'd seen the hallway. The walls and ceiling were crafted of the same stone as his room, but black tiles so smooth that they reflected the lamplight covered the floor. The hall wound round the inside of the tower. Doors lined either side at regular intervals.

"Follow me," said Talieth, and she started walking.

Lewan scrambled to keep up. "Lady, I, uh . . . that is—"

"Is this about the girl?"

"Y-yes."

"Put it out of your mind," said Talieth. "Ulaan was sent to serve your needs. Judging from what I saw, she is doing so. But if she displeased you, we'll find you another."

Lewan opened his mouth to reply, but then realized he had no idea what to say—and that Talieth was leaving him. So he simply followed her down the hallway.

Talieth led him down a long series of stairs winding around the inside of the tower. In a large hall at the base of the tower, she stopped before two massive doors and pulled a heavy cloak and hood of dark green velvet off a rack beside the door. She turned and faced Lewan as she put them on. "Pull up your hood," she said.

Lewan obeyed her, but managed a hesitant, "Why, lady?"

"Remember our words yesterday, Lewan," Talieth said, her voice low. "You walk in the midst of conspiracy. In this tower, you are safe enough. There are not many here, and those who are belong to me. But outside these doors, you speak to no one. I speak for you. You keep your hood up and your eyes down. Do you understand?"

"Yes, lady." Lewan hunched inside the robe and pulled the hood down as far as it would go. He kept his eyes fixed firmly on the hem of Talieth's skirt as she opened the doors and proceeded outside.

The fury of last night's storm had passed, but the air outside was still thick. Something heavier than a mist but lighter than a drizzle drifted in the air and made a faint sizzling sound as it hit the stone. Talieth led Lewan down wide stone steps and onto a gravel pathway. She turned left and proceeded down the path at a brisk walk.

Lewan risked a glance up. The storm had wreaked havoc on the fortress. Leaves, blossoms, and branches lay everywhere.

Talieth and Lewan had to leave the path twice and walk through the grass in order to make their way around fallen trees. Servants were busy everywhere, cleaning up the mess and hauling it away. With the sun hidden behind the sodden sky, Lewan had no idea what time of day it was, but his stomach told him that he had probably slept through the morning. The platter of food Ulaan had brought with her last night still sat on his bedside table, untouched.

They passed a set of elegantly crafted buildings with brass pillars set before huge double doors, then walked through another garden, and Lewan saw that they were passing beneath one of the tall columns on which stood a statue. The statue was bigger than a cave bear. It had been carved in the form of a rearing stallion, its mane flowing back over the spread wings of an eagle. Holding his hood so it would not fall back, Lewan made sure no one was around, then looked up. Smaller statues—all of winged horses—lined the path or sat upon pedestals throughout the garden.

They passed a fountain whose outlet was choked with detritus from the storm. A massive oak grew beside the pool, its boughs spread over the fountain so that the lowest leaves were tickled by water spouting from the mouth of another winged horse. A half-dozen men were standing under the boughs of the oak near the water. Lewan saw that Sauk was among them.

Talieth led Lewan down a narrow side path toward the group of men. Coming under the eaves of the oak, they passed out of the drizzle. Still, remembering Talieth's warning, Lewan kept his hood up and his head down. Sauk knew of his presence in the Fortress, but Lewan wasn't sure about the others. He didn't recognize any of them from the Shalhoond.

As they drew near, Lewan risked a glance up and was sorry he did. Sauk and the other men were standing around what Lewan first thought was a pile of muddy, torn rags. But then he saw that it was not mud at all. It was blood, and the rags were what remained of clothes upon bodies. How many, Lewan could not be sure, for the pieces were jumbled together. His gorge rose. He'd seen slaughter before, but animals—deer, bison, elk, cattle, sheep. Only twice before had he seen people slaughtered with such savagery.

"What happened here?" said Talieth. Lewan heard the rage and shock in her voice.

Sauk spared Lewan a glance, then fixed his gaze on Talieth. "We think it is Vasilik, Draalim, and perhaps Peluris. The others . . . well, we're still looking for the rest. There aren't enough pieces for whole bodies. We think some might be in the water."

"Why were they outdoors last night? I gave orders!"

The men around Sauk looked away, blanching under the lady's fury.

"They were keeping a vigil," said Sauk.

"A vigil?"

"The Old Man told them that the faithful must be ready, ordered them to prepare and contemplate." Sauk shrugged. "Looks like they weren't prepared after all."

Talieth stood a moment, looking at the carnage. "Get this cleaned up," she said, "and have men search the pool. I don't want pieces floating up once the weather warms." She turned to Lewan. "Come."

Raising her skirts over the blood-soaked leaves, she went round the men and led Lewan back along the path. As Lewan walked, he kept his head low, and thus could not help but look right upon a bloody torso with everything but half an arm and the remains of a neck torn away. But through the blood and shredded clothing, Lewan saw one wound clearly. He might have thought nothing of the claw marks and their size—except that he and Berun had spent several days tracking those very prints. A steppe tiger.

Lewan's eyes widened and he glanced toward Sauk. The half-orc caught his gaze and smiled.

Talieth and Lewan left the garden, passing under a stone arch covered in mistletoe. She said nothing, but her gait was stiffer than before. Whether from rage or shock, Lewan couldn't be sure—he had been around no ladies of such social standing in his life and could not read her—but he was certain there was very little grief in her mood. She had ordered the men to clean up the torn corpses as if ordering a servant to sweep up a broken plate.

A great domed building stood at the end of the path before them. Pillars ringed it—Lewan counted four on the near side alone—and he was surprised to see smoke wafting out the top. Not pillars, then, but great chimneys, each one covered in the odd angle-patterns that seemed to dominate the fortress's architecture.

Talieth glanced back and saw him gawking. "This is the Dome of Fire," she said. "Get your head down."

Lewan obeyed, and she led him down a brick path along one wall of the dome to a narrow stairway that began at ground level and descended into the earth. Ten steps down, the darkness was broken by lamps set in alcoves along the wall. The air felt cool but close, and water from the storm ran down into the earth through gutters on either side of the path. Twenty more steps and the stairway turned left and doubled back, their way lit by more lamps. Farther from the fresh air, Lewan could smell the lamp oil, scented with some kind of spice.

The stairs doubled back twice more, then ended before a yawning blackness. Lewan hesitated, but Talieth stepped toward the right wall. Just at the border between light and shadow was a stone column about waist high. The odd angular patterns and strange runes covered it, and atop it, set within the stone itself, was the top third of a crystal sphere. In the murky light cast by the last of the lamps, the crystal seemed black as dreamless sleep. Talieth placed her open hand on the crystal and stroked it.

Lewan gasped and jumped back as fire flared to life in the darkness beyond—leaping from a ledge that ran along the wall a few feet off the floor. It ran down the length of the hall, disappearing around a bend not far ahead.

Talieth turned around and gave him a gracious nod of her head. "Welcome to the Dome of Fire," she said, "although as I'm sure you've guessed, we're actually well below the dome itself."

"How—?" Lewan stared, open mouthed, at the long stream of flame running along the wall.

"The Imaskari were masters of the elements," said Talieth. "They are long gone, but their works endure, only waiting for the proper hand to bring them to life." A sharpness entered her eyes, not unlike the careful watchfulness Lewan had seen in the eyes of Sauk's tiger when she'd been set to watch him. "Much as we are hoping you will do with your sacred relic, yes?"

Lewan drew a breath, intending to point out that he had never agreed to aid their conspiracy. At least not yet. But that tigerlike gaze made him think better of it. Still, frightened as he was—and he didn't even try to fool himself into thinking that he wasn't frightened—he could not bring himself to give in so easily. He simply looked to the flames and kept his tone light as he said, "What would you have me do, lady?"

Talieth smiled, though the predator's eyes remained. "Follow me," she said, and turned down the hallway.

Lewan followed. The hall was wide enough for several to walk abreast. Talieth glided down the middle, Lewan behind her and slightly to the right. He drifted to one side and looked down into the channel. He could not smell or see oil or fuel of any sort—only a tiny crack along the bottom of the stone. It seemed no thicker than his thumbnail, and the flames leaped to life just above the crack.

He was near the wall, his eyes following the track of flame, when the channel ended at a doorway. Although the entrance had a thick wooden door on four stout iron hinges, the door was open. Inside, the room was dark, and the light from the channels of flame in the hall only penetrated a few feet inside the room. As they passed, Lewan could see no more than a bare stone floor, covered in dust and grit. But the smell emanating from the room was unmistakable. Blood and charnel. A hunter for most of his life, Lewan had seen countless animals butchered. In the villages and settlements in the Amber Steppes, he'd seen entire pens devoted to slaughter, the blood and offal drenching the grass and forming a putrid mud. This smell was worse. Lewan recoiled, almost trampling the hem of Talieth's skirt in front of him, and his gorge rose. For the first time since waking, he was glad of his empty stomach. This was the stench of slow death and rot.

Grimacing, Lewan swallowed bile and looked to Talieth for explanation. She kept walking, not even turning, as if nothing were out of the ordinary.

"What . . . was that?" Lewan's voice was hoarse and raw. His throat burned from the bile.

"Put it out of your mind," said Talieth, not turning or slowing her pace. "You have other concerns now."

They passed three more doors—two on the left and one on the right. Thankfully, these were shut tight, but as they passed the second, Lewan thought he heard a faint sniffling from behind the door, like the ragged end of weeping or someone breathing during the final stages of a long sickness. But the steady hiss of the flames drowned it out after they passed.

The hallway curved again, always to the right. They passed a large passageway with more stairs leading down, and not far beyond, they reached another door. Talieth lifted the black iron latch, the door swung forward on noiseless hinges, and she entered.

Lewan hesitated in the doorway, but the room before him was nothing like the one he'd passed earlier. It was opulent. The room was bigger than most houses he'd seen in his lifetime, though the ceiling was low. Heavy drapes covered the walls, alternating with several bookshelves, each of which was filled with scrolls and thick tomes. Soft couches rested upon thick rugs. Thick white candles burned in sconces on the wall and on pedestals throughout the room. In the middle of the far wall, a fire burned in a hearth so large that Lewan could have stood inside it. A brass brazier hung from a chain over the flames, and something inside bubbled, filling the room with a spicy scent. In the middle of the room, sitting upon a thick rug that looked as if it had been taken from a sultan's palace, was a plain table, four plain chairs set around it.

"This is my private study." Talieth stood just inside the room. "Enter and be welcome."

Lewan stepped inside, his footsteps soundless on the deep rug. Talieth shut the door behind him and walked to the table, where she turned and leaned against it to regard him with that predator's gaze.

"Please, sit wherever you like."

Lewan looked around, eyeing the plain wooden chairs and the soft, cushioned couches. Time to test this predator's mettle, he thought. He sat on the rug with his back firmly against the door.

Talieth's left eyebrow shot up, and one corner of her mouth followed it in an amused smile. "Comfortable?"

"Yes, my lady."

With both hands Talieth reached behind her neck and pulled a necklace of braided leather over her head. *Erael'len* emerged from the front of her dress.

"You remember of what we spoke yesterday?"

"Yes, my lady."

Talieth looked at him, her eyebrows rising a little more

with each moment that he didn't speak. Finally, she said, "Lewan?"

"Yes, my lady?"

"Are you going to be difficult?"

"Difficult, my lady?"

" 'Difficult, my lady,' " she repeated in a flat tone. She crossed her arms beneath her breasts, *Erael'len* dangling from one hand. "It's been so long since I've had to deal with a man your age, I'd forgotten how difficult you can be."

"My lady?"

"Lewan, I commend your manners, but I sense a lack of sincerity in them."

Lewan said nothing. He tried to hold her gaze but found that he could not, so he glanced away and pretended a sudden profound interest in the nearest bookshelf.

"I ask you, Lewan," she said, "have I shown you anything but kindness since you came to my home?"

"As I remember it," said Lewan, still studiously watching the bookcase, "you sent a band of killers to capture my master. He was killed trying to escape, and I was poisoned and brought here."

Silence. Soon it became uncomfortable, and Lewan decided to risk looking at Talieth. She stood in the same pose as before, but her eyes had gone cold.

"I loved Kheil more than my own life," she said, her voice low and carefully controlled. "Whether you believe me or not . . . damn it all, I honestly don't care. I care not if he took a different name and fled my father. Gods know I've considered it many times over the years."

She turned her back on him and bowed her head. A small part of him—the part that remembered his master's lessons of treating women, *especially* nobles, with deference, if not genuine respect—felt a pang of guilt. But only a small pang. Although the memory of watching his master disappear beneath that shambling manlike mound of earth was dull and unfocused in his mind's eye, he could still see it, like a fading dream, and he held on to that last fleeting image. He would *not* apologize.

Talieth turned to him. "We must make things clear between us, you and I," she said.

"Clear, my lady?"

Her jaw clenched for a moment. "Yes, clear," she said. "We are a proud people here at Sentinelspire, and whether you know or respect our code of conduct and honor, I assure you we do have one. This fortress is the pride and envy of the East and West—among those few fortunate enough to have seen it and lived. But we are not like the societies of the pampered sultans or simpering kings. Every person here must contribute something. We have no layabouts. Your task is to unlock the secrets of this relic." She held *Erael'len* up in her fist and shook it at him. "As long as you agree, as long as you *contribute*—and I do expect results—you will be our most honored guest in the fortress. You will be clothed in the finest clothes, fed the finest foods, bathed and oiled, you will sleep in a soft bed with the company of Ulaan or as many women as you choose. But you *will* help us."

"Or what?" said Lewan, and he was proud that his voice didn't tremble, for his heart was beating double-time under Talieth's imperious gaze. He expected her to say, *Or you'll find out what we do in that charnel room up the hall,* or *Sauk will let that tiger hunt you in the grounds,* or *I'll have you dragged to the top of the tallest tower and thrown off,* or any number of threats.

But she said none of those things. Instead she looked at him and said, "Or I'll see that you're given the best traveling clothes we have, as many supplies as you can carry, weapons of your choosing, and I'll have you taken out the gates and down the mountain. You can go wherever you like. And in a few days' time, or a tenday, or perhaps even a month if the gods smile upon us, when Sentinelspire explodes and shatters the land for a hundred miles, when a cloud of dust and ash and fire covers half the known world, choking babes in their sleep, killing wild beasts and livestock, and strangling sunlight from this season's crops—and very likely next season's as well—if you're far enough away to escape that . . . well, then, I guess you can live the rest of your life knowing that you could have helped prevent it. Once the fires have died, the earth cooled, and the ash blown away, you can even come to the great hole in the ground where once we lived, and you can dance on the place where we died. Where Ulaan died. Is that what you want, Lewan?"

✛

chapter twenty-one

25 Tarsakh, the Year of Lightning Storms (1374 DR)
Sentinelspire

Lewan sat on the edge of the bed to put on the soft doeskin boots. As he did so, he enjoyed the sight of Ulaan, standing before the open balcony doors in the morning breeze, the light curtains fluttering about her. She had her arms over her head as she put the last of the . . . *things* in her hair. Lewan couldn't remember what she'd called them—pointed rods of flexible wood encased in black lacquer. She'd done her hair up in some sort of topknot of intricate braids, all bound in gold ribbon.

"*Gaasur,*" she said.

"What?"

"The pins for my hair. They are called *gaasur.*"

"How . . . did you . . . ?"

She smiled a very happy smile and said, "I saw you watching me, and you had that look you get when you are thinking your deep thoughts."

"Deep thoughts?" Lewan chuckled.

Finished with her hair, she lowered her arms, considered a moment, then said, "I like it when you watch me, Lewan. I . . ."

He waited for her to finish. When she didn't, he said, "What?"

"I am glad I was told to serve you."

Serve me? Lewan scowled, the moment ruined, for it reminded him exactly what Ulaan was.

"Ulaan, how long have you lived here? In the Fortress?"

"Ten years," she said. Her smile melted. "Since I was sold to the Lady Talieth in Almorel."

Ten years. Twice as long as Lewan had been with Berun.

"Your parents . . . ?"

"My mother was a servant of a wealthy merchant who trades along the Golden Way. My father might have been the merchant. Or he might have been any number of guests whom my mother . . . served."

Lewan could see the wariness in her eyes, but he had to know. "How many . . . others—other men—have you . . . served?"

He saw her instant of shock, then she turned her back to him. When she spoke, anger as well as hurt were in her voice. "I am a servant here, *Master*. I do as I am told. If that displeases you, you may send for another."

"Stop saying that!"

"What, Master?"

"Stop calling me master!" said Lewan, anger rising in his voice. "And stop telling me that I can have another . . ."

"Another what? Another whore?"

"I didn't say that."

"You were thinking it."

Lewan growled and looked away, staring at the wall but not seeing it.

"Lewan?" The anger had gone from her voice. The hurt was still there, but there was something else as well—hope?

He looked to her again and saw that she had turned halfway round. Her back was straight, her head held high, her jaw out, the very picture of a woman in control of her emotions. But she balled her hands into tight fists, and he could see them trembling.

"What?" he said.

"You . . . you are not like . . . the others." She stopped, closing her eyes and taking in a deep breath. "When you look at me, when you touch me, when we . . ." She opened her eyes and looked right at him. He could see the sparkle of unshed tears. "Do you love me, Lewan?"

Lewan blinked. "I—"

A knock at the door—three sharp raps—then it opened and into the room stepped Talieth, dressed in a long, loose skirt and a sleeveless bodice that seemed to have been crafted from thousands of tiny links of red copper and laid over sheer red silk. A circlet made of the same material crowned her head, and dozens of rings and jewels bound her hair in a score of braids. Thick gold bracelets ringed her arms at each wrist and elbow. From head to toe she seemed the perfect image of a warrior queen.

Ulaan turned toward the Lady Talieth and dropped to a bow from which she did not rise.

Talieth spared both Ulaan and Lewan a quick glance, then looked at Lewan with a raised eyebrow and an upward curl of the corner of her mouth. "So nice to see you both dressed this time."

Lewan stood and faced her. "So nice of you to knock this time."

Talieth speared Lewan with her gaze. "Get into your robe and get the hood up," she said. "Time for today's studies."

Beneath the Dome of Fire in the private study, Talieth shut the door behind her and looked at Lewan.

"It's been five days, and you have unlocked none of the relic's secrets. Its power still sleeps. Explain yourself."

Lewan glanced over his shoulder to where *Erael'len* lay atop a linen cloth on the table, then focused his gaze on Talieth's chin. He couldn't quite bring himself to meet her gaze. "I am trying, my lady."

"You felt the tremor last night? Or was your attention elsewhere?"

"I felt it."

The metal lattice of her bodice and circlet made a soft tinkling sound as she approached Lewan. She stopped an arm's length away. He could smell a scent of cinnamon and some other spice wafting from her. "Sentinelspire is stirring, Lewan. And the Old Man is doing his best to wake her. Time is precious."

Lewan swallowed and took a deep breath. "I know, lady. I am trying. *Erael'len* sleeps as well, and so far, I can do nothing to wake it. However . . ."

"I have no time to for your dissimulations, Lewan. Speak."

Lewan's brow wrinkled. He had no idea what dissimulations meant.

"Erael'len is sacred to the Oak Father, a relic of the forest and the life in root, branch, and leaf. Yet I have sat here for days in the bowels of the earth, surrounded by ancient stone, cut off from the life of the wood."

Talieth turned and paced the length of the room while she thought. "You're saying that you need . . . greenery in hopes of tapping the relic's power? I'm afraid that's not possible, Lewan. Here, in my domain, my wards can protect you. Out in the gardens a hundred prying eyes could see you—and the Old Man has ways of seeing things without spies. The grounds around the Tower of the Sun are the wildest area of the fortress, but taking you there . . . that is well within his domain. I might as well blow trumpets and present you and the relic to the Old Man as a gift."

"That isn't what I meant, Lady. I don't need to be outside this room. I need to be outside the fortress altogether. In the wild."

Talieth still had her back to him, but she looked over her shoulder, a sly look in her eye. "Is this some plot to escape, Lewan?"

"Lady, you told me that you would shower me with gifts and show me on my way. I am here because I choose to be. Or am I now a prisoner? Have you reconsidered your offer?"

She turned to face him then, and gave him the last thing he'd ever expected from her: a gracious bow. "Forgive me, Lewan. You are right. Other than my own people here, most of my dealings are with nobles and the wealthy who desire my services. Every gesture and tone with them holds hidden meanings. Perhaps I have been a plotter for so long that I now cannot help but see plots where there are none. I meant no insult. You are, of course, still our honored guest. And yes, my offer stands."

Lewan was so stunned by her apology that for several moments he could do nothing but stare.

"Do close your mouth, Lewan," said Talieth, a smile taking the sting out of her words. "Standing there with it hanging open makes you look stupid."

Lewan snapped his jaw shut and forced his attention back to the matter at hand. "I must ask you something, my lady."

"What is it?"

"You said that here, in your private study, I am free from . . . prying eyes," said Lewan. "Why do you bring me here every day? Why not keep me in my room? I could just as easily study *Erael'len* there."

"Two reasons," said Talieth. "First, with Ulaan in the tower, your room offers too many . . . distractions. Secondly, the tower is not warded against those 'other ways of seeing without spies' that I spoke of."

"Then why keep me there?"

"Because if the Old Man should have reason to spy on you there," she said, "and I can't imagine why he would, he would simply see my latest acquisition to our blades. The Old Man is many things, Lewan, but he is the *Old* Man, and he has precious little interest in watching how you and Ulaan spend your nights. He has not called for a woman of his own since my mother died."

Lewan blushed. "Th-that is part of what I want to speak to you about, lady."

"Ulaan? What of her?"

"Lady, I believe *Erael'len* will continue to sleep while locked away in this stone fortress. Master Berun had a word for it he learned from his master. *Shuret*. It means . . . 'in civilization,' cut off from the wild, from growing things. Allow me to go outside, into the wild—even if only on the nearby mountainside. I believe *Erael'len* might give up its secrets more freely in the wild. And . . . and I—"

"Yes? What?"

"What I . . . have done with Ulaan."

"I've told you that is no concern. She is yours to do with as—"

"No!" said Lewan, more heat in his voice than he'd intended. Talieth's eyes narrowed dangerously and he softened his tone. "I mean that what I have done . . . I fear that I have become . . . impure in the eyes of the Oak Father. Perhaps this is why *Erael'len* does not speak to me. If I could return to the wild, if I could undergo a rite of purification—"

An exasperated sigh escaped Talieth. "You Oak Children and your obsession with purity. Does your god really deny you the pleasures of the flesh? Of women? I thought Silvanus was the god of wild and growing things. You do know where baby wolves and deer come from, don't you, Lewan?"

"To control one's desires is not to deny them," said Lewan, then he added a belated, "Lady. My body is . . . *was* sworn to the Oak Father and his daughters."

"If the girl is polluting your body and soul, I will have her removed," said Talieth. "Given that we need his favor, I would not want to offend your god."

Lewan thought he detected more than a little insincerity—or was it disdain?—in her tone, but she looked entirely serious.

"No!" said Lewan. "But . . . but Ulaan concerns this also."

"Indeed?" said Talieth. "How so?"

"If I help you, if I can figure out how to use *Erael'len* to stop your father, I want you to honor your offer. Give me enough supplies to survive and see me on my way."

"We have covered this ground already, Lewan."

"But I want something else."

"Ah," said Talieth, a knowing look on her face. "Do tell."

"Ulaan comes with me. If . . . if she wishes it."

Talieth cradled one arm in another and tapped her lips with one finger. "You are a puzzle, Lewan. First you plead help in purifying yourself, and with the next breath you ask for the little corrupting influence as a gift."

"Don't call her that."

"*I* didn't, Lewan. You did. Dress her in leaves and put flowers in her hair all you like. Ulaan is still no dryad."

Lewan flinched. After a moment's thought, he said, "That's my concern, not yours."

Talieth turned and paced the room again, causing the candle flames to flicker in her wake. She stopped on the opposite side of the table from Lewan and placed her hands to either side of *Erael'len*. "I agree to your terms," she said. "You may leave the Fortress with the relic and go 'into the wild,' as you say, to try to discern its secrets and perform whatever rites suit you. If you succeed, I will shower you with gifts, and you and the girl can go wherever you like. All this you will have . . . with one condition."

Lewan tried to swallow, but his mouth had gone dry. Despite the innocent girl smile on Talieth's face, she had that predator's gaze in her eyes again. "What condition?" he said.

"You must not go into the wild alone. These are dangerous lands, Lewan, and I will need to send someone with wards I shall prepare that—I hope—will hide you from the Old Man."

"Someone?" said Lewan. "Who will go with me?"

"Who better to guard you in the wild than the wildest of my blades?" said Talieth. "Sauk will go with you."

✛
chapter twenty-two

Sauk found them waiting just inside the main gate. Carvings decorated the arch beyond them. One side was all fair maidens with hair flowing down their backs, their arms reaching out to handsome men on the opposite side, their braids and beards carved in the style of the ancient Imaskari. The two sides' outstretched arms seemed both to reach out to the other and to bid welcome to those entering the gate.

Talieth wore that dress of hers that seemed half silk and half copper mesh. Sauk was warrior enough to know it was all for show; that pretty metal lace would never turn a blade. Talieth didn't need such things. The boy wore clothes suited for traveling.

Taaki padded along just behind Sauk. After several ministrations from the Fortress's healers and a long rest, her mood and energy were back to normal, though the cavity where her eye had once been was now no more than a puckered scar of pinched flesh and fur.

As Sauk and Taaki emerged from the late morning shadow cast by the statue of a four-headed hound, Talieth saw him. She spoke something to Lewan and approached Sauk, stopping him well away from the boy.

"You have it?" she said.

With one finger Sauk pulled at the fine silver round his neck, and the medallion emerged from the loose sackcloth shirt he wore. The medallion was only slightly larger than a coin, plain and unadorned save for the image of a broken ram's horn carved into the middle.

"Keep it on you at all times," she said. "And don't let the boy out of your sight."

"On the mountainside, I can see a long ways."

Talieth frowned at Sauk. "You're taking him to the woods. When you're out there, if you can't see him, you've gone too far. Understood?"

Sauk nodded and dropped the medallion into his shirt. "Anything else?"

Talieth glanced over her shoulder to make sure Lewan wasn't listening. He didn't seem to be. He had one hand protectively over a leather pouch at his belt, the other held a walking staff, and he was staring at the tiger, who was staring right back. The boy didn't look happy to see Taaki.

"One thing," whispered Talieth. "You recall our conversation on the mountainside?"

Sauk gave her a flat look. "Yes."

"Be on your guard out there, Sauk," she said. "Just because you're this close to home doesn't mean you're safe. He mi—" Her breath caught in her throat. She swallowed and finished. "*He* might still be alive. If he comes back, if he finds the boy out there . . ."

"Talieth." Sauk towered over her. The top of Talieth's carefully braided hair did not even reach to his chest. Looking down into her eyes, he saw more than a little of the young woman—no, she'd barely been more than a girl then—who had fallen in love with Kheil so many years ago.

"What?"

"I saw the earth swallow him. He's dead, Talieth."

Talieth's eyes went cold, and for a moment Sauk considered reaching for the long knife he had sheathed behind his back.

"You've said so before," she said, her voice still low. "He's proved you wrong once. Do *not* let your guard down, Sauk. Not for any reason. You or your damned tiger."

"You know me," said Sauk. "I never let my guard down."

Talieth watched him for a moment, perhaps searching his face for any hint of impudence or sarcasm. Apparently satisfied, she nodded at the long, thin bundle Sauk carried over one shoulder. "What is that?"

"Something between me and the boy."

Talieth's eyebrows rose.

"Nothing like that," he said. "He's safe from me."

When Sauk said no more, Talieth shrugged and told him, "Let me know what happens out there."

"I will."

"The moment you return."

Sauk grunted and walked past her. *"Neyë,* Taaki!" he called. He passed Lewan without sparing him so much as a glance and walked into the yawning tunnel through the canyon wall that marked the gateway out of the fortress. "Come along, boy," he said. "Some of the things in the shadows are just statues. But some aren't. So stay close."

Behind him, he heard the boy scramble to catch up.

That walk past the main gate was one of the longest Lewan had ever taken. Thirty paces in, and the darkness encased him. The open gateway behind was a great panorama of light, open air, and greenery. But before and all around him was only blackness, thick and close. Lewan walked blind, wedged between the half-orc in front of him and the tiger behind. Taaki nudged him once or twice with her muzzle, urging him closer to Sauk.

The farther they walked, the closer the air pushed on him. He could feel the stone closing in around them through the many twists and turns and down shallow steps. He could tell by the varying echoes of their footsteps that they sometimes passed corridors to either side. Occasionally they took one,

Sauk never hesitating or slowing his pace. Once, Lewan heard something skittering away before them—something that sounded like the feet of an insect, but far larger. Lewan wondered if any of the great spiders out of the Khopet-Dag had ever made it this far east.

"How much farther?" he whispered.

"A ways," said Sauk. "We'll be in the Gallery of Stone Faces soon. Stay by me. I'm warded to pass, but if you stray . . ."

Sauk didn't finish the thought, and Lewan wasn't sure he wanted him to.

"C-can you see?" Lewan could not, though from the way the stone threw their voices back at him, he knew the walls to either side were very close, but if there was a ceiling above, it was very, very far away.

"I see fine," said Sauk, "though I could walk this way with my eyes closed."

The floor was smooth as any Lewan had walked inside the fortress, though a fine layer of sand and grit crunched beneath their boots. After a while he was surprised to realize that he could see. Not much at first—just a large shape outlined before him. It was Sauk. Really no more than a deeper darkness against a slightly-less-darkness beyond, but there was no mistaking it. Light ahead.

A bit farther on, the walls began to widen, only a bit at first, but then they fell back altogether and the echoes of their footsteps came from far away. Lewan could see quite well. Tiny shafts of sunlight, stray motes of dust wafting here and there, rode on thin sunbeams that fell from the ceiling far, far above. It was barely any light at all, but Lewan's eyes were so used to the dark, his pupils so wide and hungry for any illumination at all, that he could take in most of what Sauk had called the Gallery of Stone Faces. A huge room—larger than any king's court; larger even than many castles' outer courtyards—of unworked stone. But in the midst of the gallery, set haphazardly across the floor in no discernible pattern, were dozens and dozens of statues. A few were smaller than Lewan, but most were at least man-sized, and some were far larger. All were hideous—demons, devils, monsters, misshapen beasts, twisted humanoid forms, and more. The statues seemed to look down on Lewan and his two companions as they walked the maze between them. Again Lewan heard something skittering in the nearby gloom.

Lewan figured they were about halfway across the gallery when he caught sight of a moth as it flew between the sunbeams. The gray light caught in its wings, making them seem unnaturally bright in the dimness. Lewan watched it flutter off into the darkness. He had just lost sight of it off to his right when he heard a sharp *snap!* from that direction, very much like the sound of jaws closing over a moth that had flown too close.

Perhaps it was just being in the dark for too long, but as they walked, Lewan began to think he could see movement out of the corners of his eyes—stone heads that turned to watch as they passed, a muscular manlike thing with a bat's face whose grin seemed to grow after Lewan's first glance. Now and then, he thought he could hear a scraping, like the twisting of stone, over the sounds of their boot heels on the grit-covered floor. But each time Lewan whipped his head around to follow the movement or look in the direction of the sound, he saw nothing but leering faces, motionless and cold as stone.

When they emerged into the full light of day again, Lewan breathed a great sigh of relief. After a life lived in the open, sleeping under stars or boughs more often than not, Lewan had begun to feel trapped by all that stone.

Squinting as his eyes readjusted to the light, Lewan turned back to see the way they had come. Around the passage, carved into the stone itself, was a monstrous, leering face. Its open mouth formed the entrance to the tunnel, and its eyes, lacking both iris and pupil, seemed to stare down upon them.

The tiger emerged from the yawning mouth and padded over to her master.

"Taaki, *gu th'nukh*," said Sauk, and the tiger bounded away.

Lewan watched her go, and saw that they had emerged into a narrow canyon that wound its way down the mountainside. The walls were so tall that only a narrow strip of sky broke the view of stone, and all the canyon lay in cool, dry shadow.

Sauk turned to Lewan. "Talieth said you need woods, preferably with running water."

"Yes," said Lewan.

"Then follow me."

The half-orc switched the long, narrow bundle to his other shoulder, then turned and began walking down the canyon. Lewan followed.

Early afternoon though it was, the sun had long since sunk behind the jagged cone of Sentinelspire when Sauk led them into the woods—a steep, narrow valley choked with larch trees and smaller scrub brush. Lewan had neither seen nor heard the tiger since they'd left the tunnel. A stream rushed down the valley, tumbling over rocks and roots, but here and there it widened into little pools, none more than a few feet deep.

"This suits your needs?" Sauk asked him.

Before Lewan could answer, a low rumble rose in the earth beneath them, then grew to a roar, and the entire mountain shook beneath their boots. Sauk stumbled but managed to keep his feet. Lewan was not so lucky. He sat down hard on an exposed tree root and decided to stay there. Under him, he could feel the wood of the tree humming like a plucked harp string. Rocks tumbled down the mountain.

A final, long groan like dying thunder, and the trembling stopped. Small stones continued rattling down the mountainside, and in the distance Lewan thought he heard boulders crashing to canyon floors. Lewan saw the half-orc looking up the mountain and followed his gaze. There, between boughs full of their new spring clusters of light green needles, Lewan could see the jagged cone of Sentinelspire. White steam, looking almost like a wisp of cloud, was rising into the wind, which quickly blew it away.

Sauk turned to Lewan, seemed to consider something, then walked over to where he sat on the root. The half-orc towered over him, deep in thought.

Finally Sauk pulled the long bundle he'd been carrying over one shoulder and handed it to Lewan. "Take this," he said.

Lewan did. "What is it?"

"See for yourself."

Something hard was wrapped inside the canvas. Lewan untied the knot and unwound the leather cord. He pulled back the cloth, and one glance inside told him what it was.

"My master's bow."

"It seems a fine weapon," said Sauk. "I considered keeping it myself. Even if I weren't smart enough to recognize those runes as words of power in whatever language you leaf-lovers use in your rites, I could still feel the power in that bow. But it isn't for me."

"It is sacred to the Oak Father," said Lewan. "Only those sworn to him may waken its power."

"You know how to"—Sauk's lip twisted in a sneer, but Lewan caught a spark of curiosity in his eyes —"*waken* its power?"

Lewan shrugged.

Sauk looked down on him, and when Lewan said nothing more, the half-orc snorted and said, "Keep your secrets, then." His countenance grew suddenly grave, and he said, "Take the bow and go."

"What?" Lewan blinked, not sure he had heard Sauk correctly.

"I have no arrows for you," said Sauk. "That would have roused suspicion."

"You're . . . you're letting me *go?*"

Sauk took a medallion out of his shirt and pulled off the necklace from which it hung. He held it out to Lewan. "Go fast. Wear this until you're at least five leagues from the mountain, then bury the damned thing and keep running. If your god favors you, maybe you can make it far enough before . . ."

Lewan looked at the medallion. It seemed rather plain, almost crude, the edges uneven. Engraved in the middle of it was the image of a broken ram's horn. "What is it?" he asked.

"It will keep the mountain's guardians away from you," said Sauk. "And it will keep the Old Man from seeing you until it's too late for him to do anything about it."

"What about Talieth?"

"Leave her to me."

Lewan could tell by the flatness of the half-orc's eyes that confronting Talieth was not something he looked forward to.

Lewan did not take the medallion. He looked at the half-orc and asked, "Why?"

"Why what?"

"Why are you helping me escape?" asked Lewan, because he wasn't sure the half-orc was. That talk that Sauk and Talieth had together before they left the Fortress—what had that been about? Was this some sort of test? If Lewan took the medallion and started walking, would Sauk cut him down? Or would he watch him go, that sly smile on his face, then summon the tiger? Lewan remembered all too well the corpses in the garden, and at least one of them had been mauled and torn apart by a tiger.

Sauk lowered the hand holding the medallion and shrugged. "Why? That's not hard. Talieth's plan has failed. Our one hope was finding Kh—er, your master, and that druid's relic he carried. But your master's dead."

"She hopes that I will be able to use *Erael'len*'s powers," said Lewan.

Sauk snorted. "I mean you no insult, Lewan, but you are just a boy. It was a fool's hope to think that even your master could help us. Given years of study and training . . . who knows? I think I see a hunter's heart in you." He looked at the mountain top. "But we don't have years."

"That's it?" said Lewan. "You mean to send me on my way while you go back to die? That's your plan? That's what passes for honor with you? Some sort of noble death?"

Sauk looked down on him, an amused look on his face. "Nothing noble about death, boy. Death means you lost. If I die, I'll die fighting, and the Beastlord will greet me with my enemy's blood on my teeth."

They looked at each other in silence for a moment, then Sauk held out the medallion again.

"Here," he said. "Put leagues behind you before dark."

Lewan looked at the medallion, then up at Sauk. "I can't," he said.

"Why?"

"It's . . . complicated." Lewan stared at the nearby stream, at the sparkling of sunlight on the water.

Sauk's words had stung him. *You are just a boy. A fool's hope.* Was he right? Was Lewan a fool to think he had any hope in learning *Erael'len*'s secret? Still . . . *I think I see a hunter's heart in you.* Lewan thought that was as close to high praise as the half-orc ever came. Would he ever be anything more than a scared boy if he ran now? Even if it was a fool's hope, he had something else calling him back to the fortress.

"Women are complicated," said Sauk.

Shocked that Sauk seemed to have guessed his thoughts, Lewan looked up at the half-orc. Sauk grinned and shrugged. "There are many secrets in the Fortress of the Old Man, but who is sharing whose bed is seldom one of them. You think you love her, but you don't. That feeling you're feeling isn't love. It's just the excitement of the first legs you've ever parted."

Anger rose in Lewan, and he stood. He'd intended to face Sauk, but even as he came to his full height, he found himself looking up at the half-orc's chin, and fear joined his anger. He swallowed, took a deep breath, and said, "You don't know what you're talking about."

"No?" Sauk smirked.

"No."

Sauk looked down at the medallion in his and sighed. "Your death is on your own head, then. I tried. One thing, though."

"What?"

"Best not to tell Talieth of this conversation. I did you a kindness with the offer. Now do me one and forget my offer. Agreed?"

Lewan felt a pang of pride that he managed to hold the half-orc's gaze. "You're afraid of her," he said. It wasn't a question.

"Damned right I am," said Sauk. "You should be too."

✦
chapter twenty-three

What was the little fool doing? Sauk wondered.

He'd found a good spot—a ways uphill from the boy, well-shaded by a large larch, but still with a good view of where Lewan sat next to the pool. Taaki was off to Sauk's left, settled and comfortable in a patch of soft sand beneath an overhang of the mountainside that offered her a wide view of the entire stretch of wood. Sauk couldn't see her, but through the bond he shared with her as a *zuwar,* he knew right where she was. He could've pointed to her like a man with his eyes closed could point to the noonday sun.

Afternoon was turning to evening, and the air up on the mountain had turned cool. Still, the boy hadn't moved in a long while. After Sauk had left him and settled in to watch, Lewan had stripped off his boots and clothes and bathed in the pool. The way the boy moved in the pool and ladled water over his torso with his cupped palms had more the look of ceremony than a true washing. This struck Sauk as nothing unusual. Most faiths had rites of ceremonial cleansing—his included, though the Beastlord's worshipers slathered themselves in blood more often than water.

Sauk knew that earlier that morning, Talieth had ordered servants into the gardens with a list of things to gather— acorns, mistletoe and holly leaves, a sprig of oak leaves. So early in the season, the acorns had been the most difficult, but they had found them at last in the tangled maze of greenery that grew round the base of the Tower of the Sun. Since the old druid had taken up residence there, all sorts of odd things grew in and out of season.

Sauk watched as Lewan sat, still naked, at the water's edge and used a stone from the stream to crush the acorns and some of the leaves. He then dipped three fingers of his right hand into the greenish-brown concoction and painted a series of symbols on his forehead, the backs of his eyelids, across both lips, round his heart, and the patch of skin between his navel and groin. Sauk scowled and muttered, "Damned leaf-lovers."

Lewan then piled a small cushion of young larch needles at the base of the nearest tree, sat on it with his legs crossed and his hands on his knees, leaned his head back against the bole of the tree, closed his eyes—and didn't move for a long while. Sauk sometimes thought he could see the boy's lips moving, but he was too far away to be sure.

And there Lewan sat as the shadows in the wood turned a deeper shade of blue and the cool of evening began to whisper down the mountain. Although he couldn't see them through the trees, Sauk knew that the first stars were skirting the eastern horizon.

A jolt, almost like a muscle spasm, struck Sauk. But this was in his mind, in his heart of hearts, that deep part of his soul entwined with the tiger. Someone was approaching. And not from a distance. Someone was already well into the wood, within an easy stone's throw of the boy. How someone had gotten so close without Sauk—or especially Taaki—being aware of them, Sauk had no idea. It put his hackles up. Sauk sensed Taaki rising from her hiding place and stalking down the slope, keeping to the shadows under the trees.

No, Sauk told her. *Easy. Let's see.*

Sauk drew his knife and waited. The boy still hadn't moved. If he heard the figure approaching, he'd shown no sign of it.

Sauk saw movement before he could make out any features. Just a different shadow moving through a wood that was quickly dimming to the uniform shade of evening. The figure made no attempt at stealth and moved without haste. Lewan still hadn't moved, though he'd have heard the figure by now—unless he'd fallen asleep.

The figure made its way round the last of the trees. A man. Sauk could tell by the way the figure walked. But his features were completely hidden within the folds of a loose robe and a deep hood. In the gloom of the oncoming evening, the robe looked black.

The man stopped a few feet away from Lewan. The boy opened his eyes and started at the sight of the robed man standing near him. The man reached up with both hands and pulled down his hood. Sauk got his first good look at the man, and he felt all the blood drain from his face.

Lewan had been aware of someone approaching for some time. Believing it to be Sauk, he paid it no mind, though he did note that he heard him coming quite clearly. Days ago, on the trek through the Shalhoond, Lewan had been surprised at how someone as large as Sauk could move with such grace through the woods. Perhaps Sauk was purposefully making noise to announce his return.

When the sound of footsteps stopped nearby, Lewan opened his eyes. He gasped and barely caught the scream in his throat, for it wasn't the half-orc after all, but someone wearing a dark robe and hood. Lewan could just make out a man's chin within the deep shadow under the hood.

"Forgive me," said the hooded man. His voice was deep and rich, but Lewan could hear the rasp of old age in its timbre. "I did not mean to startle you."

The stranger lowered his hood, and Lewan faced an old man. His thinning hair, mostly gray but with streaks of black, just dusted his shoulders. His skin was not as dark as Lewan's, but it had the darker tone of someone from southern regions, and though he was wrinkled as worn leather, his eyes were bright and sharp.

"Wh-who are you?" said Lewan. The man did not appear hostile, and Lewan's hammering heart was beginning to slow. Lewan leaned over, grabbed his trousers, and covered his nakedness.

The man smiled and gave a slight bow. "Forgive me again," he said. "Though you have been a guest in my home for some days, I have not yet greeted you—though I understand you have been partaking of my hospitality. Well met, Lewan."

"Your . . . house?" said Lewan. "You mean, you're . . ."

"The Old Man of the Mountain. Master of Sentinelspire."

Lewan's mouth went dry, and his heart began to hammer again. "Uh . . . w-well met, Master. Thank you for your, um . . . hospitality. Your daughter the Lady Talieth has made me most comfortable."

"Has she?" The Old Man chuckled. "She does like them young, but I would have thought you were a bit young even for her."

Lewan blushed and averted his eyes. "That was not my meaning, my lord! I—"

"And now," the Old Man cut him off, "I must ask your forgiveness a third time. I know what you meant, young man. I was simply having a bit of fun. But I am glad you have met Talieth, for it is she about which we must speak. She and the half-orc and their little . . . what would be the word?"

"Word, my lord?"

"You and I have just met, Lewan. I am trying to mind my manners, as they say. Put a polite term to their very impolite . . . plotting."

"Plotting, lord?"

The Old Man frowned. "Don't dither with me, boy. You're an honest young man. Your master brought you up right. Six days in my fortress, and you are already practicing the arts of deceit. Please allow me to be brutally honest with you, Lewan. You're no good at it. Don't try. Remain true to yourself."

He knows, Lewan thought. Knows it all. Knows Talieth is trying to stop him. Knows Sauk is in on it. Knows I'm helping them. He might even know the bargain I've struck. Lewan's fear paled into something approaching sheer terror at that, and he thought, Oh, Ulaan . . .

"I've not come to kill you, boy," said the Old Man. "And your girl is safe from me."

Lewan's eyes widened and his mouth dropped.

The Old Man threw back his head and laughed. "Oh, dear boy! Don't look so shocked. I'm no wizard, reading your thoughts like a tome. You wear your thoughts plain on your face. However . . ." The good humor left the Old Man's face and he looked down on Lewan with utmost solemnity. "I will not tell you not to fear. Be *very* afraid, Lewan. Talieth and her little conspiracy . . . well, I'll forsake politeness for bluntness on this point. They are lying to you. They are *using* you. Do *not* trust them."

Doubt began to course through Lewan, like a poison slowly working its way through the veins. It occurred to him to wonder why he had never seriously questioned Talieth's tale or her motives. True enough, a large part of it at first was that he'd believed himself a prisoner without much choice. But there were the earthquakes, that plume of steam from the mountaintop earlier, and the Old Man was a lord of assassins, after all, a master of murderers. Then the obvious question occurred to Lewan.

"Why—?"

"Why haven't I done something about it?"

Lewan nodded, unable to speak.

The Old Man shook his head. "Well, let me just say that the time is not yet right."

"The . . . time?"

"Let me guess," said the Old Man. "Talieth, Sauk, maybe even a few of the other blades, have told you that I have gone quite mad and am intent on destroying all they hold dear. To assure your sympathies, they have probably even told you that my nefarious plans will destroy all you hold dear as well. Do I hit close to the mark?"

Lewan said nothing and had to force himself not to nod. He didn't know who or what to believe.

"Truth is a rare gift, Lewan," said the Old Man, "but I will give it to you now. I am not out to destroy the world, but to save it—save it from Talieth and those like her, whose greed and ambition would destroy anyone and anything that gets in their way."

The sounds of crickets and night birds began to fill the wood, as Lewan simply sat there, staring into the pool. In the past tenday, his entire world had been cracked. He felt raw, drained, and utterly and completely confused. He put his head in his hands, and without looking up, he said, "Why are you telling me all this? What if I don't believe you? What—?"

He stopped himself. He'd been about to say, *What if I go back to the fortress and tell Talieth everything—that you are on her trail, aware of her entire conspiracy?* But he caught himself just in time. Saying that would be as much as admitting he was involved, confirming the Old Man's story, and no matter how sincere the man seemed, Lewan could not ignore the fact that he was sitting naked and alone in the middle of nowhere with a complete stranger, one who controlled some of the best assassins in the known world.

"Despite what you may think of me, boy, I hold no ill will toward you, and it grieves me to see you so ill used. Taken from your master, held captive, used as a pawn in Talieth's game. I am no monster. You have never done me any harm, and as a guest in my home, it is my duty to help you. However, I must confess that my motives and my reasoning for meeting you here are not entirely . . . altruistic."

Lewan wasn't sure what that word meant, but he took the general meaning behind it.

"If Talieth asks you what we spoke about," said the Old Man, "tell her. Hide nothing. As I said, deceit is not one of your strengths. Do not be ashamed by that. Revel in it. Sauk will certainly ask you. He's watching us now, I'm sure, though I don't know if he's close enough to hear." He shrugged. "It does not concern me. As soon as I'm gone, I'm sure he'll be along. Tell him everything. However, to answer your question at last—why I have come to speak to you. To put it plainly: in a short time, I will need your help."

Lewan chuckled, though it was from sheer exasperation, not humor. He'd been captured, watched his master die, and involved in a conspiracy to depose a supposed mad master of assassins, and now the very man he'd been asked to help defeat was standing here and asking for his help—while Lewan himself was naked and shivering. Lewan felt trapped in some sick bard's tale, and all he really wanted was to take Ulaan and go far away from all this.

"How could I possibly help you?" he said.

"Nothing too drastic," said the Old Man. "I'm not expecting you to grab weapons and defend me against the assassins of Sentinelspire. Your word, Lewan, is all I ask. In a short time, I will need your word of support. My plans will still succeed without you, Lewan. But things will go better for a great many people—yourself included—if you speak on my behalf. But don't worry yourself too much. I am not asking for your false witness. When the time comes, you will want to support me. You will see things my way. All I ask is that you take the courage to do what your heart knows is right."

Lewan heard the man walk away, and when he looked up a few moments later, he saw no sign of him. The Old Man of the Mountain had faded into the gathering gloom of evening. Something occurred to Lewan in that moment. The Old Man had called him Lewan. Repeatedly. Lewan had never given the

Old Man his name. He was sure of it. Still . . . Talieth had told him that her father had ways of seeing things beyond spies, and he certainly seemed to know a great deal already. If he knew what had happened to his master, knew of Talieth's plans against him, knew even of Ulaan, then the Old Man knowing Lewan's name hardly seemed notable. Still . . . Lewan could not shake the feeling that there had been something oddly familiar about the Old Man.

✤

chapter twenty-four

When Lewan reached the door to his room, he was breathing heavily and his legs felt like they had turned to granite. After the Old Man had left him on the mountainside, Sauk had come running up, his eyes as large and hard as river stones, and demanded to know what had been said. Lewan told him everything, even that the Old Man told him to tell everyone and that there was nothing Talieth's conspiracy could do about any of it. When the tale was told, Sauk simply stood there, staring at Lewan and chewing on his bottom lip. Lewan couldn't tell if the half-orc was furious, or terrified out of his mind. A little of both, he decided.

"Impossible," Sauk had said, seemingly to himself, then broke into a long string of curses in his own tongue.

The rant seemed to stoke his agitation rather than calm it, and Sauk had ordered Lewan to get his clothes on. Hadn't even allowed him a moment in the stream to wash the pasty symbols off his skin. Lewan had scarcely pulled on his boots and grabbed Berun's bow before Sauk was pulling him to his feet and rushing him onward. They'd run the whole way back, even after full dark caught them on the mountainside. Lewan's boots were scuffed and his toes hurt from bashing into rocks and roots.

The journey through the statue-haunted passageway had been the worst. Sauk had clutched Lewan's wrist and dragged him through the maze. He'd been none too careful, and they'd brushed up against several statues. More than once, Lewan could have sworn he'd felt a stony hand or claw reach out and brush his shoulder. But perhaps that had simply been his fear and exhaustion overtaking him in the dark.

Back at the fortress, Sauk had barreled through the guards at the gate, knocking one man flat on his behind. He'd pushed Lewan up the stairs to the tower, opened the door, told him, "Get to your rooms and stay there!" then bounded off.

Lewan watched him go until he was little more than a blur in shadows between pools of lamplight. Then he'd made the climb to his room.

He stood before the door—his hair, skin, and clothes drenched with sweat, dust caking him, his chest heaving, and his legs feeling as if they were about to collapse. Lewan was not soft. He'd lived in the wild most of his life, running for miles without rest. But the day had drained him. Physically, emotionally, and spiritually, he was spent. He scarcely had the energy to twist the knob of his door.

Lewan stepped inside, and an array of scents hit him like a blow—spiced candles, cherry wood burning in the hearth, expensive oil burning low in two lamps, an array of blossoms strewn about the room and on the bed, and set in the middle of the floor between the miniature oak and holly, a huge brass tub. Ulaan, wearing a blue silk gown, her hair loose and flowing down her torso, stood next to it. She saw him and smiled.

"Lewan! Oh, you look ready to fall over." She went to him, pulled him into the room, and shut the door behind him. "I've had a bath brought into the room tonight. I knew you'd be tired after a day out on the mountain with Sauk." She dropped her eyes and smiled. "And I thought we might not want to have to walk so far from the bath to bed tonight."

Lewan took her hands and pulled them off him. "Ulaan . . . I must speak to you."

He saw a slight widening of her eyes, a quick intake of breath—but she hid it quickly. "What is it, Lewan?" she said carefully.

He looked to the bedside table. A platter of food—fruits, bread, white cheese, wine—waited there. She'd even found a sprig of red holly and put it on the edge of the platter. He walked over, threw the bow on the bed, then poured the wine into a goblet and drained it in one gulp. As the warmth began to suffuse his head, he looked to Ulaan, put all the gentleness into his voice he could, and said, "Don't look so worried."

She would not look at him. "Do I have reason to be?"

Lewan put the empty goblet on the platter. He saw that his hand was trembling. "I'm not sending you away if that's what you're thinking."

Ulaan did look up then, her eyes rimmed with tears. She smiled and rushed at him with open arms.

Lewan took a step back and placed his hands on her shoulders to keep her at arm's length. Even through the grime coating his fingers, he could feel how thin her dress was and how soft the skin beneath.

Her eyes narrowed, not so much in hurt as confusion. "Lewan, I . . ."

"Please, Ulaan. You must listen. We . . ." Lewan swallowed and took a deep breath. Damn it all! Exhausted as he was, he was still blushing like a little boy. "We cannot . . . be together. At least not for a while."

"I don't understand. You said you weren't sending me away! You said—"

"No!" Lewan shook his head, cutting her off. "I mean, we can't . . . you know. Love."

Ulaan sat on the bed. "You don't love me." She seemed to be talking more to herself than him. "Earlier today, I thought . . . when the Lady Talieth interrupted, I was so sure you were about to tell me y—"

"I love you, Ulaan." There, he had said it, and he felt a surge of pride that he'd said it, plain and simple, no hesitation. "I do. But you must understand. I—"

"If you love me, then why can't we share our love? You said—"

"Ulaan, please!" He said it with more force than he'd intended. "I'm sorry, Ulaan. I'm just so tired, so confused. I can barely think. You must understand, my faith . . . the ways I was taught, the path of the Oak Father I have sworn to follow . . ."

He trailed off, struggling for the right words to make her understand. They wouldn't come to him. His exhaustion was pulling him down, and the wine wasn't helping, either.

"I took an oath, Ulaan. Being with you, I . . . I betrayed that oath. Today, I purified myself, and if I am going to get us out of here, my only hope is to remain pure. To seek the Oak Father's aid. I—"

"Us?" said Ulaan. "Get *us* out of here. Lewan, what do you mean? You mean . . . *leave?*"

She looked at him a long time, then stared at the wall. He could tell she was not seeing the stone, but all the possibilities before her.

"Yes," he said. "Leave the Fortress. Leave Sentinelspire. Come away with me."

She looked at him. "Where?"

"I have no idea," he said. "One problem at a time. But you'll be free. No longer a sla—" He caught himself. "A servant. You'll be with me."

"Your woman?"

"No. You'll be *your* woman. Free. As for you and me . . . we'll figure all that out once we're long gone from here. But it will be up to *us,* not Talieth or Sauk or the Old Man or any other madman who falls from the sky in a puff of smoke, asking for my help."

Ulaan's eyes seemed troubled. "Lewan, you aren't making any sense."

"I know. I'm sorry. I'm tired. So tired."

Talieth lived in a series of opulent rooms in the upper floors of a mid-sized tower that hugged the Dome of Fire. Other than her servants and guards, she was the only resident, and even the servants didn't reside there so much as sleep close enough to be at her beck and call.

Either the two guards at the main door knew Sauk was expected or they saw the expression he wore and quickly stepped aside. One offered a quick bow. The other made sure he was well out of the way before Sauk threw the door open and stormed inside.

The winding passage up the stairs that ringed the interior wall of the tower alternated between pools of light and wells of shadow. Only half the candles were lit, and many of them burned low. The wake Sauk left behind snuffed out several.

Two more guards—Talieth's favorite Damaran and Shou, more elegantly garbed and more heavily armed—stood outside the heavy double doors that led into Talieth's main apartment. Both had been at ease, but seeing Sauk, the Shou stepped forward and the Damaran put a hand to the short sword at his belt.

The Shou raised a hand. "My apologies, Lord Sauk. The Lady forbids any entrance. She is—"

Sauk's foot slammed into the man's gut, knocking every bit of wind out of him. He went down like a wet sack. Sauk stepped over him.

The Damaran drew his blade and held it on guard before him, but his shaking hand showed he was scared.

Sauk stopped so that the blade, trembling slightly, rested

lightly on his chest. "You, I'll put out the window if you don't sheathe that steel and step aside."

"Lady Talieth ordered—"

"Lady Talieth ordered me to report. You can stand aside and obey her—and me—and sleep in your bed after your watch. Or you can go out the window now. Your choice."

The man took a deep breath, blinked twice, then sheathed his short sword and stepped aside. "Let it be on your head, then," he said.

"It always is," said Sauk. He pulled the door open and stepped inside.

The room held an assortment of couches, a table where Talieth sometimes dined with guests, and two hearths, both burning low. Candles were set about the room, but none were lit. The room was dim, lit only by the dying fires and a lamp set amidst a wreath of apple blossoms on the table.

Kiristen, a Calishite beauty and Talieth's chief maidservant, lounged on a divan by the fire, dozing with an empty goblet in one hand. Hearing the door open, she leaped to her feet, the goblet falling onto the rug.

"Sauk! What are you doing? Out of here, this instant. The Lady has ordered that no—"

"The lady herself ordered me to report the moment I returned." Sauk gave a bow, hoping his sardonic manner was coming through. "I have returned. You may bring the Lady out, or I'll go in."

"She is abed. I will not—"

Sauk started to pass, but she stepped around the divan and in his way. She put both hands on his chest. He stopped.

"She is abed," said Kiristen, then lowered her voice. "But she is not alone. Come back in the morning, Sauk. Please."

Sauk took a deep breath through his nose and looked down at her. "Are you going to move?"

"No. Sauk, please list—"

Sauk picked her up by the waist and tossed her over the divan. She landed in a pile of cushions and pillows piled near a couch. Before she could disentangle herself from her skirts, Sauk was at Talieth's bedroom door.

"Sauk!" Kiristen gave a final plea.

Sauk pushed the door open and stepped inside.

"What in holy gods—?" said a man's voice in surprise and exasperation. Valmir was standing before the ornate fireplace, a crystal glass of wine in one hand. He wasn't wearing a stitch of clothing. Seeing Sauk enter the room, Val grabbed a pillow off the couch before him and held it in front of his loins.

Sauk kicked the door shut behind him, cutting off more of Kiristen's protests.

Talieth rose from the couch in front of Val. She glared at Sauk a moment, then grabbed a black silk robe from the couch, threw it on and tied it shut. "What are you doing here?"

"You told me to let you know what happened out there. 'The moment you return,' you said. As you can see, I have returned."

"So I smell," said Val. "Gods, did you run the whole way? You stink like a—"

"Be silent," said Talieth.

Valmir scowled—though Sauk knew he wouldn't have dared had Talieth's back not been to him. He finished his wine and stared daggers at Sauk.

"You have good reason to interrupt us, I take it," Talieth said to Sauk.

"You take it damned right. We've got a severe problem. I was watching the boy do whatever it was he went out there to do, and I saw *your father* come and speak to him. Had quite a long conversation with Lewan."

"My father?"

"Saw him with my own eyes."

Talieth paced the room, staring into space and chewing on the back of one knuckle. Valmir, who had gone white as a

cloud, followed her with his eyes. At last Talieth said, "That's
. . . impossible. It's impossible, Sauk. You know that."

"I do know it. Which means we have a big problem."

"Tell me everything he said."

Lewan knew that if Ulaan put her hands on him or
helped him bathe, his resolve would crumble. So he sent her
from the room, ostensibly to fetch him clean clothes and a
pitcher of water—his head would take no more wine. But
in reality, he simply needed her gone while he undressed
and scrubbed away the grime of the day. He'd also asked for
more blankets.

When she returned, he was clean and almost dry, standing before the fire and wrapped in the thick fur coverlet from
the bed. He asked her to turn away while he put on the fresh
clothes. She protested at first, insisting that she help him, but
she gave in without much argument.

"Ulaan," he said as he pulled on the linen shirt.

"Yes?" She turned around.

"What I said earlier . . . you can still stay here tonight. Take
the bed. But I think it best if I sleep out on the balcony."

"The balcony? Why? Won't you—"

"I've spent most of my life sleeping under the stars," he said.
"In truth, I've always found this room a bit . . . close. Besides
. . ." His eyes took in the way her gown accentuated the curves
of her body. "The cool air will do me good."

And so he bedded down on the balcony, amidst the ivy and
blossoms closed against the night. The breeze off the mountain felt wonderful, and for the first time in many days, he felt
somewhat at ease. The purification had done him good.

Then he noticed clouds coming in from the north—a thick
blackness blotting out the stars—and lightning flickering in
the far distance. Rain by morning.

"Wonderful," he said to himself. He turned back to the open doors, reconsidering a night in the open. Fresh air was one thing. Sleeping in the rain was quite another.

But then he saw Ulaan, peeling off her gown before getting into bed. All the candles were out, and the warm light from the fire settling to its rest painted her skin in glowing curves and soft shadows. She saw him watching. She returned his stare and arched one eyebrow. She said nothing, and even though Lewan had known her only a few days, he knew what she was asking. *Are you sure?*

Lewan took a deep breath, swallowed hard, and closed the balcony doors. Perhaps a cold shower was just what he needed after all.

✚
chapter twenty-five

That day in the foothills of the Khopet Dag, Lewan had not been entirely truthful with Sauk.

You ever killed anyone? Lewan had evaded the question, then let Sauk believe whatever he wanted. *I'll take that as a no.*

But Lewan had killed. And not just the animals he'd told Sauk about. He'd killed a person. He'd been only twelve years old. For years after, that day had haunted him, recurring again and again in his nightmares, and the images and sounds coming to him with sudden clarity in the middle of the day while he was in the midst of a task for his master. Years had dulled the nightmares, and even the waking memories now seemed distant and hazy.

Even as a young boy, working the fields with his father or helping his mother cook, he'd seen death. Lambs that did not survive a hard birthing. Sheep or hens slaughtered for feast days. He had seen death. But the first person he'd ever killed . . .

Most likely, the raiders from the Ganathwood had waited outside the village most of the night. They'd waited until the eastern sky was just light enough to cast the village in a muted glow. The first shepherds had just been walking bleary-eyed out of their homes to tend the fields when the first raiders slew the guards and threw the gates open wide. Lewan didn't know how or when his father had been killed. He hadn't seen the body until it was all over and the raiders were dragging him away.

The sound of his home's front door being kicked in and his mother shrieking had woken him instantly. Outside, the flocks were bleating.

He'd sat up on his straw mattress and started to call out for his mother, but hearing the raucous voices, the main room's table being thrown aside, and his mother continued screaming had filled him with a sensation he'd never known before: sheer terror. As a small child, Lewan had been afraid of the dark, and thunderstorms had often sent him scurrying to the pallet his parents shared in the main room. But this was something entirely new. His hearing and vision sharpened, but his heart was pounding so hard he could feel his temples pulsing. He felt cold all over, like he'd been rolled in snow.

His mother's screams intensified, but amidst the shrieks Lewan had heard the creaking of the ladder that led to his loft. Someone was coming up. His breath coming in ragged sobs, Lewan rose. Taking steps that were far too slow—he'd barely been able to get his feet to move at all—he staggered to the far corner, where their croft's roof almost touched the floor and the shadows were deep and dark. A pile of dirty clothing and his heavy winter blanket in need of mending lay there. He'd crawled under them and waited.

The hatch on the floor next to the far wall slammed up. A wild-haired, unshaven man thrust his head and arm through the opening. That hand held a knife. He looked around— looked right where Lewan lay curled in the shadows—then called down, "Empty! Just a loft. My turn. Now you hold her!" And he'd leaped down, leaving the hatch open.

His mother's voice rose to one long, agonized shriek, then broke into quiet sobbing. With the hatch still open, Lewan could hear at least two men chuckling and another breathing heavily. How long it went on, Lewan could never remember, but in his nightmares of the following years, those sounds went on and on and on, mingling with terrified screams and angry shouts from outside.

"Done?" a man's voice said, then, "Finish her. We'll start the roof."

Lewan heard the man leave, heard his mother cry out once more, a short burst of air, almost as if she'd fallen and had the wind knocked out of her. Then more footsteps, and the only sounds were those from outside the house.

Peeking from beneath the blanket, Lewan had been unable to look away from the open hatch, sure that at any moment the wild-haired man would return. And that's where he was looking when he saw the first ember fall. He gasped and looked up. A large area of the thatch was black, and little specks within the black were glowing like orange stars.

We'll start the roof. The men had torched the thatch!

Still shaking, Lewan crawled out from under the blankets and made his way to the hatch. More sparks were falling. One lit on the back of his hand, and the sudden pain almost broke his shock and sent him into full panic. He shook it off and scrambled the rest of the way. He peeked over the edge.

The croft's main room was in shambles, their table and water basins shattered, the door cracked almost in half and hanging on by one hinge. His mother sprawled on the dirt floor, her homespun nightshift torn up the middle, leaving her nakedness exposed. She lay in a dark puddle that Lewan first thought was the blanket she shared with his father, but then he saw it had the gleam of wetness. Thickest around her head, it formed a sickly mud on the floor, but where it had soaked into her shift, even in the dim light of predawn, Lewan had seen it was red. And worst of all, the dark blotch under her chin that had seemed like a shadow at first glance . . . his eyes seemed drawn to it, and he saw that his mother's throat had been cut open from just under her left ear to her collarbone.

"Mother!" Lewan had called, then rushed down. In his

haste, he'd slipped and fallen, landing in the mud surrounding his mother. A bit of it splashed onto his face.

Closer to her, he could see the lifeblood trickling out of her, a new wave with each beat of her heart.

"Mother . . ."

She'd turned her head at the sound of his voice. The blood pulsing out of her neck splattered her cheek. Her jaw hung slack, the tip of her tongue protruding between her lips, the slightest hint of her teeth showing. She swallowed and tried to speak, but all that came out was a horrid groan.

That had snapped some semblance of thought back into Lewan. He remembered his father slaughtering the sheep. One careful swipe across the throat, and the sheep would bleed out in moments.

He rushed to his mother on his hands and knees. The mud squished between his fingers. He grabbed a fistful of her ruined shift and pressed it to the wound.

"Mother, make it stop!" he said, and it was then that the tears had begun to fall. "Make-it-stop-make-it-stop-make-it-stop!"

The fire was growing. Lewan could hear the great roar and crackle of the flames consuming the roof, and large chunks of burning thatch began to fall in his loft. Sparks and cinders rained down the open hatch, and the loud pops all around told him that the fire was catching in the timber itself.

"Mother, we have to get out. Mother!"

She was still trying to speak, making that terrible wet moaning sound. One hand, shaking like an old woman's, rose to reach for him, but fell halfway.

Smoke was filling the room, and the sound of thatch falling in the loft overhead was a constant patter.

"We must leave, Mother!"

Lewan let go of his mother's shift. It was completely saturated with blood. He stood, grabbed one of her wrists, and pulled. She didn't budge. He pulled harder, and his feet slipped in the mud. He came down hard on his bottom and sobbed.

"Mother, please get up."

He scrubbed away the tears, and when he looked down at her again, she was watching him. She blinked once, hard, then swallowed and said, "Lew! Don't . . . let . . . me . . . buh . . . burn!"

She coughed, and the blood flowing from her neck spurted out like a fountain.

His mother tried to speak more, but all that came out was a frantic whisper. Her hand, twisted clawlike, reached out for him, missed, and raked through the bloody muck.

Lewan grabbed her wrist and tried again. Still she didn't move. Her skin felt chilled, but the room was growing hotter with each breath. Lewan coughed. His eyes were starting to sting and well with tears as smoke filled the room.

"Burn!" his mother croaked. "Lew! No . . . burrrr—!"

A large hunk of thatch, blackened and filled with tongues of flame, hit the floor at the bottom of the ladder. The fire began to lick at the wooden ladder, blackening it. More cinders followed, and the sound of the fire overhead became deafening.

Covered in bloody grime, tears running down his cheeks, Lewan stood and stumbled over to the hearth. The black kettle his mother used to prepare their meals still hung over the gray coals. Lewan grabbed the handle and lifted it off the hook. It was heavy. Twelve years old, he was small for his age, and the kettle was made of thick iron. It probably weighed almost a third of what he did.

A fit of coughing grabbed him, and his vision clouded over. The tears flooding his eyes were as much from the smoke in the air as his fear and grief.

Dragging the kettle behind him, he stumbled to where his mother lay in her own blood. She was still trying to speak. One hand reached out for him—and again failed.

Crying like a little baby, Lewan stood over his mother and gripped the iron kettle. Her eyes followed him. She was too weak and in too much pain to smile, but he thought he saw something like relief in her eyes.

Straining, he lifted the heavy iron over his head. His sobbing increased, and he inhaled a great deal of smoke. His lungs constricted and he coughed, almost dropping the kettle. Instead, he used the momentum and threw his strength into it, bringing the heavy iron down on his mother's head.

Over the roar of the flames, over the crackling and popping of the fire catching the timber, even over the screams from outside, Lewan heard the *crack* of his mother's skull, felt the shock of it go up his arms. The cough and the force of his blow caused him to lose his balance, and he fell. He fell over his mother and felt her limbs give a final spasm. His cheek hit her blood-slick shoulder, and he was close enough to hear her last breath leave her lungs.

Sickened, he pushed himself away, scrabbling through the mud. Still, he hadn't been able to look away.

His mother's forehead caved in—

—the skin broken and bloody—

—bits of bone showing.

Her eyes stared sightless at the ceiling, that last look of relief—the last look his mother had given him—was utterly gone. Her eyes were cold and lifeless as stones.

But then she sat up. Not with the sickening, desperate motions of a woman bleeding to death, but quickly and with purpose, like a sleeper wakened by the knocking of someone at the door. Blood ran down her face, one trickle running through her left eye. But she did not blink, and the eyes that she turned to him were still empty, the only light in them that of reflected flame.

"Lewan," she said, but it was not his mother's voice. Lower, more solemn, and with an underlying timbre that was beyond human.

Lewan tried to step back, to find the door and run. But his

feet would not move. His legs were heavy and slow in the way of nightmares.

"You must listen, my son," the voice said through his mother. "Death comes. When death comes for you, you must see clearly. You must not run. You must find your courage."

Lewan looked down. He was not the little boy anymore. He was seventeen, grown tall and with a lean strength from a life in the wild. He stood in the burning house naked, and the muddy symbols of the Oak Father he'd painted on his skin were still wet. They steamed in the hot air.

When he looked up, his mother was standing, her throat still savaged, the crown of her head a ruined mess, mud and worse caking her hair. "I will show you," she said.

She reached with both her hands—hands that had become claws—and grabbed the skin between her bare breasts. The claws dug into the skin and kept digging. Lewan heard bone cracking, the sound mingling with the burning flames growing in the timbers of the house. His mother's fingers were all the way inside her, and she pulled. Her breastbone broke with a great *crrrack!* and the skin tore as she pulled open her chest.

Lewan's eyes went wide with horror, but he could not look away. Instead of blood and his mother's inner organs spilling all over the floor of their croft, a light burned inside—green but warm, like the late afternoon sun shining through a canopy of new spring leaves.

"See," said the voice—

—and Lewan saw, falling into the green light.

The green glow dimmed and he found himself surrounded by blue, broken only by high, thin streaks of white. Clouds. The white was clouds. He turned, and below him stretched hundreds of miles of golden grassland. The Amber Steppes. And directly beneath him was a mountain, which rose into a broken cone. He'd never seen it from this high up, but he recognized it immediately. Sentinelspire.

As he watched, an entire face of the mountain—scores of miles of stone, soil, and greenery—fell, collapsing in upon itself. The landslide had scarcely started sliding down when the entire mountain—and several miles of ground around the mountain—exploded. For a heartbeat, a lightning-flash moment, Lewan thought he saw a white-hot center of fire, but then all of the remains of the mountain and surrounding country-side spread outward in a great cloud of blasted rock and fire, moving faster than the sound of the explosion. The fire-shot darkness swallowed him.

When he could see again, before him was the greatest wonder he'd ever seen. The world stretched out before him. He saw the yellow haze of the Endless Wastes, the darker smudges of mountains and woods, the Great Ice Sea to the north, and hundreds of miles in every direction. So high was he that he could see the curve of the world falling away in every direction. But directly beneath him he saw again Sentinelspire's explo-sion, as if time had sped up. The great cloud of ash and fire rose farther than the highest clouds, spread out as the wind caught it, and still grew and grew, covering thousands of miles of land in darkness. Beyond the great cloud where the ash thinned, still it spread a murky haze for tens of thousands of miles.

His vision shifted again, back down to woods and forests. He saw rivers choked with ash, dead fish floating downstream to rot in lakes. He saw rain filled with soot and sulfur poi-soning streams and fields. He saw fruit wither on the vine and crops rot in the fields from the lack of sun. Summer did not come to many lands, and the following winter was harsh beyond recorded memory. Starvation and disease ran rampant, in man and beast alike. Wars erupted as nations invaded the lands of their enemies—or their allies—in a desperate bid for food. Entire cities burned. Villages were laid waste. Tens of thousands died in the first year. Then even the armies broke apart or turned upon their own ranks as soldiers starved.

But as the seasons passed, the winds and rain cleansed

the air, and though Sentinelspire—no more than a gigantic crater—still oozed steam and smoke, the wild recovered. Civilization crumbled as men, elves, and other civilized people tore at one another and became savage in their bid for survival. But forests took root where once men had tilled fields. Trees grew in the midst of ruined castles. Beasts made homes in the broken bones of once-proud cities. Years passed. Where rivers had once run foul with the sludge of sewage from cities, they ran clean again. Sunrises and sunsets were no longer sullied by thousands of fires from cities. Even the great crater hundreds of miles south of the Great Ice Sea cooled and filled with water from clean rain and melting snow. It seemed almost a—

Paradise.

The image remained clear, but a new sound broke Lewan's sense of peace. He heard horns, cries of alarm, and people shouting. He looked around, and the image of the new world dissolved and faded, like smoke on the wind.

Lewan opened his eyes and sat up, dislodging the blanket he'd wrapped around his body. A light rain was falling on the balcony, rippling the leaves of the vines clinging to the stone. Clarions sounded from somewhere inside the fortress, echoing off the canyon walls. He heard people shouting.

The door to the balcony opened, and Ulaan stood there, the thick fur coverlet from the bed wrapped round her shoulders. She had lit a lamp in the room behind her, and it outlined her in a dim, flickering light.

"What's happening?" asked Lewan as he struggled to bring his mind out of the dream and back into the world around him.

"The Fortress is under attack."

Part Three

✠

THE RETURN

chapter twenty-six

16 Tarsakh, the Year of Lightning Storms (1374 DR)
The foothills of the Khopet-Dag

Berun hit the ground rolling, careful to keep his blade away from his body, and came to his feet. The tiger was already rounding on him, her lips pulled back over her teeth. Sauk and his men fanned out behind her. Berun crouched and kept the knife out before him, hoping the smell of blood on the steel would discourage the tiger. She gave it a swipe, testing him. He jerked the knife out of the way just in time and stepped back. On the edge of his vision, he could see Lewan trying to force himself to his feet but not having much success.

"Surround him!" Sauk called out. "Get behind him and close in. He's done running. He runs and Taaki'll be on him!"

The tiger backed up and crouched, baring her teeth and tightening her muscles. Berun knew she was about to pounce. He might be able to avoid the brunt of her, might even slice into her with the knife, but he knew it wouldn't be a killing blow. He'd either teach her a little caution, maybe buy himself a little time, or he'd get her so angry that she'd come at him, blade or no blade.

Berun prepared to make his own leap when that slight tickling in the base of his brain suddenly flared.

Perch hit Taaki, right on her head, coming down in a fury

of claws and teeth. Taaki roared in shock and anger and began shaking her head back and forth to dislodge the treeclaw lizard. But Perch held, and Berun knew through the link they shared that Perch's claws had burrowed beneath the fur and well under the skin. One claw was scraping along bone. Still, the tiger was a thousand times stronger than the lizard, and she dislodged him. Keeping a tenuous hold with his front claws, Perch's lower body fell on her face.

Berun saw her flex her right paw—claws fully extended—and he knew what was coming.

"Perch, *drekhe!*" Berun shouted, and at the same time urged him *flee!*

Taaki struck, and the little lizard leaped away just in time—so close that Perch felt the fur of the tiger's paw tickle his back in passing. The tiger's claws ripped into her own eye and the flesh around it. She screamed—a roar that began deep but then went up into an almost human-sounding screech—then she bounded away, running Valmir down as she passed.

Sauk roared in fury and charged. Berun could see from the look on his face that any orders of taking Berun alive were forgotten. Time for bloody murder.

The half-orc brought his sword around in a backhanded blow, all of his strength and rage behind the swing. Berun threw himself back, hoping that the downhill slope would grant him some added momentum. It did, but too much. His foot slipped on the sodden ground and he went down hard, sliding a ways downhill into a thick brake of holly. He felt the ground shaking under Sauk's heavy tread.

He pushed himself to his feet. Forest detritus and muck covered him, but he knew he didn't have time to concern himself with any of it. Sauk was almost upon him. Another moment—

The ground in front of Berun erupted, scattering leaves and branches and shattering a rotted tree into countless pieces. The moist earth swelled until it stood almost as tall as the young trees themselves. Seeing it, Berun's eyes widened in shock, for the earth was shaped almost like a man—a thick, malformed man. Leaves and mud sprouted from the great lump between its shoulders, almost like a living crown. Broken branches and old roots protruded at odd angles, and even as its thick, loamy scent hit him, Berun could see earthworms wriggling on its surface, some falling away while others burrowed back inside.

The mound of earth rose, as if dirt from the torso were being forced upward, then split into a mouth. It kept growing, the bulk of the thing's body shrinking as it formed into the jaws. The mound of earth leaned forward, towering over Berun, then fell.

When the tiger had knocked him to the ground, Berun thought he'd felt every bone in his body scrape together. This was a hundred times stronger and completely unrelenting. The tiger had struck and bounded away. This kept coming and coming and coming. He felt millions of grains of wet dirt undulating over his skin and falling down his shirt, filling his nose, burying him. Roots and rocks scraped and bruised him.

It was cold. Worse, Berun could not breathe. Dirt filled his nose, and he knew that if he opened his mouth, he would choke on the wet earth. He pitched and kicked and punched, but it was like fighting the wind. The earth flowed around every strike. He felt his knife swept away in the flood of earth. For an instant, he thought he heard Sauk screaming, but then it was gone, and there was only the roar of the earth surging around him.

Berun's kicks and punches were no longer a matter of fighting. With no air, his body had completely separated from his mind and gone into the throes of sheer panic.

Lights danced in his vision. Were his eyes open or clenched shut? He could not remember, but neither could he feel them any longer. The lights coalesced, bleeding together, and deepened into a shade of verdant green, like dawn's light on the dew of spring grass.

The light rippled, a green glow playing over shadow, and the ripples formed an outline, then a face.

Chereth.

It was Chereth, his master. Older. His face drawn. Even haggard. But there was no mistaking his master's visage.

"Berun," said Chereth, "you must help me. I release you from your oath. Come to me, my son. Come to me!"

✛

chapter twenty-seven

19 Tarsakh, the Year of Lightning Storms (1374 DR)
The foothills of the Khopet-Dag

Wake-wake-wake!
An urgency. A will tinged by worry.
Wake-open-eyes! Wake-open-eyes?
Then he heard—really heard, not just in his mind—the chittering, almost birdlike but harsher.

He didn't move his limbs or even turn his head. He wasn't sure he could and was afraid to try. Part of him was afraid that opening his eyes would show him nothing, only the smothering black of being buried alive in the deep earth. But he could breathe. Not well. His nostrils were clogged, and something was partially blocking his lips.

Berun opened his eyes. Blue sky. Not entirely blue, no. Clouds low and gray floated like islands in a sea.

The chittering came again, and Berun dared to move his head, looking up just a little. Jagged shapes broke his view of the sky. Branches. Blackened branches. Blackened by lightning. He was lying under the lightning blasted tree where he had agreed to meet—

"Lewan!"

Berun sat up. He heard a startled rustling overhead and looked up in time to see Perch scrambling down the tree.

Halfway down, the lizard leaped and alighted on Berun's shoulder.

That was when Berun got the first good look at himself. He was covered—head to fingertips to heels—in mud. It had begun to dry, and his sudden movement sent cracks across the dark surface.

Perch chittered in his ear.

Wake-wake-wake?

"Yes, Perch. I'm awake." He smiled and ran a finger down Perch's back. His arm trembled.

He felt weak, his limbs heavy, no strength in his muscles, the way he felt after running dozens of miles across the open steppe.

Berun looked around. Other than himself and Perch and a few butterflies fluttering through the grass, no one was around. No sign of Sauk and his men, nor of Lewan. The last thing Berun could remember was the earth creature attacking, seeming to swallow him and push him down into the earth. Then the green light and Chereth's face. *Berun, you must help me.*

And then he understood. Somehow, even from his prison far away, his master had sent him aid. Sauk would have killed him. Berun had little doubt of that. Even if Berun managed to best Sauk—and he knew the unlikelihood of that—that still left the other assassins and the tiger. He never could have beaten them all and escaped with Lewan. So Chereth had summoned some sort of earth spirit to save him.

He raised his eyes and looked to the east. Higher hills lay between him and the steppe, and beyond, a thick haze. He could not see Sentinelspire. But from where he sat he knew it was well over a hundred miles as the crow flies. Over the hills and valleys on foot, it was probably closer to two hundred. His supplies were gone. His knife, his bow, *Erael'len* . . . everything but the clothes he wore were either with Sauk's band or buried in the earth. And the clothes wouldn't count for much. He brushed at the mud on his sleeve to try to get the worst off, and the fabric ripped. His pants and boots, filthy as they were, were still useable. His shirt was a loss. The dirt grinding him down had done it in. The mud was probably the only thing holding it together.

Berun, you must help me. Had it been a panic-induced dream? Berun didn't think so. Besides . . . Lewan. Sauk had taken Lewan. As far as Berun knew, the boy was still alive.

His limbs still trembling, Berun pushed himself to his feet. He winced. Mud and grit had filled his boots. He'd have to find a stream very soon and clean himself up, or walking the first mile would rip all the skin off his feet.

Berun sat down and removed the boots. He'd go slower barefoot, but until he could find a stream, he had little choice.

"Let's go, Perch," he said, "and let's hope we don't run into any spiders too big for you to handle."

A stream wasn't hard to find. The little creeks running between the hills were loud and full. Berun cleaned himself up as best he could, but as he'd feared, washing the shirt ruined it. The homespun fabric fell to pieces in the stream. He saved enough strips to braid a small roost he could sling around one shoulder on which Perch could sit. With no shirt, if the lizard insisted on riding the whole way, he would tear Berun's skin to shreds. The job done, he let the final remains of his shirt float away, finished cleaning the rest of his clothes and boots, then set out.

He returned to the place where he and Lewan had spent the night. He searched for a trail but found nothing. The rain had ruined any signs, washing away even the blood. The bodies were gone.

As he stood there in the wood, cursing his ill luck and worrying over Lewan, he considered searching for the portal of which Valmir had spoken. He knew they'd spent the day heading up into the mountains. It had to be up there somewhere. But unless he managed to find their trail, he could spend months looking for the portal, and even if he found it, without the proper key, it would be useless to him. And the farther he went up the mountains, the more dangerous his path would become. With no weapons, he'd be no match against the larger spiders—and there were worse things than spiders in the Khopet-Dag.

"East it is, then," he said, more to himself than Perch. If he ran, he might make it to Sentinelspire in a tenday—if he didn't have to spend much time foraging for food. Once he hit the steppe again, he might be able to beg or steal a horse.

He searched long enough to find a good, stout stick. Not great in terms of a weapon, but it was better than nothing. The sun was riding high in the sky, approaching midday. Berun turned east and started running.

✛
chapter twenty-eight

Dusk found Berun in the last of the true foothills. The land was not as steep, but this meant going back into the Shalhoond, and the woods thickened. Dark would come fast. Thinking of Lewan, and with Chereth's plea still fresh in his mind, part of Berun wanted to push on. But he knew that he had to pace himself. He wouldn't be much help to either his disciple or master if he showed up at Sentinelspire half-dead, so he began to look for a place to spend the night.

As the last light was fading from the sky and the east was deepening to purple, the brightest stars came out in force. Berun found a quiet glade, partially open to the sky. A massive oak, its branches sprouting new spring leaves, dominated the glade. It had starved out most of the nearby trees. Two of the oak's roots spread out, and between them a stream ran down the hillside to feed a quiet pool. With the thickest of the spider country behind him, Berun had re-entered a part of the wood where insects and birds were more plentiful. Fireflies played over the water, and the evening was alive with the sound of crickets and night birds. Seeing the great oak, hearing the breeze whispering through its leaves, and surrounded by the scent of healthy greenery and clean water, a profound sense of peace settled over Berun.

He sat down beside the pool, and it wasn't until he was still that he realized how exhausted he was. His hands shook, and his arms and legs felt empty. It was too dark to have any hope of catching a fish in the pool or stream, and it was still too early in the season to forage for acorns. The thought of a supper of fireflies, crickets, and earthworms didn't excite him, but he had to keep up his strength.

He shook his shoulder to wake the lizard, who had been dozing. "Hey, Perch."

The lizard twitched. Seeing that they'd stopped, he scrambled down Berun's back and began rustling through the grass.

Berun closed his eyes, widening the link he shared with the little lizard, and sent one strong image—*Eggs.* He didn't like the idea of robbing nests, but without some nourishment soon, he wouldn't even have the strength to search for food.

Eggs-round-round-breaks-eggs-in-trees-eggs?

Eggs, Berun told him again. *In trees, yes. Bring eggs. Try-try-try not to break.*

Through the link, Berun sensed that Perch had detected a cricket that had strayed too close. The lizard lunged and snatched the insect in his jaws. He crunched and swallowed it down, then shot off through the grass. Berun listened to the sound of his claws as they scratched against the wood of the oak, then Berun began unlacing his boots.

Perch returned not long afterward, when Berun had just finished a long drink from the pool. The lizard had a small egg in his jaws, and wonder of wonders, it was unbroken.

Good, Perch! More, please. More eggs-in-trees.

The lizard took off again, and Berun used his thumbnail to crack open the top of the egg. He sucked out the inside, grimacing at the taste, then opened the shell and licked the inside clean. Going back and forth, Perch managed to bring another four. It wasn't much, but it would last Berun until morning, when he could forage or maybe even catch a fish.

The breeze picked up, and shirtless as he was, Berun knew it would be a cold night if he couldn't get a fire going or find something to cover himself. Leaves wouldn't be much, but they would be better than nothing. If he could find enough dry grass, he could stuff it inside his trousers for insulation, maybe even find enough to put a layer between his bare skin and a blanket of leaves.

Still . . .

Something about the pool called to him. Light still lingered in the sky, but the surrounding woods were mostly varying shades of shadow. Most of the pool seemed black, shaded as it was by the oak canopy. But on the far edge there was a sliver of water that reflected the first evening stars, and with the fireflies, it almost seemed as if some of the stars had come to life and danced over the water. He was suddenly very conscious of how filthy he was. Running most of the day, he'd poured sweat, and the sweat had accumulated every bit of dust and dirt he had touched or passed. Pushing his way through the brush, his skin felt raw with hundreds of tiny scratches, and some of the leaves made him itch. Cool or not, he knew he'd sleep better if he were clean.

Perch had gone off to hunt, hoping for a juicy spider but content with the crickets and fascinated by the fireflies. Berun pulled off his boots, then stood and stripped away the rest of his clothes. The grass by the shore felt wonderfully soft between his toes. He stepped into the water. He wished he could dive right in, but he had no idea how deep the pool might be, so he took his time, advancing step by sliding step. The water was cold but wonderfully refreshing, the bottom soft with mud and leaves. It proved to be about chest-deep in the middle, but Berun plunged under, enjoying the soft silence of being underwater, the only sound the faint tinkling of the streams feeding and draining the pool.

When he emerged from the pool, someone was standing on the shore watching him.

Berun blinked and wiped the water from his eyes, but when he looked again the figure was still there. The stranger began moving out of the deeper shadow, and Berun could tell by the movement that it was a woman. As she came out from under the oak canopy, a bit of the light from the sky reflected off her dress. It had seemed downy gray in the shadows, but as she stood under the sky, it sparkled like frost, catching the violet light of evening and reflecting some of it back against her skin. Berun followed her with his eyes, and as she stopped, the first edge of the moon broke over the treetops, shedding the glade in her pale light. It gave Berun his first good look at the woman.

She was strikingly beautiful, and her body had the leanness of an elf. Her sleeveless gown stopped just above her ankles, and it seemed to be made of many strips of fabric, so light that they fluttered in the breeze, reminding Berun very much of new spring blossoms. The fabric seemed pale against the darkness of her skin. Her hair fell well below her waist, and she had flowers and even tiny sprigs twined within her tresses.

"Good evening to you, lady," Berun called out.

"Peace to you, Berun," she said. He found the melodic lilt of her accent very pleasing.

"How do you know me, lady?"

She stared at him in silence for a long while—so much that Berun became uncomfortable. Finally she looked up to the sky and said, "Have you forgotten what night this, Child of the Oak Father?"

"I—" Berun stopped, realizing that he had given no thought to the day. What day was it? He might have been in the earth under Chereth's spell for years for all he knew. "I . . . don't know."

"Tonight is the *Jalesh Rudra*," she said. "I am Lebeth, daughter of the Oak Father. You must play for me. Fulfill the covenant."

Berun blinked and looked away. The *Jalesh Rudra*. That meant it had been three days ago that Lewan had been taken, that the earth had risen up to swallow Berun. To fulfill the covenant, he would play the pipes for the daughters of the Oak

Father, and if he found her favor, she would give herself to him for a night's coupling beneath the trees.

Still standing up to his chest in the water, Berun bowed his head and said, "Forgive me, lady. Great misfortune has overtaken me, and I have lost my pipes."

"I know of your needs," said Lebeth. "Our father knows of your needs. I will meet yours, but you must meet mine, according to the covenant."

She held out her hand, and the pale moonlight reflected off a small set of pipes, one of the finest he had ever seen. He could not remember if she had been holding them the whole time. She might have summoned them from the moonlight, for all he knew.

"So be it," said Berun. He waded to shore. It struck him then that Lewan should have been there, that Berun should be leading him through his first *Jalesh Rudra;* that if not for Sauk and the Old Man, his apprentice would have awoken tomorrow a boy no longer, but a man in the sight of the Oak Father. Berun's heart quickened in anticipation of what was to come, but his mood was tinged with sadness at Lewan's absence.

He came ashore where he thought he had left his trousers and boots, but they were gone.

"Your clothes are gone," said Lebeth, and when Berun turned she was standing only a few feet away. Though they were beneath the trees, the sparkle of starlight had not left her gown. Indeed, tinier sparkles dotted her arms and cheeks. This close, he caught the scent of her—night breeze through spring blossoms, but beneath it, a hint of something musky and primal. "You will not need them." She held out the pipes to him. "Play for me now."

Berun took the pipes, and in so doing his finger brushed against her hand. Berun swallowed and wet his lips. Damp as he was, the breeze made him shiver, but a warmth was growing beneath his skin and spreading outward.

"Sit," she said. "Sit and play."

Berun sat upon the soft grass and put the pipes to his lips. He blew a hesitant note, then began a simple melody, the first Master Chereth had ever taught him. He didn't even know its name.

Lebeth turned her back to him, though she continued to watch over her shoulder as she began her dance. She began with a rhythmic swaying of her hips, then her hands moved up her body to tangle her fingers in her hair. Blossoms rained down to her feet. A few caught in the breeze and fluttered to Berun. One came to rest on his cheek, and his head spun for a moment at the sharp, sweet scent.

Dusk faded to night, the sky going from deep purple to a blackness broken only by the moon and stars, but Berun noticed that it was not getting darker in the glade. If anything, he could see more. Still keeping the pipes to his lips, he turned his head slightly and saw that a warm green glow was emanating from the water. At first he thought that the moonlight had simply taken on an odd sheen, but then he saw that the light was coming from the pool itself.

A rock struck the pool, startling Berun so that his melody faltered. The sudden ripples caused the light to flicker in the glade. He returned his gaze to Lebeth, who had ceased her dance and was watching him. She had thrown the rock.

"You have all your life to stare at water," she said. "You have me only tonight."

Berun began to play again, this time a more lively tune. Lebeth resumed her dance, her hips undulating to the melody and her arms moving over her body. She joined in the music herself, stamping her foot or clapping her hands as she danced, her hair flying about her, blossoms falling at her feet.

She danced closer, bathing Berun in her scent, and looked down on him. "Be wary, son of the Oak Father," she said, almost in a chant.

He did not cease his playing, but his brows creased in a quizzical expression.

She danced away again, and as she did, some of the fabric came away from the bottom of her gown, exposing her legs below the knees. The bits of fabric floated like goosedown on the breeze and broke apart in the air until they were no thicker than smoke, enveloping Berun. It smelled like summer rain.

"My roots run deep," she said, glancing back at him again. She tossed her hair over one shoulder, and the fabric of her gown slipped down. She did not pull it back up. "I sensed the earth spirit during the storm."

The one that saved me, Berun thought.

"Even from afar," she continued, "I sensed . . . wrongness within it, like the beginnings of rot in wood."

Berun pulled the pipes away from his mouth. "I don't understand."

Lebeth stopped her dancing and looked down on him. Her lips twisted in a mischievous smile. "Play for me, Berun. Fulfill the covenant."

Berun resumed the tune, this time, a melancholy air of low notes over the longest pipes.

"Like the beginnings of rot in the wood," Lebeth continued, and this time her dance was slow, almost more of a swaying, and she drew closer to him step by step. "Do not trust visions of the cold earth, where stone is strong and growing things struggle against the dark. Earth, soil . . . its life comes from death, from the decay of once-living things. Life comes from death. Of this is the Balance. But in earth where death grows too strong . . ." Berun thought he saw a shudder pass through her that was not part of her dance. "Beware, son of the Oak Father. Even truth can deceive, when the seeker walks darkened paths."

The rest of her gown, still sparkling like starlight on frost, melted away. The remains caught on the wind and showered Berun. He closed his eyes and breathed in her scent, the last of his melody fading away on the breeze. When he opened his eyes again, Lebeth stood naked before him, still slightly swaying, the breeze playing through her hair.

"To see the light, child of the Oak Father," she said, her voice low, almost a whisper, "to protect light for us all, you must bring vengeance to the Tower of the Sun."

She knelt in front of him, so close that the breeze tossed her hair round his shoulders and face, tickling his skin.

"I am . . ." Berun set the pipes aside and looked at Lebeth. Her face was all in shadow, but he could see a radiant starlight glow in her eyes. "I am not an assassin," he said, his voice choked. "Not . . . not anymore."

"You are a son of the Oak Father." Lebeth leaned in so close that he could feel her breath when she spoke. "Your sworn duty is the Balance of all living things. For too long the Blades of the Old Man have dealt in death. Gold and power are their currency, but blood is their profit. So much blood. Too much. Too much death. Berun, son of the Oak Father, it is time to restore the Balance."

Lebeth leaned in, all warm curves and sweet scent, her lips seeking his. Berun lay back on the grass, pulling her on top of him.

✛ ✛ ✛ ✛ ✛

A riot of birdsong woke Berun, and when he opened his eyes, he saw that the sun was already above the treeline, reflecting white fire off the pool. He had slept late.

Berun rose and brushed grass, leaves, and dirt off his skin, hoping that Lebeth had remembered to return his trousers and boots. He looked around and saw that she had not, but had done him one better. At the base of the great oak's trunk, where the largest of the roots hemmed in the pool, lay a pile of clothes, supplies, and—best of all—weapons.

The trousers and shirt were both green as winter pine needles. At first Berun thought they were of dyed linen, but as he picked them up and ran his fingers over them, he was no longer sure. The fabric was soft and thin as linen, but seemed strong as tentcloth. The sleeveless jacket seemed to be made of tanned skin, but he could not tell what kind of animal it had come from—and Berun knew every animal in the Endless Wastes and hundreds of miles beyond. The knee-high boots were of the same material. The belt was thickly woven from some fibrous plant, strong yet supple. The buckle, though cool and smooth, was not metal; it had the feel and sheen of shell or stone.

The cloak and hood were strangest of all. Spreading it out, he saw that it would just touch the ground when donned, but the fabric and color he could not identify. It was heavy as oilcloth, and under the shadow of the oak it seemed the dark green of forest leaves, but here and there, as bits of the sun peeked through the canopy, it reflected bright as the sunlight itself. It seemed to gather shadow and reflect light. Berun thought that in the deep woods—or even in the tall grass of the steppe—he would be almost invisible in the cloak if he kept still.

Under the cloak was a small waterskin, already full. Berun found a cache of food wrapped in large green oak leaves— dried fruits and nuts, mostly. Wrapped round the mouth of the waterskin was a necklace, woven of the same material as the belt, though much finer, the material flexible as dwarf-forged chain. Dangling from the end was a round starstone, though its glow had a greenish tint, like sunlight reflecting off dew-covered moss.

Two weapons leaned against the trunk of the oak. One was a blade, slightly longer than the knife he'd lost, but just shy of being a true short sword. He ran his fingers along the sheath. It felt like aspen bark, soft and smooth, but it was black as river mud and cool. Blade and hilt were all one piece, carved from bone or antler. Berun drew it. Single-edged, it ended in a slight curve. He tested the blade against the thick callus of his first bowfinger. It cut through the tough skin easily as a steel razor.

The other weapon was a hammer, handle and head together as long as Berun's forearm and fist. The handle was a dark, heavy wood, and it bound a heavy stone, smooth and black. Leather had been braided round the handle to form a grip, and the braid ran off the handle so he could tie it round his wrist or use the weapon as a sort of flail. Both weapons had images of oak leaves, trees, and vines etched into them, and the etchings had been colored with a substance that smelled faintly of resin. They were easily the finest weapons he had ever held in his hands.

As he picked up the hammer and tested the weight with a careful swing, the breeze gusted, whispering through the oak leaves, and Berun fancied he heard Lebeth's whisper—*Berun, son of the Oak Father, it is time to restore the Balance.*

Berun gently laid his palm against the oak where the root met the main bole of the tree, and for a heartbeat he felt again the sensation of Lebeth's thigh beneath his caresses.

"So be it, Oak Father," he said, then looked up at the tree. "Thank you, Lebeth. Lewan, Master Chereth . . . I'm on my way."

✛

chapter twenty-nine

25 Tarsakh, the Year of Lightning Storms (1374 DR)
Sentinelspire

Janas hated guard duty. He'd been inducted into the ranks of the Blades of the Old Man only three years ago. And he'd been involved in the Lady Talieth's little conspiracy for only a few months. He had no particular love for Talieth nor hatred for the Old Man, but he'd always been smart enough to know which way the wind was blowing and set his path thereby. Changes were happening in the Fortress, and he'd be damned if he didn't end up on the winning side. Life here was too precious to risk. He wanted for nothing. He slept in a soft bed with any woman of his choosing, drank the finest wines, ate the finest foods—which were prepared for him—and all he had to do in return was put his considerable skills at murder to good use. A good life, all things considered.

Except for guard duty. Given all the traps set about the Fortress and littered about the mountain and the Lady's particular expertise at scrying, usually only the main gate held a permanent watch. But something had happened earlier—something involving Sauk and that new whelp—that had sent Lady Talieth into a flurry of orders. The guard at the main gate was tripled. Crews went out to make sure all the traps were armed and ready. A watch was set at the head of the falls. Men watched the passageways between the main gate and the Gallery of Stone Faces, men watched the passageway beyond, and Janas hid in the rocks beyond the leering stone face.

He understood why he'd been chosen. A Nar, he had more than a little orc blood in his lineage. Not a full half-orc with true night vision like Sauk, still Janas could see better than nearly anyone else at night. Strong moonlight was almost like noonday sun to him. But storm clouds had started building around sunset, and by full dark there was no moon or starlight of any kind. Still . . . always be prepared, he often told himself, and was glad he'd worn the special ring that Talieth had given him upon his induction into the Blades. It wasn't much to look at, but it enabled him to see in the dark. Not as well as daylight, to be sure. He could see no colors, but his eyes drank in the dimmest light. The downside was that he was nearly always the one chosen for nighttime guard duty or a patrol outside the walls. Only Sauk could see better than Janas in the dark, and Sauk was too high up to be assigned guard duty. Sauk did not guard. Sauk hunted.

The night flickered in sharp relief under approaching lightning, and soon after, thunder shook the mountain. Smelling the breeze, Janas knew he'd be sitting in the rain before long.

As the last of the thunder's echo faded to the east, Janas heard something skittering across the rocks down the path. He flexed his fist around the ring and narrowed his eyes. Nothing. Just boulders and rocks through which little eddies of grit and dust were stirred up by the oncoming storm. Just when he was about to relax and look away, he heard it again—a light *scritchity-scritchity-scrititch*. Definitely coming up the path. He waited, listening as the sound grew closer.

He saw it. A small shadow moving up the path. Smaller than Janas's forearm, at first he thought it was a snake, but as he watched, he saw that it didn't move with a snake's smoothness. More like the quick, jerky movements of a grounded bird or even a lizard. But its movements seemed erratic and pointless.

Now that it was in his sight, it stopped coming up the path. It stayed near the last of the large boulders on the path, running through the dust and pebbles and twisting on its back, then flipping back around. Almost like it was hurt or having a fit of some sort.

You watch like a starving hawk, Sauk had told him earlier. *Talieth says there may be trouble soon. Don't you let so much as a bat get past you.*

Bats don't go through our tunnel, Janas had told him. It was true. The bats that haunted so many of the caves and crevices of the mountain never entered the tunnel leading to the Fortress.

If one does and you don't see it, Sauk had responded, *it's your life, Janas. Anything gets past you, and you'll answer to me.*

Janas had heard what the half-orc had done to Chiganis. There were truly very few Blades of the Old Man who frightened Janas, but the half-orc was one of them.

The thing on the path continued to thrash in the dirt. The first raindrops began to patter into the dust.

Janas slid his short sword out of its scabbard. Holding it under his cloak so that another lightning flash wouldn't gleam off the blade, he rose from his hiding place and began a careful advance down the pathway. He risked a quick glance around the canyon and back toward the leering face of the tunnel. Nothing in sight but that thing on the path and wind-tossed sand.

As he drew closer, the little thing skittered back down the path a short way, then stopped and resumed its odd twitching. Janas stopped near the large boulder. It was more flat than round—a large shard broken from the mountain in a past earthquake, most likely—and slightly higher than his waist. He placed his free hand on it and squinted at the moving shape.

Definitely a lizard. Not much bigger than a bird, though it had large claws and a tail that looked stumpy, as if it was growing back. It had a fanlike skin of some sort between its limbs. It continued its thrashing, twisting and turning its body, sometimes even flopping onto its back.

"Like the damned thing has an itch it can't scratch," Janas said to himself. "Or like it's a fish out of water."

"Or a worm on a hook," said a low voice from behind him.

Janas gasped and whirled, bringing his short sword up and out. He had a brief look at a club or hammer descending upon his face. There was a brief flash—lightning or pain?—then darkness.

Berun knelt beside the corpse. His cloak gathered in the darkness so that he appeared no more than a strangely shaped boulder next to a dead man.

Perch pattered up to him, back to his usual self. He looked up at Berun and chittered.

"Well done, Perch," Berun whispered. He reached out and the lizard climbed up his arm to burrow under the hood round his shoulders.

Berun's hands were shaking. He'd just killed a man. And not in defense. Not really. He'd lured the man out into the dark and smashed in his face with the hammer. The sound of the bones shattering had reminded Berun of a green branch snapping, but the shock of the blow the hammer had sent up his arm . . . that had been the worst. That's what put cold fear into his gut.

He was scared. Not because he was infiltrating one of the most fearsome fortresses east of Thay. Not because men were waiting to kill him. No. Berun was scared because after all he'd been through, after all he'd done to make sure Kheil stayed dead, here he was, back where he had reveled in his life of murder, and he'd just killed a man. Killed him. Felt the blow ending a man's life.

And Berun had *enjoyed* it.

The sprinkle of rain increased, falling down the mountain like a shroud drawn over a man's last glimpse of life. Berun couldn't stop his hands from shaking.

Lurom didn't like the outer tunnels during thunderstorms. The thunder itself wasn't so bad. But the roar of the rain and the howl of the wind amplified through the stone passageways so that the caverns seemed to hum a malevolent tune. He turned to Ferluk, his fellow guard. "You think we should check on Janas?"

Ferluk didn't move from where he leaned against the stone wall. Beside him at chest level, the one oil lamp they were allowed sat in a niche carved into the stone in ages past. "Just a storm," he said. "Man's got his cloak. Besides, he's a Nar. Spring rain like this probably is warm to him."

Thunder boomed outside, and Lurom could feel the stone beneath his feet shaking. They were too far inside the entranceway to catch the flicker of the lightning, but by the force of the thunder, Lurom guessed it had been a close strike.

"We should look on Janas," said Lurom.

Ferluk scowled. "Look on him if you want. But leave the lamp."

"You expect me to walk in the dark?" Lurom looked down the passageway. It was narrow—scarcely larger than one of the servants' halls in the tower where he had his rooms. The light from their lamp reflected off the stone a good twenty feet in either direction. A few feet beyond that was only dim shadow. Beyond that lay utter darkness and the heavy drone of the storm.

"I don't expect you to take an open flame into the rain," said Ferluk. "Besides, you know the way. And if you're going out, you'll want your eyes adjusted to the dark. Janas won't have a light."

Lurom looked into the darkness. "Maybe if the storm lets up. Then we—what's that?"

He pointed and Ferluk looked.

"Just a lizard," said Ferluk. "Probably came in to get out of the rain."

"Animals don't come in here," said Lurom. "Even bats won't. You know that."

But it was a lizard. Not a very big one, all mottled brown and still glistening from being out in the rain. It cocked its head at them and blinked.

"So chase it off," said Ferluk.

Lurom took a few steps toward it. The little lizard stood on its haunches and hissed at him. Lurom stopped, not taking his eyes off the little creature, and said, "You think it might be poisonous?"

Ferluk rolled his eyes and pushed himself away from the wall. He drew his short sword as he passed Lurom. "Won't matter if I have this," he said.

He raised the sword and approached at a careful crouch so that a strike from his blade would reach ground level. "Go on!" he said, and swiped the sword at the lizard.

It hissed back at him and flexed its front claws. They were small but looked sharp.

"Brave little thing," said Lurom, and forced a laugh.

"Not for long," said Ferluk, and he lunged, swinging at the lizard.

It shot away, but rather than retreating down the passage, it ran around Ferluk, skirting the wall. Lurom leaped back, not wanting to be anywhere near the thing's teeth and claws if it were poisonous. But the lizard ran past him, not even slowing. For a moment Lurom thought it would keep going, but it skittered up the wall, its claws finding enough grip that it scampered up like a spider.

"The lamp!" Ferluk shouted, but it was too late.

The lizard blundered into the niche, knocking the lamp

out, then leaped away. The brass lamp hit the floor with a clang, oil spilling onto the stone. The flame guttered, and for one moment Lurom feared it would die and he'd be left in the blackness of the passageway that still seemed to hum to the rhythm of the storm. But then the flame caught in the spilled oil and flared. It burned low and blue in a pool along the floor, giving off only a fraction of the light the lamp had.

"Pick it up before all the oil spills!" Ferluk shouted.

The darkness moved behind Ferluk, coming for him.

Too shocked to form a coherent warning, Lurom screamed.

Too late.

An arm of shadow whipped out, the meager light glinting off something pale, like bone. Ferluk had begun to turn when the pale shard passed through his throat. Blood sprayed the wall, and over the sound of the shadow's approaching footsteps, Lurom heard a hundred tiny droplets patter to the stone like rain. Ferluk's blade clattered to the ground only an instant before his body.

Lurom reached for his own blade and drew in a breath to scream, but it died in his throat.

Berun shambled through the passageway. Hunched over inside his cloak, the tiny light of the starstone shedding a deep green light before him, and dragging a dead man behind him, he looked like some herald of Kelemvor, dragging the latest doomed soul to the City of Judgment.

The weight of the guard's corpse slowed Berun, but there was no helping it. He needed the man's key to pass through the Gallery of Stone Faces, and the key might have been anything—a ring, a medallion, a coin, a pin, or even an arcane symbol etched into the man's skin. Berun had no way to know and no time to bargain with the man for his life. So he dragged the guard's corpse behind him through the twisting tunnels. It had been years since he'd last walked this path, and it disturbed him how familiar it all seemed. His starstone lit the way before him, but he thought he might have been able to walk the way with his eyes closed. It was not a comforting thought.

In his heart, he prayed that there would be no more guards before he reached the Gallery of Stone Faces. The weight of the dead man was nothing compared to the weight on his soul. He tried to remember how many men he had killed since Sauk had come back into his life. It frightened him that he couldn't remember. In that moment, only the thought of Lewan and Chereth, both ahead of him on the far side of these dark tunnels, kept him going.

✦ ✦ ✦ ✦ ✦

"What is that?" Galban whispered.

"Where? " said Bennig. "What is what?"

The two assassins had been assigned to watch the main passageway just outside the Gallery of Stone Faces. Bored and more than a little bothered by the oppressive dark, Galban hadn't taken his eyes off the main passage. Not too long ago, he'd thought he'd heard something skittering down the corridor, like a large insect or small lizard. That had raised his hackles, since the only things that moved in these tunnels were in the Gallery of Stone Faces—and you didn't want to see them moving. He'd never seen the source of the noise, but he'd been watching the main passage since. Bennig had been either lightly dozing or deeply snoring since they first settled in.

"Keep your voice down!" Galban rasped. "I just saw a green light down the main passageway. Damn me if I didn't."

"Then damn you," said Bennig. "But I see nothing. You must've dozed off and dreamed it."

"I wasn't the one sleeping. A faint glow. Greenish. It crossed our path. We need to have a look."

"You have a look," said Bennig. "Don't wake me when you get back."

"If Sauk finds out you were sleeping, he'll have your ears for a necklace."

"He won't find out unless someone tells him. Will he?"

"There!"

This time, Bennig saw it too. A faint green glow crossing their tunnel, only this time it was headed back toward the Gallery of Stone Faces. He thought he might have caught a glimpse of a large form near the light, then it was gone.

Galban heard Bennig push himself to his feet and the whisper of his dagger coming out of his scabbard. Galban drew his own blade.

"Let's have that look," said Bennig. "Nice and quiet."

"Light?" said Galban. He had a sunrod tucked under his belt.

"It'll give us away," said Bennig. "Just stay close."

The two assassins made their way back to the main passageway, the soft soles of their shoes silent on the smooth stone of what had probably once been a lava tube. Just as they were coming to where the tunnels crossed, Galban saw light glowing on the stone walls. But it was coming from their left. They had seen the green glow going down and right, toward the Gallery. Both men stopped and waited, their steel held ready.

But it was only three of their own men coming up the tunnel. Jerumillis, a cutthroat from the Sword Coast, led them. He held a saber in one hand and a glowing sunrod in the other.

"Douse that light, you fool!" said Galban.

Jerumillis scowled. "You care to choose your words again?"

Galban looked at the saber in Jerumillis's hand, then glanced at the two men behind him. Neither seemed particularly interested in the conflict. One was eyeing Jerumillis and looked as if he were preparing to leap aside. The other was looking past them where the light from the sunrod failed and the passage continued into the dark.

Galban sighed and said, "You care to put your light away so you don't let anyone and everyone know where we are?"

Jerumillis's scowl eased, and he slid all but the last bit of the sunrod into his sleeve. He closed his fist over the rest, plunging them into the dark. "You saw it too?"

"The green glow?" said Galban. "Yes. Bennig saw it first, then we both saw it again, headed back toward the Gallery."

"What was it?" asked one of the men behind Jerumillis.

"You tell me and we'll both know. A green light. That's all I saw."

"It scarcely seemed brighter than a firefly."

"You ever see a greenlit firefly?"

"Enough talk," said Galban. "Jerumillis, you have the saber. I suggest you go first. Everyone else fan out and follow."

"Narrow tunnels like this," said Jerumillis, "a dagger should go first. I say you go first, Galban."

There was a tense moment of silence, then Galban said, "Fine. But if I go first, *you* go last."

The five assassins spread out and began a careful, quiet walk toward the Gallery of Stone Faces. It was not a long walk, but it seemed a great distance in the dark.

Bennig felt the thunder before he heard it—a slight rhythmic hum to the air. But as they proceeded he could hear it quite clearly, and as they rounded a bend in the tunnel, he saw the flicker of lightning. Not light, really, not yet, but more of a lighter shimmer on the walls against the impenetrable dark.

They rounded the last bend in the tunnel—the gallery was no more than a few dozen paces ahead—and when they did, they saw the green glow ahead of them. Bennig was right behind Galban, and he could see the man profiled in the light. Galban stopped a moment, then continued on, his blade held behind him to keep the light from glinting off it—and to be ready to strike. Bennig followed, so close that he could have reached out and touched the tip of Gal's blade. Ahead of them, he could hear rain dripping through crevices in the gallery's ceiling.

As they entered the Gallery of Stone Faces, Bennig was able to make out more details around the green light. A statue, a crouched demonlike figure with a horned head and wide, leering lips. Its stone tail curved around, its forked tip dangling over the lip of the pedestal. Hanging from the lower fork was a necklace. Nothing lovely, it looked like no more than braided leather or perhaps a rough thong, but the small stone on the end of it gave off a faint green glow.

Lightning flashed outside, sending down a few shafts of bright white light that disappeared as quickly as they'd come. Thunder shook the gallery, a great explosion that faded into a rumble down the mountain.

"Oh, damn," said Galban, and knelt a few feet before the statue.

Bennig stepped around him and saw the reason for Galban's curse. By the green glow, Bennig could clearly see smears of something dark along the stone and floor. It was impossible to tell for certain in the green light, but Bennig thought it looked like blood.

"What is it?" said Jerumillis as he entered the gallery last. He opened his fist slightly, and a bit of the sunrod's light leaked from his fingers. The light was meager at best, but in the green-tinged gloom of the gallery, it seemed a small sliver of the sun. As the light spread about the nearest of the statues and the back wall, Bennig saw them—two pale eyes watching from above the doorway to the main passage, and around the eyes the dark mass of a figure.

Bennig drew in a breath, but then the eyes dropped. "Jeru—!" Bennig shouted, then he saw the flare of a cloak, and Jerumillis went down beneath it, and the sunrod's light with him. The light in the cavern was again only the faint green glow.

The other assassins cried out. One scrambled away, but Galban and another man ran for Jerumillis. Bennig followed them, opening his eyes wide to adjust to the dim light.

"What—?" said Galban.

Bennig looked down at the body. It wasn't Jerumillis. It was Lurom, his skull over his right eye smashed in, blood caked round his face and down his chest. His mouth hung open and his eyes stared sightlessly at the comrades who had come too late for him.

"Where is Jerumillis?" said Bennig.

The man who had fled into the dark cried out, "Sound the ala—!" followed by a sharp *crack* of something heavy smashing bone. Then another sound—one Bennig had heard many times in his service for the Old Man—the sound of a body striking the floor.

The green light winked out and there was only darkness. Quick as it took him to draw a breath, hold it, and crouch, two thoughts occurred to Bennig.

One, their keys that protected them from the guardians in the Gallery of Stone Faces had failed—or someone had found a way to dampen their power. But he discounted that. If one of the guardians had been after them, all of the guardians would have been after them, and in their moments of light he hadn't seen a single one moving.

Two, someone was in the tunnels with them. Sauk and the Lady Talieth had known something was wrong and had set guards in the tunnels for a reason. A reason they hadn't explained. But Bennig realized that the reason had come, and he had to think quickly.

Two down. But Berun knew that there were three others in the room, all armed—and any number could still be lurking in the far tunnels. He'd been expecting only the three he'd seen farther up before he'd retreated back to the Gallery. Where the other two had come from, he couldn't be sure. One of the side tunnels, surely. And if there were two, there could be twenty, still waiting.

He'd been crouched on the ledge above the doorway when the guards entered. It had not been an easy climb, carrying the dead guard with him, but he knew that this was the worst place in all the mountain to be without a ward. When the guard had seen him, he'd dropped the corpse on the nearest man and followed after. He'd killed the man with the saber and took his body instead, leaving the first one, hoping it might cause some confusion among the survivors. It had, just enough for him to strike again.

He'd managed to get one man's sunrod and douse it, and after killing the leader, he'd retrieved his starstone. He had to end this quick.

The gallery lit up as lightning split the sky over the mountain, the edges of its bright light leaking through the cracks in the roof.

"There he is! By the—"

Thunder drowned out the rest.

Four guards huddled just inside the main gate of the Fortress. Two had been assigned to watch the tunnels and to sound the alarm should anyone try to pass without the proper words. The other two were to keep an eye on the grounds around the main gate. But once the storm began in earnest, the wind off the mountain driving the rain horizontally at times, all four had sought refuge just inside the tunnel. The torches set on posts just inside the gate had long since been drowned by the storm, but the brazier set inside the tunnel still gave the guards a decent light. Whatever powder Velugis had sprinkled on the coals had turned the tiny flames blue, and it kept the fire going. Three of the guards huddled near the brazier, taking comfort not only in the warmth but the light, though they all took turns complaining about the foul odor.

"What did you put on the coals, Velugis?"

Velugis, the fourth guard who stood apart from the rest, just at the edge of the circle of light, was from Thay. Beyond that, no one knew much about him, nor cared to ask. He kept to himself most of the time, shut up in his rooms when not on assignment. Word around the Fortress was that he never even asked for one of the slaves for his bed, and he never drank anything but water. But one thing everyone knew was that Velugis was a master of potions and poisons, second only to the Old Man himself.

He turned his head a bit, not so much to look at his companions as to make sure his voice was heard. "Just something to keep the coals going in the damp. They burn hot, yes?"

"Hot, yes. Like hot horse piss. Is there nothing you can do about the stench?"

"I do have something I could sprinkle on the coals," said Velugis. "A powder of my own design. It would burn with the scent of honeysuckle."

"Well, let's have it then," said one of the other men.

"I think not."

"Why not?"

Lightning struck somewhere up the mountain, bathing the Fortress in harsh light for a moment. The ensuing thunder was so loud that it drowned out even the sound of the wind and rain.

"Because those sweet fumes would kill you within five beats of your heart." Velugis turned again to face the darkness.

The three guards muttered amongst themselves a moment, occasionally sparing a withering glance at the Thayan.

"Why you standing over there, Velugis? Don't care for our company?"

"Two reasons," said Velugis. "First of all, we *are* supposed to be standing guard. And second, the coals *do* smell like scalded horse piss."

"You aren't cold?"

Velugis said nothing, but his posture went suddenly very stiff and he leaned forward into the darkness.

"Hey! You hear me, Velugis?"

The Thayan drew his dagger with one hand and reached into his large belt pouch with his other. "Someone is coming," he said.

The other three men spread out and drew their own weapons. Two had heavy cudgels and the third a sword.

More thunder rumbled from somewhere far off on the eastern grasslands. When it faded, all four men could hear it—footsteps coming up the tunnel.

Velugis stepped back amongst the other three, so that all four guards blocked the tunnel.

"Who approaches?" called out the guard with the sword.

No answer.

More lightning struck, and if anyone answered from the darkness, they could not be heard over the thunder.

"Name yourself!" the swordsman called.

A man stumbled into the light cast by the brazier. He wore no cloak or coat, and his left sleeve was a bloody tattered mess. It was hard to tell ripped cloth from shredded skin, but the sliver of bone protruding from his forearm was quite clear. What had once been his left eye now hung out of the socket, and the entire left side of his face was a cut and torn wreck.

He looked at the four guards with his remaining eye, which went wide, then he fell to his knees.

"Oh, gods," the man said. "Sound the alarm. Hurry!"

Part Four

✠

The Old Man of the Mountain

✚

chapter Thirty

25 Tarsakh, the Year of Lightning Storms (1374 DR)
Sentinelspire

The door between the balcony and the room opened, and for a moment it was Lewan's mother who stood there, outlined by fire.

Death comes. When death comes for you, you must see clearly. You must not run. You must find your courage.

But then the dream faded. His mother was gone—many years gone—and it was Ulaan standing there, the thick fur coverlet from the bed wrapped around her shoulders, a dim, flickering light outlining her. Not the light of burning thatch and timber—she had lit a lamp in the room behind her, its yellow glow weak and guttering from the wind of the storm.

"What's happening?" asked Lewan as he struggled to bring his mind out of the dream and back into the world around him.

"The Fortress is under attack." Ulaan's voice held a slight tremble.

"Attack? I—?"

"Those horns are the call to arms," she said. "Please come inside, Lewan. We should lock the doors."

Lewan stood and gathered his blankets. He was dripping wet, his hair sodden and clinging to his forehead, and his blankets were heavy with water. How had he slept through such a storm? Still, his body felt strangely hot. Not fevered, for he felt strong and full of vigor.

"Lewan, *please* come inside."

He did, and Ulaan pushed the balcony doors closed behind him. Lewan's mind still felt foggy.

The knob of the hallway door rattled, startling Lewan. Finding the door locked, whoever was on the outside pounded on the heavy wood. "Open!"

Lewan recognized Sauk's voice.

"Open the door or I'll kick the damned thing down!" said Sauk.

Lewan looked to Ulaan. She stood very still, huddled up to her chin in the blanket, a look on her face like a denned rabbit who can hear the fox coming down the hole.

"Stay here," said Lewan, though he wasn't sure where else she could go.

He walked to the door, raised the iron crossbar, and twisted the latch that opened the main lock. He reached for the knob, but the door flew open before he could twist it. The edge of it caught him in the knee as Sauk pushed his way in. The half-orc's skin was flushed, his hair and clothes wet, and he held his short sword in one hand.

"You're wet," said Sauk, looking Lewan up and down. "And already dressed, I see. Well and good. You're about to get wetter." He grabbed the front of Lewan's shirt and dragged him from the room.

"My boots!" Lewan protested.

"No time," said Sauk, and threw Lewan in front of him. When Lewan tried to stop, Sauk pushed him onward.

"Lewan!" Ulaan called. He looked back and saw her standing in the open doorway.

"Go inside and bar the door!" he said, then Sauk pushed him round the bend in the hallway. Even if the half-orc had not held two feet of naked steel in his hand, Lewan knew he would be no match for Sauk, so he went along. "Where are you taking me?" he asked.

"Out," said Sauk.

"Why? What's going on?"

"Someone made it inside the walls," said Sauk as they walked down the stairs. Sauk took them two at a time and saw to it that Lewan did the same. "Got through the guardians on the mountain and inside the tunnels. Took out the guards we set—either killed 'em or hurt 'em so bad that they wished they were dead." A feral smile lit the half-orc's face. A wolf's smile. "Only two people alive know the tricks of the tunnels and could do all that."

"I don't understand. Who—?"

"Me, for one."

"And the other?"

"Kheil."

"Kheil is dead."

Sauk snorted. "Berun, then."

"Berun died too. You saw it yourself."

They reached the main floor and Sauk forced them into a slow run. "That man cheated death once already," he said. "Looks like he's back again. Damned if Talieth wasn't right."

The obvious question hit Lewan then. "Why drag me out?" He gave Sauk's short sword a meaningful look.

Sauk stopped at the door. Hand on the lever, he turned and grinned at Lewan. "Kheil's a killer, a hunter. You want to catch a hunter, you put out the thing he's hunting."

"You mean bait," said Lewan.

"I mean you." Sauk pulled open the door and dragged Lewan out into the storm.

They were not alone. A group of five, cloaked against the weather, waited for them at the bottom of the stairs.

Talieth stepped forward and eyed Lewan, but she spoke to Sauk. "Did you have to drag him out bootless?"

"You said hurry," said Sauk. "I hurried."

"No matter." She looked to Lewan, her hood up against the rain. The lamps set to either side of the door gave off ample light, and he could see her face, could see the regal look she turned on him. It was not the look of a benevolent queen, but of a ruler ready and eager to pronounce judgment. "What happened on the mountainside today," she said, "what you saw, what you were told. We will speak of it later. At length. For now, you're with us."

"I won't help you capture him." There. Lewan had said it, though it took all of his courage. He half expected to be slapped, maybe even beaten to submission and tossed over Sauk's shoulder.

Instead, Talieth turned to face him and said, "I'm not out to capture your master, Lewan. I'm out to stop him from doing more foolishness. He's already killed several of my men. I'm hoping that your presence will be a . . . calming influence upon him."

"But," said Sauk, and he laid the full weight of one hand on Lewan's shoulder, "you *are* coming with us. One way or the other. Don't make it the hard way."

"Truly spoken," said Talieth, and she turned away. Her men followed in her wake. Sauk pushed Lewan after her, and he followed. For now.

The first sight of the Tower of the Sun only increased Lewan's fear. The physical layout of the Tower seemed unchanged since the last time he'd looked upon it. But something set Lewan's teeth on edge, almost as if the Tower hummed at an octave just out of his range of hearing. It had a . . . *presence* to it. Something inside that tower was watching him.

As they drew closer, Lewan saw the lights. Like bits of mist that glowed, the lights filled the garden in the courtyard below the Tower. Lewan had no gift for the arcane, but even he could recognize magic of this magnitude. Some of the lights were no larger than fireflies, but some were big as faces, and they seemed all too watchful as they wafted soundlessly through the boughs and climbed the Tower like sparks lifted by the heat of a fire.

"I don't like this," one of the guards muttered.

"Be silent," Talieth ordered him. She led the way round the wall to the main gate.

Six men stood before the entrance, and Lewan could see the eldritch lights reflecting off bare steel in their hands. Talieth walked up to them, and they bowed before her.

"Lady Talieth," said one of them—a pale-haired man with a rapier. His bow deepened, but he did not put away the blade.

"Erluk, is it?" said Talieth.

"Yes, my lady. At your service."

"Why are you here? Has the Old Man ordered you to stand watch?"

"No, my lady. When we heard the alarm—"

"You were to take your stations." She cast her gaze over the other men. "*All* of you. So I ask you again: why are you here?"

Two of the men looked down at their feet, but the others only stiffened, and Lewan saw one of them flexing his hand around a thick dagger. This did not bode well.

"Forgive me, Lady Talieth," said Erluk. "We thought it best to see to the Old Man's safety."

"You thought it best?" said Talieth.

"Yes. I did."

Erluk held her gaze, and by the looks her guards gave, Lewan knew he was not the only one to notice the omitted *my lady*.

"The Old Man rules the Fortress," said Talieth, "and the Tower is his inviolate domain. But *I* order the blades of Sentinelspire. As you can see, I have brought men to guard the Tower. You men will go to your stations. Now."

"Our place is here," said one of the men behind Erluk.

"Is it?" said Talieth.

Erluk opened his mouth to answer, but before he could, Sauk struck. The half-orc thrust Lewan aside and brought his short sword down into the space where Erluk's neck joined his shoulder. The sheer force of the blow slammed Erluk to the ground. His comrades were so stunned that Sauk's follow-through, a backhand strike, beheaded the man stepping away from Erluk before the others had even raised their weapons.

It was over in moments. Talieth's guards struck down three others, almost with ease, while a sole survivor fled for the open gate. He made it no more than a half-dozen steps before a dusky shadow hit him from behind. Taaki bore the man to the ground with her claws. Her jaws grabbed the screaming man by the back of his neck. Lewan heard the bone snap and the man went limp.

Talieth had barely moved through the entire confrontation. She looked at the six corpses lying in pools of blood and said, "Throw them in the foliage and take your positions. Lewan, you are with me."

✠

chapter thirty-one

The Fortress had changed since Berun had last seen it nine years ago. The buildings, statues, and canals were much the same. The interior had always been verdant—cultivated gardens, fountains, flowers, and fruit in every street—but the greenery inside the walls was lush to the point of choking out the stone. Some structures were completely encased in vines. The building that had once been used to house prisoners was now roofless, one wall fallen, and trees grew in the midst of the floor. Even the youngest of them stood well above the building's walls.

In that crumbling, brush-infested building, Berun hid, huddled with his back against the wall, the branches of an oak keeping the worst of the rain off him. Perch clung to his forearm beneath his cloak. The treeclaw lizard was shivering, partially from the wet and cold and partially from the excitement. When the last tunnel guard had made it past Berun and fled, Perch had gone after him. The lizard hadn't been able to stop the man, but barring a particularly talented healer or cleric, the man would be no threat to anyone for many days to come.

The alarm horns had stopped some time ago, but the streets were thick with patrols. Berun had already been forced to kill three more people since entering the walls. They'd been cloaked against the rain, and in the dark he hadn't been able to see any of their features, but the last one Berun had taken down . . . in the instant before the hammer cracked the skull, Berun could have sworn that the voice crying out was a woman's. He could still hear that final desperate shriek ringing out in his mind, then cut short. His arm still felt the shock that had rattled through the hammer and up to his shoulder.

Berun took a deep breath and squeezed his eyes shut. Part of him wanted to throw the hammer into the brush and sneak out of the Fortress again. Killing all those people with the hammer and the blade Lebeth had given him, it had felt . . . *good*. And that scared him. Scared him more than anything had ever scared him. Kheil had reveled in blood. Seeing the last light of life leave his victims' eyes had once brought a pleasure beyond any spiritual bliss or sexual delight. It had been the closest he had ever known to defining true ecstasy. But Kheil was dead. Dead and gone. Executed. *Justly* executed, he told himself. Stabbed and sliced and bled out on the Tree of Dhaerow.

But life had brought him back. No, not life. That didn't quite describe it. The sheer power of *Livingness,* of all living things, had pulled him back, had put breath into his lungs and hot blood pumping through his veins. Berun—and Berun alone, not Kheil—knew one thing more than he had ever known anything: the absolute preciousness of life. He knew it, though he doubted he could put words to it. *Love* was the closest word he could find—the love for life had been imprinted on his consciousness. Death was cheap. Worse, it was easy. Life . . . there was no price for it. That his heart now beat fast and his breath came quick at the thought of killing, of taking the lives of others . . .

All your life you have dealt death. Now the god of life calls you. Time to answer. The words spoken so long ago. Master Chereth's low voice, just beginning to rasp with the onset of old age.

Then another voice, softer and warmer and more recent—
*Beware, son of the Oak Father. Even truth can deceive, when the
seeker walks darkened paths.*

Crouched in a crumbling building in the night, listening to the storm and the cries of the patrols looking for him,
smelling the blood of dead men mixing with the sweat and
rain on his skin and cloak, Berun felt as if he were on a very
dark path indeed. He felt . . . lost.

The temptation to flee was strong. The assassins knew he
was inside the Fortress. They were hunting him inside the
walls. It would be all too easy to make it back through the tunnels where they wouldn't be looking for him, to find his way
down the mountain and disappear into the Endless Wastes.

But there was Lewan. Somewhere in this Fortress, Lewan
was still a prisoner. If there was even a sliver of hope that the
boy was alive, Berun knew he had to find him and help him.

Never had Berun felt so confused. So frightened. Finding
Lewan and fleeing would change nothing. He had died to the
life of an assassin. Had he been raised to life, tried so hard to
make a new life, only to find himself being used to kill again?
Whether it was the Old Man, paying him in pleasure and
profit for his skills, or the Oak Father, cloaking his actions
in terms like justice and vengeance and the Balance . . . it all
amounted to the same thing: he was here to kill. The fact that
he found himself enjoying it only frightened him all the more.
In his heart of hearts, he had hoped for more, wanted to believe
that there was more purpose to his life than killing.

Sauk would have laughed at that notion. Life was struggle,
death the ultimate reward for everyone. To balk at killing only
meant that you stood a good chance of getting your reward a
lot sooner than most. To hunt and kill the strong only made
you stronger.

It was true, Berun knew, but as his master had been so fond
of telling him, it was only one leaf on a branch on a tree whose
roots ran very deep. And so, Berun sat in the dark, listening

and trying his best to see the rest of the tree—maybe even glimpse the forest—and so find the Balance.

Berun, you must help me. Chereth's words, sent to him in a vision. *Come to me, my son.*

And the words of Lebeth. *To see the light, child of the Oak Father, to protect light for us all, you must bring vengeance to the Tower of the Sun.*

"To see the light," Berun said to himself. He needed that now more than he ever had. "So be it."

Berun took a deep breath, steeling himself, and prodded the link he shared with Perch. *Ready, Perch?*

The Tower of the Sun was not far from where he hid. One tree-lined garden, a low wall, and a building separated him from the great spire.

Ready eat-and-eat then sleep-sleep. Tired-tired-so-tired.

"Me, too," Berun whispered.

Eat and sleep soon-soon?

Lightning flashed in the distance. Berun saw the light flickering off the ruined walls and leaves in their midst.

Soon, I hope. We must hunt a while still. Then sleep.

It occurred to Berun that the sleep he might be walking into was the eternal sleep, but he tried not to let that thought seep through to Perch.

Thunder rolled over the Fortress. He felt Perch's claws flex, piercing his shirt and pricking his skin. *Hunt-hunt.*

Yes, hunt-hunt. Perch, I need you to look. Search the shadows. Search the leaves and trees. Find the tiger.

Malicious glee surged through Berun's mind from Perch. He couldn't help but smile. The treeclaw lizard had developed a most intense dislike for Taaki. Spiders knew their match and did their best to get away, fighting only when cornered. Perch had never fought a creature as large as Taaki that would hunt and fight back with such ferocity. The lizard might have been afraid of the tiger at first, but twice he had faced her and won. The victories had filled his little heart with an eager boldness.

The link Berun shared with the lizard flooded his mind with emotions and images—*Fight-fight tiger. Claw and bite and leap-leap and claw-claw-fun-fun-fun!*

Only if you have to, Berun told Perch. With his bow and poisoned arrows long gone, his only hope was to avoid the tiger. His hammer would only anger her. The bone knife might bite deep, but for him to get close enough to use it, the tiger would have to be on top of him, and it would hardly matter how deep his blade bit if that happened.

Perch crawled out from under Berun's cloak and scampered away, all the while giving off a constant chatter of *tiger-tiger-tiger-hunt-tiger-fight-fight-tiger-tiger-tiger.*

"Yes," Berun said to himself, "time to hunt."

Nine years ago, the Fortress of the Old Man had been well lit, even at night. Torches burned in sconces along pathways. Slaves tended braziers where the larger paths crossed, and in the gardens and along the main thoroughfares, oil lamps burned behind colored glass. But tonight, under the storm, the pathways were dark. Wind and rain had doused the torches and braziers, the slaves hid indoors, and the oil burned low in the lamps, casting only weak puddles of light. Shadows welled thick in the fortress, and Berun stayed in them as best he could.

He skirted the tree-lined garden and went round several smaller outbuildings so he could approach the Tower of the Sun from the east. The entrance to the tower's courtyard and the main doors were to the west, but Berun knew they would be well guarded. Better to have a look around first.

His first sight of the tower up close stunned him.

Nine years ago, carefully tended fruit trees, a few fountains, and stone benches had filled the courtyard. All were gone. A small forest ringed the base of the Tower, the trees, vines, and creepers topping the courtyard wall and spilling onto the path outside. The trees swayed in the wind and millions of leaves trembled beneath the onslaught of the rain. But within the boughs and drifting overhead round the lower stories of the tower were dozens of bluish-green lights, wispy round the edges, their light undimmed by the rain. Far too large to be fireflies they floated without sound and seemed completely impervious to wind and rain, moving of their own accord. Berun sensed nothing natural in those lights.

Look-look-look! The message from Perch hit Berun so strong and sudden that his vision blurred and he swayed on his feet. He leaned against the building and closed his eyes.

You've found the tiger? Berun asked.

Found tiger. And others-others-others. Found big-big two-legs brother of tiger.

Sauk? Berun asked. Names meant little to Perch. He recognized his own and a few beyond that, but Berun sent the knowledge of the half-orc in a way that the lizard could understand. *Big two-legs with long hair.*

Yes-yes-yes. Big-big two-legs smells like death. He has little two-legs brother! Has him! Has him!

Berun's eyes snapped open.

Where, Perch? Tell me where!

"You're certain he'll come here?" Talieth asked Sauk.

Talieth and Sauk stood just outside the open gateway of the courtyard of the Tower of the Sun, the vines and flowers on the wall dripping rain into puddles behind them. Still barefoot, cloakless, and thoroughly soaked, Lewan stood just in front of Sauk. He was shivering, and his feet felt cold as winter river stones.

Sauk didn't take his eyes off the shadows of the far buildings and gardens. In the pouring rain, and cool as it was, he still stood without cloak or coat. His canvas shirt had soaked up all the rain it could, and water poured off him in a steady stream. He didn't seem to mind. "Only two things he's coming for—the old druid and this young one. One way or the other, he'll make his way here."

Talieth turned and looked behind them. Under her long cloak and deep hood, Lewan could only see the tip of her chin. The wispy lights haunted the trees and wound their way around the tower. Something about the shadows in the trees seemed . . . watchful. "I don't like being this close," she said. "We're taking an awful risk."

"You really think that being farther from the tower would do any good if the Old Man wanted to stop us?"

Talieth turned her back on the tower. She was silent for a while, then said, "Taaki can't find him?"

"She could," said Sauk. "But we want him to talk, not fight. Yes?"

"Of course."

"Then Taaki stays where she is."

"Where is she?" asked Lewan, turning his head to look at the half-orc.

"Don't you worry about that." Sauk still had one hand firmly on the boy's shoulder. "You cold?"

"Yes," said Lewan.

"Worse things than being cold." Sauk smiled, and when he saw Lewan blanch, his smile broadened. "Think warm thoughts. I'm sure Ulaan will be willing to—"

Sauk grunted—every last bit of air in his lungs exploding out at once—and pitched forward into Lewan.

The lights gave off neither heat nor cold and made no sound—and they made Berun nervous. He'd scaled the eastern courtyard wall of the Tower of the Sun—an easy task with all the thick vines and foliage encasing the wall—and dropped into the greenery beyond. To call the garden overgrown would have been to call the ocean wet. It was an uncontrolled mayhem of growth—trees, shrubs, untrimmed hedges, buds, early spring fruit, vines, and creepers of every sort. The lights played amongst them, shedding their unnatural light within the greenery.

They never came very close to Berun, and none seemed to linger for long. Still, the lights made his skin crawl. Worse was the deeper darkness of the shadows—especially up in the trees. Nine years in the wild had taught Berun to trust his instincts, and he knew from the first moment he set foot inside the courtyard that he was being watched. But there was no help for it. He knew for certain that Sauk, Taaki, and at least half a dozen men were spread around the main entrance to the courtyard. To have any chance of getting to Lewan before he was surrounded, Berun's only hope was to come at them from behind, charge fast, and hit hard.

Berun took his time, making his way through the foliage to the western side of the tower and the main gate. Although the trees and brush were thick enough to hold off the worst of the rain, the way before him seemed strangely clear of branches and vines. Even the wet grass and leaves beneath his feet were soft, so his footfalls made little noise. The only sound was the rain pattering on the canopy overhead, dripping down the leaves, and a steady stream of water than ran down the sides of the tower itself.

There.

About ten paces from where Berun crouched under the shadows of an oak bough, Sauk stood just outside the main gate, one hand on Lewan's shoulder in front of him. Another figure, cloaked and hooded against the weather, stood to the side.

Berun untied his hammer's leather strap from around his wrist. He knew that Sauk's senses were exceedingly sharp. He'd have to risk a throw rather than a charge. Carefully so as to minimize the sound of his sleeve rustling against his cloak, Berun brought his left arm out, tightened his grip around the haft of the hammer, brought his arm back—

—and hesitated.

At one time, Sauk had been his . . .

No. Not Berun's. Sauk had been Kheil's friend. More than just a friend. Blood brothers. Sworn to live and die for one another. Dead Kheil might be, but his memories lived in Berun, and Berun knew that Sauk was a hunter who reveled in the chase, in the kill, and had no remorse for most who had died by his hand. But there was little malice in him. Sauk did not prey upon the weak. To hunt and kill those weaker than himself was the utmost shame to Sauk, and he refused to take part in it.

Kheil had been there many times when Sauk stood in the way of the Old Man's blades, refusing to let them kill for killing's sake, because there was no honor in it. Sauk stalked and killed to prove himself, to test himself against stronger foes. And, Berun knew, to fight the demons that haunted his past—growing up among orcs who derided him, under a father who despised him, and amidst brothers who recognized how much better he was than them and hated him for it. Had Sauk not fallen under the wing of the Old Man, had his fate taken him under brighter skies, Berun knew that Sauk could have been a great force for good in the world. Perhaps even a hero.

And so Berun hesitated.

All that stood between him and Lewan was Sauk and whoever was under the cloak. More assassins were likely scattered nearby, hiding in the shadows, but if he could remove Sauk and his companion from the situation, he and Lewan could lose the others.

Easier said than done. Incapacitating a foe quickly was not as easy as bards' tales told. A knock to the head that fell too lightly might only annoy a very dangerous foe. Too heavy, and

mark sehestedt

you could just as easily kill your target as knock him out. And despite everything that had happened over the past tenday, despite the blood he had already spilled that night, Berun could not bring himself to strike at Sauk. Not to kill.

If he could strike the soft tissue between Sauk's jaw and left ear, it would daze the half-orc at the very least. Might even knock him unconscious if he hit with enough force. But again, too much, and it might kill him.

Berun closed his eyes and offered a silent prayer to the Oak Father, adjusted his grip on the hammer, swung it round once to gain momentum, and threw.

Sauk was halfway through a sentence. "I'm sure Ulaan will be willing to—"

—and the weighty stone head of the hammer struck.

Sauk pitched forward, his knees buckling. Lewan stood just to one side and so barely managed to avoid being crushed under the falling half-orc. Berun was moving even before Sauk hit the ground.

The cloaked figure beside Sauk gasped and turned. Hearing Berun's approach—perhaps even seeing the eldritch light glinting off his blade—the figure looked up.

"Kheil, no!"

Berun turned his strike just in time. The blade sliced through the fabric of the figure's hood but missed the throat within. Even after nine years, he recognized the voice at once. It was Talieth.

Berun heard footsteps approaching from the surrounding paths. Several shapes were coming out of hiding from buildings across the street. Berun caught the blur of an arrow just in time. He bowed to the side and heard the *whisk* of the arrow go past his head before it shattered against the wall behind him.

Talieth threw her hood back and turned, both arms upraised. "Stop! I'll flay the next man who looses an arrow. Stop where you are!"

Her men obeyed.

Sauk was stirring, one hand moving to rub his neck while he struggled to his hands and knees.

Berun darted forward, grabbing Talieth from behind. With one hand around her waist, he pulled her close and set the point of his knife against her neck. "Lewan, grab that hammer and get behind me!"

"Kheil, please!" said Talieth. "You don't understand!"

Lewan stepped around Sauk, snatched up the hammer, and moved behind Berun.

"Order your men back," Berun told Talieth. Even through her heavy cloak, he could feel the shape of her body. Although his mind tried to resist, his body remembered how she felt against him so many times. To hold a knife against her now . . .

"I already ordered them back, Kheil," she said. "Now *listen*, pl—"

"You ordered them to stop. I want them gone."

Sauk stood, and from somewhere above and behind Berun, the tiger roared like thunder on the mountain.

✚

chapter Thirty-two

Ihat hurt," said Sauk, rubbing his neck and jaw with his left hand. His other hand rested on the pommel of the sword at his waist. "Definitely going to bruise."

Lewan crouched just behind his master, his heart beating a frantic rhythm in his chest as he glanced between Sauk before them, the tiger crouched on the wall above, and an array of assassins spread just beyond Talieth along the path. Every way, he and Berun were surrounded.

"Kheil never struck from behind," said Sauk. "Thought it was cowardly."

"If Kheil were here," said Berun, "you'd be dead. My—"

"Name is Berun," said Sauk. "Yes, I know."

"Stop this!" said Talieth. She spared a glance at the blade near her neck. Although both of her hands were free, she did not struggle against Berun, and her face showed no sign of fear. Even her voice sounded more angry than frightened. "Both of you! Kheil, listen to—"

"I said get those men out of here!" said Berun.

"Berun, listen to me," said Sauk, his voice much calmer than Talieth's. "Let her go and we'll talk. You continue this nonsense and I'll have Taaki take your boy."

"You'll *all* leave now," said Berun, "or I'll kill her."

"No, you won't," said Sauk. He shook his head, and the smile on his face was almost sad. "Even Kheil would never have done that—not to her. And as you have said so many times: You are not Kheil."

Lewan looked at his master. The Berun he had known would never kill a person in cold blood. But had he ever *really* known Berun? In all their years together, Berun had never once mentioned Kheil, Sauk, Talieth, the Old Man, or any of this.

"Ask your boy," said Sauk. "We have shown him nothing but kindness. Even got him a girl to warm his bed. Eh, Lewan?"

Lewan paled. The guilt and shame of his actions brought before so many was bad enough—but before his master . . . "Master Berun, I . . . I . . ."

"Berun," said Sauk, his tone soft, almost gentle, "let her go. And I swear to you on the brotherhood we once shared that no harm will come to you or Lewan. We only want to go somewhere and talk."

Lewan saw his master risk a glance up at the tiger, then survey the half-dozen assassins around them. Four had blades in hand and two held bows with arrows nocked.

"Your boy is cold," said Sauk. "I'm going to count to three, Berun. If you haven't ended this by then, I'm going to have Taaki end it. One . . ."

Lewan glanced up at the tiger. Her rear haunches twitched in preparation to strike. "Master, I—"

"Two," said Sauk—

—and Lewan heard the rustle of foliage overhead. He turned in time to see the tiger coming down on him, a huge dusky shape that in the gloom seemed to fill the sky.

Taaki hit Lewan, and he went down beneath her bulk. Had her claws been extended, Lewan surely would have had the skin and flesh ripped from his chest. Lewan hit the brick pavement hard, his eyes squeezed shut, not so much out of pain but because more than anything, he did not want to see Taaki's teeth closing round his throat.

But the tiger did not put her full weight upon him. As soon as Lewan was down, she was gone.

Lewan opened his eyes. The tiger had bounded away but was coming round again, her eyes fixed on Berun. Talieth was on the ground, and Berun was doing all he could to avoid swing after swing from Sauk's sword and fist. The half-orc was much taller than Berun, and the length of his sword gave him a much farther reach than Berun's knife. But Lewan noticed that Sauk swung with the flat of his blade—once, he managed a glancing blow off Berun's forearm.

"Sauk, stop this!" Talieth said.

The other assassins closed in, but they were hesitant to get too close to Sauk's swing. Both archers had their bows bent and fletching held to their cheeks.

"Either of you loose and you are dead!" shouted Talieth. "You men fall back! Kheil! Sauk! I command you to stop!"

The assassins stepped well back, but Sauk and Berun continued to swipe at each other. Berun ducked a swing of Sauk's fist and his blade flicked forward. When Sauk stepped back, blood ran down his forearm.

"He does still bite!" Sauk said, and renewed his attack.

Berun fell back before the onslaught, ducking and stepping away from the blade and blocking the half-orc's fist. But Lewan saw Sauk's tactic at once. The half-orc was leading Berun toward the tiger, who crouched ready just inside the open gateway of the courtyard.

"Master!" Lewan called. "Behind you! The tiger!"

Berun shifted his retreat to the right, circling away and putting Sauk between himself and the tiger.

Talieth was on her feet, her hood down and her cloak thrown back. The incessant rain had plastered her hair to her face. "Lewan, he'll listen to you. Tell him to stop this! I *swear* to you that no harm will come to you or your master."

Lewan opened his mouth and took in a breath to shout, but then he remembered the words of the Old Man on the mountainside. *Talieth and her little conspiracy . . . they are lying to you. They are using you. Do not trust them.* But had not Sauk offered—even *urged*—Lewan to flee? And there was something else, something Talieth herself had said to him earlier, something he had not been able to get out of his mind.

He didn't know what to do. He wasn't sure to whom he was speaking, but he picked up the fallen hammer, stood, and shouted, "Stop it! Just stop!"

The half-orc held his sword back, prepared for another swipe, but he did not bring it forward. He stopped and risked a glance at Lewan.

Berun used the opportunity to step back and look around, surveying the situation. Sauk hadn't moved. The surrounding assassins were keeping their distance, and Talieth stood not far from Lewan, both hands curled into tight fists.

For a moment, everyone simply looked, the only sound that of the rain in the leaves and on the pavement.

Then the tiger growled.

Berun snapped around.

Lewan saw her less than five paces from his master, crouched and ready to strike. Her lips curled over her fangs, which glowed an unearthly blue in the eldritch lights round the Tower.

The tiger's front paws had just come off the ground when a small shape struck her on the head. Perch!

Taaki's lunge turned into a fierce back and forth swing of her head as she tried to dislodge the treeclaw lizard. The tiger shrieked and slapped at her own head—but she remembered her previous injury and kept her claws retracted.

For the first few swings and shakes of her head and slaps of the tiger's paws, Perch managed to avoid the strikes by shifting his grip and twisting his own lithe body back and forth. But then the tiger rolled onto her back, scraping her head and neck along the brick pavement.

Perch bounded off just in time. Had he fled into the brush,

he would have been safe. Instead, he twisted around, rose on his hind legs, and hissed at the tiger, amazingly loud for such a small creature.

"Sauk, call her off!" Berun shouted.

The half-orc's lip had twisted into a sneer at the sight of the lizard, and he shook his head once. "Lizard took her eye," he said. "He's got this coming."

Taaki rolled onto her feet, took one look at the offending lizard—she didn't even roar—and jumped, reminding Lewan of a barn cat lunging on a mouse. Perch avoided the first strike, but he was not quick enough to dodge the second. The tiger struck again, trapping the lizard between paw and pavement. The tiger's head ducked down. Her back faced Lewan, but he heard her massive jaws snap closed. She shook her head left and right once, then threw her head back as she swallowed the treeclaw lizard whole.

"Perch!" Berun screamed.

Sauk laughed. "Don't cry too much. Your little friend got her eye. A lot more than most of her prey get. But only the strong survive. Your little lizard never had a chance."

Sauk backed away and lowered his sword. Berun just stood, looking at the tiger.

"Stop this now," said Sauk. "Before someone else you care about gets hurt. Drop the knife. *Now.* Drop it or Taaki takes you down."

Berun stood still a moment, then he stood straight. Lewan gasped, and the hammer wavered in his hand. Was it over?

Then Berun grabbed the clasp of his cloak. A twist, and the heavy fabric fell to the ground. Unencumbered, he dropped into a defensive crouch and brandished the strange ivory blade.

"Your choice," called Sauk. He pointed his blade at Berun and told the tiger, "Taaki, *anukh!*"

The tiger came in slowly, each paw placed carefully on the wet pavement before her, her head low to the ground. Lewan knew that a knife would be no match against the tiger. He brought the hammer back, preparing to throw—if he could hit the tiger in the head, it would stun her long enough for his master to get away.

But before Lewan could throw, Taaki went still as stone. She crouched, unmoving, and Lewan counted five quick beats of his heart. Then a tremor passed through her, so violent that she sprayed thousands of tiny droplets of rain out of her fur. She twisted around, snapping at her midsection with her teeth.

"Taaki?" called Sauk, his voice thick with worry. "What's wrong?"

The tiger screamed—high, pitiful, and with such strength that Lewan flinched and covered one ear with his free hand.

"Taaki!"

The tiger bit at her side several more times, then threw herself onto her back and began to flop and writhe like a live fish thrown onto a hot pan. Again and again she screamed, drowning out Sauk's cries. She writhed and squirmed, her rear paws kicking the air, and then she clawed at her own torso with her front claws. Fur wet with rain flew—and then fur wet with blood and bits of skin—and still she screamed. Lewan had never heard such cries of agony.

A few assassins ran over. One of the archers approached Sauk, his bow in hand and arrow still on the string. He pointed it at the tiger. "Sauk, shall I—?"

Another shriek from the tiger drowned out his last words.

The bowman raised his bow, pulled shaft to cheek, and pointed the sharp steel at the tiger. Sauk snarled and cut off the man's head with one backswing of his sword. The archer's body fell one way, his head the other, and blood flew up in a great gout over his companions, who were quickly stepping back.

Talieth was screaming something, and even though she was only a few paces away, Lewan could not make out her words over the tiger's cries.

Sauk dropped his sword and tried to approach the tiger, but as soon as he came within reach of her claws, one raked across his leg, gashing a wide red swath through his trousers and skin. Grimacing in horror, he backed away.

Taaki slapped her torso with both paws three times in quick succession—with such force that Lewan was shocked he didn't hear bone snapping. Then she arched her back and let out a long, final scream that rose and rose until it was beyond human hearing. Her muscles seemed locked in that position, the middle of her back arched almost a foot off the ground, when Lewan saw it—

The torn fur and skin high up on her stomach . . . *bulged*—

—then fell back.

Her back relaxed, and she hit the pavement. Her stomach bulged again, larger this time, and kept expanding until the skin ruptured and tore. The lights hovering over the tower courtyard brightened from a pale blue to a bright green, and Lewan saw a tiny claw emerge from the torn skin. Then another, scratching and raking at the bloody flesh. The rupture widened, and Perch's horned head emerged—his skin black from blood and other fluids, but when he opened his eyes, they reflected the unearthly green light.

✙
chapter thirty-three

Sauk roared, his own cry of grief fierce as any tiger's, and raised his fist to smash the treeclaw lizard. His arm was halfway through its descent when Berun tackled him. The two combatants struck and slid across the pavement in a great splash of rain and blood.

Sauk used the momentum to throw Berun off and away. Berun hit the courtyard wall—had it not been thick with green ivy and moss, he would have had broken bones—and then fell to the ground. The half-orc scrambled for his sword, and Berun regained his feet.

Talieth turned to her men. "Stop them! Hurt them if you must, but do *not* kill them!"

But Sauk was beyond reason. The rage of a maddened beast filled him, and he came at Berun swinging with all his strength, no longer using the flat of his blade. It was all Berun could do to avoid each strike, stab, and swipe.

The assassins advanced, none of them exhibiting any enthusiasm. Lewan had no idea where Perch had gone.

Sauk and Berun's battle took them under the arch of the gateway and inside the courtyard. The lights seemed to gather round them, bathing the combatants in eerie green light.

One of the assassins ran forward and tried to grab the half-orc's free arm. "Sauk, plea—"

Sauk plunged his blade into the man's gut up to the hilt,

roared in the man's face, and pushed him away. Another man tried to grab the half-orc's sword arm, but was either too slow or Sauk's rain-soaked skin was too slick. A backhand swipe, and the man was missing a hand. Screaming and spurting blood from the stump of his wrist, the man fell back onto the pavement.

Talieth ran toward them, but stopped well out of range of the combatants.

"Sauk!" Talieth screamed. "Stop this at once! I command you!"

Sauk ignored her. Lewan wasn't sure if he'd heard her. The half-orc's face was twisted by grief and fury, and his eyes were fixed on Berun.

Talieth twisted the clasp of her cloak, threw it off, and raised both hands, her fingers twisting in an intricate pattern. She closed her eyes, took a deep breath, and said, *"Targelu engethlimek!"*

Sauk hesitated in his advance.

"Sauk," Talieth said, forcing calm into her voice. "Listen to me, Sauk. We need him."

Sauk snorted like a bull and shook his head, almost like a sleeper shaking off a fading dream. His lip twisted in a snarl, the green of the lights gleaming off his silver tusk, and he leaped at Berun.

But the distraction had given Berun time to back away. He tried to make it out of the courtyard, but one of the assassins lunged for him. Quick as a serpent, Berun's knife-hand shot forward and back, but then he had to turn to face Sauk.

The assassin lurched backward, both hands at his throat. He turned and stumbled into Lewan. The hands gripping his throat were dark with blood. He opened his mouth as if to scream, but he only made a choking sound as he fell to his knees, one hand at his throat while the other clutched at Lewan's shirt. His death grip and heavy weight pulled Lewan to his knees. The man's body was trying to breathe, but he was drowning in his own blood.

Horrified—more at his own actions than the dying man—Lewan brought his hand with the hammer around in a swing. *Crack!* went the assassin's forearm . . .

The sound of the arm breaking brought it all back to Lewan—his mother's pleading, agonized face. The look, almost of relief, in the moment before Lewan brought the black iron kettle down on her skull. That day, he'd thought all hope of happiness had left him forever. With Berun, he'd found, if not happiness, then at least hope. Perhaps even meaning. And all of that hung like a heavy stone caught on a spider's web, sinking and about to snap at any moment—

Lewan pulled himself to his feet and backed away. The assassin fell to the ground, squirming and kicking as his body fought for air that would never come.

Only two of Talieth's guards were left. One of them, holding a bow, ducked round Talieth to get a good aim. He raised it and brought the arrow to his cheek, the steel point aimed right at Berun.

All of the fear—fear at being hunted, captured, at the future of the world supposedly hanging in the balance—poured out of Lewan then in a desperate cry. He charged. The bowman adjusted his aim as Berun and Sauk's battle danced about the courtyard. Lewan brought the heavy weight of the hammer around, putting all his strength into the blow. The stone hammerhead struck the bowman's left shoulder. Bone shattered like chalk and the man went down, his arrow flying into the leaves.

The momentum of Lewan's charge would not allow him to stop, and he stumbled over the fallen archer. He managed to keep his feet, and when he'd regained his balance, he found himself face to face with the last of Talieth's guards. The man—his eyes glistening brightly under the green light—looked at the hammer in Lewan's hand, glanced at his mistress, back to the hammer, over to Berun and the half-orc . . . and then he turned and fled.

Seeing him go, Talieth turned the full weight of her gaze on Lewan. "This ends now!"

Talieth began to weave another incantation, even as Sauk brought his sword arm back for another strike. But his fist and blade caught in a thick tangle of vines dangling from an oak branch. The half-orc yanked his hand free and continued his advance.

But then Lewan saw that the half-orc had not simply tangled his hand in the vines. The greenery above and behind him was moving of its own accord—branches flexing like stiff fingers, vines and creepers writhing like charmed snakes. So intent was Sauk on killing Berun that he didn't see the danger upon him.

"Sauk, get out of there!" Talieth shouted, and Lewan realized that she had seen the slithering vines as well. Her hands stopped moving. Confusion and horror passed over her face, and Lewan realized that the moving vines were not her magic at work. This was something else.

Berun stumbled and went down. Sauk stopped, towering over Berun, and swung his sword arm back. A leafy vine shot out and wrapped around Sauk's wrist. Shocked, the half-orc pulled, but the vine held tight. Judging from the amount of blood that began to run down Sauk's arm, Lewan thought the vine must have been thick with thorns under all those leaves. Sauk reached up with his other hand to try to free the sword, but more vines snaked down, wrapping both hands together. Roaring in anger and frustration, Sauk began to thrash, trying to dislodge his arms, but he only succeeded in bringing more of the vines down upon him. In moments only his legs were visible, and then the vines contracted, lifting the half-orc up into the branches of the oak. Even after his legs disappeared into the tree canopy, Lewan could still hear the half-orc screaming and cursing.

Talieth, eyes wide and mouth hanging open, looked up where Sauk had disappeared. But then she shook her head and rushed for Berun.

"Kheil, I—"

More vines shot downward, ignoring Berun and aiming for Talieth. She shuffled backward, her hands and fingers moving in an intricate pattern. *"Gerulu tserulek!"* she shouted, then clenched her right fist and punched the air. An orange light glowed round her fist, flared, then shot forward in a shaft so bright that it burned its after image into Lewan's eyes.

The shaft of light hit the vines, and they exploded in a burst of ash and smoke. But more were coming, snaking along the ground or undulating through the air in several directions. Three more times Talieth invoked the magic and sent it shooting outward to burn and shatter the foliage. But for every strike she made, more vines took their place.

She backstepped as she struck, trying to keep the vines in sight, but one was too quick and wrapped around her left forearm. Talieth yanked at it, but the more she struggled, the more the vine tightened and pulled back, dragging her step by step into the thick foliage.

"Erbeluth draglen!" Talieth's free hand shot out, hurling a tiny ember of fire that gathered momentum as it sailed through the air. It tumbled upward, growing in strength and fury as the air around it caught fire. It was the size of a knight's shield—and still growing—when it struck the thick bank of foliage from whence most of the vines had come.

Fire caught in the leaves and branches, and the vines reaching for Talieth fell to the ground, lifeless, their ends smoldering.

His eyes had adjusted to the dim light cast by the floating orbs round the tower, and all of the sudden brightness made Lewan wince. The stench of the burning greenery filled Lewan's head, making him choke and gag. The scent was . . . *wrong* somehow, whether from the arcane flames or something twisted and unnatural in the foliage itself, Lewan did not know. Nor did he care much. He only knew it was time to leave.

"Where is he?"

As Lewan's eyes began to adjust to the light, he saw Talieth standing beside him, her hair and clothes sodden, her left arm wet with rain and blood where the thorns had raked her skin.

Lewan looked past her. There was no sign of the half-orc. The bodies of the assassins lay where they'd fallen, one man still moving feebly. The archer whom Lewan had struck with the hammer was gone, though his bow still lay on the pavement next to a haphazard pile of a half dozen arrows. He saw nothing of Berun, save the cloak he'd tossed aside. Beyond the burning brush, the light from the fire only seemed to thicken the shadows in the courtyard. But Lewan could see that the shadows were moving—and not from the fall of the rain. Talieth's spells had hurt the army of vines and creepers, but more were coming.

Lewan cried, "Lady, there—!"

Talieth whirled, bringing her right arm up to cast another spell. But it was too late. Vines shot downward, their leaves rustling like the hissing of a serpent, and wrapped around Talieth's waist. Before she could complete her invocation, more wrapped round her arms and tightened. The Lady of Sentinelspire thrashed and screamed, but like Sauk, the more she struggled the more she entangled herself. More vines wound out of the forest to grapple her.

"Kheil! Lewan! Help me!" But then she was gone, pulled out of sight into the branches.

Lewan froze, crouched under the tree, the hammer in his hand. He was too frightened to move, afraid that more vines might come for him. But none did. He could still hear thrashing overhead, Talieth and Sauk screaming. An occasional branch or leaf fell, but no more vines dangled down.

"Lewan."

He turned to see his master. With his knife still in hand, Berun rushed out of the shadows and embraced Lewan.

Lewan squeezed him back. "Master, what just happened?"

Berun pulled away. He glanced up at the boughs where Talieth and Sauk were still screaming. Then he looked back at Lewan and said, "I think they have displeased the master of this tower."

"The Old Man?"

Berun nodded. "I never knew him to possess powers such as these. It seems what Sauk told me is true. He has learned to bend my master's power to his own will."

"I've seen him, Master!" said Lewan, and it all came out in a rush. "The Old Man. He came to me. On the mountain. He said . . . he said that Talieth and Sauk were lying, that he was out to save the world. He said he needed my help, master! He—"

"Lewan," said Berun. Not a shout, but enough force to cut off Lewan's stream of words. Berun held him by the shoulders and smiled. "It is good to see you again. I feared the worst. They didn't harm you?"

"N-no, Master. They—"

"I'm sorry, Lewan," said Berun, his smile fading and his face becoming grim. "I pray you'll be able to tell me all about it later. Now, you must find someplace to hide."

"What? Where are you going?"

Berun looked up at the tower. "I was given a task. During the *Jalesh Rudra*. I must fulfill my oath."

The *Jalesh Rudra* . . . Lewan had so much to tell Berun, so many questions, so much to confess.

"I'll come with you," he said.

"No, Lewan. Listen—"

"No!" Lewan shouted. All of the terror and secrets and worry rose up in him, boiling over and turning into white-hot anger. "No, *you* listen! You can't just order me to run off and hide every time it gets dangerous. Look how that worked last time! I begged—I *begged* to go with you, but you ordered me away without so much as an explanation. I'm hunted down by a bunch of murderers looking for you, dragged off and told that everything you ever told me was a lie!"

"I never lied to you, Lewan."

"You never told me about Kheil!"

Berun flinched at that, but his heavy gaze returned to Lewan. "No. No, I didn't. But I didn't lie. Kheil died—and he *deserved* to die. Who I am now—"

"I don't *know* who you are anymore!"

Berun dropped his hands but he would not drop his gaze. "I have much the same problem."

"Then let me come with you. Whatever you're going to face in there, we can face it together."

"No, Lewan."

Above them, the screaming had stopped, though they still heard occasional thrashing.

"What makes you think you can stop me from following you?" said Lewan.

"Nothing," said Berun. "I am sorry I missed your *Jalesh Rudra*. But one thing you must learn about the difference between being a man and a child is doing the *right* thing, not the thing you want. If even half of what Sauk told me is true . . . we stand on the razor's edge. If we fail . . ." He shook his head, and his expression hardened. "Time to grow up, Lewan. You need to realize what your limitations are. I'm more proud of you than I know the words to tell, but you must understand that if you go with me, you will limit what I can do. My concern will be for you. I can't have that. I need you gone. The world needs you gone. Go to the Shalhoond and find one of the Circles. Beg for their aid."

"My place is with you," said Lewan. "To aid *you*."

"No, Lewan. Where I am going you could not aid me. My concern—my *love*—for you would only hinder me. It's going to be all I can do to stay alive in there. I can't worry about you, too."

"I'm not a child anymore."

"I know you aren't. Now it's time to make the man's choice. If I fail here—even if I succeed here—we may still need the aid of the Circles. You can find them. Tell them everything you know."

"And how do you expect me to get out?" said Lewan. "I've been through the tunnels. Without a guard warded against the guardians—"

"You've been through the Gallery of Stone Faces?"

"With Sauk," said Lewan, and he was surprised to find that he had already accepted Berun's order. How had he given in so easily? Why?

"Listen to me," said Berun. He gripped Lewan's arms again and crouched to look him eye to eye. "If you can get there quick, find one of the bodies I left behind."

"B-bodies?"

"The guards. They had keys to pass the guardians. Drag one of the bodies with you. Keep it with you on the mountain as well. As long as you can. I know it will slow you, but there are guardians on the mountainside. Once you reach the steppe, you should be safe."

"What if I can't find a body?" said Lewan. "What if others have come and taken them already?"

Berun looked at him long and hard, then glanced at the hammer in Lewan's hand. "Then you'll have to get your own. It's the only way." Berun pulled Lewan to him, holding him in a fierce embrace, then pulled away. "You've been like a son to me, Lewan. Get out alive. Get out of here and far away."

Berun turned and ran through the eldritch light-haunted courtyard to the steps of the tower. The doors had been thrown back—had they been open the whole time? Lewan wondered. Beyond lay only darkness. Lewan watched as his master disappeared into the dark, then he turned and walked away. In four steps, he was running.

✠
chapter thirty-four

As Berun entered the Tower of the Sun, the first thing that struck him was the smell. Back when he—when *Kheil*—had lived in the Fortress, the tower had been a crumbling relic, an ancient testament to the genius of the Imaskari. The Old Man had renovated the tower and put his own mark upon the place—priceless rugs, tapestries, furniture from east and west. All that was gone.

Berun left the arcane-tinted light of the courtyard and entered the first halls of the tower, and the scent hit him—the thick moist smell of growing things. He pulled the starstone necklace out of his shirt, and its green light lit the hallway about him, confirming what his nose had already told him. Vines and thick stalks of ivy, dripping in black berries, clung to the walls and hung from the ceiling. And it was not new growth. Where rugs and carpets had once covered the cold stone of the hall, at least two seasons' worth of old leaves now made a sort of dry carpet that rustled and shifted with his every step. Berun knelt and swept aside the leaves until he found the floor beneath. Moss and lichen covered the stone beneath the leaves, some of it old enough that it had already begun to crumble the stone. Not far ahead, the shoot of a young tree broke through the rock. How it thrived without sunlight or rain was mystery, but its branches were thick with new spring leaves.

Berun stood and began to make his way forward. The

tower had dozens of rooms—some only small storage rooms, while others took up an entire floor. Chereth could be in any of them or in the warren of cells beneath the tower. But Berun knew he had to deal with the Old Man first. Once that was done, he could find Chereth, but until the Old Man was dealt with, neither he nor his master would be safe.

He took the stairway on the left, which hugged the wall of the tower as it wound up to the next floor. As his foot touched the first step, the large double doors at the entrance slammed shut behind him. Berun jumped at the noise and stood stock still, ready in case something else happened. But only a few leaves, shaken loose from the vines by the force of the blow, fluttered to the ground.

Berun turned to the stairs before him. Stealth, at this point, seemed foolish. The Old Man would have to be either deaf or dead not to have heard the fight outside. But the vines that had come to his rescue, entangling Sauk and Talieth . . .

He'd inferred to Lewan that the Old Man had done that. But had he? If so, why? Why aid Berun against Sauk and his own daughter? If the Old Man was truly aware of the conspiracy then why not catch Berun as well? If he knew that Sauk and Talieth were conspiring against him, then surely he knew they had approached Berun in hopes of securing his aid. And surely the Old Man knew why Berun had come. Why help him now?

Was he wrong about the vines? If it had been Chereth who helped him in the Khopet-Dag, sending the earth spirit and the vision, then could not it have been Chereth who captured Sauk and Talieth outside? If his master could still wield such power, why hadn't he escaped? Where did that leave the Old Man?

Only one way to find out, Berun told himself, but before he continued forward, he quieted his mind and prodded that deep corner linked to the treeclaw lizard.

Perch?

Nothing.

Perch, are you well? Where are you?

Ever so faintly, like the last fading sound of an echo, Berun felt his friend respond. The lizard was outside in the courtyard. The leaves and vines taking on a life of their own had thoroughly unsettled Perch, and he was huddled deep inside the den of a trapdoor spider. The den's owner had provided the lizard with a welcome meal to refresh his energies. *Killed the tiger!* Perch was ecstatic. *Tiger swallowed this Perch. Claw-and-bite-and-claw-claw-claw out of the wet darkness.*

Yes, you did, Berun told him. *You killed the tiger, my friend. Well done.*

More fight-fight?

Not now, Perch. Rest. You have earned it.

Perch was strangely silent for a moment. Berun sensed something unusual in his friend. Something almost like pensiveness, which had never existed in the frantic treeclaw lizard. *Look and smell and listen and taste-taste the air. Big stone tree*—Perch's understanding of the Tower—*smells rot-rot.*

I'll be careful, Berun told him, and continued up the stairs.

The second floor—a series of rooms arranged like spokes round the hub of a wheel—proved much like the first. Thick vegetation crowded every surface, even the floor on which Berun walked. Passing by a window, Berun caught the faint glow of the lights outside, but the window was so choked with vines and waxy green leaves that he could see outside only through tiny gaps in the foliage.

Berun kept going up. At the top of the stairs, a door blocked the way between the last step of the second floor and the main landing of the third. Berun tested the latch. It creaked like moist iron that had not seen oil in far too long, but it opened. He pushed it, and in the hall beyond, he heard small things scuttling away through the foliage. Keeping his knife ready in one hand, he held forth the starstone into the hall. Only an empty hall, also covered in leaves, vines, and twisting branches that clung to the stone. Some of the leaves moved, as insects and small lizards fled from Berun's light.

He entered the hall. The foliage was even thicker, the footing uncertain, for the floor was a mass of thick, woody vines with clusters of long leaves shaped like double-edged blades. It seemed that the farther he went up the tower, the thicker the vegetation became, almost as if it had grown from the top of the tower down.

The door closed behind him. Not a slam this time. But he heard it creak shut, and when he turned to look, three woody vines were falling away from the door, like arms going back to rest after having done their duty.

The knife in Berun's hand went suddenly cold, like grabbing an icicle through silk gloves. When he turned to face the hall, eyes were watching him from the darkness just beyond the reach of his light. Three sets of eyes—he saw one of them blink slowly—reflected his starstone's light back at him. Two glowed from about a man's height to either side of the hallway, but the third set—slightly farther back—was looking at him from near the ceiling. From their odd angle, Berun realized that the watcher was hanging upside down, as if clinging to the vines.

Everything around Berun seemed to come into sharp focus, and although his heartbeat did not increase, it beat with a stronger rhythm, and his breath came in deeper draughts, as if his body were seeking to draw in and sort every scent. Berun recognized his body's reaction at once. Fear. The old childhood fear of the dark and the unknown, the first true emotion he'd understood as an orphan on the streets of Elversult. As a young man under the tutelage of the Old Man of the Mountain, Kheil had learned to harness that fear and ride it into a formidable aggression. *Take your fear and give it to your enemies,* Alaodin had told him. *Make them fear the dark. Make* them *fear the night. You must become fear. You must become the night.*

Berun crouched and brought the knife up into a guard position. Another set of the eyes blinked. Berun brought back his hand holding the starstone, intending to throw it farther into the hall so it would bathe the three watchers in light while leaving him in shadow. But in the instant before his arm came forward, he felt something wrap round his forearm and constrict. He tried to pull away, but the grip tightened, and another snaked around his right leg up to his knee. He looked down and saw that the vines were wrapping round him, just as they had around Sauk and Talieth in the courtyard.

He slashed at the vines with his knife. The blade cut through them as easily as a new razor parting cobwebs, but even as he pulled his arm free, more vines rose up, grabbing both arms and then his waist. He managed one more slash before his knife arm was caught. The feeling of the vines and leaves moving against him, gentle but unyielding, almost brought a scream to his throat. But the sound of the vines was the worst. The leaves rustled and hissed, not like a breeze through boughs, but more like a snake through spring grass.

The more Berun struggled, the tighter the vines squeezed, and more came, detaching from the walls and ceiling, even rising from the floor. In moments his entire body was wrapped up to his chin, though the starstone still dangled from its leather cord in his fist. The vines tightened and pulled, lifting his feet from the ground so he was suspended from the ceiling. He hung there, slightly swaying, like a dressed pheasant hung from the eaves.

From out of the darkness, the eyes came forward, and as they entered the nimbus of green light cast by the starstone, Berun saw their true forms. Berun's first thought was that they were elves, but he dismissed that almost at once. Their ears had sharp points like elves, and their eyes were angled so as to gather even the faintest light. But their limbs were lithe and too long for elves, and the tint of their skin was only a shade lighter than the surrounding foliage. All three were male. Two of them walked, and they moved as if their joints did not fit together in the usual fashion. The third was creeping along the ceiling, either holding onto or being held aloft by the thick vegetation. As they came near, Berun caught their scent. It reminded him of a rain-freshened breeze blowing through spring blossoms. But there was an undercurrent, too, something bestial and primal.

The two walkers stood in front of him, the third still hanging from the ceiling, all watching him, expressing neither malice nor compassion. Merely curiosity. The one on Berun's left reached out and plucked the knife from his hand. Holding it with both hands, he closed his eyes, brought the knife just under his nose, and inhaled, like a nobleman testing the bouquet of a fine wine. As he did so, the fine etchings of vines and leaves that ran along the blade glinted green, then faded to a glow, almost as if a spark had lit in dry leaves before fading to an ember.

The creature opened his eyes and smiled at Berun. But there was no humor or goodwill in the smile, merely a drawing back of the lips over teeth that were pointed and sharp. Quick as a scorpion's tail, the creature's hand flicked out with the dagger, drawing a shallow gash across Berun's cheek. Berun winced and tried to pull away, but the vines held him fast. The creature reached out with one finger, wiped a bit of the blood, then brought the redness to his tongue. His companion stepped forward and did the same, but the one on the ceiling only watched.

"What are you?" Berun asked.

The one holding the knife cocked his head at Berun, but did not reply.

"They are called killoren," came a voice from the darkness. A voice Berun recognized.

Berun heard the sound of footsteps along the leafy floor, and a figure emerged from the shadows. A cloaked figure in a deep hood. In the dimness of the hall, the fabric seemed dark as winter pine needles.

"Ashai!" said the three creatures. The two standing drew back from Berun, and the one on the ceiling dropped to the floor. All three bowed.

The figure ignored them and stood before Berun. Two hands emerged from the folds of the cloak and pulled down the hood, revealing a wizened face, hardened by the years, but still the face Berun knew.

"Welcome to my tower, Berun," said Chereth. "I have missed you, my son."

✛
chapter Thirty-Five

Lewan ran, his bare feet slapping the brick pavement and splashing through puddles. The paths through the fortress were dark, many of the braziers and torches having been drowned out by the rain. The worst of the storm had blown over, fading to a steady drizzle. Running through a garden, a contingent of guards ordered him to stop, but he only slowed, yelling, "The Lady Talieth and Sauk are trapped in the courtyard of the Tower of the Sun! I'm going for help," and he ran on, hoping that the guards did not follow him.

They didn't, and Lewan ran on, though he did not go to the main gate as his master had commanded. Instead, he ran back to the tower where he'd been staying. He took the front steps three at a time, threw open the doors, and continued up the inner stairs and down the hall to his room.

The door was locked. "Ulaan! Ulaan, it's me, Lewan. Let me in."

He heard her work the locks, then the door opened. She stepped out and embraced him. "Oh, Lewan, what happened? You're drenched! I was so worried."

Lewan pushed past her. "Do I have any dry clothes?"

"Yes," she said, closing the door behind her. "Why?"

"We're leaving. Tonight. Now. Where are the clothes?"

"On the hearthstone," she said. "Leaving? Lewan, I don't understand. The Lady Talieth—"

"Is in no position to stop us. It's now or not at all. Do you have a key to get past the guardians in the tunnels?"

"A key?" Ulaan shook her head. "No, I—"

"No matter," said Lewan as he stripped off his wet clothes. He tossed them aside and began to pull on the dry clothes. He looked at Ulaan, still dressed in the robes of a serving girl. "Can you find yourself something more suited for traveling?"

"I have nothing."

"Then find something suited for me. You can wear it. Quickly."

"But the Lady Talieth—"

"I promise you, Ulaan, she is in no position to stop us right now. But we must hurry. Now go and find yourself some traveling clothes. And try to get us both a cloak. Something heavy to keep out the rain. Now, Ulaan. Go!"

Although fear filled Ulaan's eyes and he could see her hands trembling, she left the room, shutting the door behind her.

Lewan pulled on the last of the dry clothes and put the hammer Berun had given him through his belt. It was heavy, but he felt better having it there. His master's bow was still propped in the corner, wrapped in the rough canvas in which Sauk had given it to him. Lewan had checked it earlier. The bow's string was still good, but he had no arrows.

He was lacing up his boots and considering whether to take the bedclothes with them—they'd need blankets out on the steppe—when the door opened. A figure walked in, and at first glance Lewan thought that he'd waited too long, that one of Talieth's blades had come for him.

"It's me," said Ulaan. She was dressed much like Lewan in plain breeches, boots, a loose shirt, and a long vest, over which she wore a heavy cloak with a deep cowl. She had another wadded in her arms. She shut the door behind her and lowered the cowl. Her skin was pale and her eyes wide. "Lewan,

304

if we are caught escaping"—she swallowed and took a deep breath—"I will be killed. You? I don't know. Perhaps. Perhaps not. After tonight . . . I don't know."

Lewan stood and went to her, putting his hands on her shoulders, much as Berun had done to him not long ago. "Ulaan, if we don't get away, it's only a matter of time before we're dead anyway. And not much time, I think. We'll need to go far and fast." He paused a moment and made sure he had her gaze, then said, "You do want to come with me, don't you?"

"I don't want to die."

"You'd rather risk staying here . . . a slave?"

She stepped closer and embraced him. "I don't know what to think. I'm so scared. But I trust you."

He held her, one arm across her shoulders, the other round her waist. "Then let's go. We must do one thing first."

He tried to step away but she held him tight. "What?"

"We need to get through the tunnels and past the guardians. I . . . I need to look for one of the men my master killed."

She looked up at him, and behind her eyes he could see her emotions warring.

"What is it?" he asked.

Ulaan swallowed and looked away. "That won't be necessary."

"What? I don't understand. We must have a key to get past the guardians. I need—"

"You don't. I can get us past the guardians."

Lewan tensed. "Is . . . is there something you want to tell me?"

"Later," she said. "When we're far away from here."

They followed the same path Lewan had taken with Talieth days before. The rain had stopped, but the clouds still hung low over Sentinelspire, and the few lamps that remained lit could not cast their light far in the mists that drifted along the pathways between the buildings. Just past the elegant buildings with the brass pillars—ahead, Lewan could see the hedge marking the garden where the assassins had been dismembered the night of the *Jalesh Rudra*—four men stepped from behind the corner of the building and blocked the path. All were cloaked against the weather, but even in the flickering orange light cast by a brazier on top of the building's steps, Lewan could see that they all had steel in their hands.

One stepped forward and brandished his sword so it caught the light. "Name yourselves!"

"I am Lewan, guest of the Lady Talieth, and this is my servant."

"An intruder is loose on the grounds," said the man. "Go back to your rooms at once and lock the door."

"I know," said Lewan. He remembered Talieth's proud demeanor that she had used on him to such great effect, and he tried to put some of that into his voice. "I am on an errand for the Lady. Most urgent. You must let me pass."

" 'Must,' he says?"

The three men behind the speaker spread out, blocking the street and flanking Ulaan and Lewan.

"The Old Man still rules here," said the guard, "and the only thing we *must* do is watch for intruders. I have heard of Lady Talieth's guest, and I've been told what he looks like. Now lower your hoods. Both of you."

Lewan hesitated. If the man knew of him, perhaps this would all be over soon. He held the bundle with Berun's bow in one hand. With the other he lowered his hood and risked a glance over his shoulder at Ulaan. She lowered her hood as well.

"Well, look who it is," said the man nearest Ulaan. "Your . . . servant, you said?"

Lewan took a deep breath. His heart was fluttering. "The Lady Talieth gave her to me to serve my needs during my stay. Bataar, is it?"

Ulaan lowered her eyes and bowed. "Ulaan, Master."

"Ulaan, yes," said Lewan. "Forgive me."

The leader looked at Lewan long and hard, then glanced at Ulaan, and back at Lewan. "Well, *Master* Lewan," he said, "you go back to your room and lock the door like I told you. Let Ulaan . . . serve you, but you stay inside. Do this, and you and I won't have any trouble tonight."

"But my errand—"

"Will wait. You're going to do as I tell you. One way or the other."

"But—"

"Enough!" said the man. With his free hand, he motioned toward Lewan and Ulaan. "Dayul and Turan, take Master Lewan and his woman back to his room. Ulaan, you know the rules. You'll serve your master well if you see that he stays there."

One of the men put a heavy hand on Lewan's arm and tried to turn him. "Come along."

Lewan shook his arm free. "No! You don't understand. I—"

"No," said the leader. *"You* don't understand. Now you can walk back or be carried. Your choice."

"Master," said Ulaan. "Please. Let's go b—"

Lewan's left arm shot out of his cloak. After shrugging off the guard's arm, he'd reached for the hammer and pulled it from his belt. The guard was reaching for him again, but Lewan swung the hammer and brought its heavy head down on the man's wrist as hard as he could. He heard the bones shatter like eggshells, and the man screamed.

"Ulaan, run!" said Lewan.

She turned to run but the guard grabbed her, catching her sleeve and pulling her toward him. Lewan brought the hammer back and started toward her, but the other guard and the leader rushed him. The leader reached him first, and Lewan swiped at him with the hammer.

The leader stepped back. "Stop this! Stop this now or you are dead, guest of Lady Talieth or not."

Lewan raised the hammer again. His other hand, still holding the unstrung bow in its bundle, he waved before him to ward off any strikes. "Let the girl go."

"Wrong answer," said the leader, and he came at Lewan, this time with his sword ready.

Keeping most of his attention focused on the man's blade, which he held low, Lewan struck the sword with the bundled bow, knocking it out of the guard's hands. He swung the hammer at his face, but the man ducked, reached out, and caught the haft with his free hand. A quick twist, and he yanked the hammer out of Lewan's hand. Lewan lashed out with the bow, but the guard caught it, yanked it from Lewan's grasp, and tossed it onto the pavement.

"Little bastard broke my wrist!" said the guard whom Lewan had struck.

The leader hefted the hammer, seeming to enjoy its weight in his hand. "An odd weapon," he said, "but effective." He retrieved his fallen sword, sheathed it, and looked to his injured man. "Have at him, Dayul. Don't kill him. But he's earned a hard lesson."

"No!" Ulaan shrieked, but the man holding her yanked her away.

Dayul stepped forward, cradling his broken arm against his torso. His other hand held a dagger. "You hold still," he said, "and I won't use the sharp part."

The man struck. Lewan saw it coming and tried to dodge, but Dayul was far too quick. The brass pommel of the dagger smashed into Lewan's cheek, tearing the skin. He went down onto the wet gravel, a dozen orbs of light dancing in the world around him.

"Get up," said Dayul. "I didn't hear a bone break. You broke me. I'm going to break you."

"No!" said Ulaan. "Leave him alone! Please. Please, I'll take him back to his room."

"You stay out of this," said the leader. "Your new master earned this."

"Get up," said Dayul, "or I'll kick in your ribs right there."

Lewan took a deep breath and began to push himself back to his feet. He didn't even have a knife. The hammer and bow had been his only weapons, and they had been taken from him with ease. He knew that any one of these men could best him easily. They were trained assassins. Out in the wild with a bow, Lewan might have stood a chance. Here, outnumbered in the dark, the best Lewan could hope for was to take his beating and sneak away once they'd finished with him. He stood up.

"Leave him alone!" Ulaan cried.

"Quiet!" The man holding her yanked her arm.

Ulaan twisted in his grasp and slammed the heel of her hand into the man's nose. Lewan heard a *crunch* as his nose shattered, but he kept his grip on Ulaan. She used it, pulling him close. In three quick motions her hand shot forward, grabbed the man's knife from his sheath, and plunged it into his side just above his belt. He screamed, releasing her, and fell back.

Ulaan turned and dropped into a practiced fighting stance, the bloody knife in her hand. She glanced at Dayul, then fixed her gaze on the leader. "I serve the Lady Talieth," she said. "You fools are interfering with her orders. Dayul, you will apologize to Lewan, then Master Lewan and I will leave. Anything else, and I'll kill you all. Right here. Right now."

The man she'd stabbed was pushing himself up with one hand, the other grasping his side. Blood leaked between his fingers, and his face was a grimace of pain. "You're no servant girl."

"I serve the Lady Talieth"—Ulaan gave Lewan a look full of apology —"in many ways."

"You're one of her personal blades," said Dayul.

"I am." She gave a curt nod but did not relax from her fighting stance. "Which means I don't give idle threats. Dayul, if the next words out of your mouth are anything but an apology, you are a dead man."

Dayul stood before Lewan. He looked down on Lewan, saying nothing, and Lewan could read the reluctance in his stiff stance. But there was fear as well. Now the only question was whether the fear would win out in the man's mind—or his pride.

Behind Dayul was only the darkness between two buildings. The man took a deep breath, but before he could speak, the darkness behind him took form and struck. Whatever it was, the dim light revealed no features other than a slight green sheen. It grabbed Dayul's cloak and pulled with such force that the clasp snapped and the heavy cloth flew away, pulling Dayul onto his back. The man cried out as his injured arm hit the ground, then it turned into a full-throated scream as hands reached out from the darkness and pulled him in.

"What—?" said the man Ulaan had stabbed. At the same time their leader said, "Inside! Get inside!"

Lewan turned, intending to grab Ulaan and run, but what he saw stopped him. Dark shapes, vaguely humanlike but moving with grace and dexterity beyond any human, were scuttling down the brass pillars of the building—some of them head first, clinging to the wet metal like spiders.

The stabbed man pushed himself to his feet. "What are they? Gods, Weilus, *what are they?*"

But Weilus—the leader who'd been doing most of the talking—turned and ran, heading for the hedge that marked the boundary to the garden where only days before Lewan and Talieth had seen Sauk and his men gathering the remains of slaughtered assassins.

"Weilus!" the guard called, but Weilus didn't even make it halfway. A half-dozen of the shapes charged him, quick as leopards, and the man went down screaming.

Ulaan ran to Lewan's side. She still had the bloody knife in her hands, but she looked up at him, fear in her eyes, and said, "I . . . I'm sorry, Lewan. I—"

"Later."

The two remaining guards stood back to back, their eyes wide, their blades trembling in their hands.

"What do we do?" said Ulaan.

Lewan looked around. He could not make out any distinct features on the creatures, just a vague glimmer of green where the light reflected off them, and eyes that burned with a cold light. He stooped to retrieve the bundle with Berun's bow, but couldn't see where the hammer had gone. "Be ready to run," he said.

The creatures struck, avoiding Lewan and Ulaan altogether, and swarmed the guards. One of the men lashed out with his sword. Lewan thought the blade struck home, but the creature didn't even slow. Both guards went down shrieking, and Lewan could hear the sharp snap of tendons tearing and flesh being ripped from bones.

Lewan's face ached where Dayul had hit him, and he felt his cheek swelling. The pain snapped Lewan's fear. Part of him knew that he and Ulaan were about to die, but the pain triggered a primal need to survive.

"Back to the room," he said. "Run. Run and don't look back. Go!"

He grabbed Ulaan's arm and ran. After seven or eight strides, they came up against a wall of the creatures. Heart pounding in his chest and breath coming in ragged gasps, Lewan pulled Ulaan the other way—right into more of the creatures. They skidded to a halt on the wet gravel.

The dark shapes crouched before them, their posture and slight movements more like animals than people. They made a slight chittering sound, not unlike Perch sometimes did. A few of them came closer, not charging like they had against the guards, but hesitant and slow. Curious, almost. The faint light from the brazier still reflected from them more green than orange, and Lewan thought their skin—or was it their clothes?—had the texture of leaves. Two stopped, still crouched low, and sniffed the air. One kept coming until it was only an arm's length away. Its scent washed over Lewan. Even in the damp air, it was strong—the scent of gentle rain over new spring blossoms. But wafting through it was a darker aroma, as if the blossoms grew over a predator's den.

The creature stood up straight in a posture that was almost humanlike. Still, something about the twist of the joints or the cant of the thing's head told Lewan that the position was completely unnatural. Close as it was now, Lewan could see that it had the lithe build of the elves, even the pointed ears and tilt of the eyes, but its way of moving made it seem a wild reflection of any elf he had ever seen. The icy light from its gaze was not the shimmer of the brazier, but came from inside the creature's eyes.

Lewan raised a trembling hand—a last effort to keep the thing at bay, though he knew it was probably futile.

But the thing flinched back just slightly, then leaned in, almost hesitantly, and sniffed. Then the thing's mouth opened, and a dark tongue flicked out, like a lizard tasting the air.

"Lewan . . ." Ulaan rasped. He felt her hands clinging to him, trembling. "It's . . . them. The dark things from the Tower. The Old Man's hunters."

The creature tilted its head, almost birdlike, and looked at Ulaan. The cold light in its eyes flared briefly, almost like a breath washing over an ember, then the creature returned its gaze to Lewan and gave a deep nod, almost a . . . a sort of bow.

"*Lur'ashai,*" it said. It stepped aside as one of the other creatures came forward. It also gave a semblance of a bow and then extended both hands. Resting in the creature's palms, glowing faintly, was the hammer Berun had given Lewan.

The creature proffered the hammer. Part of Lewan wondered if this was some sort of bestial warrior's code, if they would not kill him until he had a weapon in hand. But no. If this were Sauk, then maybe. But these creatures were unlike anything Lewan had ever seen or heard of. This had not been battle for them. They had ripped those men apart, like wolves taking down an elk.

Lewan reached out and took the hammer.

"Lur'ashai," said the first creature. *"Jankhota saalthua."*

"I . . . don't understand," said Lewan.

The creature who had carried the hammer suddenly stood to its full height—as tall as Lewan—but was unnaturally stiff, as if bound to some unseen board. Its arms stood out from its sides, and its fingers splayed. The creature's eyes blazed, and it threw its head back.

"Little master," it said, but Lewan knew at once that the voice from the creature's throat was not its own. No. Lewan recognized this voice. It had spoken to him that day on the mountain. "The time has come. Your word, Lewan, is all I ask. The time has come."

✠
chapter thirty-six

Berun lay on a bier of fresh leaves and flowers. The creatures had carried him here. Trussed in vines like a caterpillar in its cocoon, Berun had not even struggled as they grabbed him and bore him up the stairs. Up and up and up to the roof atop the Tower of the Sun. Open to the air as it was, still the scent of rampant vegetation permeated the air. A stone table lay near the northern ledge. There, they laid Berun upon a bed of new leaves and blossoms, his head cushioned by soft larch branches.

He had been too stunned to resist, to even wonder where they might be taking him and why. Over and over again, he saw it in his mind and heard the words. Chereth, his beloved master, the man who had restored him to life—and more importantly taught him how to live—standing there saying, *Welcome to my tower.*

. . . my tower.

. . . my tower.

And then, *Bring him.*

And the creatures had obeyed.

. . . my tower.

It couldn't be true. Chereth was master of the tower. Impossible. And yet it was the only explanation.

All he had been through in his life—*both* lives—

An orphan in Elversult, living as a thief, scrabbling for

survival. Fighting. Beating and being beaten. Running. Hiding. His first kill.

Alaodin, the Old Man of the Mountain, finding him and taking him in. Giving him a life. A life of murder.

Sauk. The brother he'd never had. One to fight beside. One to die for. And kill and kill and kill and kill . . .

Talieth. Love? No. Neither Kheil nor Talieth had really known love. But they had known passion, had connected in a way that Kheil never had with any other woman.

And then death. Death by Chereth's word. And life. Again by Chereth's word. And more importantly, a *way* of life. Something to believe in. Something to strive for. Meaning. He became Berun.

But Chereth had left him. Left him to . . . to what?

"Questions," said a voice. Nearby. Very close. Chereth's voice. "You have questions, I'm sure."

Berun felt the vines around him loosen, heard the rustle of the leaves, then they fell away.

"Your questions shall be answered," said Chereth, still unseen but very close. "And if the answers spawn questions, those shall be answered as well. But first we must see to your wounds. Sleep now. *Olirith.*"

The last word held the tinge of magic, and Berun's awareness fell away.

Berun slept beyond dreams, but he did not sleep for long. Slumber fell away from him. He heard thunder shaking the sky far away, and he opened his eyes. It was still dark, but wispy, glowing orbs filled the air over the roof, floating like cottonwood seeds on a breeze. Berun sat up. His shirt was gone, and all of the cuts he'd taken under Sauk's assault were no more than lines of white scar tissue. Runes and holy symbols covered his arms and torso. The paint, smelling faintly of pine resin, was still damp. He could feel more on his face and forehead.

Berun took in his surroundings. Kheil had been here many times, the rooftop that was the highest level in the Tower of the Sun. The Imaskari had named it the Eye of the Four Winds, for standing at any of the waist-high ledges, one could see for miles in every direction. The stone tubes that wound their way up the tower connected to portals deep beneath the mountain—portals that opened to the elemental planes. With the proper spells, one could funnel both fire and water to the heights of the tower, so that in high summer, the fountains were always fresh and cool, forming falls that went over the heights of the tower. In the cold of winter, fires burned for light and heat.

Water flowed, giving off a clean scent, its song inherently soothing as it bubbled out of fountains, one at each corner of the roof. Fires burned, not from the tubes, which sat quiet and cold, but from a few braziers and several lamps, their flames low, their glow an orange as a dusty sunset. The light cast as many shadows as pools of light. In the nine years since he had last been here, the Eye of the Four Winds had been filled with vines, fruit trees, flowers, bushes, ivies, creepers, and even long strands of moss drooping off the stone.

"It is good to see you again, my son," said a voice behind him.

Berun turned, and Chereth emerged from the shadow cast by the arm of an oak that grew from the floor and spread its branches over the ledges and up to the sky.

"Master?" said Berun.

Chereth had been old when Berun had last seen him, and he wore the past nine years heavily. His hair had lost none of its thickness, but it was bone-white and flowed well past his shoulders in a wild mane. Leaves and flowers peeked out from the strands, and Berun thought some of them might actually be growing there. Chereth leaned upon his staff, and his posture had a stoop to it that Berun had never seen before. Even his gait was slower. Not quite a shuffle, but it was the pace of a half-elf much closer to his grave than his birth.

The old druid came round the bier and stopped before Berun. He placed his free hand on Berun's arm and squeezed. "My heart rejoices to see you, Berun. Truly."

"Master Chereth . . . I . . ." Berun didn't know what to say.

Chereth smiled at him. "Many, many questions, yes?"

"Yes, Master."

"Our time is short, my son," said Chereth. "But tonight, all your questions must be answered. I have long waited for your coming, and the rest of this night I give to you. All must be made clear before we finish what we began."

Berun felt suddenly weak. He feared his legs would not hold him, so he sat back on the bier. "Finish what, master?"

"That should be your last question, I think," said Chereth. "Better for your understanding if we begin at the beginning, yes?"

"I . . . I don't know where to begin, master."

"I should begin before you came to me," said Chereth. "Before you were Berun. Before you were even Kheil perhaps, for I have walked this path many long years. It began when I was not much older than you are now. As a child of the Oak Father, I served among the Masters of the Yuirwood for many seasons. We saw many victories and many defeats. *Many* defeats, both in the Yuirwood and in other places where my service to the Oak Father took me.

"Always I saw blight, corruption—both natural and arcane—assaulting the woods so beloved to our god. Every year I saw the forests grow a little smaller—if not in one place, than another. Villages, towns, cities . . . as they prospered and grew they dumped their filth into our rivers, our lakes. They fill the air with their smoke and stench. They cut and destroy and do not replant. Kings and their nobles hunt for sport, leaving animals to rot where the hunters' arrows take them.

These nobles will retrieve their arrows, but they leave bears, foxes, and wolves to rot, their death meaning only a moment's amusement for pampered fools.

"I swore my life to the service of the wild. To communion with all living things. Yet year by year I saw the wild shrinking. Saw it polluted. Defiled. And so the Masters of the Yuirwood and other Circles sought to heal, to repair, to foster the wild. But over the years, after so many defeats, I saw this for what it was—a long defeat. For every grove we preserved or fallow field we filled with trees, ten groves were cut and the wild grew ever thinner.

"I began to search for an advantage. What the assassins of this place might call 'an edge,' something that would allow our efforts to go on the offense for once. Traveling through many lands, I sought lore, artifacts, relics, items of power of any sort, and allies to aid my work. I met many whose wisdom added to my own. I found the ancient works of the Imaskari, who were masters of the portals, using them to travel vast distances as if crossing the room. But they also used them to travel to other worlds—some strangely similar to our own, and others different beyond our imagination. Such . . . power this offered.

"The ancient histories all agreed that one of the greatest of the Imaskari wonders lay in the Endless Wastes. My studies led me to believe that this was none other than Sentinelspire itself, and all the scrolls I studied and tales I gleaned spoke of a fortress hidden on the mountain. And thus I first began to learn of the Old Man of the Mountain and his . . . *cult* of assassins.

"Perhaps two years before Kheil and I first crossed paths, I found some of Alaodin's contacts in Glarondar. Unlike most who approached Alaodin, I did not want anyone murdered. I requested an audience with the Old Man of the Mountain, for I greatly wished to come and study the Imaskari lore at Sentinelspire. Why he granted my request I don't suppose I will ever know. Nor do I care. He probably thought he could find a use for whatever knowledge I unearthed, or perhaps he saw me as a potential contact within the Yuirwood.

"Alaodin sent an escort for me—a quiet, secret thing that most of his blades did not even know. Using the portals, they brought me to the Fortress, and I spent many long days and nights studying in the vaults and libraries of the Fortress. Alaodin, despite being one of the world's foremost murderers, had gathered an impressive collection of lore and relics of power—both Imaskari and otherwise. One item in particular was the relic you carried for so long."

"Erael'len?" said Berun. "It came from Sentinelspire?"

"It did," said Chereth. "How such a holy relic to our faith came to be in the possession of the Lord of Assassins I do not know. He had never been able to unlock its secrets, though he sensed the power within it. And here, I must confess that I defiled the rules of hospitality. I stole *Erael'len* and fled. I had no choice. For such a holy relic to rest in the hands of someone so unworthy . . . my heart would not bear it. During my escape, I was forced to kill several of Alaodin's men.

"Alaodin felt that his honor had been insulted—that, and I'm sure he wanted the relic back. And so Alaodin gathered his very best assassins and sent them to kill an old druid in the Yuirwood. And here, my dear son, is where you enter this tale."

Berun's mind reeled. When the Old Man had ordered him to lead the blades into the Yuirwood and kill an old druid, Berun had not asked why. The opportunity to kill had been enough. The order to hunt and kill in lands he'd never seen had been . . . intoxicating. There had never been any word of retrieving a relic. At least not to Kheil. If that had been part of their mission, it had been only for the ears of one of the other assassins.

"Kheil and his band," Chereth continued, "killed many of my people. But the old druid Chereth? Me, they missed, and Kheil was captured by my best wardens. And at my word, they put him to a just and deserved death. But the mysteries of the Oak Father are beyond comprehension. From death comes life. And so, by the grace and power of the Oak Father, I called you back to serve, to serve the will of the god and all we hold precious—growing things, the wild, life itself." The old half-elf smiled, and his voice became raspy with emotion. "And you did, my son. You did. Served beyond all my hopes and dreams for you."

Chereth turned, walked away, and began to pace the roof, the strange lights playing about him.

"But still my quest continued. I shared my desire with others of my Circle and other Circles. I pleaded with them of the need to strike a blow for the wild, lest it be lost beyond repair. But they failed to see the wisdom of my words. They failed to see the depth of civilization's stain upon the world. And so I left, and together we sought the final pieces I needed."

"Why, master?" said Berun. "Why did you never tell me any of this?"

Chereth stopped his pacing and held Berun's gaze. "You were strong. Never doubt that, my son. Strong like a diamond. But, like a diamond, I knew that one strike in the wrong place and you would shatter. I knew you had taken to your new life, becoming *berun* for me and for the Oak Father. But I could also see that your old life still haunted you, that still you had to struggle with the corruption of Kheil in your soul. This is why you took so readily to the wild, I think. In civilization, in the cities, towns, even in the villages . . . Kheil's desires began to reawaken, did they not?"

It was true. The fear, the memories, and all the horrors endured by a little boy forced to survive on his own in the streets channeled that into an anger, a bloodlust, that could never be satisfied. Yes, that had been Kheil. And in the cities—hearing the call of merchants, the plaintive cry of animals caged and penned when they longed to roam, the bickering, the laughter, all the thousands of little sights and sounds and scents of civilization . . . they woke the old fears, and the fears sought the one comfort they had found: The desire to kill, to slay the things that had used and abused him as a child.

All this was true, but Berun simply said, "Yes."

"Yes," said Chereth, and he resumed his pacing. "Besides, I did not want to draw you into the petty bickerings of the Circles, of men and women whose minds were too small to see what ought to have been plain as summer sun before them. And so we left, you and I, wandering, doing what good we could in the lands where I continued my search for the final keys that would allow me to accomplish my desire.

"Five years ago, during our wanderings through the Ganathwood, I found the last piece I needed. I knew that to begin my plan, I had to return to Sentinelspire—the one place in all the world you could not go.

"And so, return to Sentinelspire I did, anticipating a great battle. I even prepared for my own death. But other events had happened in my absence. I'm sure that the death of Alaodin's god sixteen years ago was a severe blow to his power. His faith was shaken, but the lack of power also shook his authority within the Fortress. An old half-elf druid managed to enter the heart of the Fortress itself, kill many of the Old Man's blades, and rob the place of a valuable magic item on the way out, then when the Old Man's best assassin was killed in quest for retaliation . . . well, the resentment and ambition that had been building for years boiled over. While you and I were wandering the wild, the Old Man had to put down two rebellions among his own people. He won both times, but the last one was particularly savage, and almost half the blades of Sentinelspire ended up dead. Good for me, since they were still cleaning up the mess when I arrived. Already weary, both physically and emotionally, from slaughtering their brothers, the surviving assassins were in no position to offer much beyond a token resistance to my powers.

"To make a long tale short, I killed the Old Man. Killed him not far from where you now sit. Rather than seeking to avenge the death of their master, most of the assassins hailed my arrival. For I brought the thing they lacked—vision. I promised them a new way, a new vision of the future, in which my followers will rule as kings and queens of a new Faerûn."

Berun shook his head. It was all too much to take in. "A new way? A new Faerûn? I have no idea what you mean."

"Ah, and here we came to the thing for which I have labored and hunted all these years. My final solution. But for that, I must have a witness. Someone I am sure you will be gladdened to see." He looked up, his gaze fixed on the shadows gathered round, and said, "Bring the boy."

The shadows moved, taking form, and Berun recognized the creatures that had met him in the corridor and brought him here. They bowed to their master and disappeared down the stairs.

chapter Thirty-seven

Surrounded by at least a dozen of the dark creatures, Lewan stood once again before the courtyard of the Tower of the Sun. The rain had slackened to a heavy drizzle that seemed to hang in the air. The grounds were much as Lewan had last seen them. The bodies of the assassins and the tiger still lay amidst the foliage. Rain had diffused the blood, but there was so much. Most of the inner courtyard was soaked in it, looking more black than red on the wet pavement, and much of it was slowly seeping into the street. Lewan was shocked at his utter lack of revulsion. Had he changed so much already? Seen too much death for it to have an effect upon him? He did not like the thought of that.

"What happened here?" Ulaan whispered. "Did . . . *they* do this?"

Lewan glanced at their escorts. If the creatures had understood her words, they gave no sign of it.

"No," he said. "This was mostly my master, Sauk, and the trees."

"The . . . trees?"

"And the vines. It all happened so fast."

"I don't want to be here, Lewan. Let's go. Like you said. Just run away."

The creatures were not close—the nearest of them a few paces away—but still, he and Ulaan were hemmed in. Lewan and Ulaan had not been bound, nor once prodded on the way. But there was no mistaking the creatures' intention. "I don't think that's possible anymore," he said.

"I'm scared."

"Me too."

Shuffling his feet, Lewan felt something under his boot and looked down. They were standing in the midst of the arrows the archer had dropped during the fight. Lewan counted at least five of them within easy reach. He spared a cautious glance at the creatures, then knelt and put his hand over one. Two of the creatures looked at him, then looked away, seemingly unconcerned. Encouraged, Lewan picked up the arrow, then gathered the other four. With the hammer tucked into his belt, he was able to carry the arrows and his master's bow in one hand. Ulaan reached for his other hand, but he pulled away.

"Lewan," she said. "About . . . what happened . . ."

Lewan waited, but she could not seem to find the words.

"I . . . suspected already," he said.

"What?"

"Earlier today, Talieth said something to me. About you. When I bargained for your freedom, she told me, 'Ulaan is still no dryad.' But I never mentioned the dryads to her, nor the *Jalesh Rudra*. But she knew about them. Which means that either she was watching us—or you told her." He looked down on her, hoping to seem angry and resentful, but he knew his face reflected only his true feeling—hurt. "I'd hoped she was watching—sick as that might seem."

Ulaan looked away. "I . . . I am sorry, Lewan. Truly."

"I thought . . ." He looked away, unable to finish.

"What?"

"I thought you had feelings for me," he said, "like . . . like I had for you. That hurt at first. Hurt me to think of all the other men who'd had you." He looked at her again, and this time he knew the anger was coming through in his gaze, for she flinched back. "This . . . this hurts worse."

She held his gaze. "You . . . were not wrong," she said, "about all of it. Not everything I told you was a lie, Lewan. My mother was a slave, and my father could have been anyone. Lady Talieth bought me and trained me. As an assassin. And part of being an assassin is learning the skills to . . . to get close to someone."

"Like me."

"Yes," she said.

He let the silence hang while he gathered his own thoughts. The creatures around them seemed heedless of the conversation. At last he said, "Back in my rooms as we were preparing to leave, you almost told me then, didn't you? All this?"

"Yes."

"Why?"

She thought a moment, then said, "You weren't wrong. I have been with other men. But none of them looked at me the way you do. They saw me as warm flesh to use. You see a person." She opened her mouth to say more, but then looked away.

"You really were going to go with me?" said Lewan. "Away from here?"

She looked at him then, and looking into her eyes, Lewan saw—perhaps for the first time—the real Ulaan. Not the meek servant nor even the deadly assassin. He saw strength, courage, and a determination bordering on ferocity—but also a need that looked to him. "Yes," she said. "I *will* go with you."

The creatures around them went suddenly very still, then a few of them cocked their heads, as if listening. A murmur passed through their ranks, then they were moving forward again, Ulaan and Lewan in their midst.

Ulaan reached out and grabbed Lewan's hand. He did not pull away this time. He could see the fear in her eyes, but still she smiled at him and said, "This was not quite what I had in mind."

A shudder passed through Lewan as they walked through the gate and entered the courtyard.

"What's wrong?" said Ulaan.

"It's just—"

"Ulaan!" came a cry from above them.

They stopped and looked up. Under the lights and shadows, Lewan could not see clearly more than a few feet into the trees, but he thought he could make out something paler than the surrounding foliage. Skin? Given the size and shape, it had to be a face.

"L-lady?" Ulaan called out.

It was Talieth, still trapped by the vines up in the trees.

"Ulaan!" Talieth called out. Lewan had never heard her voice like this. The proud queen, the temptress, was gone. She sounded weak and frightened. It was taking the last vestiges of her courage to call out. "Ulaan, call for help! Please! Tell the blades the night is red! Call for—!"

The leaves rustled and thrashed, and Talieth's cry ended in a shriek.

The creatures pushed them onward. Not roughly, but there was no resisting them.

"Boy!" It was Sauk, calling out from above. "Hear me, boy! You're going up there, you tell your master I'm coming for him! I'm going to eat his heart! Tell him!"

There was more thrashing, much more violent, and Sauk's roaring did not end. Lewan could still hear it echoing off the stone as he and Ulaan were led inside the tower.

Halfway up the stairs, Ulaan stumbled and fell. When she didn't rise, Lewan stooped and grabbed her arm with his free hand. The creature nearest him hissed.

"I'm just helping her up," he said.

The creature blinked at him, displaying no emotion or acknowledgment that he understood—or cared.

Lewan looked down at Ulaan and helped her to rise. He thought he heard her murmur something.

"What?" he asked.

"What?" she said as she regained her feet.

They continued walking up the stairs.

"I thought I heard you say something," said Lewan.

Ulaan did not answer.

At the top of the stairs before a stout wooden door, the creatures stopped. The door opened, and by the sound of rustling leaves and creaking branches, Lewan knew that the vines wrapped around it were doing the opening. Beyond the doorway were more stairs, encased in an arched stone hallway.

The creatures turned to him and bowed. One of them hissed and said, *"Lur'ashai, ash sissaan."*

"They want us to go up, I think," said Lewan.

"Do we have a choice?" said Ulaan.

"You want to tell them no?"

She considered a moment, then said, "You still have your hammer?"

He patted the stone head of the hammer protruding from the top of his belt. "Yes."

A moment's silence, then she said, "You go first."

Lewan led the way. The door shut behind them. The steps, wide and shallow, wound around the tower several times, then passed through a large opening in the ceiling.

Lewan and Ulaan emerged onto a wide roof, lit by a few braziers and several lamps, their flames low and weak in the drizzle. But dozens of the meandering lights had climbed the tower and floated about, making the shadows seem to cringe and gasp in their passing. Great columns of stone, twisted in the Imaskari fashion, stood at each corner. Statues of ancient Imaskari heroes—or perhaps they were gods—stood atop them, and each supported the end of one of the great stone tubes. One, a beautiful woman, held forth a silver urn, still untarnished by the years, and clear water poured from it. Opposite her, a bearded man stood amidst stone waves, and from the tip of each wave, water streamed out in fountains. The water filled a pool before running off in channels and through sluices over the edge of the tower. The other two—one holding aloft a stone sun, the other pounding stone flames over a graven forge—stood cold. Vegetation dominated everything—trees growing up through broken stone, vines and creepers covering stone and trees, moss carpeting many surfaces, petals and lily pads floating in the water.

"And there they are!" said a voice behind them.

Lewan turned. On the far side of the roof stood an old man, dressed in a long robe and leaning on a staff made from twisted branches. Lewan knew the voice at once—the voice of the man he'd met on the mountain, and the voice that had spoken through the creature after rescuing Lewan and Ulaan from the guards. Behind the Old Man, Master Berun sat shirtless upon a wide stone table covered in leaves and flowers. Most of his exposed skin had been painted with runes and holy symbols, and his wounds were gone.

"Master!" Lewan called out. He ran to Berun and embraced him with his free arm. "I could not get away," he whispered. "Forgive me. I tried."

Berun returned the embrace, then pushed Lewan away gently. "There is someone you must meet."

Lewan stepped back from his master and turned to the other man. Closer now, he saw that it was not an old man at all. The sharper features, the slight cant to the eyes amidst the high cheekbones, and the points of the ears protruding from the tufts of white hair showed Lewan that he was a half-elf—a very, very old one.

The half-elf smiled and bowed. "We have met, have we not, Lewan?"

"Uh, I . . ." No mistaking it. It was the same voice. But this half-elf looked nothing like the man Lewan had met that day on the mountainside.

"You must forgive our young disciple, Berun," said the half-elf, "though I fear the fault for his confusion must be laid at my feet. Observe."

The half-elf closed his eyes and murmured. He drew in a deep breath and . . . flickered. The light and shadow of the floating orbs played over him, and his image seemed to blur and shift. When it steadied, an altogether different man stood before them. A human, still past middle-age, but taller, darker, and possessing an aristocratic bearing. It was the man Lewan had met that day on the mountain.

Berun's eyes went wide with shock and something like horror.

The man laughed, and his image flickered again. When it steadied, the old half-elf stood before them again.

"A small joke on my part," said the half-elf. "I came and spoke to your disciple several days ago while he was undergoing a vigil on the mountainside. I knew that the half-orc was watching, and I knew that the sight of Alaodin emerging from the woods to talk to Lewan here would . . . rattle Talieth's little conspiracy."

"Conspiracy?" said Lewan. "I'm sorry, masters. I'm . . . I'm confused." He looked at the half-elf. "You aren't the Old Man of the Mountain?"

The half-elf chuckled. "Oh, but I am! And I am not. The Old Man of the Mountain—Alaodin, master of assassins, feared the world over . . . well, I fear he met his just and deserved end many years ago. At my hand. But the Oak Father smiled upon me, and rather than fight his remaining subjects, they swore loyalty to me. And so I became a 'new' Old Man."

The half-elf sighed. "But alas, the oaths of assassins are not to be trusted. Seeing my vision, the beauty of what I would bring to the world, some of the blades of Sentinelspire joined me. But some want only to sate their own appetites, to horde power for themselves no matter the cost to the world. And these . . . these found a willing leader in the Lady Talieth. Almost from the beginning, she has conspired against me."

"You killed her father . . ." said Berun.

"I did," said Chereth, "though it was no grief to her. I don't suppose you two had time to speak much tonight, have you? I killed Alaodin, true. But it is also true that the last rebellion the Old Man put down before my arrival—the one that almost succeeded—was led by Talieth. Even she recognized what a blight Alaodin had become to the world. The day I killed her father, Talieth was locked in a dungeon beneath the Fortress, waiting for her father to decide what to do with her. I had hoped she might treat me with some gratitude. I succeeded where she failed, and I freed her. Still . . . Talieth will never serve" —he cast a quick glance at Berun—"or love anyone but Talieth."

"Then why—"

The sharp look from the half-elf stopped Lewan. Master Berun had always permitted—even encouraged—Lewan to question him.

"Why did I allow her to live?" said the half-elf. "Her and Sauk and the rest?"

Lewan nodded. Berun did nothing. His eyes held a hollowness that Lewan had never seen before.

"I am no murderer, Lewan," said the half-elf. "I kill only when left with no other choice. I had no desire to kill Talieth, despite her plot to kill me. But . . ." Something like mischievousness crossed the half-elf's features, not unlike a little boy hiding a secret. "In truth, I spared her out of my love for you, Berun. Once my plan reaches its fruition, the world will need to be filled again. Filled with the faithful who will not defile the natural world. I knew, both from things you had told me and things I learned of Talieth, that she was the only woman you had ever loved. I spared her in hopes that she might come to see the folly of her ways, to accept the truth and beauty of what I seek to do. I hoped she might be your bride in our glorious new world, the mother of many children who will carry on our legacy."

"And Sauk?" said Berun. "Why spare him and the others?"

The half-elf smiled. "Truthfully? I like Sauk. Make no mistake, he's a bloodthirsty killer, but if there is malice in his soul I have never found it. He does not prey upon the weak. To do so would be the gravest sin, in his mind. To him, glory is hunting and killing those stronger than him. In our new world, we will need hearts like his."

"New world?" Lewan looked to his master, hoping for an answer, for guidance of any sort, but he saw nothing.

"Yes, my son," said the half-elf, and he laid a hand on Lewan's shoulder.

Something in the half-elf's touch made Lewan want to pull away. It reminded him of the time out on the steppe when he and his master had made their camp too close to an old hill that housed a colony of snakes. Lewan had woken with one in his blankets.

"And here we come to the reason I have summoned you," said the half-elf. "I intend for the two of you to rule by my side. We are about to see the birth of a glorious new world, a world free of the corruption of civilization, where the peoples of Faerûn live in harmony with their world. Tell me, Lewan. The night after your vigil, you dreamed, did you not? Tell us of your dream."

"What?" said Lewan, and his breath caught in his throat. How could Chereth know? If he knew of the dream, then he also knew of Lewan's mother . . . and how she had died. Had he told Berun?

"Long ago my own master taught me the art of communicating through dreams," said Chereth. "It is not something I have forgotten. I was able to contact you, Berun, that night in the Khopet Dag, yes? And you, Lewan, on the night after your vigil. I was able to send you a vision of my goal. You saw the mountain, did you not? Sentinelspire?"

"I . . . I did, master," said Lewan. "I saw Sentinelspire. But not from here, from the Fortress. It was as if I saw it from a great height. Like . . . like an eagle might see it, far up in the clouds."

"Yes," said Chereth. "Yes, that was it! Now, Lewan. Now is the time we spoke of on the mountain. I told you I would need your witness, your word. It is time to give it, my son. Tell your master what you saw. Tell him everything."

Lewan closed his eyes, trying to recall every detail of the dream. It had been so strange, yet so vivid, and as he searched his mind the memories came back easily.

"I saw the mountain . . . fall. It just collapsed, like a tent whose pole snaps. Much of it was still falling when it all exploded. For an instant, I saw fire in the center of it, white-hot like the sun, then rocks, dirt, ash, and fire . . . so much fire . . . spreading outward. Spreading and spreading. It didn't slow. Miles and miles, almost like the ripples of a pond. And then . . . then the darkness and fire filled everything.

"But then I could see again. I was still up above the world—but higher than any eagle. Higher even than a dragon could fly, I think. Hundreds of miles stretched out under me. I could see the edge of the world curving away into blue sky and black night. But below me—far, far below—I could see the smoke and ash from the mountain. It spread over hundreds, maybe thousands of miles, the wind carrying it far. It spread like . . . like a brown haze over the world, and then . . . then I was back down, closer to the land. I could see forests covered in ash. Rivers turned to mud and sooty muck. Fish died in the streams, animals on the land. Summer did not come. Beasts and men starved. Disease crippled entire cities. Entire realms burned as kings made war on their neighbors for food and unpoisoned fields. Then the armies turned on one another.

"Seasons passed. Winds and rains cleansed the air, more every month. Forests grew where once entire villages tilled fields. Trees and vines grew in the midst of castles fallen to ruin. Animals lived in the shells of dead cities. Rivers ran clean again. Lakes became clear. No more did fires burn in cities, their smoke turning sunsets brown. And . . . and here, the mountain . . . gone. Blasted away. Only a great hole in the ground remained, and over the years it filled with rain and snowmelt, forming a lake clear as diamonds held against the sky. It was . . ." Words failed him.

"Beautiful," said Chereth. "Perfect. The very image and heart of that for which our Order strives. Men, elves, dwarves, and all thinking peoples will survive, will even thrive in time. But the stink of civilization will be pushed back for hundreds of generations. The wild will recover. We shall breathe free air again."

Lewan looked on the half-elf, the horror of what he meant beginning to dawn on him. "You mean that you are going to going to *cause* this? All those people—"

"Dead, yes," said Chereth. He hung his head, but Lewan did not sense any real sadness or regret in the gesture. "So it must be, much to my sorrow. To save the body from infection, sometimes one must cut off a limb."

"But all those innocent people . . ."

"People die every day, my son," said Chereth. "Innocent and guilty alike. This, too, is part of the Balance. You yourself have been used by people who profit from murder. That is the world that people have made. But it was not always so. Before the rise of cities, of rivers of sewage and sludge . . . people lived as one with the wild, giving and taking in equal measure. Today, we have a world of rot, and you know that the only way to save a tree from rot is to prune the sick limbs."

"One who tends the trees must prune, yes," said Berun. "But you aren't talking about trimming a few rotten branches. You are talking about burning the whole wood! And what good to us if we prune ourselves? If what Lewan saw is true, we will not be around to see your vision fulfilled."

"Oh, but we will!" said Chereth. "You know full well that we stand in the midst of a fortress riddled with portals to points across all of Faerûn—and beyond. Once I wake the mountain at last, we will go elsewhere. I have prepared a place for us. I have not sat idle these years, but I have even taken many of the animals from this world and sent them there so that we may bring them with us when we return. Return as—"

"Conquerors?" said Berun.

"No," said Chereth. "As teachers. Guides. We will lead by example, not force."

"Destroying civilization," said Berun. "That isn't force?"

Chereth scowled. "Of course it is. A necessary force. Necessary to cleanse the world, to establish paradise."

Lewan had no idea what to say. He sensed the wrongness—more, the *vileness*—of what Chereth planned. But he could find no reason or argument to refute it.

"Murder," Chereth continued, "greed, blind ambition . . . destroying innocent lives. Were the both of you not orphaned by the greed of those more powerful than you? Filth, corruption, the sacrilege of undeath holding sway over entire regions—it must end, my sons. *We* must end it."

"Vengeance," said Berun, and an odd expression lit his face, almost like epiphany. "All this talk of justice, of cleansing, it all comes down to simple vengeance. Vengeance in the Tower of the Sun."

Chereth scowled at his odd choice of words. "No, my son," he said. "Vengeance is hurting one who has wronged you."

"And civilization—the stink of cities and their sewage, as you put it—has not wronged us? Has not wronged the wild we love and swore to defend?"

"No, my son!" Genuine distress clouded the old half-elf's features. "The desire for vengeance, for retribution . . . those are the desires of lesser men. I speak of the Balance, of righting

the scales so long wronged by"—his lip curled round the word
—"*civilization.* We must be above such petty concerns."

"But Sauk said . . . I was told—"

"Lies!" said Chereth, and his face flushed with anger. "That
murdering bitch and her half-orc lackey told you nothing but
lies. Ask your beloved disciple. Lewan"—the half-elf turned
his gaze on Lewan, who flinched away—"tell your master.
Have you not been well treated, even pampered, during
your entire stay? Your every desire"—he glanced in Ulaan's
direction—"quenched?"

"Y-yes," said Lewan, and he took an involuntary step away
from the old druid.

"Yes! Yes, of course you have." His voice lowered, calming,
becoming almost kind again. "But my dear boy, it was all a lie.
Sauk gave you just enough truth to cloak Talieth's lies. From
the beginning. Talieth has used you. She even sent a spy into
your bed to corrupt you."

Lewan's heart lurched at the look of shock that passed over
Berun's face. Both his master and the half-elf turned their gaze
on Ulaan.

"What is this?" said Berun

"I . . ." said Lewan. "It . . . it isn't what you think."

"No?" said Chereth. He glared at Ulaan. "You stand in this
holy place and tell my son that you were not sent to his bed by
your mistress to gain his sympathies and spy upon him?"

Fear lit in Ulaan's eyes. "Lewan—"

"Do not look to him!" said Chereth. "You have defiled him
enough already. Trained in the arts of murder *and* seduction.
What better way to get close to your victim?" Chereth turned
to Lewan. "Talieth sent her to you to turn you to their cause. To
stop me. To stop the world from returning to purity. To murder
me and continue their little cult of death dealing. Once they
were done with you, she'd have tossed you out . . . or worse."

"No!" said Ulaan. "At first, that's all it was. Duty. But now,
we—"

"Lies!" said Chereth. "Even now her honeyed tongue drips its poison. She is nothing more than a seductress, using you to get what she wants." The half-elf faced Ulaan, a look of malice twisting his features. He raised his staff and shouted, *"Ebeneth!"*

"Wait!" Lewan shouted, but it was too late.

The plants and vines struck. Some rose up and twisted like snakes, while others lashed like whips. The thickest struck Ulaan's side, knocking her off her feet, and a thick tangle of leaves and creepers caught her and twisted. More and more wrapped around her, binding her tight. With a flick of the old druid's staff, the vines dragged her back to him until they held her only a few paces away. She thrashed and kicked and screamed, but succeeded only in amassing a crisscross of scrapes and cuts across her skin.

Berun stepped forward. "Master Chereth, what—?"

"Even now she betrays us!" said Chereth. He shook his staff at Ulaan. "Did you think I would not know. *Did you?*"

Ulaan shrieked and thrashed. Blood streaked her face.

"Stop it!" said Lewan. "Stop! You're hurting her!"

"Do you know what she has done?" said Chereth. "The die is cast. She has used her little trinket"—the half-elf stepped forward, reached amidst the vines into Ulaan's shirt, and pulled out a silver chain upon which hung a red jewel —"to summon the assassins to rescue her conniving mistress." He released the jewel and it fell back against the girl's chest.

Lewan remembered Ulaan stumbling upon the stairs. He *had* heard her murmuring something. A signal. A cry for help.

"Release her!" said Lewan. "Please. Please, I beg you!"

"I can sense them now," said Chereth. His gaze seemed distant, and he gave no sign that he'd even heard Lewan. "In the courtyard. They are setting fire to my gardens." He chuckled. "They think that will protect them. *Fools.* Soon they will burn, and all they hold precious—and all the world will be my garden."

Ulaan stopped screaming. Her breath came in ragged gasps. Her eyes, pleading, looked to Lewan, then at Chereth.

"Still," said Chereth, "I cannot have them interfering. Berun, my son, I fear we cannot perform the last rite until dawn, when the stars and planets align, pulling upon Faerûn to release the energies I need."

"If all the assassins have come," said Berun, "we cannot withstand them all. They are too many." His voice sounded oddly flat. Emotionless and . . . resigned.

"*We* need not do anything," said Chereth, "save perhaps listen to the screams of the dying."

The druid raised his staff again and half-closed his eyes. Lewan heard him murmuring something. He looked to Ulaan, afraid that the druid was about to inflict some new torture upon her, but nothing changed. She lay there, encased in vines, smeared with her own blood and shivering from terror.

"What are you doing, master?" said Berun.

The druid lowered his staff, leaned upon it, and opened his eyes. "Sending forth my *loyal* servants. The ones who brought you both here tonight."

The dark things. Lewan shivered at the thought. He had watched them tear those four assassins to pieces. If they were going after Talieth's blades . . . the poor souls wouldn't stand a chance.

"What of those among the blades loyal to you, master?" said Berun.

Chereth smiled. "I have you and Lewan. I have the only ones I truly need."

"What of Talieth?" said Berun. "You said you'd saved her. For me."

The half-elf closed his eyes a moment, then looked at Berun, almost sadly. "That is up to her now."

"Master!" said Lewan. "You can't—"

"Be silent," said Berun. But the look from Chereth truly silenced him.

"And you, Lewan?" said Chereth. "Your master begs for his woman. Do you wish me to spare your little whore? Were the Oak Father's daughters not worth waiting for?"

"Don't kill her," said Lewan. "Please."

"Purified yourself, have you?" said Chereth. "You think so? Washed her scent and sweat from you? You heard what I said. To save the body, one must cut away the corruption."

"Please!" said Lewan. "Let her go. I beg you. I'm sorry. I'll never touch her again. Just . . . don't kill her. Please."

"Oh, I will not kill her," said Chereth, and the malicious smile returned. "*You* will. Prove your loyalty to me now. To the vision the Oak Father gave me. Kill this vile thing and enter into bliss."

Lewan's knees trembled. He tried to steady them, but all strength left his legs and he fell to his hands and knees. He dropped the bundled bow and the arrows he held. Unbalanced and top heavy, the hammer fell out of his belt and thunked on the leaf-covered floor. "No," he said.

"My son," said Chereth. Lewan heard the shuffle of feet, and when he looked up the druid was looking down on him, sadness in his eyes. "You have done it before. To spare those you love from pain. Now you will do it to purify yourself." Chereth nudged the hammer with his foot, pushing it toward Lewan's hand. "And if it helps you . . . to save her from pain."

The druid walked away and raised his staff.

"No!" Lewan cried.

"Naur illeth!" the druid cried out.

Thick smoke billowed from the vines encasing Ulaan, and Lewan could see tiny tongues of flame catching in the foliage. Ulaan screamed.

✠

chapter Thirty-Eight

Valmir led a half dozen assassins—four men and two women—through the storm-slick streets. He knew he was very likely heading toward his own death, but it was not the thought of death or even life that was running through his head.

The thought that kept coming to mind was that the gods of magic, despite being feared and revered throughout Faerûn, must have one sick sense of humor. He'd at least halfway understood Talieth's lessons on the necessity for components to spells—how their inherent qualities, both natural and arcane, helped summon and strengthen certain magical forces. But the fact that one of the main ingredients of one of his most deadly spells was something that came out of the south end of a northbound bat often made him wonder if the gods were more than a little insane, or if they just liked to test the mettle of their servants. They were hundreds of miles from the nearest apothecary, so Valmir had to search the caves for his own bat excrement, and that only made it worse. Still . . . he knew the effort would be worth it.

The night is red! The night is red! The ni—

The call had come not long ago. He'd feared it since Talieth first laid out their plan this morning—feared it and prepared for it. Still, that it had come not from Talieth or Sauk but from one of Talieth's pets that was currently sharing the boy's bed . . . that bothered Val. It meant things had gone from bad to worse to—

"What in the unholy hells is that?" said the man walking behind Val.

Valmir had been so lost in his thoughts, his attention so focused on getting them to the Tower of the Sun, that he'd almost stepped on . . . whatever it was. At first he thought it was merely a pile of refuse that a servant had been taking out, dropped on the street, and left when chaos broke loose. But then he caught the stench—blood and offal.

One of the other men, the one holding the lantern, came round. His light fell on the bloody wreck. "I think that was Dayul."

Whoever it was, he hadn't simply been killed. He'd been torn apart. Limbs ripped off the torso, skin and flesh ripped from bones, intestines scattered. Not even the tiger would have done something like this.

"Dayul?" he said. "How can you tell?"

"I recognize the boots . . . uh, boot," said the lantern man. He pointed. Lying a few paces away from the thickest mass of gore was half a leg. It still wore a fine leather boot with brass buckles. "Dayul loved those boots."

"Not anymore," said Valmir. "Let's move. Be ready."

"Ready for what?" said one of the women.

"Wish I knew," said Val, and he reached inside a pouch for the small clump of bat excrement. He grimaced, but damned if it didn't feel comforting just then.

Nearly two dozen of the blades were already at the Tower of the Sun when Valmir arrived. The assassins stood on the path outside the main entrance of the courtyard. Several held lanterns, but most of the light came from the odd orbs floating round the tower and among the brush. A few of the assassins had ventured under the archway, and one of them—an old veteran named Merellan—called to Valmir.

He walked past the others. "Where's Talieth?" he asked.

Merellan swallowed and looked inside the courtyard. "Trapped. Up there in the trees."

"Trapped?" said Valmir, both confusion and anger in his voice.

"Wrapped up in vines."

"What are you waiting for?" The confusion gone, Valmir's voice was all anger. "Get her out!"

"We . . . we tried. The woods in there—they're alive, Valmir."

"Alive? Of course they're alive you damned fool. They're plants!"

"Not like this. See for yourself."

The man motioned to another to bring up his light. He opened the lantern's shutter. Valmir held the wad of bat droppings and brimstone mixed together, just the way Talieth had taught him, and he rolled it between his thumb and fingers as he advanced, the words of the spell playing round and round in his mind.

He heard something approaching through the foliage, and he stopped. Then he saw that it was the foliage itself moving—vines covered in leaves and thorns, and thick braid-like strands of creepers—snaking over the ground and swaying through the air toward him. He quickly backstepped out of their reach.

"*That's* what I meant," said Merellan. "Alive."

"What do we do, Valmir?" said one of the assassins in the street.

"Valmir!" called a voice from inside the courtyard. A woman's voice.

"Talieth?" Valmir shouted. "That you?"

"He captured us," said Talieth. "Sauk and me both. We're caught up in the vines."

"How bad you hurt?"

"We'll live," said Talieth. "You need to get us out. We have to get up there and stop the druid before it's too late. Burn it. Burn the woods."

Val looked round at the other assassins. They wore the same shocked, fearful look that he knew was on his own face. "But that will burn you, too."

"The vines are coming from the thick foliage near the base of the tower. One cluster has me. The other has Sauk. Hit them—burn them all—and I think the vines will release us. But be ready to cut and drag us out quick."

Valmir took a deep breath. "What if it doesn't, Talieth? What if it burns and you stay right where you are?"

There was a moment of silence, broken only by the patter of the drizzle on the leaves and the rustling of a few branches in the wood, then Talieth said, "Burn the cluster holding Sauk first."

Valmir smiled. "That I can do."

✚
chapter thirty-nine

No!" Lewan grabbed the hammer and forced himself to his feet. Gripping the weapon tightly, he charged Chereth.

He'd gone only three steps when a heavy shape bowled him over. Lewan went down hard, the breath knocked out of him and his shoulder bruising even on the carpet of leaves. He rolled up and saw Berun standing before the smoldering net of vines around Ulaan. His master held his long knife in his hand and raised it.

"No!" Lewan shrieked.

Berun brought the knife down in a ferocious arc—but not at Ulaan. He struck low, hewing at the braided vines that held her off the floor. One swipe, and a thick mass of vines parted as easily as old cloth. Berun's backhand chop cut another thick, smoking bundle. The weight of the girl was too much for the remaining vines, and she toppled. Berun caught her with his free hand and sliced through the last of the greenery.

Chereth simply stood there, leaning upon his staff and watching.

But Berun ignored the half-elf. Ulaan was still screaming, her voice becoming shrill and almost inhuman as tangled vines and her clothes still burned. Berun grabbed her and dragged her to the nearest fountain. Five long strides, and he heaved her in. She landed with a splash and a hiss as the water drowned the flames. Still encased in smoldering vines, the girl kicked and thrashed, but Berun forced her all the way under the water.

Lewan pushed himself to his feet and stumbled over to his master. Berun pulled the girl and mass of scorched foliage out of the water. Ulaan was coughing up water, which Lewan took as a good sign. Coughing meant alive. Many of the leaves and vines were withered and burned, but still firmly wrapped their victim.

"Thank you, master," said Lewan.

Berun set the girl on the ground and looked up, an expression of profound sorrow upon his face. He still held the knife in one hand.

Lewan's blood was pounding in his ears, but as it began to calm, he heard screaming. For a moment, he thought it was Ulaan again. Her screams and the smell of burning dredged up memories of Lewan's mother, but he squeezed his eyes shut and forced them away. He could still hear the screaming—faintly, but there was no mistaking it.

Then he realized it was coming from outside, far down below. Men and women screaming. Chereth's dark creatures had found Talieth and her assassins, and the bloodbath had begun.

Talieth's plan had worked. Even more amazingly, Valmir's spell had worked. He'd spoken the incantation, completed the last of the hand motions, and a tiny ember had shot forth from his fist, growing in size to a great globe of fire before striking the thick mass of foliage to the left of the tower's main doors.

The arcane fire burned fast and hot, and as Valmir and the other blades stood just outside the main gate, watching the woods begin to burn, Sauk—wrapped in vines and branches—had fallen from the canopy. He hit the leaf-covered pavement hard and began thrashing and roaring. None of the assassins—Valmir included—were bold enough to go inside the courtyard yet, especially with an enraged Sauk. With the base of the vines in flames, the tops of the plants had been reduced to no more than ordinary vines, and though they reduced his clothes and some of his skin to shreds, the half-orc managed to free himself in short order.

He stomped over to the nearest corpse, retrieved a long knife from the belt of one of the dead assassins, spared Valmir a glance that was pure rage and disdain, and disappeared into the shadows of the wood.

A similar strike released Talieth, though she demanded help in freeing herself from the thorn-thick vines. With the fires destroying the main clusters of vines, several of the assassins had worked up the courage to venture into the courtyard.

Standing, Talieth was bruised and her exposed skin was bloody from dozens of scratches and cuts inflicted by the thorns, but the wounds only strengthened her resolve and stoked her fury.

"We must get inside that Tower," she told her assembled blades, "and we have to do it fast. Before—"

"Lady Talieth!" said Merellan, pointing up to the tower.

Talieth and the gathered assassins looked up. Dozens of shapes were shambling down the outer walls of the Tower.

"What are those?" said someone behind Valmir.

"I think those are what happened to Dayul," said Valmir.

Chereth still leaned upon his staff, watching Berun and Lewan. He heaved a great sigh and said, "I am most disappointed in you both. Lewan cries for a lying whore, and my trusted disciple rescues her from justice."

"This was not justice." Berun stood. Water from Ulaan's thrashing had splashed onto him, and the runes and holy symbols were running off his skin in long, dark streaks. "That was simple cruelty."

"Cruel?" said Chereth. "That would imply she didn't deserve it. Pitiless? Perhaps. But justice must often be pitiless, lest it become weak."

Berun held his master's gaze a long time, then looked at the knife in his hand. "Do you remember the autumn before we left the Yuirwood?"

"What of it?" said Chereth.

"Blight had infected the Seventh Circle's grove. It was beyond saving, so we burned the grove. Trees that had been old when our ancestors were young . . . we had to kill them. When this grieved me, do you remember what you said?"

"That was many years ago," said Chereth, his voice still cold. "But I know what I would say now. Corruption must be rooted out, rot destroyed, blight burned. Yes?"

"Yes," said Berun. "But do you remember why?"

"What?"

"You told me why it had to be so. Because an infected tree, once it is beyond saving . . . its greatest danger is in nurturing the corruption that might spread to others."

"Quite true. All the more reason to kill corruption wherever we find it."

Berun fell to his knees. He still held the knife, but in a limp hand, and there were tears in his eyes. "Don't you see? This place . . . this cursed place . . . *is* corruption. It is death and murder and"—Berun looked around, the eldritch lights reflected in his eyes as he searched for the right word —"pitilessness. To kill without mercy. Without thought for the life ending. To kill only for what the killing will gain. Can't you see it, master? You cannot live in such disease without becoming infected by it. I . . . I know this better than anyone. Oh, master, it has infected *you.*"

Chereth's eyes narrowed, and at first he paled, but then blotches of color—purple, in the arcane light—began to rise in his cheeks. "You impertinent, ungrateful little . . . whelp! You presume to rebuke *me?*"

Berun, still on his knees, fell into a deep bow. His wet braid fell on the leafy floor before him. "Forgive me, master. I . . . beg you. Destroying so many . . . killing thousands . . . *thousands* of thousands! That is not our way. That is not the Balance of the Oak Father. Please, master, let us go far from here. Tonight! Far away and we will take a vigil together to seek our Father's guidance."

"You think I have not sought the Oak Father's guidance? I have taken more vigils in my life than you have taken meals. And yet you presume to counsel me." Chereth slumped, and he shook his head. "I see that I left you too long, my son. You have forgotten—"

"Nothing," said Berun. "I have cherished your every word, master. Everything you ever taught me. Not a day has gone by since you left me in the Ganathwood that I have not meditated on your teachings. Those teachings guide me now. Death, killing, *murder* . . . cannot be the will of the Oak Father. This is not the wisdom that guided me."

"You little fool," said Chereth. He threw back his head and laughed, but it was a burst of exasperation, not humor. "I *made* you. You would be nine years to rot if it were not for me. And this is the gratitude you show me." The half-elf stood straight, then, his staff held in a firm hand, no longer leaning upon it. "This is your judgment, then? You will not join me? You will not aid me?"

Berun went even lower, putting his head upon the floor. "Forgive me, master." He looked up, his cheeks wet with tears, but a fierce resolve filled his eyes. "If I cannot turn you from this madness . . . I must stop you."

Chereth laughed again, this time in mockery. "You? Oh, Berun, I do admire your foolish courage. The day I left you, I was ten times stronger than you. My power has grown since then. What makes you think you can stop me?"

"Bring vengeance to the Tower of the Sun."

"What . . . ?"

"The night of the *Jalesh Rudra*," said Berun. "A servant of the Oak Father came to me. Those were her words, the Oak Father's command to me. I understand them now. Bring vengeance to the Tower of the Sun."

Sadness filled Chereth's face. Genuine regret. But then his eyes hardened. "This is your final word, then?"

"Not mine," said Berun. "The words of the Oak Father. I am merely his hand. I am vengeance."

" 'I am vengeance,' " said Chereth. "Those are the words of Kheil the killer, not Berun, son of the Oak Father."

Lewan could see his master's gaze turning inward as he considered the old druid's words. But then Berun blinked, his eyes cleared, and he said, "It seems then that Kheil must become the son of the Oak Father. *Berun Kharn kienelleth.* Hope must become vengeance."

"Then I have no choice," said Chereth. "I am so sorry, my son. I must destroy you."

The druid took in a breath, raised his staff with both hands—

And a dark shape hit him. The half-elf went down under the dead weight. Eyes wide, Lewan saw that it was one of the druid's dark creatures.

But quite dead. Broken and bloody, in fact, its throat a mangled mess. Not cut, it had been ravaged by teeth.

"Oh, no," said a hoarse voice. "That bastard is mine."

An even larger form dropped down from the ledge at the edge of the roof, then stood up. What was visible of his skin showed greenish gray under the floating lights, but he was covered in a black wetness that Lewan knew was blood. More coated his heavy blade and the hand that held it.

It was Sauk.

✠

chapter Forty

The half-orc had not only killed one of Chereth's dark creatures—he had scaled the tower carrying the dead weight, then thrown it on the druid. Sauk stood near the edge of the roof, covered in gore—much of it his own blood. His skin was a collage of cuts, scrapes, and scratches. He bled from a deep gouge on his left shoulder.

Sauk fixed his gaze on Berun, who still knelt on the ground. "On your feet, you bastard. Your skulking little lizard killed Taaki." He hooked three fingers like claws and raked them across his face and heart. "Now I'm going to eat your heart. *Dam ul dam.* Blood for blood."

Completely unhurried and seemingly unconcerned, Berun pushed himself to his feet. He still had the knife in his hand, but it hung in a relaxed grip at his side. "Talieth . . . ?"

"Doesn't matter," said Sauk, and he approached Berun. "All that matters now is you and me."

"You *dare!*" Chereth crawled out from under the dead weight of his servant and regained his feet. Blood from the dead creature smeared his robes, and he trembled with rage. The lights drifting over the roof flared brightly and took on a red tint. *"Ebeneth!"*

The foliage around Sauk erupted, vines snaking forward and branches grasping for him. But the half-orc was prepared. He leaped away, and when the plants came too close, he slashed at them with his blade, cleaving vines and sending leaves flying. Dodging the first assault, he tried to charge the druid, but more plants rose up to block his way and try to trap him. Sauk slashed and jumped. A few meager creepers managed to grasp one leg and arm, but he ripped away.

Chereth raised his staff and pointed, as if directing the attack. More and more leaves and branches surged after the half-orc, driving him away. Sauk cut and punched and kicked his way out of them, but he was being steadily forced toward the ledge.

Berun raised his knife and charged the old druid.

But Chereth saw him coming. He took one hand from his staff, held it palm upward before his face, and said, *"Naur telleth!"*

A burst of flame erupted in Chereth's palm, painting his manic features in a devilish light. He curled his hand into a fist, thrust it outward, and the flame shot straight for Berun.

Berun put his forearm in front of his face and tried to dodge, but the flame followed him and struck his midsection. Berun screamed and fell.

"Master!" Lewan called out.

His blistered torso smoking, his face twisted in pain, Berun pushed himself onto his feet and looked to Lewan.

Lewan took one step forward and tossed the hammer. It tumbled end over end in a long arc. The druid cried out and threw another gout of flame at the hammer. With his free hand, Berun reached out. The haft of the hammer slapped into his palm, he gripped it, twirled, and swung. The heavy stone hammerhead struck the ball of flame in midair, scattering it into a cloud of bright sparks.

Roaring like a wild animal, Sauk was still trying to find a way past the vines, but no matter how much he dodged or slashed, more always rose to take his place, pursuing him.

A weapon in each hand, Berun resumed his advance, more cautiously this time. A large patch of skin on his stomach and chest was blistered and torn, and he was obviously in pain.

Lewan turned and crouched next to Ulaan. She was trembling, her eyes wide. Lewan tried to peel back some of the vines and leaves. Some that had been burned crisp broke away, but most of the foliage still twisted tightly around her. He could see that her clothes had taken most of the flames. Only the skin of her hands and one cheek showed any injury from the fire. Her shivering was more from fear and shock than severe physical harm.

"Ulaan, can you hear me?"

Her eyelids fluttered and she looked at him. She didn't speak, but her gaze seemed to acknowledge his presence. Lewan pulled and tore at the vines. Whether they had been weakened by the flames or because the druid's magic was focused elsewhere, Lewan made progress, if too slow for his liking. Some of the vines had thorns that gouged and ripped his skin, but he ground his teeth through the pain and kept at it.

Lewan pulled and twisted at her bindings, snapping a thick tendril and freeing her left arm. "I don't suppose you could call for help?"

"Th-they're dying, Lewan," said Ulaan. Lewan could see that she had the jewel of the necklace clutched in her hand. "M-my . . . sister." A sob shook her and she squeezed her eyes shut. "They're all dying."

Lewan looked over his shoulder. Sauk was only a pace or two from the ledge, the vines and foliage still pushing and whipping at him. More vines had risen to try to seize Berun, and Chereth continued to lob balls of flame at them both. Sauk managed to duck or dodge most, though he had a large burn on his forearm. Berun was avoiding the fire or swiping it away with the hammer.

Lewan knew there was little he could do to help his master. But he might be able to help Ulaan.

"If I can get this off of you," he pulled off another long vine, "do you think you can walk?"

"Get me out of here, and I'll run," she said.

Lewan smiled and tore at the greenery. Some of the smaller creepers had burrowed into Ulaan's cloak, and bits of fabric ripped away as he pulled the foliage.

"Lewan?"

"What?" He kept at his work, not looking her in the face.

"I meant what I said. That I care for you."

"We'll talk of that later."

Behind him, Sauk roared.

"If there is a later."

A great many of Talieth's blades lay dead or dying. Only the most skilled of her assassins had lasted past the first assault, for their steel did little to deter the druid's creatures. The monsters hurled themselves on the assassins' steel, and if they felt any pain, it only seemed to fuel their fury. The assassins who could cast spells lasted longer, and Talieth was foremost among them, hurling fire and bolts of arcane energy at the creatures. Flame seemed the only thing that gave the creatures pause—and even that did not last long against their cunning, for they came in great numbers, some throwing themselves at their prey, distracting them, while others lunged in from behind.

Talieth lost sight of Valmir, concentrating all her attention on killing anything that came too close. It didn't take her long to realize that the creatures were slaughtering the assassins only as a means to an end. They were coming for her.

The assassins nearest her seemed to realize it as well, and they fled, leaving Talieth standing alone in the heavy mists, surrounded by a ring of the druid's minions. They moved in slowly, their eyes reflecting the light of the fire Talieth held in her upraised hand. It sizzled and hissed as the rain struck it.

One of the things stepped forward, crouching and keeping a wary eye on Talieth's fire. It reached out a hand toward her, then its entire body stiffened, its head shook, and its eyes rolled back. "Talieth," it said, though she knew that it was not the creature's voice, but something speaking through it. "Bring it to me. You fought a good fight. You lost. Give me *Erael'len,* and even now I will forgive you. Come to Kheil. Join me in our new world."

A shudder passed through the creature, and all stiffness left its body. It was fluid grace again. It watched her, waiting for her answer.

Talieth took a deep breath and squeezed her hand shut, extinguishing the fire. "Take me to him," she said.

Berun struck a gout of flame with the hammer and dodged another. From the edge of his vision, he saw Chereth muttering, and he knew the druid was toying with them. His power was beyond anything that he or Sauk could hope to withstand. Berun's heart dropped as he watched his old friend. His master, the one person in the world that Berun had held as an ideal, had gone mad. Whether it had truly been the seductive evil of Sentinelspire, the druid's own blind ambitions, or a combination of both . . . at this point, did it matter? All that mattered was stopping him.

Despite Berun's delusions to the contrary, Chereth had indeed become the Old Man. No matter what Chereth told himself, his motives were little different than Alaodin's. Alaodin had sought power and dealt in murder, but he'd rationalized it, believing it necessary to protect himself and those he loved. Was Chereth any different? And had he always been that way?

Swinging the hammer, Berun deflected more fire. It shattered into sparks and singed his bare arm. Berun backed away for a moment's respite and risked a glance behind him. "Lewan!" he shouted. The boy had succeeded in getting most of the vines off the girl. "Get out of here! Run!"

Lewan did not look up from his efforts. "Trying!"

"Enough of this!" Chereth called out, and he thrust his staff toward Sauk.

The writhing vegetation surged like a wave over rocks and hit the half-orc. Sauk struck at the greenery with his arm, but it did no good. The thick mass of vines, leaves, and writhing wood slammed into him, his legs struck the stone ledge, and he toppled over. His feet went up over his head and then he was gone, tumbling over the tower's edge.

Chereth swept his arm around, and a mass of leaves and branches rose and enveloped Berun. He lashed out at them with the hammer and knife. The blade sliced through a few branches before the vines wrapped round both his arms and pulled them to his chest. More snaked around his legs and torso. He screamed as the sharp leaves and prickly vines tore into the blistered skin along his stomach and chest. The mass of vegetation constricted, pulling his limbs tightly against his body so Berun could move only his head. He felt himself lifted up and borne toward the druid. He looked down upon the half-elf, who was not even breathing heavily.

"You see the power I now wield?" said Chereth. "You see the folly of opposing me? Forsake this foolishness, my son."

Chereth turned away, leaning upon his staff as he walked across the roof. The vines holding Berun bore him along after the half-elf. Chereth stopped before two statues—one of a winged lion, the other of a great stag whose antlers spread wide, reaching toward the lion's wings and forming a sort of arch. The druid reached inside his robes and withdrew a rod carved from white wood, or perhaps bone. He spoke a string of words in a language Berun did not recognize, and the air under the arch shimmered and blurred like a summer haze on the horizon.

"See?" said Chereth. "This portal leads to a realm of endless wild, where bricks and mortar are unknown, and the highest creatures live in harmony with the lowest. There, I will dwell while this world cleanses itself of Sentinelspire's fire and ash." He faced Berun again. "Do you still wish to oppose me? To die here amongst those who would trample upon all we hold dear?"

Berun looked down on his master. He would not give in to despair. He'd been dead before. To die now . . . at least he would have the hope of being found worthy to join the Oak Father. Such a fate might be welcome after the horror of the past days. But Berun knew that if he died here, he had to take Chereth with him. Otherwise, untold numbers of people—entire nations—would die as well.

"Ah," said Chereth, looking past Berun's shoulder. "Look who is back."

Berun craned his neck around to see Sauk climbing over the ledge of the tower. He no longer held his blade.

"I thought you might be too stubborn to fall," said Chereth. "Hail and well met, Sauk."

"I . . ." Sauk dropped to the ground and sat, his chest heaving. "I have no quarrel with you, Old Man. I'm here for . . . for him." Sauk pointed at Berun.

"Taaki truly meant that much to you?" said Chereth.

"Why ask what you already know?"

"Your devotion is commendable, Sauk," said Chereth. "It is one of the many things I admired about you. Had you taken a different path in your early years, you might have been a disciple to make me proud."

Sauk snorted. "Damned leaf lover."

Chereth smiled, though a dangerous glint filled his eye. "This leaf lover just beat you like a cur."

"I seem to remember your leaves beating me," said Sauk. "*You* haven't faced me yet, *Old* Man."

"Old I am, yes. But it seems I'll outlive you. Look."

Chereth pointed to the east. The clouds of last night's storm still hung heavy in the sky, but they did not reach quite to the horizon, where the bright glow of dawn was already peeking over the edge of the world.

"The time approaches," said Chereth. "The stars, the Tears of Selûne, the Dawn Heralds, the Five Wanderers . . . all are in perfect alignment, pulling the molten blood of Faerûn into the beating heart of Sentinelspire. Soon, the new world begins."

Chereth walked to the very center of the roof. The vines holding Berun pulled him behind. The druid looked at Lewan, who had almost finished removing the last vines from around Ulaan's legs.

"You could have been a prince in paradise, boy, with your choice of women," said Chereth. "You chose poorly." He looked at Berun. "A third time now, I offer my forgiveness, for the affection I still bear for you and the loyalty you once gave me. I will not offer again. Join me in a new paradise. Teach our ways to a new world. Or die here. Now."

Berun tried to move his arms. He could feel his weapons in his hands, but the vines held him tight. He sighed and said, "What you offer isn't paradise. It's just a greener hell. You can rot there on your own."

Chereth's jaw stiffened and his lip twisted into a sneer. "So be it."

He turned to face the entrance to the stairs and said, "Come!"

Two killoren emerged, moving with their unsettling, almost-human grace. Behind them walked Talieth, her clothes torn, her hair a tangled mess, skin scratched and bloody. Still, she walked like a queen. She took in the scene around her, glancing at Sauk, Lewan, and Ulaan. Her eyes widened when she saw Berun.

"Kheil, I—"

"I'm sorry, Talieth," said Chereth. "It seems that your former love will not be joining us after all. He would rather die here than live with you in paradise."

Talieth stopped, glanced again at Berun, then fixed her gaze on the druid. "I will not leave without him."

Chereth returned her gaze for a moment, then sighed and said, "You have ruled here too long, it seems. You misunderstand me. You no longer command anyone or anything. I am not bargaining with you. I am offering you the chance to live, and serve me in a new world. Or you can die here." He shrugged. "Understand—I don't need you. I only need what you carry. And I can have it."

Chereth raised his staff and pointed it at Talieth. The killoren leaped away as vines rustled forward, wrapping around her and pinning her arms. She struggled, frantically at first but then giving up entirely. One of the killoren grabbed a leather cord from round her neck and pulled, yanking *Erael'len* from Talieth's bodice. Before the killoren could get a look at *Erael'len,* a long tendril of ivy darted out, grabbed the relic, and whipped it into Chereth's waiting hand. Raising his staff, the druid began a long chant.

Berun heard rustling in the leaves that carpeted the roof, and looked over to see Sauk charging Chereth. The half-orc was still several paces away when Chereth glanced at him, almost casually, and flicked his staff. Vines snapped forward, seized Sauk's legs, and the half-orc hit the ground, where more vines entangled him. The druid resumed his chant.

Berun felt it before he heard it—a low rumble, like distant thunder, only it did not dissipate. It grew, all the leaves on the roof rattled, and then Berun could feel the stone of the tower shaking beneath him.

"Lewan!" Ulaan screamed and kicked the last vines off her legs. Her limbs tingled as the blood began to flow again. A few burned twigs and leaves still clung to her clothes. "Lewan, we have to run!"

"It won't matter now." He looked at her, resignation in his eyes, then grabbed her in a fierce embrace. It hurt her burned skin, but she didn't care.

The trembling increased, and Berun could hear the stones rattling. Chereth kept up his chant, his voice rising over the rumbling of the mountain.

Furtive shapes came up the stairs, ignoring Lewan and the girl, walking right past them. The killoren—all that had survived the battle below. They moved quickly, and Berun saw something in their eyes for the first time—fear. The killoren knew what was coming. More climbed over the tower's ledge. Some ran and some shambled, almost beastlike, but all headed for the air shimmering between the statues and walked through, back to their world. Those who had been guarding Talieth joined their brothers, passed into the hazy air, and disappeared.

"Chereth!" Berun called out. "Master! Stop this! Stop it before it's too late!"

Chereth turned to face him, an exultant smile on his face, but he did not cease his chant. He was still smiling when a dusky brown shape hit him in the face, all biting teeth and scrabbling claws. The druid's voice broke and rose into a shriek. He dropped both staff and relic and slapped at the treeclaw lizard ravaging his face. As soon as the staff left his grip, Berun felt the vines around him lose their strength, and he dropped to the floor. He could feel the tower shaking, but the rumble in the air was quieting, and the tremors losing their strength.

Berun thrashed and kicked. Broken twigs and thorns jabbed his skin, cutting bloody swaths in his back and arms, but he didn't care. He kept fighting.

Chereth's cries stopped, and Berun dared to look up as he continued his efforts to free himself. The half-elf's face was a ruin—bright red blood surrounding darker patches of shredded skin and flesh. Both eyes were intact, and they burned with fury.

"*Damn* you!" Chereth shrieked.

Berun heard a screech and saw Perch not far away, standing on his hind legs amidst the leaves. His forepaws hooked into savage claws, Perch looked up at the druid with his jaws open in a fierce show of aggression.

Chereth bent and retrieved his staff. He raised it, but even as he took in a breath to summon his spell, Sauk plowed into him from behind. They hit the roof hard, and Perch had to scramble away to keep from being crushed beneath them.

It gave Berun the distraction he needed. He lunged forward, tearing loose from the last of the vines, half rolling and half stumbling, then he dropped the hammer and reached out. His hand grabbed *Erael'len*.

"No!" screamed Chereth.

Berun looked up. Chereth stood again, staff raised, his face a mask of blood. Behind him, a tangle of vines had wrestled Sauk to the ground. The half-orc thrashed and cursed and screamed, but he could not break free.

Even as Berun watched, Chereth flicked his staff at Perch, and a smaller tangle of vines shot out and engulfed the lizard.

Chereth turned his bloody visage upon Berun. "Give that to me!"

Berun stood. Even as the last tremor passed through the tower and the stone stilled, Berun could feel *Erael'len* coming to life in his fingers, its warmth spreading through his hand and arm.

"No," said Berun. "This madness ends now."

Chereth's chest heaved from exertion and pain. Blood dripped from deep cuts on his forehead and cheeks. His eyes seemed very bright, even savage. His lip curled into a snarl and he turned, pointing his staff at Lewan, who was huddled with the girl not far from the stairs. Vines shot out with so much force that some cracked through the air like whips.

They struck the boy, tearing skin off his face and hands, then wrapping around him. Lewan screamed but the vines kept coming, wrapping him tight and lifting him off the ground. One wound round and round his neck, then constricted, cutting off Lewan's screams.

The druid turned to Berun. "Give me *Erael'len,*" he said. "Give it to me now, or the boy dies."

Berun stood, wincing at the pain from the burns across his skin. *Erael'len*'s power was pulsing through him now, like blood, only a thousand times more alive, more vital, more *powerful.* "If I give you *Erael'len,* the boy dies anyway."

The vine around Lewan's neck tightened even more. His face was turning purple. Ulaan began screaming and pulling at the vines, but her efforts were futile.

Chereth risked a glance at the boy, a flicker of indecision passed across his face, then the vines round Lewan's throat slackened. Just enough for the boy to draw in breath.

"It need not be like this, my son," said Chereth. His words were soft, cajoling, but Berun could see the cunning in his eyes. "I threaten, you relent. You threaten, I relent. Such are the ways of lesser men. They are beneath us. Give me *Erael'len,* Berun. Its glory is beyond you. Give it to me, and I will leave you to whatever you wish. You may follow me—or not. Give me the relic and let me go my way."

"Your way is death for us all," said Berun.

Chereth's eyes hardened, and the vines tightened round Lewan's throat again. Ulaan yanked at them and began to sob.

"Your way is death for the boy," said Chereth. "A slow, agonized death while you watch. While he knows in his final agony that it is all your fault. His last choked breath, his last sight of the world as it fades to black . . . your fault. I'll have my way, anyway. Or you can give me the relic and go as you will with the boy. Your choice."

Berun swallowed. The top of the tower was strangely quiet. Even the drizzle had stopped, and there was no wind. So quiet that Berun could hear the vines tightening round Lewan's throat. Through his heightened senses from *Erael'len,* he could even hear the thorns tearing through the skin of Ulaan's fingers as she tugged at the vines.

"Talieth!" Berun called.

She was still trapped in vines. She looked up at him, and even from so far away Berun caught her scent. The sight of her and the scent of her skin brought a flood of memories to Berun. Kheil's memories, true, but they hit him still—he and Talieth in the height of their passion had often come here at night, where they could enjoy the clean air, the sight of the open sky, and the quiet. It had been dark during their first visits, which did not hinder their purpose. But later, Talieth had learned to use the portals crafted by the Imaskari, calling up water and cool air through the tubes to the top of the Tower, to cool the lovers as they enjoyed each other's company. Even in winter, when dark came early, the moon rose pale and clear over the steps to bathe them in her cold light, and frost gripped the tower from top to bottom, Talieth had called forth fire from other worlds, the flame roaring up the sides of the Tower to bathe them in light and warmth.

Berun could see that she was hurt, disoriented. He knew that she had seldom faced such a desperate situation. But that was good. Berun knew that Talieth was never more dangerous than when she was desperate.

"Remember the winters, Tali!" Berun called out. "Remember our nights by *the fires.*"

"Enough of his!" said Chereth. He spared a glance at Talieth. Apparently deeming her no further threat, he returned his attention to Berun. He clenched his fist and the vines round Lewan's neck tightened further. His face was a deep red, darkening to purple. Ulaan screamed.

Berun took a deep breath and concentrated on the power flowing through him. It was not a part of him. Not exactly. More like a conduit, it joined his lifeforce and his will to all living things around him—including the vines and plants that Chereth was bending to his will. Berun felt their life, their vitality, their *anger*—

But that was Chereth. Berun knew that plants were far more complex than most people believed, but anger . . . no. That was the half-elf. Berun felt that fury, understood its contours within the web of living things around them, then formed his own—a sharp, direct point of will—and struck.

The vines holding Lewan went limp, and the boy struck the ground and gasped for air. The mass of branches and creepers round Talieth slackened, and she fell forward, free at last. Berun felt the will giving strength to the plants that had buried Perch. He struck that power, shattering it, and the lizard scrambled out of the leaves. In the deep part of his mind, Berun sensed Perch's confusion and terror. Fighting steppe tigers was one thing, but plants that crawled like snakes . . . too much. Still, he could not bring himself to abandon his brother. Perch sat in the leaves, frozen by his own fear and indecision.

For a moment, Berun considered freeing Sauk as well . . . but no. In his present state of mind, the half-orc would be just as likely to attack Berun as Chereth.

Chereth looked at Berun in wide-eyed shock. Even Sauk, still pinned to the ground by the vines, only able to move his head, stared at Berun, disbelief and wonder warring with the rage in his eyes.

"I fear I wasn't entirely truthful with Sauk some days ago," said Berun. "I am no master, certainly, but I have had nine years to study and commune with *Erael'len*. I have unlocked more than a few of its secrets."

Chereth stiffened again, the haughty arrogance returning to his posture, and he said, "Pray it will be enough."

Time slowed for Berun. All around him, he felt the very substance of the air, and within those millions of tiny eddies and flows, he felt a charge swelling, crackling, and building as it gathered. Chereth pointed his staff at Berun and spoke a word of power. The charge in the air coalesced and lightning shot out from a half-dozen directions, every bolt arcing right for Berun. But through *Erael'len,* Berun's will was tied to the power, and he turned the bolts away. Some struck patches of vegetation, shattering them in an explosion of scorched vines and leaves. One narrowly missed Lewan and Ulaan, striking the top step and cracking the stone.

Chereth stepped closer, his staff held at the ready. "Impressive," he said. "Your faith, your *power,* would be worshiped in my new world, Berun. *Berun*—'Hope,' I named you. Do not betray that hope now. You have so much to offer a fresh world, a world of life, a world ready to grow according to our will."

"*Your* will, you mean," said Berun. "You're no different than any tyrant or upstart warlord. Your way or no way. That is not the way of the Oak Father. That is not the Balance."

Chereth snorted. "Stupid fool," he said. "You know so little. Your half-orc is subdued, your boy and his whore are whimpering on the ground, and your woman"—he turned to look at Talieth, who had stumbled over to the statue of the Imaskari hero holding the sun —"mad, apparently. You stand alone, Berun, and you have made me very, very angry. Give me what is mine *now,* and I will grant you the mercy of dying beside your friends. Otherwise, I'll kill you here, take what is mine, and I'll take little Lewan with me as a pet for the killoren. They have developed quite a taste for manflesh here at the Fortress."

"Lewan!" Berun called out, but he did not turn to face the boy.

"Yes, master?"

"You remember two summers ago, hunting the bear?"

A short silence, then, "Yes, master."

"Take my bow and go, Lewan! Run! Get out of here, now!"

A longer silence this time, then, "Yes, master."

Berun saw Chereth glance toward the stairs. He did the same. Just in time to see Lewan—Berun's bow in hand—leading Ulaan down the stairs.

"You think I will not find him?" said Chereth.

"Threats," said Berun, "cruelty . . . those are not the ways of the Oak Father."

"The wild can be cruel," said Chereth. He stopped only a few paces from Berun. *"Must* be cruel to survive."

Something grabbed at Berun's legs and he went down. He was halfway to his feet when the vines that had tripped him began to wrap themselves around him. Rather than struggle and fight them, he calmed his mind, concentrating on the power flowing through him by his connection to *Erael'len*. He sensed the power controlling the vines. Bending them to his own will would have meant a war of minds with Chereth—a war Berun wasn't sure he could win—so he snapped the connection. All mobility left the vines, and they were ordinary vegetation once more.

Berun rose to his feet. Chereth stood only a few paces away. Berun eyed him, needing him to move to his left a bit. Talieth stood ready beside the statue, her hand poised to begin her spell. The golden sun in the hands of the statue connected to the Imaskari tube, a window-sized portal that wound its way down and around the exterior of the tower before plunging deep into the heart of the mountain.

Keeping his eyes fixed on Chereth, Berun called out, "Ready, Talieth?"

Silence. For a moment, Berun feared she was dumbstruck—or worse, misunderstood his reference to the winter nights and the fires. But then he heard her, her voice haggard and rough, beginning the incantation.

Erael'len in one hand, knife in the other, Berun charged. He kept the relic behind him—well away from Chereth—and brought the knife around in a swipe aimed at the druid's throat. Chereth took a half-step back and blocked Berun's first strike with his staff, the second with his forearm, then countered by jabbing the end of his staff at Berun's face. Berun dodged and the blow merely scraped the side of his check.

Berun stabbed, forcing Chereth to leap back to avoid the blade. Berun backed away to catch his breath—and to keep Chereth right where he stood.

"You could have been a king in a new world," said Chereth. "Now, only I will remember you, and I will not mourn you, Berun. I was wrong to name you Hope. In all my years, you have proved my greatest disappointment." He shook his head, raised his staff, and said, *"Ebeneth!"*

Most of the vines in which Berun stood did not move, but one strand shot forward, quick as a cobra, and snatched *Erael'len* from his grasp. He let it go, his senses returning to normal, and the vine slapped it into the open, bloodied palm of Chereth.

The druid's eyes lit with exultation, and the madness in that gaze was clear to Berun. How could he not have seen it before?

"You have defied me for the last time," said Chereth. "You will—"

Berun shouted, *"Now, Tali!"*

Fire—a great river of it, like a dragon's fury—erupted from the stone sun where Talieth stood. It shot outward, straight for the old druid. Perch screamed and ran to the edge of tower.

Chereth simply smiled and raised *Erael'len*. The fire washed over him, so hot that it singed Berun's skin from several paces away, but Chereth did not move, and his smile did not falter. He simply stood there, letting the flames wash over him.

The fire sputtered and died, a few flames dancing around the sun-disc before flickering away. The stench of burned vines and leaves filled the air, and near the edge of the tower, Talieth slumped to the feet of the statue. "I'm . . . sorry," she gasped. "I . . . could not hold it . . . any longer."

Chereth shook his head as he walked over to Berun. "You

think I didn't hear your little signal?" he said. " 'Remember the winters! Remember our nights by the fire!' How touching. But I have had years to study and master what the Imaskari left behind. Nothing in my tower can harm me."

Holding *Erael'len* in one hand and raising his staff in the other, Chereth summoned two great masses of vines forward. One wound round Talieth and bound her to the statue. The other grabbed Berun, sharp thorns shredding his clothes, and threw him against the bole of the oak tree in the center of the roof. Berun's breath exploded out of him, and he felt and heard his ribs break. The vines kept coming and coming, wrapping round him and the tree, binding him there with arms outstretched.

Simply breathing was agony. The vines constricted, grinding Berun's broken ribs together, and darkness threatened to overwhelm his vision. But then the foliage slackened slightly, and the pain eased. Still, Berun could hear a cracking sound. It took him a moment to realize that it was not his bones or even the vines, but someone approaching. He looked up and saw Chereth walking over the carpet of leaves. Blood and gore still covered the druid's face from Perch's attack, and his hair and robes were a tattered, tangled mess from the fight.

"Damn you," said Chereth through clenched teeth, and Berun saw that he was trembling with fury, tears mingled with the blood on his cheeks. "Damn you to the darkest, deepest hell, you ungrateful, ignorant whelp. Your futile attempt, your . . . *foolishness!*" Words failed him. He squeezed his eyes shut, took a deep breath, then looked at Berun again. "The world has turned too far. It will be months before I can complete my plans. Months!"

Berun said nothing.

"But you haven't won," Chereth continued, "only delayed the inevitable. You have done something else, though." The half-elf's eyes narrowed, and he looked upon Berun with hatred and contempt. "You know what I am going to do while I wait? I'm going to kill your woman over there. Then I'm going to hunt down that little pup of a disciple of yours—him and his whore. I'll kill him last, after he's watched me kill her. And I'll kill him slowly. And the whole time he will know it is you that brought this upon him, when he could have had paradise—or at the very least, a quick death in glory."

"No," Berun said, though it was agony to speak. "You . . . won't."

"Oh, but I will." Chereth smiled, a truly horrific sight through the mask of blood. He raised his staff, and the vines binding Berun's left arm tightened and stretched, so it seemed that Berun was holding the knife out to Chereth. "First I'm going to take care of you. Once and for all. You've been too full of surprises today. Best to end it now. What was it you told Talieth's little bed warmer out in the Shalhoond?"

Berun's eyes widened.

"Oh, yes," said Chereth. "I have watched you for many long days, and once Sauk found you, I watched closely. That night by the fire during your escape, what was it you said? 'The greatest weapon is the weapon at hand and the willingness to act.' The first thing the Old Man ever taught you, you said. After all you have done to me, I certainly have the willingness to act. And look"—he reached out and took the knife from Berun's hand —"a weapon, literally 'at hand.' Let's put it to good use."

Chereth brought the knife up and slammed it down, plunging it through the vines and deep into Berun's flesh, right where his neck joined his shoulder, right into the large vein. Chereth pulled out the blade and blood spurted all over them both. It seemed to fuel the druid's fury. He turned the knife and stabbed—

"I—!"

Again.

"—am—!"

Again.

"—through—!"

Again.

"—with—!"

Again.

"—*you!*"

He stopped and let go, leaving the blade stuck between two of Berun's ribs. The second—or had it been the third?—strike had pierced one of Berun's lungs, and he could feel blood beginning to fill his chest. He coughed once, bringing out a spurt of blood. He could hear Talieth crying.

Berun smiled.

"What?" Chereth stood there, panting from exertion. "Why are you smiling?"

"The . . . second—" Berun coughed again, spraying more blood.

"The second?"

"—thing!" Berun had to pause between each word to gather enough air, and even then each one came out wet with blood. "The . . . Old Man . . . taught . . . me."

A small spark of curiosity overtook the fury in Chereth's eye. "And what was that?"

"Al—" Another cough, this one so hard that blood filled Berun's nose and leaked out. "Always . . . watch . . . your back!"

Chereth whirled.

Next to the stairway stood Lewan, Berun's bow in hand, arrow pulled back to his cheek—the steel point aimed directly at Chereth. Lewan's fingers, grasping the bowstring, opened, and as the curve of the bow straightened, snapping the string forward with a sharp whisper of air, the runes etched into the bow glowed a brilliant green.

The druid raised his staff and spoke a single incantation.

Berun did not know if his life was failing so fast that his brain had already begun its long sleep, or perhaps it was simply the blessing of the Oak Father upon the bow, but in that instant he thought he saw a flash in the air as Chereth's magic failed him. The arrow flew straight and true, burying itself in the half-elf's chest. It struck with such force that it spun him around, and when he fell upon his hands and knees, he was facing Berun. By the time he gripped his staff and pushed himself to his feet, he was shaking like an old man with palsy—

—and Lewan had another arrow drawn and nocked. But only for a moment.

Chereth opened his mouth in a last, desperate attempt to call forth his magic, and the arrow struck him there, passing between his teeth. The steel point bored through his skull before the wood of the arrow stuck.

The old druid fell back onto the vine-covered roof, his legs kicked twice, and he died staring at the sky.

✚
chapter forty-one

The bowstring was still vibrating when a great mound of vines and leaves erupted. Sauk rose to his full height, snapping branches and raking thorns down his skin as he freed himself. A few thick vines round his shoulders would not give, so he swiped at them with a dagger until the severed ends dangled behind him like some bizarre, thorny half-cloak. He spared Lewan and Talieth a quick glance, dismissed them, and fixed his gaze on Berun. He stomped toward the oak, and Lewan heard a growl growing in the half-orc's throat.

"Lewan . . ." said Ulaan.

"Stay back," he told her, then took another arrow from his belt, laid it across the bow, pulled the arrow to his cheek, and aimed the steel point at Sauk. "Stop, Sauk! Stop where you are."

The half-orc's gaze flicked to Lewan. Sauk saw the threat and stopped. He turned to face Lewan and smiled. "You think you can take me with that twig tosser"—he spat blood onto the leaves —"before I get to you? You'll only get to loose one arrow before I reach you."

"I've been a hunter most of my life," said Lewan. "Once chance is all you ever get."

"Stop this! Both of you!"

Lewan heard movement behind him, and from the corner of his eye he saw Talieth step up beside him.

"Sauk," she said, "I know you. I know your code. You won't prey upon anyone weaker than you."

"This isn't about honor anymore," said Sauk. "This is about blood. Berun killed Taaki."

"No. His lizard did—and only after Taaki almost killed him. It was survival, Sauk. Life and death. You would have done no different in the same situation."

Sauk snarled, the growl building in his throat, blood running off his good tusk and the silver one. His grip tightened around the knife.

"I am truly sorry about Taaki," said Talieth. "But understand this. The only one on this tower stronger than you right now is me, and *I* am telling you that if you take one more step toward Kheil with murder in your eyes, it will be the last step you ever take."

Talieth's voice sounded weak and strained, but Lewan heard the truth in her words. It was not the first time he'd been told that Sauk believed that killing those weaker than him was dishonorable. The bow, drawn and ready and aimed at Sauk, made Lewan a formidable foe. And though it took every ounce of will he had left, Lewan slackened the bow and lowered it—though he kept his fingers with a tight grip on the arrow.

Sauk ignored the gesture, keeping his eyes fixed on Talieth. Lewan noted that the half-orc gripped the knife so tightly that his entire arm trembled.

Sauk threw his head back and roared. Talieth took a half-step back and raised her hands, a spell already forming on her lips, but when Sauk lunged, it was behind him. He buried the knife in Chereth's chest. Lewan heard bones break like shattering stone. Sauk pulled the knife down, cutting through muscle and shattering the dead druid's ribcage. Lewan stared wide-eyed as Sauk tossed the knife away—with such force that it sailed over the edge of the tower—ripped open the half-elf's chest cavity, and tore out the heart with both hands. He held it in his fist, raised it over his head, and shouted something in his own tongue. The only word Lewan understood was the last —*"Malar!"*—then Sauk bit into the heart, tore out a chunk with his jaws, threw the rest away, and looked over his shoulder at Talieth. Fury filled his eyes, and great hurt, but Lewan could see thought there as well. Sauk the Assassin was returning, though Sauk the Predator was not entirely gone.

Talieth held her stance a moment longer, then relaxed. She arched one eyebrow and said to Sauk, "Are you done?"

Sauk chewed, drips of blood leaking out of the corner of his mouth as he considered. At last he looked down at Chereth's mutilated body, spat out the heart, and said, "He's done."

Lewan, Ulaan, Talieth, and Sauk stood before the oak, facing Berun. Although the druid's magic had left the vines, they still bound Berun to the tree. Only his head was completely free, and it hung limp. Lewan still held the arrow on the bowstring, and he kept an uneasy eye on Sauk, but the half-orc, while certainly far from calm, seemed to have control of his rage. Talieth had dismissed Sauk entirely, and she stood with her hands outstretched, seeming hesitant to touch Berun.

"Is he . . . ?" said Talieth.

At the sound of her voice, Berun's eyelids fluttered and remained half open. He coughed, and a thick gout of dark blood sprayed onto Talieth's outstretched hand.

"Oh, Kheil—" she said, her voice breaking. But when she turned and looked at Lewan, her eyes were cold and hard as new steel. "Help me get him down. If we can find a healer—"

"No!" Berun croaked. The one word brought another fit of coughing, and he splattered them both in blood. Neither cared.

"I won't lose you again, Kheil," said Talieth, looking to Berun again. She held his face in her hands and lifted it so he could see her. "Chereth is dead. We can—"

"No," said Lewan.

"Silence!" She turned a look on Lewan that bordered on murder. "You *will* help me."

Lewan did not flinch or even resist. He held her gaze a moment, then looked to his master. Tears welled in his eyes, and he said, "He's beyond saving, Lady. Let him die upon the Oak. It's what he wants."

"No!" Talieth threw herself forward and tried to embrace Berun. "Do *not* die! If you do, I swear I'll drag every priest of every faith here until one of them can call you back."

"I . . . will not . . . *answer!*" The last word came out of Berun in a wet gasp, and a fit of coughing seized him, bringing up more blood. But then he settled, and his next words were clearer, though scarcely above a whisper. "I go to my Father." He managed to find some last bit of strength, and he lifted his head to look at Sauk, Lewan, and Talieth. "Good to . . . have you three . . . here. At the end."

Berun let out a final, bubbling breath, then his muscles went slack. He hung upon the oak, a dead weight in Talieth's arms.

Talieth let out a long cry that Lewan felt sure could be heard on the distant canyon walls, then she slumped to her knees and wept at Berun's feet.

Lewan heard a frantic rustling of leaves off to his right, and when he looked, Perch crouched upon the ledge. The lizard seemed to realize that his master was gone. He threw back his head and let out a long, trilling wail.

Sauk growled and took a step toward the ledge.

Lewan half-raised the bow and pulled the string back. "Don't," he said.

The full light of a clear morning shone down on Sentinelspire when four figures emerged from the Tower of the Sun. Lewan, hollowed-eyed and covered in blood, supported Ulaan with one arm and carried Perch on his left shoulder. Behind them walked Talieth, the Lady of Sentinelspire. All were scratched, cut, smeared with blood, and their clothes were little more than rags. The proud gait of the queen was gone from Talieth's bearing. She looked defeated.

The woods of the courtyard were in devastation. Many of the trees and much of the foliage had burned, scorching even the rain-soaked grass beneath. Bodies and pieces of bodies lay everywhere. Most were the assassins of the Fortress, but here and there lay the darker shapes of the creatures that had served the master of the tower. The dead tiger lay on her back in the blood-soaked grass, her innards splayed over her torso.

A group of figures huddled on the lawn outside the courtyard. When they saw the trio emerge from the tower, two of them ran over. Lewan recognized one as Valmir, but he'd never seen the other man. They had weapons in hand, but when they came close enough to recognize Talieth, they lowered them. The stranger slowed to an easy walk, but Valmir ran forward to embrace Talieth.

"Gods," said Valmir, "you look like . . ."

For once, Valmir was at a loss for words, and the impudence was altogether gone from his eyes.

"What happened," said the other man, and he nodded at the tower, "up there?"

Talieth said nothing. She didn't even look at the men, just gazed at the buildings across the street, obviously not seeing them. Her eyes seemed . . . haunted, Lewan thought.

"Everyone's dead," said Lewan. "The Old Man, Master Berun . . . everyone except us."

"And Sauk," said Ulaan.

"Where is Sauk?" asked Valmir.

"When we left, he was just sitting up there," said Ulaan, "staring into space. As far as I know, he's still there."

"Gorin, why don't you go up there and check on him?" said Valmir.

Gorin snorted. "Right after you hug me tight and call me mother. You go check on him yourself."

Valmir scowled at Gorin, then looked up at the tower. "I'm sure he's fine."

✦ ✦ ✚ ✦ ✦

Atop the Tower of the Sun, before the great oak tree, Sauk sat. The morning breeze off the mountain set the tree's leaves to whispering and tosse d the half-orc's unbound hair into his face.

After a long time, he looked up at the body on the tree. Sauk's knife was gone. He made the sign of the Beastlord— three middle fingers curled like claws—on his forehead, dug his middle nail deep into his skin, and opened a fresh gash down his forehead and across his cheek.

"Dam ul dam, Malwun."

He sat there, looking up at Berun, and tears mingled with the blood on his cheeks.

LISA SMEDMAN

The New York Times best-selling author of *Extinction* follows up on the War of the Spider Queen with a new trilogy that brings the Chosen of Lolth out of the Demonweb Pits and on a bloody rampage across Faerûn.

THE LADY PENITENT

BOOK I
SACRIFICE OF THE WIDOW
Halisstra Melarn has been a priestess of Lolth, a repentant follower of Eilistraee, and a would-be killer of gods, but now she's been transformed into the monstrous Lady Penitent, and those she once called friends will feel the sting of her venom.

BOOK II
STORM OF THE DEAD
As the followers of Eilistraee fall one by one to Halisstra's wrath, Lolth turns her attention to the other gods.

BOOK III
ASCENDANCY OF THE LAST
The dark elves of Faerûn must finally choose between a goddess that offers redemption and peace, or a goddess that demands sacrifice and blood. We know what a human would choose, but what about a drow?

June 2008

ed Greenwood

presents

WATERDEEP

Time passes and so do men, but Waterdeep remains the same—
dangerous, full of intrigue, and in desperate need of heroes.

BLACKSTAFF TOWER
Steven E. Schend

In the wake of the Blackstaff's death, schemes and peril abound
over who will be the next to command Blackstaff Tower.

September 2008

MISTSHORE
Jaleigh Johnson

One woman must learn to stop running away—from the Watch,
from her powers, and from her past.

December 2008

Explore the richly textured city of Waterdeep with
master storyteller Ed Greenwood as your guide in an
action-packed series of adventures that will leave fans
of the FORGOTTEN REALMS® world breathless.

A Reader's guide to
R.A. Salvatore's
The Legend of Drizzt™

THE LEGEND
When TSR published *The Crystal Shard* in 1988, a drow ranger
first drew his enchanted scimitars, and a legend was born.

THE LEGACY
Twenty years and twenty books later, readers have
brought his story to the world.

DRIZZT
Celebrate twenty years of the greatest fantasy hero
of a generation.

This fully illustrated, full color, encyclopedic book celebrates the
whole world of The Legend of Drizzt, from the dark elf's steadfast
companions, to his most dangerous enemies, from the gods and
monsters of a world rich in magic, to the exotic lands he's visited.

Mixing classic renditions of characters, locales, and monsters
from the last twenty years with artwork by Todd Lockwood and
other cutting-edge illustrators, this is a must-have
book for every Drizzt fan.